INTO THE WOLF'S MOUTH

Wayne Slater

wayneslater.com

Dedication

To Kate Slater, my Queen of Hearts.

About the Author

Born in Salford in 1958, I have spent most of my working life performing on the stage with my comedy magic act, *El Loco*. Over a 30-year period, I was fortunate to perform more than 4,000 shows worldwide in various venues that included theatres, cruise ships, hotels, holiday parks and social clubs. Unfortunately, one fateful night aboard a cruise ship off Dubai, I suffered a life-changing heart attack before a performance, bringing down the curtain on my career.

At a loose end, and having an encyclopedic knowledge of stage performance and magic, it was suggested I should write a book to fulfil my creative need.

This is my first novel, *Into the Wolf's Mouth*.

Based in Nottinghamshire with my wife Kate, we have two wonderful sons, Charlie and George, who with their partners, Corazon and Becca, have three little miracles - Reuben, Charlotte and Ezra.

Wayne Slater

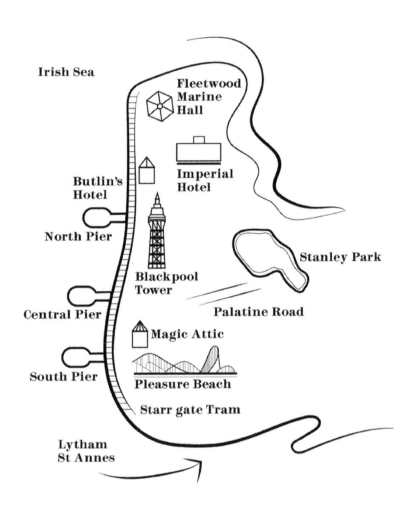

Irish Sea

Fleetwood
Marine
Hall

Imperial
Hotel

Butlin's
Hotel

North Pier

Blackpool
Tower

Stanley Park

Central Pier

Palatine Road

Magic Attic

South Pier

Pleasure Beach

Starr gate Tram

Lytham
St Annes

Prologue

Blackpool, 1969
The Games People Play

By the end of today, and for all the wrong reasons, the Marine Hall in Fleetwood would remain a permanent scar in my memory. Tonight's entertainment showcase should have been like any other – a variety of performers displaying their unique talents for bookers and agents alike. Except Neil Armstrong put paid to that at 3.56am when he became the first man to walk on the moon, ensuring tonight's conversations between booking agents would be more about the impression left on the moon than any on the stage. Until the closing act.

I'd arrived at the Marine Hall by mid-afternoon, even though my performance was not due to start until around 9pm. Most showbiz folks tend to share camaraderie, which is why I arrived early to help two of my fellow performers. Sarah, aka "Snowflake", required help selecting the right piece of music. Neil Armstrong made my selection easy after his early morning stroll - "Bad Moon Rising" by Creedence Clearwater Revival. It would provide the perfect introduction for her new illusion, Discombobulation; a routine regarded so dangerous that experts doubt it possible. Danny Mac's request for assistance was far more complicated.

With his stage assistant Julie unavailable, he needed help with The Bullet Catch, an infamous illusion he hadn't performed for over 12 months. Danny was an established illusionist, but not a great one. Always in need of substance before a performance, the empty pill packet and pint pot in his dressing room declared he'd needed both that day.

'Helps settle my nerves, young Gee, 'was his justification for opening another bottle of beer - not a good idea when you're attempting to catch a bullet travelling at 1,200 miles per hour in your teeth. Danny Mac was unpredictable. You were never quite sure which Danny would turn up – the downcast, dejected depressive, or the cheerful, cheeky cockney.

As with many magic illusions, there is no single way of performing The Bullet Catch. The method can vary depending on the performer. In its simplest form, an audience member selects then signs the bullet, and it is then inserted into the rifle. The target through which the bullet must pass, usually a glass screen, is set to destruct. The performer must palm one bullet for another, ensuring the signed bullet ends up in his mouth until he is ready to spit it onto a plate. My friend and mentor, Gordon Kingsley, was going to be the marksman firing the rifle; Danny Mac, the heroic bullet catcher. However, Gordon's shop, The Magic Attic, didn't close until 5pm. By then, it would be too late to rehearse. So in the meantime, I stepped in to help Danny perfect his angles before going through a full rehearsal, including firing the rifle.

'It's really quite simple, Gee, 'Danny stated. 'You insert the bullet, then push it down the muzzle using the ramrod. When the ramrod is removed, it'll hide the bullet in its chamber. Then you palm the bullet and pass it to me as you hand me the plate.'

I hated this trick. I didn't trust the ramrod to catch hold of the bullet correctly, and under stage lights, with my dodgy left eye, I couldn't see if the bullet had attached or not. We both took up our positions, exactly 23 feet apart. As always, I touched the birthmark on my shoulder for luck. 'Ok, I'm ready,' I uttered across the stage.

'Remember, keep your eyes – sorry, eye – open and squeeze the trigger gently,' Danny called sarcastically, with a sudden frown.

I couldn't help but think if this went wrong, and without any witnesses, I'd be charged with murder. Whether it was fear or anticipation, I didn't know, but the rifle felt a little clunky. I rested the butt against my shoulder. Taking aim, I gently squeezed the trigger as instructed. BANG. My shoulder jolted backwards. Danny collapsed to the floor. Instantly, the warmth from the rifle butt morphed into a block of ice, trickling down my neck. I froze like a verglas statue, watching as blood flowed from one corner of Danny's mouth and he laid motionless on the floor. This was my worst fear. Holy cow, how would I explain it? Had I been set up? Sarah Todd stood to one side, open-mouthed, fear etched on her face. Slowly and from opposite sides of the stage, we walked to where he lay deathly still. Danny's shoulders started to shake. He burst out laughing like a demented circus clown. He stood upright and spat the blood-stained bullet from his mouth onto a plate.

'You bastard,' I snapped. 'How could you do that to me? I thought I'd killed you!'

Danny continued to laugh at his own prank, took a hankie from his pocket and wiped the remaining blood from around his mouth and chin. 'Did you like the fake blood capsule? I made it this morning,' smirked Danny as he walked away whistling Colonel Bogey. Thankfully it was the cheerful, cheeky cockney who turned up that day. Though I wish he hadn't, as I later found out that his assistant, Julie, couldn't attend because Danny had broken her nose in a violent attack the previous day.

Entering my dressing room, the smell of rising damp nudged me to open a window, inviting in a welcome breeze off the Irish Sea. With several hours to go until tonight's show, I pulled up a chair and sat by the window. Soon the dressing room would be full of chatter as the performers arrived. Before they did, I carried out my pre-show ritual. I opened a pack of cards, removed the 7 of hearts, the joker, and the ace of spades, and shuffled the three cards until I no longer knew which order they were in. The first card I turned over would determine the outcome of tonight's show.

1. Turning over the joker meant my show would go well.
2. Turning over the 7 of hearts meant the whole show would go well.
3. Turning over the ace of spades meant death.

Slowly I turned over the top card, revealing the ace of spades.

Chapter 1

Blackpool, 1948
Nature Boy

Annie Camberwell climbed the last few stairs of her four-storey guesthouse. A task made all the more difficult as she approached her seventh month of pregnancy. Overcome with dizziness, she paused outside room 9. Gripping the bannister rail, she fought to replace the oxygen into her five-foot frame for both baby and herself. Running a nine-bedroom guesthouse was not how husband Tom had promised. The short summer months brought 16-hour working days and the much-needed cash to survive the long winter months.

Capri Guesthouse was one of many such terraced establishments halfway down Palatine Road, which is why last night's late check-in was so unexpected. Few people visited Blackpool out of season, let alone two foreigners. The couple, who spoke little English, were wrapped in headscarves - not to hide their identity, more to protect themselves from the bitterly cold February wind. The young woman's high cheekbones underlined her black pupils, reflecting like black pearls in the hallway's bare lightbulb. The young man's eyes were unengaging. Perhaps the warmth of the name "Capri" had attracted them to the property. Whatever the reason, the added income was undoubtedly welcome at that time of year. Annie delivered her usual instructions to the one-night-only guests.

'No food or alcohol in the room. Breakfast is served at 8 am prompt.'

That's probably why she was a little miffed that by 8.45 am the following day, the guests had still not shown for breakfast. Annie, always

The early riser, looked far too young to be running this type of establishment. She was in her mid-twenties, hair tied up in a bun and a blue headscarf, with a matching housecoat that no longer tied around her baby bump. Outside room 9, she noticed the bedroom door was slightly ajar. Knocking gently, and without a reply, she tried again. This time she called out.

'Good morning,' she said whilst pushing open the door into a room of darkness. Annie swiftly moved across to the window, hoping to startle the lazy guests by throwing open the curtains. The rain-filled light creeping into the room barely made a difference. To Annie's surprise, the bed was empty; no bedsheets or pillows, no sign of the young couple, just a blue towel wrapped into a small bundle in the centre of the bed. Blood-stained bedsheets poked out from under the bed. She felt dizzy but had no one to call on as Tom had left for work. Annie was terrified at the thought of what could be lying under the bed. She was even more terrified at what may be in the blue towel. Unable to lift her feet, she slid each one slowly towards the bed, and with outstretched, shaking arms, she gently took hold of one corner of the blue towel and peeled it away to reveal a newborn baby with patches of dried blood scattered across its tiny body. Annie noticed a large birthmark on its shoulder, oddly shaped like a boot.

There was no sign of life. Instantly she picked up the baby, its cold skin jolted her motherly instincts into wrapping the blue towel around him, and she quickly made her way downstairs, too afraid to imagine the baby may already be dead. Her mind whirled at what to do next. Capri Guesthouse had no phone. Her only hope was that Mr and Mrs Collins, who lived two doors up, were home. Thankfully, Jenny Collins' front door was open. Annie ran straight up the hallway calling for help, hoping her voice would startle the swaddled baby. Jenny immediately felt Annie's fear.

'Michael!' Jenny shouted. 'Get the car.'

Within five minutes, they arrived at Blackpool Victoria Hospital. The baby still showed no signs of life as Annie handed him over to one of the nurses. Annie was instructed to sit in the waiting room until the police arrived. *If this is parenting, the years ahead will be very stressful*, thought Annie. Agonisingly, she paced around the room containing half a dozen chairs and a coffee table. She must have picked up the old copy of *Woman's Own* a dozen times, discarding it back to the table without turning a page.

Eventually, after two hours, the same nurse returned. Annie immediately blurted out,

'The baby?'

'The baby is very poorly. He's between four and six weeks premature and weighs just over 3lb. He's unlikely to survive the day.'

'Can I see him?' Annie pleaded.

'Sorry, no, we've placed him in an incubator where he'll be monitored,' assured the nurse before introducing PC Jack Brock. Annie hurriedly explained to the policeman what had taken place from the moment the young couple arrived at the guesthouse the previous evening to arriving at the hospital today.

Tom Camberwell tended not to rush anywhere; a shrapnel wound from the Second World War had left him with a pronounced limp. He'd received news at work that there was a problem with the baby and he needed to go to the hospital. Entering the stale waiting room, Tom respectfully removed his cap. When he noticed the PC, Annie quickly reassured Tom she hadn't given birth early and told him about the abandoned baby in room 9. Tom, not a man to over-engineer his words, simply asked PC Brock,

'Can we go home now?'

Annie eagerly jumped in. 'What will happen to the baby if he survives?'

PC Brock methodically folded his notebook, like all new recruits tended to do before delivering a speech - one he had to repeat more frequently than he'd expected.

'He's what's known as a foundling, a baby without the known whereabouts of either mother or father. Should he survive, he'll be put into council care. Why? Do you fancy giving him a home?'

Tom was quick to reply. 'No, we have our own baby on the way,' he said, ushering Annie out of the door. As they were about to leave, the nurse handed Annie the blue towel that the baby had been wrapped in, which she gratefully accepted.

By late afternoon, darkness mixed with a sea mist engulfed most of Blackpool. The only sensible place to be was indoors by a warm fire. Annie was no longer in the right frame of mind to cook the Valentine's dinner she'd planned. Instead, she sat as close to the open fireplace as possible, staring at the flames that appeared to dance in time with the music on the radiogram. The glow from both was the only light in the evening lounge. With the blue towel on her lap, she wondered how anyone could abandon such a beautiful baby. Closing her eyes, she tried to remember the baby's olive skin when she first opened the towel and the birthmark on his shoulder. Clutching the towel to her face, she smelt the baby's aroma. In one corner of the towel, she noticed the initials GB.

'Tom, what do you think this means? A name? Or a place perhaps?' Tom tried to change the subject, reminding Annie it was not long before their own baby arrived, but Annie wouldn't let it go.

'Where did the couple come from, or go to for that matter? Were they French?' Annie asked.

Tom thought differently. 'No, they kept repeating the words *'va bene'*. It's Italian for ok.'

"Nature Boy" by Nat King Cole played on the radio. Annie listened intently to the song. *There was a boy, a very shy enchanting boy.* Again, Annie held the blue towel to her face, this time to dry her tears, praying the baby was still alive. She fixed her eyes on Tom. He knew exactly what she was thinking.

'Ok, I'll contact council welfare in the morning, but there is no guarantee the baby will live or that they'll place him with us.'

The rain was no deterrent as Annie nervously made her way to the hospital the following morning. She now had two babies to silently pray for; the one she was carrying was more active than usual. On arrival, she spoke with nurse Julie, who'd given her the blue towel.

'He's still alive, but very poorly. He's certainly a little fighter. We've named him Baby Gee after discovering the G and B sewn into the towel.'

Returning home, Annie stopped by the local church seeking extra insurance. The whole process became Annie's daily ritual for the next two weeks; snow, fog, and rain could not deter her. Tom stated he'd contacted the welfare department, informing them they would like to foster the baby if no one else came forward. Annie was not sure he was being truthful.

There was no formal announcement about what happened to Baby Gee. Annie made her daily visit to the hospital one day, only to be told the baby had been put into welfare care by Blackpool Council. It took several days before Annie got to speak to the correct department. By this time, Baby Gee had been placed into his first foster home with an option to adopt. Annie was devastated. The baby had been registered by the local welfare department as Gee Valentine, born on the 14th of February, 1948, at Blackpool Victoria Hospital. There was no mention of Palatine Road or Tom and Annie Camberwell.

Returning home, Annie removed her rain-soaked coat. She hadn't even noticed it was raining. She also didn't notice the Austin A40 that almost knocked her down outside the hospital. Climbing the four flights of stairs, she paused outside room 9 for both breath and courage. Inside the room, Annie found herself standing in the very same spot she first saw Baby Gee wrapped in his blue towel, the blue towel she was now holding in her hands. Annie placed the towel in the centre of the unmade bed, where she had found it. Taking one last look before leaving, she noticed the wallpaper was peeling away in one corner. She'd normally inform Tom, but it would be a long time before this room was disturbed again. She locked the door with its memories contained and was about to make her way down the stairs when something caught her eye on the threadbare carpet. It was a tiny silver heart. On inspection, she noticed SB engraved on one side. She placed it in her purse, where it remained for many years.

Later that day, Tom found himself back at the hospital. On arrival, he was informed Annie had gone into premature labour – their baby was not due for five weeks. Baby Penny was born blind, weighing just under three pounds. She entered the world on the 14th of March, exactly four weeks to the day Gee Valentine was born.

Chapter 2

1964, Blackpool
Runaway

The Fleetwood to Stargate tram was a boneshaker of a journey, accompanied by an orchestra of grinding metal along the 11-mile track. Without money to buy a ticket, I balanced on the outside metal buffers, crouching like a surfer barrelling through a giant wave along the promenade, all part of my reckless existence.

Onlookers were unsure if I was trying to kill time or myself. Blackpool was in its heyday, with the sky-pointing tower standing proud like a giant middle finger to its French counterpart. Below was the Golden Mile. Shop after shop selling all types of novelty items, from kiss-me-quick hats and candy floss to sticks of rock and saucy postcards. My destination was the Pleasure Beach, a fairground of fun with thrill rides, like the Wild Mouse, the Grand National and the Big Dipper. The only way for me to enjoy the rides was by sneaking past security. If caught, I knew the punishment handed out by twin brothers Dravern and Vincent Leach, the security guards with vicious reputations. Their way of dealing with wayward boys like me was whacking them in the back of the neck with a clenched fist, known as a rabbit punch, so painful it took your breath away. Then you were frog-marched off the Pleasure Beach before getting a kick up the arse as one of the brothers shouted, 'goodbye, donkey!'

If the Pleasure Beach was my kind of fun, living in a care home was the complete opposite. Thirty boys aged under 16, all with varying reasons for sharing the same leaking roof, bedroom, lice and rat-infested toilets.

Most postured for the position of cock of the house. Some, like me, tried to lay low and avoid the daily bullying. My saving grace was being first pick when teams were selected for a game of Split the Kipper - a daredevil game where two opponents stood three feet apart, facing each other on grass or soft earth. The first person threw a penknife around three inches from their opponent's feet. The opponent then had to move their foot to where the knife was, without moving the other foot, pick up the knife and repeat the process, doubling the distance to six inches and so on. To win, you had to force your opponent into a position where they couldn't spread their legs apart any further, causing them to fall over, hence the name. The boys in the care home thought I was gifted. That's probably why I was no longer referred to as "Wop Boy", knowing I could easily remove one of their toes with an accurate throw of my knife.

I guess it was fair to say, the first 14 years of my life had been interesting but with little compassion. The only kindness had come from nature itself. Now at five feet ten inches tall, I have olive skin, almost coal-like coloured hair and black pupils that stand out like polished marbles. I have no understanding of why I was in care in the first place. What could I possibly have done wrong that my parents deemed unacceptable? I didn't know if my mother died whilst giving birth to me or if I had any family at all. God knows I'd asked the question often enough. Just over a year ago, I asked one too many times and received a punch in the face from one of the staff.

Schooling, on the other hand, had left a different kind of mark - fortunately, top ones in most subjects. For my age, according to my teacher, I was the most advanced pupil she'd come across in over 20 years. Not that it stopped the headmaster, Mr Coil, shaking with rage as he brought down his birch cane three times onto my left hand for my constant truancy. Thankfully his timing, like his eyesight, was that of a man waiting to retire. My problem was boredom. School was just too easy, so I disrupted the class. The teacher yelled, 'get out!' and within minutes, I'd be wandering the streets of Fleetwood. Passing the time, I'd make up anagrams of the street names. Scotgate Road became "strange cod". Ideal, really, as Fleetwood was a fishing town. Hassocks Lane changed into "oh a slackness". Though my favourite had to be Old Turnpike or "polite drunk", not many of them around those parts.

By the middle of summer 1962, I was informed by the care home staff that I'd been selected to go on a two-week sailing holiday. I may have been many things, but stupid was not one. I'd overheard a conversation the previous evening. I was being moved on and would not return to the Fleetwood care home. The night before I was due to leave for my so-called "sailing holiday", I decided to break into the secretary's office, where I hoped to find details of my birth parents. I waited until 1.30 am when the night staff gathered in the canteen to eat. I wasn't surprised to find the secretary's door unlocked, though, frustratingly, the filing cabinet was. Though taught little by the care home staff, I learnt much from my fellow detainees. I removed a lady's hairpin from my pocket. Crouching down to keep out of sight, I inserted the pin into the filing cabinet lock. After several careful turns and a loud click, I was in. On locating my file, I was disappointed to read how little there was about my past.

Gee Valentine. Born Blackpool Victoria Hospital 14th of February 1948.
Parents; unknown.
Family; unknown.
Brought into care and placed with his first foster family in 1948. He was returned to care within two months.
From 1948 to 1954 he was placed in five further foster homes, always returned to the care home within two to three months.
Though educationally very bright, Gee Valentine suffers from low self-esteem, finding it difficult to become attached to anyone. From the age of 13, he's become an increasingly disruptive and troublesome child, often caught stealing from local shops and markets.
It has therefore been decided he should be put forward for migration to Australia.

Wow! I was so much trouble they were sending me to the other side of the world. I was about to be abandoned once again, only this time at the hands of those I was supposed to be able to trust. Moved on to some other unsuspecting family 12,000 miles away, with no chance of a return to sender.

(*)

Tilbury docks from Blackpool was a long, arduous 14-hour charabanc journey. On arrival at the port, there were hundreds of children milling around. Most faces were filled with fear, some with anticipation; others were expressionless. Chatter soon spread that this wasn't a sailing holiday as we boarded the magnificent *RMS Orion* for a six-week, one-way adventure, or as one boy put it: 'where a new ready-made family will be waiting for us'.

Another boy asked, 'Do you know the heat down under can get over 100 degrees in the summer?' The complete opposite of what I was used to, where freezing winds off the Irish Sea once made my ears bleed.

Up to that point, I, too, had been excited at the prospect of a new life away from the bullying, abusive care home. But what suddenly occurred to me was I already had a ready-made family, who would one day surely return to Blackpool to try and find me. They'll never think to look for me in Australia. It wasn't long before I heard the ship's engines fire up and the rigging ropes cast off, sinking into the water like my dreams of ever being found by my mother and father. Throughout the night, the rocking motion helped me flit in and out of sleep, still wrestling with the decision I'd made the previous day; a life changed forever, no turning back the clock, what's done is done. When the rocking motion suddenly stopped, I stretched out my spindly legs and kicked at the metal doors where I'd been cooped up all night, eventually bursting them open.

My eyes could not focus due to the sea spray blowing off the waves. Squawking seagulls bombarded my ears. I knew exactly where I was. As I wiped away the salty tears, a broad beaming smile spread across my face. I looked up at Blackpool Tower from the coach park. A tower stretched up to a bright blue sky. I was sand-grown, Blackpool born and bred, convinced my parents would one day return and reclaim me as their son, and when they did, they'd be proud of how I'd turned out.

Fourteen hours earlier, I'd sneaked off *RMS Orion* via the service gangplank as she was about to set sail, then hidden inside the charabanc luggage hold, which I'd just kicked my way out of. I wouldn't be returning to a Fleetwood care home for more abuse. From now on, Gee Valentine would make the decisions about his life. *No one will ever abandon me again.* Today was a new opportunity, a gift waiting to be unwrapped.

Chapter 3

Blackpool, 1962
Return to Sorrento

The only items I now possessed, besides my Split the Kipper penknife I was wearing. With my belly grumbling like a fairground ride, it prompted me towards the Pleasure Beach. It was late July and the schools were out for the summer. Blackpool was now at its busiest; holidaymakers and day-trippers were everywhere - easy pickings for a boy in need. By the time I arrived at the Pleasure Beach, this boy was in desperate need of food.

Driving my hunger pains was the smell of fresh bread, attracting me like a bee to pollen. Following my nose, I made my way down an alley next to the Pleasure Beach. I came across a large window which reflected the sun into the eyes of those queuing. A lady with a mass of bright red hair was poking her head through a serving hatch, looking like a giant candy floss on a stick. I could almost taste the fresh bread and cakes on view.

Penniless, I was trying to work out a way of stealing without being caught when I was handed my first bit of luck. The man ahead of me in the queue left his change on the countertop; two silver shilling pieces begged to be claimed. Quickly I moved forward with my left-hand index finger outstretched. I pointed to the bread while simultaneously covering the coins on the counter with my right. Feeling flush, I also ordered two doughnuts. Handing over one of the shillings, the lady turned to sort my change and greedily, I snuck a small cob into my pocket. As she handed me my threepenny bit change, her untrusting eyes blinked like the shutter of a camera, storing my image in her mind.

My task complete, I sat on the bottom step of a wooden staircase running up the side of the bread shop. By the time I'd scoffed my way through the bread and doughnuts, my face almost matched the lady's hair. Feeling flush, I took the threepenny bit from my pocket, ready to place it into the gumball machine, until I remembered this was the only money I had. Faintly the sound of soft music from above led me up the wooden stairs. At the top was a half-glazed door. *Kingsley's Magic Attic* was written in gold leaf on the obscure glass. Through it, I just about made out a man playing the saxophone. The music tugged at me to enter, and as I opened the door, I was greeted by a service bell. Ignoring my entrance, the man continued to play, and at that very moment, my life changed forever – my second stroke of luck in a matter of minutes.

The room was unlike anywhere I'd been before. No more than 20 feet square, a dark wooden counter ran the full length of the wall opposite my entry point. There were no windows, but floor to ceiling cabinets filled the room, all crammed with magic tricks. At the time I had no idea what they were as my eyes took in coloured silks, steel rings, ropes, playing cards, coins, paper flowers, clocks, candles and bottles. Pride of place in one corner was a 9-feet high guillotine. Below was a basket complete with a false head - at least I hoped it was false. My eyes continued to scan; the shelves behind the counter were lined with hundreds of books, probably carrying as much dust as words. On the counter, I noticed a threepenny bit. I felt this really was my lucky day until I tried to pick it up and realised it was glued down.

'Stop thief, stop thief!' A voice screeched so loud I had to cover my ears. I looked up to see a bright green bird with a splash of red above its beak, perched on the mezzanine bannister. Suddenly the music stopped, the saxophone now sat back in its stand on top of the counter. The silence between us was about to be broken.

'That's Angel, she's my Amazon Parrot, and she lets me know if someone is stealing, so you'd better be careful.' I felt Angel pin her eyes on me.

'Most people fall for the threepenny bit trick. I glued it there some years ago. Those without principles always try to steal it.' The words were spoken in a soft Scottish accent. 'Did you enjoy the bread and doughnuts?'

Shocked, I stepped backwards thinking, *how the hell did he see me from up here?* I tried to change the subject. 'What's the music you were playing?'

'*Ritorna a Sorrento.* In English, it means "Return to Sorrento".' His lips turned upwards at the word 'Sorrento' as though for one moment he was there. 'How long have you been stealing from bread shops?'

I thought carefully about my answer. 'I didn't steal them. I paid for them.'

The man moved behind the counter and gave me a distrustful adult stare I'd seen many times.

'Not for the cob roll in your right trouser pocket,' he snarled.

Confused, I averted my eyes and refocused on the magic tricks within the glass cabinets.

'How old are you?' he asked.

'Sixteen,' I responded through lying teeth. A wide smile now spread across his face. His tone softened even more as he asked my name and where I came from.

'My name is Gee Valentine.' I don't know why but I told him of the last 24 hours and why I'd come back to Blackpool instead of starting a new life in Australia. He listened intently like no adult had listened to me before. For a moment, I almost lost sight of where I was and what surrounded me in the glass cabinets.

'What is all this?' I enquired, gesturing with my hands and arms as my eyes tried to remember everything.

'This, young man, is the Magic Attic, and I am the proprietor, Gordon Kingsley. What you see here is a world of magic and illusion, a world where those who dedicate themselves to learning the art of magic will find a purpose in life.'

Gordon removed a small tree in a terracotta pot off the counter, lifted the hinged countertop and beckoned me forward. As soon as I walked behind the counter, Angel screeched,

'Stop thief, stop thief!' This time he made me smile.

Once behind the counter, Gordon revealed a 12-inch square opening in the floor. Looking down, I recognised the bread shop's countertop where I'd picked up the two shillings earlier.

'Holy cow,' I exclaimed. 'But how?'

'A collection of mirrors run under the floorboards at various angles. I keep a careful watch on my friends, and the lady who runs the bread shop is one such person,' Gordon explained with a smile that made me think the lady who owned the bread shop was more than just a friend.

'It's fascinating. A whole world I didn't even know existed until now,' I remarked as I walked from behind the counter and sullenly towards the exit door. Gordon returned the small tree to the counter.

'Let me have the threepenny bit coin from your pocket.'

I didn't argue. I simply gave it to him. He removed a white handkerchief from his waistcoat, placed the threepence into its centre, and folded it into a parcel. When he let the handkerchief fall open, my coin had vanished.

'Hey man, they're hard to come by, you know,' I complained. Gordon ignored my protestation. Standing behind the small tree, with flat open palms, he slowly and continuously motioned upwards with his hands. Astonishingly, and right in front of my very eyes, oranges started to appear out of the tree.

'Holy cow,' were the only words I could muster. I counted eight whole oranges. Gordon picked one off the end of a branch.

'Do you have a knife?' he asked. I rifled through my pocket with anticipation at what he would do next as I handed him my silver penknife. He sliced the orange into small quarters. Handing me a piece, I quickly shoved it into my mouth, allowing the juice to bring a sunshine smile to my face. As he handed back my penknife, it had changed colour to red. What followed remained excitedly in my mind for the rest of my life. From the centre of the orange, Gordon removed the threepenny bit. Handing me the coin, he said,

'Take this to the bread shop downstairs, along with the cob roll out of your pocket, and give it to Lana. She's the lady you stole it from.'

'The lady with red hair and untrusting eyes?' I asked.

'They're not untrusting, just vigilant,' he smiled. 'Then get yourself back up here. We have a lot to do before the shop opens in the morning. I could do with an extra pair of hands if you're up for it?' I did exactly as instructed.

I wasn't sure if I was awoken by the smell of fresh bread giving me the warmest of hugs or by Angel squawking, 'I'm awake, I'm awake.' One thing was for sure, it was the first time I remembered sleeping through the night. The previous evening, Gordon Kingsley offered me a six-week opportunity to change my life, allowing me to sleep in the mezzanine above the shop.

'If you can show me you want to alter your life for the better, I will help you, but if you steal from me, or anyone else for that matter, I will contact the care home in Fleetwood and you'll be back there before you know it.'

In return for helping out in the shop and delivering parcel orders around Blackpool, I would receive food and a small wage. I did not question why a stranger would help such a wayward boy. I was just grateful.

The next morning I made my way down the rickety ladder from where I'd slept on the mezzanine floor. Gordon asked me to collect the fresh bread from Lana's bakery. Gordon was an imposing character, a good two inches taller than me at 6 feet, his hanging shoulders indicated he'd been carrying a burden around for years. Oddly he had no hair or eyebrows.

After breakfast, I was given the task of cleaning every magic trick in the shop. There must have been at least a thousand, not that I cared. Over the next few weeks, I had more fun than I'd ever had. Once the shop was closed each night, Gordon taught me sleight of hand card moves and explained how every magic trick I'd cleaned operated. He also gave me my own deck of cards to practice with.

Sleep was something I usually needed little of, which came in handy sometimes. As the Magic Attic was mainly constructed of wood, any movement throughout the night brought about an eerie feeling, like a troubled mind trying to get comfortable. One such night around 2.30 am, I heard footsteps coming from the outside staircase. My whole body tensed up and I shot upright as the shop door handle turned. Putting aside my deck of cards, I positioned myself at the top of the mezzanine. Through the half-glazed door, the beam from a torchlight scanned the room. I thought about waking Gordon when I heard what I thought was a key inserted into the lock and then a click. The door handle turned, and slowly, the door opened. Quickly I made my way down the ladder and grabbed hold of a bottle from one of the shelves. The door came to an abrupt halt by a security chain. I heard faint mumbling before the would-be intruder stumbled back down the wooden stairs. Quickly I pushed the door closed and laid down on the floor next to it in case he returned. It took a while for my heart rate to return to normal, but eventually, I fell to sleep.

The smell of fresh bread was fast becoming my alarm clock. Looking up, I found Gordon standing over me by the door. Explaining what took place in the night, Gordon snarled,

'Alex bloody Lockhart! He's the resident magician and escapologist performing at the Tower Circus. He's also a bloody drunk.' Closing one eye and tilting his head to one side, he asked, 'Why are you holding that bottle?' Glancing down, I saw the bottle still gripped in my hand.

'I was going to hit the intruder over the head with it if he got in the shop.'

'Not much bloody use that would have been.'

I looked at him blankly.

'It's made from sugar,' he chortled.

Later that morning, Gordon found a scribbled note from Alex Lockhart in the letterbox stating he'd broken one of his multiplying candle props and needed a replacement immediately.

'Take this parcel to the Tower Circus and give it to Lockhart, no one else. If he doesn't give you the money, don't give him the parcel.'

'How will I recognise him?'

'You can't miss him. He's got an ace of spades tattooed on his neck. Now off you go.'

Arriving at the Tower Circus, I was sent in the direction of the performance arena. From a distance, I heard panic in the raised voices. Staff were huddled around the elephant's enclosure. Above the noise, I asked a lady if she could point out Alex Lockhart. She stared through me like I was an empty shop window. Amongst the commotion, my curiosity led me beyond the elephant's enclosure. I was drawn to the constant crack of a whip along a corridor that contained five, maybe six, metal bar cages. Inside one was a man, whip in one hand, a large stick in the other, his face full of concentration, desperately fighting to force back a snarling lion. At first, I thought I was witnessing rehearsals until I spotted two other men also in the cage with him, dragging a man along the floor, leaving behind his severed leg in a mixture of blood and sawdust.

A group of men fleeing the area in search of safety almost knocked me over. I had no idea why they were in such a hurry until, no more than a paw's swipe apart, another lion majestically strolled into the corridor. Our matching black pupils locked onto each other. All of a sudden, Australia seemed like a really good idea. Frozen with fear, I was unsure how I'd found myself here. Fortunately, the lion took more interest in its feline friend, who was swinging around the departed man's leg like a giant stick of rock. With my heart in overdrive, I placed my mind into reverse and manoeuvred backwards, sliding my feet through the sawdust and back into the elephant's enclosure - where a new kind of fear awaited. Sergeant Jack Brock, a policeman I'd had several run-ins with over the years, was trying to bring some sort of order to the chaos.

'Does anyone know the name of the man we dragged out of the cage?' he shouted above the din.

'Alex Lockhart,' replied a man nearby.

'Nobody leaves this area. Mr Lockhart has been padlocked inside the lions' cage.' The sergeant's eyes panned the area. If he recognised me, I'd be back in the care home before the next tide came in, so I quickly made my exit.

By the time I returned to the Magic Attic, Gordon had already received the news of Alex Lockhart's death.

'How did you find out so soon?' I asked breathlessly.

'My friend Tom has just been on the phone. He works at the Tower. After leaving here in the early hours, it appears Alex picked his final lock. He'd snook into the lions' enclosure, where he probably fell asleep. When he woke up, he must have panicked, and one of the lionesses mauled him to death. As Lana in the baker's shop would say, "it's a good way for a bad magician to die".' I didn't like Lana's saying.

'Tom also mentioned that Sergeant Jack Brock is asking about the identity of the boy with the parcel for the former magician.' Just hearing the policeman's name made me want to run away. I told Gordon of my run-ins with Sergeant Brock whilst at the care home.

'Ok, it's time to make a few changes,' he said, looking me up and down like a tailor sizing up for a new suit. 'I think we'll start with your name. From now on, your first name is Giovanni, Giovanni Valentino – it'll be a great stage name for your magic act,' he laughed.

'Where did the name come from?' I enquired, looking bemused.

'I was based near Naples at the end of the Second World War. Should anyone ask, I'll say you're from a family in Sorrento who helped me and I'm returning the favour by helping their son.' Again, the word Sorrento brought an expression to Gordon's face like the sun had just popped out from behind a grey cloud.

Later that day, Lana arrived with scissors. Nervously, I sat still as she cut my shoulder-length hair. I heard Gordon on the phone talking to his friend Tom about me coming from Italy on a learning programme. Replacing the handset onto the receiver, he glanced over at Lana cleaning her scissors in the sink.

'He's a good friend, a real trustworthy man.' She looked back with eyebrows raised questioningly.

'Who?' Lana queried.

'Tom Camberwell,' replied Gordon.

Chapter 4

1963, Blackpool
I Will Follow You

'You see all types of life from up here,' said Gordon. My eyes were instantly drawn to the large picture window overlooking the Pleasure Beach. Gordon called it his window on the world. This was the first time I'd been invited to his workshop, and it reminded me of the first time I'd entered the Magic Attic. Magic tricks littered the workbenches. Some were half-built. Others needed repair, like the large guillotine that had once stood proud in the shop. Its chrome blade no longer reflected the sun as dark menacing clouds brought in the evening before it was due. Through the window, the Pleasure Beach moved into full technicolour. Thousands of multicoloured light bulbs illuminated the rides and stalls, all waiting to be explored. Up to now, Gordon had warned me off the amusement park. I was itching to get out there and have fun. The deadline for Gordon's six-week trial period had come and gone without comment until now.

'Gee, I think it's time we got to know each other a little better. Firstly, we must only ever deal in truth. I don't like secrets.'

Ironic, I thought, considering he sold them for a living. I threw Gordon a puzzled look, unsure where the conversation was leading. He straightened himself like a teacher ready to take class, and I sat on a chair by the window like a model pupil.

'Both my grandfather and father were watchmakers. They also applied these same techniques to build magic tricks, some small and some large, like the guillotine you see needing repair. My grandfather built it for a famous Scottish magician named Brodie Lock. Though it may look the standard type, behind the upright wooden frame, there are more steel wires, coils and pulleys than three grandfather clocks put together. So accurate was the mechanism that once the magician released a secret pin, within ten seconds, the lethal blade would fall, slicing through human bone if it were in the way. Brodie Lock performed the illusion in many of Scotland's theatres. On one such occasion at the Empire Theatre Clydebank in 1886, Brodie Lock became infamous, and my grandfather was in the audience to witness the horror that unfolded.' Gordon opened a cupboard door by his workbench and stretched a hand in to pull out an old newspaper. He blew off the dust that fell in my direction, and I coughed and spluttered, then cleared my eyes and started to read.

Glasgow Herald, 8th July 1886
"Horror show at the Empire Theatre."
Yesterday evening at the Clydebank Empire, pandemonium broke out in the theatre as a magic illusion went gruesomely wrong. A volunteer from the audience tragically lost his life. He was decapitated by a guillotine in front of a live audience. Illusionist Brodie Lock, who performed the illusion, later released a statement claiming the guillotine, made by Donald Kingsley, was faulty, and he would be suing the watch and illusion maker for damages.

I read no further. Open-mouthed, I lifted my head. 'Holy cow.' Carefully handing Gordon the newspaper, my eyes glanced at the guillotine blade on his workbench, catching Gordon's reflection as he set about repeating to me what his grandfather told his father.

'Brodie Lock had great stage patter. In Scotsman's talk, he was always bumpin' your gums. Softly spoken, Brodie explained the dangers of the guillotine. He also proclaimed he had psychic powers, and he could stop the blade in mid-flight by simply clapping his hands together twice. As he walked downstage, suddenly and without warning, the blade fell crashing into the lunette. The noise alone brought gasps and even some laughter from the audience. Slowly and calmly, Brodie walked back upstage and reset the guillotine, explaining to the audience that it was probably faulty - hardly reassuring for any volunteer, but it was all part of Brodie's master plan, for, amazingly, there were still people willing to take the risk. A volunteer made his way onto the stage. Once his neck was fixed into the lunette, Brodie made his way downstage, again boldly stating that when the blade fell, he would clap his hands together twice, stopping the blade in mid-flight. As the blade fell, Brodie clapped his hands, but the blade continued downwards, cutting through the neck of the hapless volunteer, decapitating him instantly. The screams and wails from the audience were as real as the blood soaking into the wooden stage floor.'

'What went wrong?' I gasped, now unable to look at the guillotine blade.

'Nothing went wrong. Brodie released the pin, knowing that within 10 seconds, the blade would fall and slice through the victim.'

'You said victim. Do you mean he intended to murder him on stage in front of the audience?'

'Of course, he simply wanted to avoid paying the final 50% that he still owed to my grandfather.'

I eagerly interrupted again. 'How would killing his volunteer avoid the final payment?'

'Brodie was a cunning man. Remember, he publicly stated to the audience the guillotine was probably faulty. After the event, the safety pin was certainly made to appear faulty, and he knew my grandfather would carry the blame, being the manufacturer.' Gordon cupped both hands together, fingers entwined as if holding his entire body together.

I didn't want to ask, but I knew I had to. 'What happened to your grandfather?' Gordon untwined his fingers and nervously picked at a loose bit of skin near the top of his index finger as he raised his eyes to meet mine. He handed me another old newspaper, this time, standing from my chair, I took it from him before he blew more dust in my face.

Glasgow Herald, 14th April 1887
"Empire horror show, watchmaker to be hung."
Donald Kingsley of Edinburgh was yesterday convicted of murder at Glasgow High Court. Jimmy Robertson from Paisley, a hapless volunteer, lost his life due to the negligence of faulty equipment made by Mr Kingsley. Brodie Lock's claim for damages against Mr Kingsley due to loss of income was upheld by Judge Anderson. Mr Kingsley denied making faulty equipment, claiming Brodie Lock had tampered with the

mechanism. Judge Anderson dismissed Mr Kingsley's defence, sentencing him to death by hanging at Barlinnie prison.

The words sent my mind and stomach into orbit. I didn't know if I would faint or throw up first, so I sat back down. Gordon Kingsley's pride for his ancestors shone through his eyes like a beacon. His family ties, going back over a century, would never be forgotten. How I wished I could trace my family back that far. I scratched my head. Something didn't feel right.

'Wait a minute, so, how did you regain possession of the guillotine?' A smile returned to Gordon's face. Eyes alight, he was ready to deliver the final part of his lesson – this time it was about secrets.

'A few years after my grandfather's execution, Brodie Lock was back performing in theatres around London and enjoying his anonymity and the damages award by the judge. Lock was also allowed to keep the guillotine. One afternoon whilst setting the stage at Bethnal Green Music Hall, he was on his knees connecting the base of the guillotine when forcefully his neck was pushed into the lunette. Unable to move, the last voice he expected to hear was that of my grandfather, the very same one he thought had been hung six years earlier.'

'What?!' I exclaimed.

'My father and grandfather sounded and looked very similar. No hair, no eyebrows - a Kingsley trait. My father wore Grandfather's old work apron. With Brodie's head locked in the lunette, and enough distance between him and my grandfather, he became confused, begged for forgiveness, and admitted his guilt.'

Gordon didn't boast if his father executed Brodie Lock as an act of revenge. He simply said his father dismantled the guillotine, packed it into two cases and returned home to Edinburgh. Gordon held out a third newspaper, the headline proclaimed:

Glasgow Herald, 14th April 1897
"Magician's head found in the River Thames."

He folded the three newspapers and returned them to the cabinet. Looking directly at me, he said,

'Ok, Gee, now it's your turn. Remember, no secrets.'

Still in my chair and feeling queasy, I tried to change the subject. 'What did you do in the war?'

'You will do well never to ask me questions about the war,' came his sharp reply.

'But you told me you served in Italy.'

'Aye, aye I did, it's where I learnt to play this blasted thing,' he said, pointing to his saxophone. He leant back against his workbench, folded his arms and waited for me to speak. What was he expecting me to say? Did he know my real age? If I told him I was only 14, would he immediately send me back to the care home?

'Is the lady with the red hair in the bakery your girlfriend?'

Gordon frowned. 'Enough of your cheek, laddie. Come on, let's hear your secrets.'

I decided to keep my age to myself and stick to talking about the Pleasure Beach. 'I used to sneak onto the rides without paying, but I'd get caught by the security guards, Dravern and Vincent Leach.'

'I know of them,' said Gordon. 'They're twin brothers, real nasty pieces of work - well-known for rabbit punching little boys. Besides working part-time as security guards, Vincent also moonlights as a burglar. Dravern, meanwhile, masquerades as a magician. I've caught them both on several occasions trying to steal from the shop.' Silence fell momentarily between us before Gordon blurted out, 'Well, is that your only secret, sneaking onto the rides at the Pleasure Beach?'

'Oh, a few days back, someone tried to open the shop door in the middle of the night,' I said in a matter of fact way.

'Sadly, Gee, there are lots of cranks around here, thinking that if they steal a few tricks within a few weeks, they will become a magician.' Gordon removed a framed picture of the great illusionist, Harry Houdini, from the wall.

'Pop your head in there, young Gee.'

I looked at Gordon apprehensively. 'Will I lose it?'

'Not today,' he laughed.

Nervously I placed my head through the hole in the wall. The cold draught caused my eyes to water as I recognised the wooden stairs leading up to the half-glazed entrance door. Removing my head, I asked, 'More mirrors?'

'Yes,' he replied with a wink of his eye. 'Next time you hear someone on the stairs in the middle of the night, push the bell button behind your bed. It rings a bell in my bedroom. I'll do the rest.'

I was dumbfounded by the number of secret mirrors, tunnels, and bells. I asked myself why I was privileged to all of this. Gordon was fast becoming the fulcrum of my life.

'Follow me, Gee.'

'Where?' I asked. Without reply, Gordon walked to the far end of his workshop, standing in front of his 2x5ft tool rack stacked with various tools from screwdrivers, hammers and pliers to clamps and saws.

'Remove the orange-topped screwdriver.'

Apprehensively I asked, 'Are we being launched into space?'

Gordon looked out of the window and said, 'If you don't hurry, the Pleasure Beach Park will be closed.'

I did as requested and removed the orange-topped screwdriver. The tool rack disappeared inside a pocket in the wall as if by magic, revealing a small corridor and a fire escape at the far end. Crouching down to enter, Gordon pushed open the fire escape door, where we were immediately engulfed by a rush of wind carrying a wall of screams from the thrill-seekers, enticing us to join them on the Pleasure Beach below.

'Holy cow!' I shouted above the din as we made our way down the metal fire escape. Lana, smiling, waited for us on the bottom step, her suspicious eyes packed away for another day and replaced with a glow of friendliness. The air was thick with the smell of candy floss, and the lack of wasps indicated the lateness of the season. This time tomorrow, the Pleasure Beach would close down for winter, the last chance to enjoy the excitement of the rides. First up was the Grand National, a wooden rollercoaster Lana refused to join us on, stating it was far too fast. Next up, the Big Dipper, again minus Lana. I wanted to go on the Wild Mouse, but both Gordon and Lana said it was too dangerous for a boy of my age. We passed the glass case containing the laughing clown, roaring with laughter and mechanically rocking from side to side, backwards and forwards. We couldn't help but laugh along. Suddenly I was brought back to reality. In the glass case, I caught the reflection of security guard

Vincent Leach. I edged between Gordon and Lana in search of my security. Seeing our reflections too, we looked like any regular family out for the evening.

(*)

Once the Pleasure Beach closed, winter soon set in and Christmas was upon us; my first Christmas out of the care system. Lana and Gordon tried their best to cheer me up at a time that always had me thinking of my parents. Were they still alive? Did they live together? If so, where? So many questions, but no one to ask. One thing that put a smile on my face was Lana's cooking. Christmas dinner at the back of her bakery was the best I'd ever had.

'I hope you've saved enough room for Christmas pudding, Gee. I've made it especially for you.' The more I got to know Lana, the more motherly she became. Gordon, like the magician he was, produced a lit match from behind his coat lapel and set the Christmas pudding alight. With my last spoonful, I bit on something hard. Lana and Gordon exchanged smiles. At first, I thought I had bitten on a gobstopper. Then I removed a threepenny bit from my mouth. They both burst out laughing, though I'd no idea why until Lana explained it was the same threepenny bit she'd given me as change on my first day here.

'It's meant to bring you luck,' explained Gordon.

'Not much luck if I'd broken my tooth,' I ruefully replied.

On leaving the bakery and returning to the Magic Attic, Gordon stopped to clear the snow off the top of the gumball machine at the bottom of the wooden stairs.

'Where's the threepence from the Christmas pudding, Gee?' Gordon asked.

Ungratefully, I held it aloft like a booby prize.

'Insert it into the gumball machine and let's see what luck it brings.'

Confused, I played along, inserting the coin. I cranked the handle and a small white plastic egg was released. I looked at both Gordon and Lana suspiciously.

'Well,' said Lana. 'Open it up, slowly as you do.'

I placed it to my ear. Faintly, I could hear ticking.

'Is it a bomb?' I smiled. Prizing it open carefully, I was amazed to find a gold pocket watch inside. I looked up and smiled at Gordon, wearing a smile as bright as his Christmas tie.

'It's from Lana too,' he stated. Opening the face of the watch, a tune started to play.

'It's "Return to Sorrento",' interrupted Lana. 'Gordon made it.'

I noticed an inscription on the back of the pocket watch which read *Close the book and open your mind.*

Showing affection at times like this was something I was not capable of. 'Thank you. But I don't have anything for you,' I said in a sorrowful tone.

'Just you being here is our Christmas present. Oh, and don't forget your lucky threepence,' replied Lana.

'But it's inside the machine,' I exclaimed.

Lana's eyes switched from me to Gordon. The threepenny bit was between his teeth. I had no idea how he'd got it out of the machine without me noticing, other than believing he was actually a real wizard.

(*)

The winter of 1963 – The Big Freeze - was the worst on record. From Christmas Day until late February, the snow fell endlessly. Fortunately, this was Blackpool's quietest time of year; no holidaymakers or day-trippers. Gordon spent most days in his workshop making, mending, and teaching me magic. I spent most of my days watching Gordon go about his work. Unable to sleep, most nights I often practiced my sleight of hand moves. On one such night, I heard a noise outside the wooden staircase. Living in a wooden structure, the Magic Attic often spoke to itself throughout the night, but this was definitely not an in-house conversation. Eerily after each splinter-stepping climb, there was silence. I believed someone was trying to break in. Remembering Gordon's instruction, I pressed the bell button behind my bed. Moving to the edge of the mezzanine, I made out the shadow of a man through the glazed door. The noise that followed I'd never heard before or since. It sounded like two hammerheads colliding, followed by a continuous humming sound, akin to a swarm of bees. Gordon had given me strict instructions - under no circumstances was I to go anywhere near the entrance door. Fear flowed through my veins, but it didn't stop me from making my way down the ladder. I removed a display sword from the wall. The shadowy figure turned the door handle, and momentarily a shower of colourful sparks appeared behind the outer glass, followed by the crashes and bangs of someone tumbling down the stairs. Then silence. No shadows, no humming sound, nothing.

The next morning, the faint smell of burning sausages from Lana's bread oven brought me to my senses. Exasperated, I explained to Gordon, who was half listening, half stocking shelves for today's wannabe magicians, what took place in the night.

'Gee, why is there a sword on the shop counter?' he inquired.

'I took it off the wall in case I needed to defend myself against the burglar.'

Gordon casually picked up the sword. Shaking his head, he glanced at me whilst pushing the retractable blade back into the handle.

'Just like the sugar bottle, Gee, you have a lot to learn about magic props.'

Another lesson taught by the master to his wannabe apprentice.

Chapter 5

1963, Blackpool
I Will Follow You

Sergeant Jack Brock entered the Magic Attic. His broad, distinctive Manchester accent reminded me how vulnerable I was. Gordon had instructed me to stay up in my room until the officer completed his inquiries. Officiously, he went about his work.

'As I mentioned to you on the phone earlier, Mr Kingsley, the body of security guard Vincent Leach was found outside the bakery by Lana Kingsley at 7 o'clock this morning. Are you and the lady related by any chance?'

'Yes, Lana is my sister-in-law,' replied Gordon. Instantly I wondered what happened to his brother.

Brock continued. 'Does anybody else live here?'

'Yes, I have an Italian student.'

'And his name?'

'Giovanni Valentino.' Through the gap in the floorboard, I watched as the sergeant scribbled my name into his notebook.

'Mr Kingsley, it appears Vincent Leach was trying to break into the bread shop downstairs, probably trying to steal yesterday's cash takings.'

'He was not a pleasant man, sergeant. Can I ask how he died?'

'There are a couple of possibilities. One, he was standing on top of the gumball machine trying to remove the top window, the one with the fluorescent light behind. He probably gave himself a nasty electric shock trying to remove the tube, and the jolt probably knocked him off the gumball machine, causing him to break his neck in the fall.'

'I'm sorry to hear that,' Gordon said unconvincingly.

'One less common thief for me to deal with,' remarked the sergeant like it was a favour.

'Stop thief, stop thief,' piped up Angel. I peered over the bannister to see Sergeant Brock's hand covering the threepenny bit on the counter. As he looked up at the parrot, I quickly ducked out of sight.

'Don't you find that thing annoying?' barked the sergeant.

'No, he's company, and he lets me know when someone unsavoury is in my shop,' smiled Gordon, a smile that transferred to my own face.

'What can you tell me anything of these steel rings I found in a bag that Vincent Leach had with him?' With that, he removed seven 8-inch steel rings. 'Any idea what these are? They appear to have your shop label on them?'

'Yes, they are an ancient magic trick known as the Chinese linking rings. There should be eight of them. They must have been stolen from here as I only remove the label once they're sold.'

Listening and watching intently from above, I observed as Sergeant Brock leant on the counter with his elbow, slowly running one of the steel rings through his fingers.

'Tell me, Mr Kingsley, why is there a small break in one of the rings?'

'Tell me, sergeant, is it part of your investigation?' Brock tilted his head, looking upwards as if he knew I was listening.

'Heavens no. I'm just curious,' replied Brock.

'Well, as a member of the Magic Circle, I'm sworn to secrecy, so I'm afraid I can't tell you.'

With that, Sergeant Brock closed his book and gave Gordon an indignant look before dropping the linking rings back into his bag and turning to leave.

Gordon called out, 'Sergeant, I believe those linking rings belong in my shop.'

'No, Mr Kingsley, they're now crown evidence. The eighth ring was found around Vincent Leach's neck.' The officer opened the door, ready to leave, then turned back around to face Gordon.

'Oh, one last thing, will the Magic Circle allow you to tell me what the ace of spades card represents?'

Gordon paused, processing the question. 'Many things. Firstly, it's the highest and most valued card, but it can also represent death.'

'It certainly did for Mr Leach. The ace of spades card was jammed inside his throat.'

Sergeant Jack Brock closed the door behind him as Angel screeched, 'Ta-ra then.'

I waited a few moments before I made my way down the ladder. 'Is that what really happened to Vincent Leach?' I asked.

'Something like that.' Gordon turned on his heels and headed off to his workshop. It was the first time I realised that Gordon Kingsley was a ruthless man.

(*)

With my 15th birthday approaching, Lana and Gordon arranged a picnic for what they believed was my 17th. I still hadn't found the courage to tell them. Though February was hardly picnic weather, Gordon wanted to show off his brand new car, a white VW Beetle, in the snow of all things! He also had another surprise in store. He told me he and his friend Tom Camberwell were in a band called The Sandy Grains, and they had a gig at the Butlins Hotel on Blackpool seafront tonight. And I was invited.

'Nothing better than a chilly afternoon in Stanley Park,' said Lana as she bizarrely set up a picnic in the Italian Gardens. The never-ending snow still fell, laying like a giant white blanket across the central pond.

'No chance of playing a game of Split the Kipper today,' I called to Gordon, who shook his head. Lana passed me a cup of hot Bovril. Mockingly, I held my hands over the cup, trying to warm them. Both smiled at my attempted joke.

'There's a reason why we brought you to the Italian Gardens on your birthday.'

I sensed Gordon was about to give me some information about my parents. It was 15 years to the day since they abandoned me.

He continued. 'The more I watch your personality grow, the more I'm beginning to think that your mother and father may have been Italian.'

'Could you not have told me this back at the Magic Attic?' I asked through chattering teeth, a remark Gordon ignored.

'With your dark olive skin, jet black hair, oh and the way you explain things with your hand gestures, you remind me of an old Italian friend I once knew.' Gordon then fell silent. I felt he was holding something back. Lana tried to lighten the atmosphere by handing me my birthday present, wrapped in paper normally reserved for her fresh bread. Adding to Gordon's theory, inside was an Italian phrasebook.

'Do you want to tell me something else?' I asked them.

'Nope, the phrasebook will come in handy in case you meet up with Sergeant Brock,' said Gordon. Little did I know how useful it would become in the years ahead. Lana remarked she found it odd that there were no olive trees in the Italian Gardens.

'Probably because they would freeze to bloody death,' I complained.

'Mind your language, young man,' Gordon shouted, adding, 'You'd be better served concentrating on your sleight of hand than attempting comedy. That will lead you nowhere.'

'Looks like rain is on the way,' stated Lana. 'Better pack up. We've got to pick up the Camberwells. What number Palatine Road are they Gordon?'

'I'm not sure. I just look out for the Capri Guesthouse sign.'

A couple of minutes from the park, Gordon applied the handbrake outside the Camberwells' guesthouse. Snow had turned to drizzle, and I was sent to let them know we'd arrived. As I lifted my hand to knock on the door, it sprightly opened. I was greeted by a small plump lady who looked me up and down quizzically. I expected her to speak, but she just carried on staring.

Embarrassed, I eventually blurted out, 'Gordon sent me to let you know we're here.'

Looking over my shoulder, she waved to Gordon and Lana in the car. 'Is that his fancy new car?'

'Yes,' I replied.

'He should have chosen a coloured one. He'll never find it if it carries on snowing! Come in. I'm Annie, Tom's wife.'

'I'm Gee,' she looked at me like we'd met before, but if we had, I couldn't place where.

'Oh, you must be the Italian student. Your English is very good,' she said and gave me an even more puzzled look. Tom now appeared in the hallway proudly carrying his keyboard. He was at least a foot taller than Annie.

'Happy birthday, Giovanni. Welcome to our home,' he greeted in a slow, exaggerated drawn-out English accent. Annie continued to stare at me.

'Yes, happy birthday. Tom, his English is very good, so don't speak to him like he's a foreigner.'

Trying to move things along, I pointed towards the car. 'We'd best get going.'

Annie remarked she was not coming, so I helped Tom carry his keyboard to the car before he slowly limped back up the slushy path.

'I'll just go and fetch my little butterfly,' he called. Moments later, he reappeared. Holding onto his arm was a young girl. Lana nudged me with her elbow.

'Get out of the car and open the door for the young lady.' In doing so, I slipped in the snow. As I returned to my feet, my nose was no more than a snowflake away from the girl's face.

'This is my little butterfly, Penny. This is Gordon's Italian student, Giovanni,' announced Tom.

I mumbled a polite 'hello,' captured by her eyes and the light smell of her perfume. I moved to one side, allowing Penny to sit in the car. Tom took his place next to Gordon and we were on our way to my first ever music gig.

On arrival we were greeted by a wave of noise as we entered the hotel's cabaret room; the movement of drinking glasses, chairs and bustling conversation excited me. I recognised the performer on stage as Dravern Leach who was wearing his wannabe magician hat. His swagger wasn't matching his presentation of the multiplying clocks. When he noticed the five of us carrying musical instruments into the venue, he couldn't resist the opportunity of getting a cheap laugh.

'Hey up, the band's arrived. Do you know they are all musical in that family, even the sewing machine's a singer!' he said, to which he got a few titters from the audience. Lana looked for a table so we could watch the show. It was the first time I'd seen Penny in the light. There was something very different about her, what that something was, I was about to find out. She was tall and slim like her father, with white, shoulder-length, bobbed hair that certainly made her look different. The black sleeveless dress, interwoven with silver threads, dazzled as we weaved in and out of the tables. I tried not to stare, but her eyes wouldn't let me go. 'Would you like a drink, Penny?' Lana said sharply, interrupting my thoughts.

'Yes. Coke please,' she shyly replied.

'Come on, Gee. You can help me.' Lana gripped my arm, leading me towards the bar. 'Stop staring at her,' said Lana through gritted teeth.

'I can't help it.'

'Do you know she's only just about to turn 15, and she's Gordon's goddaughter?'

'I didn't know,' I said defensively.

'You haven't noticed something else too.'

'What?

'She's blind.'

The shock unsettled me. I was surprised as she carried herself so well. Lana went into detail about how Penny was born five weeks prematurely and had been blind since birth. I felt such sadness. There was me thinking my life had been tough without parents, but it was nothing compared to what Penny must have been through. As show time approached, every table in the room was taken, and Dravern was making his way to ours. He looked scruffy in the Butlins uniform of white trousers and red jacket. His eyes moved in opposite directions, giving the appearance he was trying to catch a fly.

'Good evening, Lana,' he said without taking his leering eyes off Penny. 'You're looking lovely tonight, Penny.'

She smiled in a kind of polite way that instantly said, *I think you're a creep.*

'He's a square and talentless,' remarked Lana as she threw back her red hair whilst stubbing out a cigarette. Dravern strutted to the stage, smugly removing the microphone.

'Hey dudes, let's get this Valentine's dance underway, give it up for Blackpool's very own, The Sandy Grains.'

Gordon and Tom were now joined by a drummer, making them a three-piece. I was amazed to hear that Gordon could sing, as well as play the saxophone. Song after song I couldn't stop staring at Penny. Her eyes seemed to be locked on mine and I didn't want the evening to end. Sadly it did. Tom took the microphone.

'You may remember the last time we were here, my daughter Penny sang the penultimate song of our set. So, I'm going to call my little butterfly up to the stage.'

Lana immediately nudged me. 'Go on, escort her to the stage,' she said in a hushed voice.

I stood, and Penny found my arm. I guided her to the stage like my life depended on it. With the audience applause fading, Penny took hold of the microphone and introduced the newly released single by Little Peggy March, "I Will Follow You". Her voice started softly and built powerfully. I was, as I had been all evening, captivated. Under the stage lights, each time she swayed, the silver threads in her black dress shimmered like stars in a black sky. I glanced at what I was wearing. I looked like a fairground attendant in a grey t-shirt and double denim (jeans and jacket). Dravern appeared next to me at the bar. Nudging me with his elbow, eyes fixed directly at Penny, he uttered,

'I would, and I bet you would too.'

Before I could react to his sick comment, he'd gone. The song ended with thunderous applause. So engrossed in the song, I'd failed to notice Dravern was the first to offer his hand to help Penny step down off the stage. I was furious with myself for not being there.

'Ok, folks, take your partners for our last song of the evening, Buddy Holly's "True Love Ways",' called out Tom over the microphone.

Gordon sang the opening line of the song. 'Just you'll know why.'

By now, I had taken hold of Penny's other hand. With fierce eyes and hostile words spilling from my mouth, I left Dravern Leach in no doubt how I felt about what he'd said at the bar.

'Now fuck off.'

Spurned, Leach walked away without replying. I didn't know if it was the music or Penny's eyes pulling us closer together. Either way, the song would soon end.

Penny whispered in my direction, 'Dance with me.'

'I'm not sure I know how,' I declared shyly.

'You will by the end of the song.'

Chapter 6

Blackpool, 1964
Sound of Silence

With Gordon often out and about helping to fix something or other on the Pleasure Beach, I was trusted to open, close and generally look after the Magic Attic alone. It was on such a day I first encountered Danny Mac, not a Scotsman as the name led me to believe, more a wide-boy cockney, the type of person who exploited the vulnerability in others. From the mezzanine, I watched him enter the Magic Attic, whistling a tune I later found out to be Colonel Bogey. Slim in build and in his mid-30s, he was the first man I'd come across with a ponytail.

'I'll be down in a minute,' I called. When I reached the bottom rung of the ladder, I heard Angel screech.

'Stop thief, stop thief.'

Danny Mac was on the wrong side of the counter.

'You'll do well to remember this is not a serve yourself shop,' I said in as deep a voice as I could muster. Danny moved to the customer side of the counter.

'Where's the governor today?' he asked in a strong London accent.

'Gordon's out, so I'm helping look after the shop,' I replied, refraining from saying, 'I'm in charge.'

'You're a little young to have an understanding of magic, aren't you?'

I returned a stare that belied my years.

Placing his palms flat on the counter, he leaned his head within six inches of mine. 'Tell me, shop boy, what do you know about The Bullet Catch illusion?' The stench of stale alcohol forced me so far back I was almost sitting on the same shelf as Angel.

Quickly I tried to remember what I'd read on the subject, but he was on my case.

'Come on. I'm waiting.'

Swallowing hard, I tried to gather speed. 'I know many people have died performing it, including Chung Ling Soo—'

Danny interrupted again. 'Do you have it in stock?'

'No, that's not the kind of item we keep on the shelf. I can ask Gordon for you when he gets back.' Before I'd completed the sentence, Danny turned on the heels of his cowboy boots and made his way out of the shop, like a petulant child denied his favourite toy.

Before the echo of Danny's footsteps faded on the treads of the wooden stairs, I'd switched on the TV behind the counter, returning to my favourite pastime of watching the old silent comedy movies. Be it Charlie Chaplin kicking a keystone cop up the arse, Buster Keaton perfectly positioning himself whilst the front of a house collapsed all around him, or just about anything that included Stan Laurel, I loved them all. What I loved most about these slapstick comedies was that everything was done without any talking. I'd begun to realise that almost anyone could learn to produce a chosen card if they dedicated themselves enough time to practice, but not everyone made people laugh. The more I watched Stan Laurel, the more I wanted to make people laugh. Gordon often caught me rocking and roaring with laughter at the antics of these comedy geniuses. Shaking his head, he'd throw me a pack of cards saying: 'Shouldn't you be practicing? There's no future in watching the keystone cops.'

In an effort to keep me away from the TV, Gordon managed to sort me a job at the Tower Circus. It was a simple enough task for a boy of my age, checking tickets and showing people to their seats. The pay was not great, but it gave me the chance to study live performances, or as Gordon said, 'Keep you away from that blasted TV.' I hoped it would also allow me to see more of Penny Camberwell.

On my first day at the circus, I got to see how imposing Blackpool Tower really was. Built in 1894, it was described as a rival to the Eiffel

Tower in Paris. Though in fairness, it is half in height and eminence. It was my first visit since seeing Alex Lockhart dragged out of the lions' cage. The history of the building was everywhere. When I walked up the long narrow corridor to the performers' dressing rooms, I was in awe. Floor to ceiling red embossed wallpaper, covered in gold motifs of the tragedy comedy mask, left me in no doubt this was showbusiness. On either side of the walls hung giant billing posters of performers and shows from yesteryear. *Bob Kellino and Doddles,* both clowns in the early part of the 1900s, occupied the first two frames. Across the hall was the largest billing photo of all, that of the great funny man *Charlie Cairoli,* which left me in no doubt that I too wanted to be a performer - of what type I had yet to work out. At the end of the corridor, the last of the billing frames grabbed my attention, probably due to its date and name, *Rossini's Traveling Circus, 14th January 1948;* just four weeks before I was born. This poster had no photos, just beautifully coloured illustrations of various acts. One, a man in his swimming trunks about to dive from a great height into a barrel full of water. Bizarrely, a bearded man named *Otto Coltelli* was throwing knives at a poor unfortunate girl tied to a wooden board. Another showed a high wire balancing act whilst eating fire. Unfortunately, the bottom half of the poster was barely readable due to light exposure from an effacing window, meaning all the performers' names had faded. Not that I fancied being a high diving, knife-thrower act who ate fire! Something about this poster caused me to stop and stare each time I passed by.

For me, the place was full of excitement. Parents watched through children's eyes; children aspired to be performers when they grew up. The smell of toffee apples and animal noises rose through the floorboards where the seated audience waited in anticipation. A circular theatre of fun, complete with a ringmaster dressed in a splendid red tailcoat and top hat, and I got to watch each live performance for free. *Mac Attack, The World's Most Dangerous Illusionist,* stated the billing poster. Danny Mac was the illusionist I met in the Magic Attic a few weeks before, along with his wife and assistant Tracey. Gordon described Danny as 'no more than a bloody box opener with little talent'. The highlight of their performance was Metamorphosis, an illusion also known as The Sub Trunk and made famous by the great Harry Houdini. Gordon did say that in fairness to box openers, this was the best illusion available. Blink and you'll miss it.

Lana saved me a seat next to Gordon on the front row. "Telstar" by The Tornadoes was the chosen music as Danny and Tracey Mac made a low-key entrance and walked to the centre of the arena before Danny sprang into life and kicked over a wooden packing crate. He removed a large, empty red sack from inside, and placed it by Tracey's feet. She stepped inside and Danny lifted it above her head, securing it with rope. Swiftly, he lifted the sack, complete with Tracey inside, and placed it into the crate. Once the lid to the crate was closed, Danny secured it with padlocks before athletically jumping on top. The music stopped. Slowly he turned full circle, dramatically holding the audience's attention like a good showman. Two stagehands passed a curtain up to Danny that now hid the crate. Momentarily, he lifted the curtain above his head, also concealing himself.

What should have followed a second or two later was Tracey standing on top of the crate, instantaneously changing places with Danny. Tracey would then remove the padlocks from the crate, lift the lid, and untie the rope securing the top of the red sack to reveal Danny shackled inside.

What followed was a reminder of how dangerous circus life can be. Danny was still standing atop the crate, but Tracey was nowhere to be seen. The music kicked back in. Danny furiously threw the curtain to the floor, like a matador no longer interested in the bull. He jumped off the crate and stomped out of the arena, ponytail swinging. Moments later, the two stagehands returned, removing the crate. Some clowns rushed on, trying to distract the audience from the failure that had taken place. I quickly made my way to the dressing room area. It reminded me of the chaos of my last visit. The two stagehands had removed the red sack containing Tracey. Danny quickly untied the rope and pulled Tracey's limp body from the sack. Fear struck as all three men jumped back. I gasped as a pale brown snake leisurely slithered out of the bright, red sack. I felt a hand on my shoulder as Gordon calmly said it was time to leave.

The next day the headline in the *Blackpool Gazette* read: "*Snakebite kills magician*".

Tracey Mac, aged just 18, died after being bitten several times on the leg by a Saw-Scaled viper. Tracey was performing with her husband Danny at the Tower Circus. A statement released by Manchester Royal Hospital said: "*Toxins in the venom had broken down the membranes in her blood vessels. She had severe swelling in her leg and sadly died five hours later."* A stagehand who witnessed what took place said the snake had probably escaped from the zoo area of the Tower, probably in search of warmth, and found its way into the sack.

I'd never met Tracey, and though Danny and I did not hit it off when we first met, I had nothing but sympathy for him. Both were accomplished magicians in their own right. Lana summed up all our feelings when she said,

'It was certainly no way for a good magician to die.'

Sometime later, I was perplexed when Danny mentioned he and Tracey operated a coin toss to decide who started inside the packing crate and who presented the illusion. Fortunately for Danny, he'd won the toss that evening, opting to present.

A few days after the initial story, the *Blackpool Gazette* published a follow-up headline: *"Snakebite mystery?"*.

An unnamed employee who worked in the reptile house at Blackpool Tower Zoo revealed they have no record of ever keeping a Saw-Scaled viper. So how did the venomous snake get inside Blackpool Tower, let alone the red sack? Had someone brought the snake into the circus and planted it? And if so, why? The newspaper also stated Sergeant Jack Brock of Blackpool Police said they had no reason to suspect any foul play, and no further investigation would be needed.

Out of respect, the circus closed for a few days. Gordon soon had me back out on his rickety old bike delivering props. If I headed north, I always cycled down Palatine Road, hoping to get a glimpse of Penny. Should I go south, then I returned via the Pleasure Beach. Due to my association with Gordon, I rarely had to pay for any of the rides, though I was still forbidden from going on the Wild Mouse. 'Not good for a young man's posture,' said Gordon. Actually, what he really said was, 'Your bloody head will fall off!.'

90 seconds of being chased by a crazy cat claimed the sign at the entrance to the Wild Mouse. It was too good an opportunity not to find out. I climbed into the front of the two-seater car, feeling a tingle of excitement. Secured into my seat by a locking metal bar, I heard someone jump into the seat behind me. The car jerked forward, crack! I felt a punch in the back of my neck.

'Now donkey, what are you doing on here without paying?'

I knew immediately it was the security-guard-come-red-coat Dravern Leach.

'I knew it was you or your brother,' I said, gritting my teeth in pain.

'You're not so brave now the blind girl isn't here.' Smack! Another rabbit punch to the back of my neck. 'Don't you ever talk about my dead brother, donkey.'

The car started a slow vertical climb. Turning slightly and with clenched fists, I threw out my arm, unable to make contact. When the car hit the first bend, our bodies jerked violently from side to side. Bang! Another punch on the back of my neck. The car descended. Leach grabbed the back of my ears, pulling them so hard I thought they'd tear off; the sound of scraping metal on metal covered my screams of pain. As the car started a slow climb again, pinning us both back into our seats, I tried throwing another punch but only moved the air. The car slammed left then right before dropping again. I felt several more painful blows, this time to the back of my head. Leach was now making a noise like a donkey. Ahead was the platform, and although dazed, I thought I'd do him over once I got out of the car. The safety barrier automatically released and I jumped out. Leach was already running away down the platform, continuing to make donkey noises as he went. Beaten and bruised, I decided not to tell Gordon what had happened. When he asked about the bruising to my neck, I told him I'd fallen off the bike. The next time I went to deliver a parcel the old bike had been replaced with a new one. It appeared I couldn't do any wrong, or so I thought.

Darkness brought a creepy, ghost-like feeling to the Pleasure Beach. Some nights I snuck into Gordon's workshop, looking out through his window on the world, watching the rats, foxes, and bats scavenging for food. I tended to think those who worked throughout the night must be like me, unable to sleep. Though it wasn't through lack of sleep that I was waiting outside the glasshouse of the laughing clown, now slumped to one side in the sleep position. It was 2.30 am. Patiently, I waited like a fisherman, but not for fish, more a rat. I smelt him before I saw him, his odour carried along on the breeze off the Irish Sea. Dravern Leach's bedraggled shadow stretched out ahead of him as he wandered around on night patrol. Though he was five years older than me, I was going to administer the surprise attack he'd caught me with on the Wild Mouse - retribution for me and all those kids who'd been abused by the Leach brothers over the years. Kids who were too frightened or unable to defend themselves.

Concerned I may damage the dexterity of my fingers, I slipped on a knuckle duster, taken from a glass cabinet in the Magic Attic. With little difference in our heights, I stepped out from the darkness and drew back my elbow like a skilled archer. His crooked eyes widened with fear, his brain too slow to do anything but take the punch full-on between the mouth and nose. I heard the sound of splitting teeth followed by air expelling from his body. His legs buckled like a drunk as he collapsed to the floor, and then he whimpered. Standing over him, I briefly shone my torch on his face. Blood was flowing freely from his nose and mouth. I switched off the torch quickly - I couldn't allow him to see his assailant. Instead, I flicked on the switch activating the laughing clown, who instantly echoed eerily throughout the Pleasure Beach as I made my way back to the Magic Attic and my bed.

(*)

The Magic Attic was the place to be and be seen for magicians, especially on Saturday mornings. Many professional magicians popped in for a coffee and a chat before going to their first gig of the day. I was about to unlock the shop door when Gordon called me to one side.

'Did you hear the laughing clown in the middle of the night?' Now if there's one thing I've learnt about Gordon, you can't pull the wool over his eyes. Chances are, he had a mirrored tunnel from his bedroom overlooking the Pleasure Beach. I decided to go with the truth, starting with riding on the forbidden Wild Mouse and Dravern Leach attacking me. Gordon listened until I was exhausted before asking,

'Did you turn on the laughing clown when you left him looking for his teeth?'

'Yes,' I replied with a cocky half-smile.

'Well, it was a bloody stupid thing to do, the Pleasure Beach manager telephoned the police.'

'He had it coming to him.'

'And you might have it coming to you when Sergeant Brock starts sniffing around. What did you hit him with that caused so much damage?'

'The knuckle duster from the glass cabinet. I didn't want to damage my hands.'

Gordon immediately removed the offending item from the glass cabinet, picked up the phone receiver and started to dial. Convinced he was contacting the police, I tried to think where I could run to.

'Tom, it's Gordon. I need a favour. Could you pop over to the shop just after lunch?' Without another word, he replaced the handset.

'Before you open the shop, remove the last of Dravern Leach's blood from under your fingernails.'

The shop was soon busy. I was surprised to see Danny Mac talking to Gordon about ordering the Bullet Catch trick so soon after Tracey's death. Tom arrived just after lunchtime. On seeing me, he asked if I would pop downstairs and help guide Penny up once she stopped chatting to Lana. Taking two stairs at a time, I dashed excitedly downstairs.

'My mam has sent you some blackberry pie.' Penny handed me a small box, adding, 'For some reason, she thinks you're a bit special, the son she never had.' I joined in with her gentle laughing to hide my embarrassment. As we reached the top stair, she let go of my arm, and for a moment, I panicked, afraid she might fall. Softly, her hands took hold of mine. As always, I was lost in her eyes, the misty outer grey, thin delicate black circle, bold planet-like pupils that held my gaze.

She whispered, 'Are you staring at me?' I realised we were still holding hands. Letting go, she ran her hand around the back of my neck.

'How did you bruise your neck?'

I had no idea how she would know my neck was bruised. 'I fell off the shop bike.'

'I don't believe you.'

Opening the door into the Magic Attic, Tom glared at me. I knew instantly that Gordon must have told him about me attacking Dravern Leach.

'Right butterfly, we'd better get going,' he said as he brushed past me. I noticed the knuckle duster in the top of his shoulder bag, confirming my suspicion. He took hold of Penny's arm, leading her out of the shop. I asked Tom if I could help.

'Yes,' he said quietly. 'Stay away from my daughter.'

I looked across at Gordon; his shoulders slumped forward. I'd added a new burden to the one he'd been carrying around for years. I tried to speak, but Gordon stopped me in my tracks and told me to go up to my room, as he needed time to think. I knew I had let him down. I'd no sooner climbed the ladder up to the mezzanine when I heard the shop doorbell.

'Sergeant Brock, no uniform today? I take it you must be here to buy a magic trick or two?' Gordon declared more cheerily.

'It's Detective Brock now. No uniform required.'

Gordon tried to exchange pleasantries, but the detective was strictly there on business.

'The only magic you can help me with is how do you think the laughing clown turned itself on in the middle of last night?'

'It's magic, it's magic,' screeched Angel.

Gordon quickly threw a blanket over his cage before adding, 'Oh, that won't be magic, detective, more a problem with the electrics. Maintenance will probably call at some point for me to take a look.'

Jack Brock raised his voice. 'Perhaps maintenance will ask you to take a look at Mr Dravern Leach's mouth while you're at it. He was punched by someone wearing a knuckle duster, similar to the version you sell.'

The detective looked into the glass cabinet, noticing the knuckle duster was no longer inside.

'It's not illegal to sell knuckle dusters, detective.'

'No, it's not, but it is illegal to punch someone in the face while wearing one,' he replied.

'Are you accusing me, detective?' Gordon hit back angrily.

'Absolutely not, Mr Kingsley, a war hero awarded the George Cross in 1942 for heroism would never stoop so low.' The detective had done his homework.

'The problem is, Mr Kingsley, it was not just a violent attack on a security guard. Dravern Leach left his post whilst he should have been guarding the day's takings. Thousands of pounds were stolen. At this point, I'm not sure if both crimes are connected. Should they be, whoever did this will go to prison.' My mouth fell open, shocked to hear that money had been stolen and hoping Gordon wouldn't think I was also involved.

'That Italian student who's staying with you, is he about so we can have a chat?'

'He left a couple of days ago, gone off backpacking around Europe he said.'

'What is he, some kind of hippie?' Brock now appeared more relaxed.

'Something like that,' replied Gordon, bored with Brock's lacklustre questioning.

'Well, when he returns, tell him to report to Blackpool police station,' called the officer, failing to close the door as he left. It seemed an age before Gordon called me down from the mezzanine. Lana arrived with some food, and dinner had a last supper feeling about it as we all sat in silence.

'This is a mess, Gee,' remarked Gordon. 'Did you have anything to do with the robbery?'

'No! Absolutely not. Look, I can see I've brought you a lot of trouble. I think it best I leave.'

Lana lifted her head from the plate, throwing me a stare I'd not seen since the first day I arrived. Gordon placed his hand on my shoulder.

'We don't run away from our problems, Gee; we steer around them. After dinner I need you to pack your clothes. Tom's pulled a few strings and managed to secure you a live-in job as a compere at the Carlton Hotel in Brighton.'

'Where the hell is that?' I asked.

'On the south coast,' interjected Lana, desperately trying to stop her tears from falling.

'How long will I have to be gone?'

'Until this has all blown over, maybe a year, possibly two, and we leave tonight.'

'Tonight!' I almost yelped.

'Look, it will be good for you. All you have to do is introduce the visiting cabaret acts. It will give you the chance to refine your own magic act.'

I couldn't believe my own stupidity had put me in such a situation. I was sad at the thought of leaving Gordon and Lana, even sadder knowing that if my parents came looking for me I would not be found. Lana gripped me, vice-like, demanding I take care of myself. We took a detour via Annie Camberwell's, as apparently she had something for me, probably more pie for the journey. Approaching Capri Guesthouse, I was relieved Tom's car was not outside. Gordon, who had not spoken since we left, at last broke the silence.

'I'll stay in the car. Annie's already waiting for you at the door.'

'Come in, Gee,' she welcomed me as always with a warm smile. I tilted my head to one side, listening to the faint sound of a guitar playing.

'Oh, that's Penny's practising with her guitar.'

'Penny plays guitar too?' I said, stunned.

'Penny is a very determined young girl, Gee.' We made small talk about my new job in Brighton when Annie, out of the blue, said,

'Gee, I have this theory, you may think I'm mad, but when you first came here I had a strange feeling we'd met before.'

'Well, I don't think we have—'

Annie interrupted. 'I was going to ask you this when Tom was here, but he's been called into work.'

Now I was feeling really nervous, what was she going to ask?

'Gee, open your shirt, please. I need to see the top of your left shoulder. If I'm wrong, I'll explain.' I knew what she wanted to see right away, but I didn't know why. Opening my shirt, I pulled it off my shoulder. Annie's eyes filled with tears. Overflowing, they fell down her chubby cheeks.

I quickly buttoned my shirt. 'What's wrong?'

'You were born here, Gee, in this very house. I thought it the first time you came here. When Gordon recently mentioned you were an orphan, I became convinced. You have your mother's high cheekbones and black pupils. The birthmark in the shape of a boot confirms everything.'

I was stunned.

Gordon appeared, saying we had to get going. But leaving Blackpool now was the last thing I wanted. Annie asked us both to sit down, then explained about the foreign couple who checked in the night before I was born and how she found me wrapped in the blue towel the next morning. Fearing I was dead, she rushed me to hospital, explaining how she visited the hospital day after day to follow my progress. That Tom and her had tried to adopt me, but I'd been placed with someone else. I sat in silence, staggered at what I heard, and then came my questions.

'Where were they from?'

'I don't know,' responded Annie.

'Where did they go?'

Annie lifted her shoulders before they dropped, along with the corners of her mouth.

'Wait, wait,' interrupted Gordon, 'it can't be Gee, he was born in 1946 not 1948.' My eyes glanced across at Gordon, quickly averting the moment he realised.

'I'm sorry, Gordon. I lied to you. I thought you would never take in a 14-year-old boy.'

'Too bloody right I wouldn't, so much for no secrets between us.'

'Now let's stay calm,' pleaded Annie. 'It's been a shock for us all, a shock that back in 1948 put me into early labour. Penny was born five weeks prematurely, which may have caused her blindness.' I instantly felt my parents were responsible for Penny not being able to see. Annie left the room, and a stony silence fell between Gordon and me. When Annie returned she was holding the small blue towel she'd found me wrapped in. Handing it to me, she pointed out the GB sewn into one corner.

'What does that stand for?' I asked.

'Sadly, I don't know. It's a question I've been asking myself for years.'

'What now?' I asked solemnly.

'Right now, we get going to Brighton,' stated Gordon.

'What about the age thing?' I asked.

'Well, you've fooled me for the past two and a half years. I'm sure you'll fool the hotel manager too.' Gordon delivered his first smile on a trying day.

'There's always your room here, Gee, when you return. Nobody has slept in it since the day you were born.' I hugged Annie like I had never hugged anyone in my life. I asked if I could say goodbye to Penny.

'Yes, but quickly,' smiled Annie. I knocked gently on Penny's door.

'Come in.' The room was in darkness except for a candlelight flickering, reflecting faintly over Penny's face, who was sitting in a chair.

'I heard everything. I suppose I should be grateful that you're not my half-brother or something like that. Brighton's supposed to have some of the prettiest girls in England.'

'Not one as pretty as you.'

Shyly, Penny's eyes lowered. Her cheeks matched the tip of the burning candle. 'When will you be back?'

'I really don't know. Perhaps we could be penfriends.' I immediately regretted the stupid words that left my mouth.

'I don't do letters,' Penny responded.

I couldn't find another word without my voice choking. Wrestling with my courage, I leant forward to kiss Penny goodbye, but she broke my movement by picking up her guitar.

'As there's no sand in Brighton, perhaps you could send a pebble from the beach.' Penny blew out the candle, asking me to close the door behind me. As I walked away, I heard the strings from her guitar and instantly recognised Simon and Garfunkel's "Sound of Silence". Then Penny's soulful voice was in full flow.

'Hello darkness my old friend. I've come to talk with you again.'

It was a song that would resonate with me throughout my life. It certainly did as we made our seven-hour journey through the night to Brighton.

Chapter 7

Brighton, 1965
The Haunted Hotel

Gordon promised to keep his eyes open for an Italian-speaking woman with high cheekbones, searching for a troublesome boy with shiny black pupils. It was a light-hearted way of saying goodbye. I waited until his VW Beetle roared off along Marine Parade and back up north. At least I was now one burden less for his hanging shoulders even if I was on my own again.

The Carlton Hotel stood proudly on Kemp Town seafront, like the grandmaster of all hotels, with four towers symbolising each of the seasons, fifty-two chimneys representing the weeks of the year, twelve floors and three hundred and sixty-five bedrooms. My room was in the basement and I shared it with a waiter named Johnny, who claimed to have slept in at least a third of the hotel's bedrooms, as it's forbidden to invite female guests back to staff quarters. Brighton in the 1960s was a real eye-opener for this 17-year-old. With London just up the road, it was probably why most locals sounded like Danny Mac. I quickly settled into my new role. Besides Penny, Gordon, and Lana, I missed little else from Blackpool.

My new boss - Walter Wilson - sounded nothing like a cockney. He was very much the English gent. He served with both Tom and Gordon in the British Army during World War Two. He seemed to have taken a real shine to me and delighted in telling me haunted stories about the hotel.

'Pull up a chair, son,' he'd say. 'You'll struggle sleeping tonight after hearing this one.' I doubt most were true, but one particular story brought home again the idea that performing magic doesn't always go to plan. As one particular event took in the Marine Ballroom, on the hotel's top floor, Walter insisted I meet him there after the evening show. When I arrived, Walter was removing a couple of folding chairs from a small store cupboard.

'Back in the 1950s, this used to be the dressing room for the visiting acts.'

I craned my neck inside to see. It was hardly big enough for one person, let alone two. Noticing my expression, he couldn't resist the opportunity to deliver a comedy line.

'The room's so small you have to step outside to change your mind.'

I couldn't help but think Walter had stolen the line from a visiting comedian as he placed both chairs in the middle of the dance floor. The high ceiling and regency carved coving gave the room a Victorian feeling. Walter set the scene like a film director, and before a final cough to clear his throat, he settled down to tell his story.

'Carl and Cynthia Dean were a long-time married couple in their mid-50s. They were both competent magicians and lived locally behind the hotel. Billed as *The Pavilions,* they were regular performers at the hotel. On my first night, back in 1956, The Pavilions performed in this very room. Sitting close to the front, where we are now, I watched their closing routine, known as The Razor Blade trick.'

I knew the trick, having sold it at the Magic Attic. I also knew how to present it, but it didn't stop Water from explaining the routine chapter and verse.

'The magician first removes five razor blades from a small box, demonstrating to the audience how sharp the blades are. The magician slices through a newspaper. Dramatically, the performer slowly swallows each blade, creating the illusion the blades have passed through the throat. After unravelling a length of cotton, some 14 inches long, that too is swallowed. The magician regurgitates one end of the cotton, pulling it out of his mouth, revealing all the razor blades have magically threaded onto the cotton.' Walter paused; I knew from previous stories this meant it was my turn to speak.

'You're saying all this like something went wrong.'

Walter smiles, clearly happy I'm contributing to his story.

'Here's the theory behind the trick. Before the routine even starts, the magician places five blunted razor blades, already threaded onto the cotton, into one cheek of his mouth. In fact, all the blades are blunted other than the one used to slice through the newspaper, which is palmed out of harm's way. When the performer appears to swallow the blades individually, he's simply hiding them in his other cheek. Unfortunately, what Carl didn't realise was that the blunted blades had been switched for razor-sharp ones. He was unaware they were slicing into his cheek, seeping blood each time he spoke. When he inserted the individual blades, also razor-sharp, they lacerated his tongue as he moved them into the opposite cheek, releasing more blood. Carl had no idea that the cotton he was about to place in his mouth had been laced with hydrogen peroxide. When the cotton came into contact with the open wounds, Carl started to gag, then choke, as a razor blade slipped down his throat, slicing through his oesophagus.' Walter paused again.

I stretch my neck and swallow hard out of compassion. 'And?' I croaked.

'Carl collapsed to the floor.'

'Did you not get out of your seat to help?' I pleaded.

'Hell no, you never can tell with magicians if the drama unfolding is all part of their routine or not. Even when his assistant Cynthia started shoving cotton wool into his mouth, I still had no idea if this was part of the show.

'What the hell did you think she was doing, making a teddy bear?'

Walter frowned at me, reminding me of Gordon.

'I just thought it was all good acting, especially when Carl's outstretched arm started slapping on the wooden stage, like a zoo penguin demanding more fish.'

'Did you then get up to help?'

'No, there was nothing I could do. Unfortunately, poor Carl choked to death on the cotton wool. So I left the room and went to bed.'

'Still, I don't understand. Why would that make the hotel haunted?' I asked.

'The date Carl Dean was murdered was October the 31st. They were performing for the Grave Diggers Association, their annual ball. Every Halloween since, guests have reported the sound of banging coming from the Marine Ballroom late at night, yet the room has been unused for years.'

'It's probably those blasted seagulls on the outside window ledges.' I suggested trying to reassure myself the hotel was not haunted.

'No, I've been in one of the rooms below. The noise is coming from the stage. I believe it's Carl's outstretched hand slapping on the wooden floorboards reminding us that his wife murdered him.'

'Wait a minute, that's twice you said Carl was murdered?'

Walter stood up and folded his chair. Like a good actor, he was about to deliver the dramatic climax to his story. 'I'd only been in the job a week when I got a visit from two senior detectives from the Brighton cop shop. They both believed Cynthia Dean had murdered her husband and charged her accordingly.'

'Holy cow! Why the hell was she charged with murder?'

Now about to deliver the *coup de grace,* Walter walked towards the store cupboard with his chair. 'The week before, not only had Cynthia Dean purchased enough cotton wool to fill an eiderdown, but she'd also took out extra life insurance on her husband.'

I couldn't help but think it sounded like a bad way for a good magician to die.

'Mark my words, this hotel is haunted,' bellowed Walter as he wished me goodnight, leaving the room. Alone, I remained in my chair until I heard the faint sound of the wind, whistling through a gap somewhere in the large ballroom. The hairs on my arms stood to attention, and I quickly followed Walter out of the door.

The following day, I returned to the Marine Ballroom. In my rush to leave the night before, I'd left my jacket on the chair. However, both my coat and the chair were nowhere to be seen. Faintly, the sound of whistling wind still swirled in the air. My eyes alerted me to the slightly ajar store cupboard door. With echoing footsteps, I edged across the wooden dance floor. I inched back the door; the whistling wind grew louder. Inside the store stood a tatty old wooden wardrobe, without doors. My coat hung neatly on a rail, softly swaying in the draught. Removing it, I saw a crack in the back of the wardrobe from where the wind whistled through.

The problem with living at the Magic Attic was that it made me think all buildings have secret passageways lined with mirrors. I peered through the crack then pushed hard on the back panel. Instantly it fell away into a hidden room. Clearing away the cobwebs, I ventured inside as the spiders raced for cover. Halfway up the opposite wall was a porthole with broken glass, which allowed the wind to gush in and only partly masked the smell of rising damp. A beam of light illuminated millions of colourful dust motes, magically floating in the secret room no bigger than 12 feet square. There was a single bed and on top were two vinyl records, one by Edith Piaf and the other by Perez Prado. On the opposite wall was a bedsheet draped over a box. I slowly removed the sheet to reveal a small cocktail bar. Shivers ran through every molecule of my body. *'Pavilions, parlour magic'* was written across the front. This must have been the stage set of Carl and Cynthia Dean, placed here after Carl was murdered, a boarded-up secret until now.

As I turned to leave, there was an abundance of artiste billing posters covering the wall where I'd entered. Chillingly I'm drawn to *The Pavilions'* 10x8 promo photo. Carl is dressed in a dinner suit, with his head tilted back as he pulls half a dozen razor blades on a thread from his mouth. Wife Cynthia, half-smiling, watches on. Her eyes reminded me of Lana's. Ducking my head to leave the room, I noticed a familiar poster - *'Rossini's Traveling Circus'* - the same poster I'd seen in the Tower Circus. Carefully I removed the Sellotape holding it in position. The date stated the show was to be held on the 14th of December 1947 at Preston Park, precisely eight weeks before I was born. Sadly, the bottom half of the poster was torn, leaving only the top half of the fire eater. I was starting to believe this circus poster just might be my lucky charm. Back in the store cupboard, I replaced the back panel, covering any trace of my entrance.

Later that day, my mind drifted back to my newfound secret room. Maybe this room could be the start of my journey as a performer, a place where I would build my own comedy act, with music at the forefront. I decided not to tell Walter about the room. Instead, I would seek his advice. After all, as well as being a great storyteller, Walter also performed as *'The Gurner'.* Removing his false teeth, Walter would take hold of the outer rim of a car tyre. Sticking his head through the centre, he'd gurn; twisting, pulling and distorting his face into various poses like a witch, baby, clown, old man, Popeye. He could even lift his bottom lip above his nose to give the impression of an alien. Though his act only lasted six minutes, he had audiences in fits of laughter. His advice would prove invaluable.

'Creating a stage show is like a recipe for gourmet dining. It requires preparation, application and dedication. Too much of the wrong ingredient and the whole show experience is ruined. There are so many aspects that need to be addressed before you try to build your comedy act.'

I listened intently as though he were delivering the secret to a long life.

'If you want to be a speciality act, you'll need a theme for your show and a type of character your audience will find endearing. You'll need to know who your target audience is and what type of venues you can perform in.' Walter's advice was clear. I just thought I needed to be funny. Turns out I needed a whole lot more. I wanted to portray a waiter in the mould of my comedy hero, Stan Laurel - silent, clumsy and forgetful, and my ten-minute routine would include inviting a female audience member to sit at a small bistro table onstage.

I spent the following months practicing funny walks, acrobatic moves and various mannerisms, listening to the many songs of Edith Piaf. Without props or words, I would serve my guest an imaginary dinner, using only the art of slapstick. It needed to be both funny and endearing and become the mainstay of my act for the next 20 years. I would bounce off ideas for my new show with Walter. He would either frown or produce one of his wide, wobbly, gurning smiles of approval. Eventually, I found the courage to ask him if I could try out my new act on him.

'Have you rehearsed?' he quizzed.

'Every day,' I replied.

'I only need to see ten minutes.'

'Ten minutes is all I've got,' I replied.

'11 pm tonight in the Marine Ballroom.'

'But I thought you said it was haunted up there?'

Walter gave me a worried frown. 'It is, but if your act works up there, it will work anywhere. Oh, and no razor blade tricks!' His laugh reverberated as he walked down the corridor.

With military timing, Walter pulled up a chair in the Marine Ballroom at 11 pm. Upon noticing my stage set of chair, table and radio sitting on top, he nodded approvingly.

'Ok, let's see what you've got, Radio Valentine.' Radio Valentine, I like that! My ten-minute routine flew by like a dream. Walter stretched back in his chair, ready to pass judgement.

'Very good. When one of the visiting acts fails to turn up, you'll get your chance. Until then, keep practicing.'

'Is that it?' I asked.

'What do you want, a bloody Oscar?' he laughed.

Whilst he was feeling jovial, I decided to quiz him about how he became friends with Gordon and Tom.

'In September 1943, I served with the 1st Airborne Division In Italy. We were sent to capture the port of Bari, which we did successfully. There were so many unexploded bombs they brought in a few extra bomb disposal teams. One such team included Tom Camberwell, an engineer, and brothers Gordon and Gino Kingsley, who were both bomb disposal experts.'

'Gordon had a brother named Gino?' I asked, surprised. Walter instantly knew he was probably revealing too much information.

'Maybe you should ask Gordon.'

I pushed Walter for more information, knowing he couldn't resist a good story.

'I suggest you just keep this to yourself.'

I promised Walter I wouldn't repeat a word.

'We took a phone call about an unexploded bomb on an American cargo ship. Tom and Gordon were on duty, but Gordon had gone AWOL with one of the local girls. Gordon's brother Gino stepped in, but he was not as experienced as his older brother. Anyway, all three of us boarded the ship. I secured the area. Tom checked the structure near the bomb position before Gino moved in to defuse it.' At that moment, Walter stopped and placed his hand on his right leg to stop it from shaking. 'I wish I'd never started this blasted story.' Walter paused again, taking a swig of courage from his flask. 'Tom was behind me; we were withdrawing from the area when the bomb suddenly exploded. We were both knocked off our feet and it killed Gino immediately. There was nothing left of him. Shrapnel peppered Tom's legs and back. The noise was so loud it left me with bloody tinnitus in both ears to this day. But, most painfully, it left Gordon without his brother.' Walter fell silent.

I realised the guilt that Gordon had been carrying all these years.

'Tom and I covered for Gordon so he wouldn't get a court-martial for going AWOL. Not that Gordon cared if they'd locked him up and thrown away the key. Shortly after, he was redeployed to Naples. Tom was shipped off to Capri to convalesce, and I served out my time in Italy until the war ended.'

I was truly saddened by the story and apologised to Walter for pushing him into sharing it with me.

'Tom and I kept in touch after the war by letter. He had terrible leg injuries, which Gordon also blamed himself for. When Tom and Annie got married, Gordon's wedding present was the deposit to buy Capri Guesthouse. At the same time, he also opened the magic shop and the shop underneath so Gino's widow, Lana, could open up a bakery.'

'What was Gino like?'

'Well, if you think Gordon was a good magician, think again. Gino Kingsley was only 28 when he was killed. Five years earlier, he'd been voted Scotland's best magician. His dexterity was second to none. After the war, Gordon and Gino were going to form a double act. It was no way for a magician to die.'

I couldn't help but feel Gordon was trapped in a lifetime of guilt, one he would never escape.

'Gee, there is one other thing you need to know.'

Looking at Walter, I wasn't sure what else he could possibly reveal.

'Like most soldiers, we all got our names shortened. I was Wal, Gordon, Gord, and Gino was known as Gee.'

Wow! Everything was starting to make sense. Is this why Gordon took me in, to push me into learning magic because I shared the same rare name as his brother?

(*)

In July, the Carlton Hotel celebrated its 100th anniversary. A Gala Ball was arranged that would eclipse anything seen in Brighton that century. The theme was Lewis Caroll's *Alice in Wonderland,* which was also celebrating the centenary of its first publication. Walter was part of the planning committee that included Blackpool-based impresario John Todd, who selected the performing acts. Walter informed me that TV star Terry Vaughan had been booked as the compere. I was disappointed my services weren't required. The bright and colourful billing posters were plastered all over Brighton. Bold in both size and colour, they read...

John Todd Entertainments proudly presents...
The Carlton Hotel Centenary Gala Ball
An Evening of Magic and Illusion

Top of the bill was 'Snowflake', the UK's leading female illusionist, and Italy's Luca Baldino, the world's fastest metamorphosis. From the USA sword magician and swallower, 'The Great Zantini', 'The Brighton Bell Dancing Girls', and many other headline performers from around the world, it was going to be a night to remember.

When the big day arrived, Walter was in a flap. The Great Zantini was stuck in a Paris airport, waiting for a connecting flight. Walter asked me to hang around the reception area and welcome the VIP guests as they arrived. After two hours of polite smiles and cheery hellos, I glanced out the main lobby window and, to my amazement, I saw Gordon's VW pull up outside. My surprise turned into excitement when I saw Penny being helped out of the car by Annie. I rushed outside like a boy who hadn't seen his family for months. Gordon gave me the firmest of handshakes, Annie and Lana the warmest of hugs, and Tom simply nodded in my direction.

'I'm still waiting for my pebble, Gee Valentine,' Penny said quietly whilst offering me the shyest of smiles. I desperately wanted to hug her but thought better of it. Walter appeared. More handshakes all round between the old army friends.

'Tom, Gordon and Gee, can we meet in my office in, say, ten minutes?' instructed Walter in an army-like voice. By the time I arrived, Tom and Gordon were already in there.

'Come in, Gee. I'm just explaining the situation we have. The not-so-Great Zanini is stuck in Paris and won't arrive until after the show starts, so we're 20 minutes short. John Todd contacted Tom last night to ask Penny to step in with a couple of songs, and Gee, you will fill the other ten minutes with your act.'

Holy cow. My legs started to wobble. Gordon reassured me that I wouldn't let anyone down. Walter interrupted him.

'I've been watching Gee in rehearsals, Gord. Providing he can control his nerves, he'll be fine. John Todd's taken my word, Gee. Go and set up your music and props. The band call's taking place right now in the Ocean Ballroom.'

I made my way past the hotel staff, who were still frantically trying to finish decorating the room. Most of the acts on the bill were going through their band calls. The Brighton Bell Dancers were pacing through and marking their positions. Sarah Todd, aka Snowflake the Illusionist, was running through her final rehearsal. I watched as one of the stage crew secured her into a straitjacket, then bound her ankles together with thick rope. Instantly she was hoisted upside down, some 30 feet above the stage. The rope hanging above her ankles was set on fire. I was captivated as she struggled to free herself, wriggling and twisting her body to release the straitjacket, or she would fall 30 feet onto a bed of nails below and certain death. My heart was beating way too fast for a boy my age. First, the jacket was removed, my eyes followed as it dropped onto the bed of nails. Hoisting herself upwards, she quickly untied the rope around her ankles before it burnt through. Now freed, she calmly took hold of a chain that gently lowered her back down to the stage.

'Far out, man,' I called. Sarah smiled at me and made her way towards me, followed by her father, John Todd, who spoke first.

'You must be Gee Valentine, the brilliant slapstick act Walter keeps rabbiting on about. You'd better be good,' he said. As he walked away, he called to the dancing girls. 'Go through the opening number one more time.'

Sarah smiled at me. 'Don't worry about Daddy, his bark's loud, but he's a pussy cat really.' At just under 5 feet tall, Sarah's build was slender, to say the least. Her eyes were wide, like her smile, and her waist-long hair was more white than blonde. She was the first friendly person of my age I'd met since leaving Blackpool. Within seconds her warm personality had shone through, helping to put me at ease. She introduced her boyfriend.

'This is Micky. Should you ever need an illusion building, he's your man.'

I'm not sure if Micky partly smiled at me or silently tried to pass wind.

His face was as round as his tinted orange spectacles, which clashed with his ginger hair.

I heard the drums and keyboard from the far side of the stage, informing me that Penny was onstage with her opening song, "I Will Follow You". Hearing her sing again calmed me down. After looking for tonight's running order, I find it pinned to the stage manager's door. I'm the third act on the bill. Controlling my nerves was a must. If I froze, this would be my opening and closing night all in one go. I head off in search of what becomes a pre-show ritual, sleep.

Chapter 8

Brighton, 1965
After the Ball

I knew I'd arrived early, as the Alice in Wonderland characters were still adding the finishing touches before the guests arrived for dinner. Balanced on top of the shoulders of Tweedledum was Tweedledee, holding onto one end of the banner. Meanwhile, The Mad Hatter climbed the ladder, some 20 feet away, attaching the other end of the banner to a hook above the entrance doors that led into the Ocean ballroom. *'Welcome to the Mad Hatter's Ball. 100 years in the making'*, it read.

A dozen or so dwarfs dressed as Alice characters were milling around. I snook past them and into the ballroom. Around 100 tables were set for dinner, each with an Alice in Wonderland character centrepiece. Making my way to the dressing rooms, I came across John Todd sitting cross-legged at the front of the stage. He was a larger-than-life character, though not in height at only 5ft 9, but certainly in weight (all 18 stone of him). He had a shiny, bald head with a grey handlebar moustache that flapped about his chubby cheeks when he spoke. Tonight, he was immaculately dressed in a dark blue tailored suit, white shirt and stand out bow tie to match his red shoes. Walter had mentioned his eccentricity and smart business brain had brought him much wealth. Walter also warned there were three things you should never try and get close to - his daughter, his wallet and his breath, as he's a constant chewer of raw garlic.

In a quieter version of his normally booming voice, he said, 'Opportunities like these can shape a young man's future. Don't let it pass you by.' A genuine smile spread his handlebar moustache across his face, touching his ears and showing a softer side, just like Sarah had said. I rolled under the safety curtain and onto the stage, finding myself at the feet of the Italian performer, Luca Baldino, setting up his Sub Trunk illusion. Trying out what little Italian I had learnt from my phrasebook, I greeted him with,

'*Ciao* Luca, *mi chiamo* Gee.'

His reply is so fast I don't catch a word. Embarrassingly, I have to ask if he speaks English.

'Sure, no problem, I just thought you were Italian?'

'I'm not sure if I am or not,' was my meek reply.

'You're not sure? How can you not be sure? Italians are always sure of being Italian,' he replied with confidence. Standing 6 feet tall, he was wearing a slim-fit black outfit, topped off with hair as black as my pupils.

The only pathetic response I could muster was, 'My parents abandoned me as a baby. Many people think I might be Italian, though, because of my skin tone and mannerisms.'

'And your Roman nose!' Luca smirked as his arms and hands moved like a keystone cop from an old movie.

'I have a Roman nose?' I inquired.

'Yes, oh, and your jealousy! I saw the way you glared at the stagehands when they ogled your girlfriend in rehearsals.'

'I don't have a girlfriend.' I said, trying to play it cool.

Luca blew out his checks, mumbling, '*Pazzo.*' Luca helped me to my feet as I dusted down my trousers. His performance of the Sub Trunk was claimed to be the world's fastest, at just under three seconds. Offering Luca one of my pear drops, I mentioned I was witness to the slowest Sub Trunk presentation ever performed when Tracey Mac, unfortunately, lay dead inside a crate, bitten by a venomous snake.

'I remember that story from the Italian newspapers. Snakes are definitely not part of my Sub Trunk routine,' he replied, shaking his wrist in a wary kind of way.

'Anyway, the girl who assists me would have probably bitten the snake first!'

'Where is she, in the trunk?'

Luca's puzzled eyes glanced at the trunk and my attempted joke fell flat. I could only hope this was not a sign of things to come for the evening.

'No, London, she's an art student, probably won't arrive until ten minutes before the show.'

'Wow, does that not scare you?'

'We've performed the Sub Trunk many times together. I know she won't let me down. *In bocca al lupo.*'

'*Sì,*' I return without a bloody clue what he was talking about and a mental note to check my phrasebook later. Reaching my dressing room, I was greeted by the compere.

'Hello, I'm Terry Vaughan. You must be Gee?'

I nod politely, still feeling out of my depth.

'Afraid we're sharing a dressing room.'

Gordon and Lana popped in to say, break a leg. Lana told me I was already more reliable than The Great Zantini because at least I'd shown up! The nerves had really started to get to me, so I went looking for Penny to wish her luck. The door to her dressing room was open just enough to see Annie fixing Penny's silver necklace. Gone was the girl I first saw at 14, she was now replaced by a shapely, mature, young woman, wearing a three-quarter-length, figure-hugging gold dress. I pushed open the door and gave a wolf whistle, announcing my presence.

'Gee Valentine, don't you know it is bad luck to whistle backstage?' Penny said with a shake of her head.

Embarrassingly I replied, 'No.'

'Well, you should, and you've just cursed tonight's show. Now leave the room, turn around three times, swear, then knock on the door and come back in.'

I gave a puzzled look. 'Really?'

'Yes, really, go on.'

I don't know why I agreed to carry out the silly task, other than there was probably nothing I wouldn't do to win the affection of Penny Camberwell. When I re-entered the room, the look on Annie's face said she knew I was smitten with her daughter.

'How can I help you, Gee?' asked Penny, giggling.

'I just came to wish you a break your leg,' I said, and they both burst out laughing.

'Break a leg, silly, not break your leg,' laughed Penny. Overtures and beginners were being called over the intercom.

'That's you, Gee.' Annie informed me. Back in my dressing room, I continued my pre-show ritual. Opening a new deck of cards, I removed the 7 of hearts, the joker, and the ace of spades, mixing all three cards until I no longer knew their order. I turned over the top card, revealing the 7 of hearts. Silly, I know, but it brought a strange kind of reassurance. Looking into the dressing room mirror, I looked every part the French waiter. Black trousers, long white apron, white shirt, black dickie bow and long black tailcoat.

I waited in the wings of the stage and readied myself. Nine hundred guests dressed in their finest clothing were waiting for the next act. Terry Vaughan was about to introduce a boy into the world of showbiz, a world I didn't know if I was born into or just destined to be in. I heard the words 'Radio Valentine', touched my birthmark for luck and walked on stage to Perez Prado's "Guaglione". The audience reacted warmly to my clumsy walk, which ended in a me double somersault and landing on a chair next to my bistro table. The chair collapsed to the floor. Roars of laughter turned into applause as I picked myself up along with the chair. With one vigorous shake, I restored the chair to its original condition. Casually, I removed an imaginary tea towel and polished an imaginary wine glass. One quick flick of my hand, and I was holding a real glass that reflected in the stage lights.

'Bravo!' a lady called out from one of the front tables. Immediately I felt a sense of belonging; concentration now my ally, the audience my family. I made my way downstage; the audience was in fits of laughter. I pretended to have no idea that the bistro table was dragging behind me, caught in my tailcoat, thanks to a powerful magnet. Reaching the top of the stairs which lead down to the audience, I tugged at my coat before stumbling and crashing down the stairs. Gasps from the audience turned into more applause as I landed upright. People all around the room were standing to try and get a better view. The music changed, as did the tempo. Edith Piaf's "Lovers For a Day" filled the room as I held out my hand to the 'Bravo' lady. Placing her hand in mine, I led her back to my bistro table on the stage. I pulled the chair forward for her to sit on, but having seen it collapse once, she smiled and shook her head. I jumped up onto the chair and stamped my feet to demonstrate its safety before backflipping off. I landed on my feet and held onto the chair back.

My guest took her seat. The music fitted perfectly as I offered her an imaginary menu, which, through giggles, she accepted. I paused, looking puzzled at my guest and then the audience, before taking the imaginary menu off her and turning it the correct way up! After more miming, the sound of thunder and rain brought a speedy conclusion to my debut show. I picked up the stem of the bistro table and used it as an umbrella to escort my guest to her seat. As a final flourish, I produced a red rose from my bare hand and handed it to my volunteer. My performance had gone by in a genie's puff of smoke. I was dripping in sweat as I took my centre stage bow and exited to my right. My newfound family were standing, clapping and cheering. Terry Vaughan called me back to take another bow and I was stagestruck. Back in my dressing room, I slumped into the chair as my tears fell. I buried my head into my blue towel as the anger inside took over my emotions. Why the hell were my parents not here to watch their son?

'Where did a performance like that come from?'

Removing the towel, I look up to see Gordon with a smile as wide as the doorway.

'Probably all those silly old silent movies, the ones you said I was wasting my time with,' I replied, returning the smile as I wiped away my tears.

'Well thankfully, you didn't listen to me!'

'Quite the opposite, Mr Kingsley,' I answered, removing the pocket watch from my tailcoat he and Lana gave me. 'What were the words you engraved on my pocket watch?' I ask.

Gordon's face twisted as he searched his mind. 'Close the book and open your mind,' he said, spoken like a proud parent.

'John Todd thinks you are the most refreshing act he's seen in years. He wants to meet with you after the show. Whatever he offers, accept it. He knows what he's doing.'

I had a feeling my life was about to have a purpose.

Taking up my viewing position at the back of the room, I watched as Luca Baldino was about to perform the world's fastest Sub Trunk illusion, providing, of course, his assistant turned up. It was 12 months since

Danny Mac's failed attempt. I only hoped I'd get to see the conclusion this time. Luca's choice of music surprised me, "The Twist" by Chubby Checker. Stylishly, in that Italian kind of way, he twisted on from stage right, dressed immaculately in a black dinner suit. Simultaneously, his assistant twisted on from stage left. Dressed in a blue mini skirt and cropped top, both matched her wildly swinging blue hair. They came together centre stage. She stepped into a white mailbag by Luca's feet. Quickly, he raised it above her head and secured it with a double rope knot. Swiftly he scooped it up and placed it into the sub trunk, draped in an Italian flag. Luca sealed the lid with four padlocks. Instantly jumping on top of the trunk, he grabbed another large Italian flag and swished and swirled it around like a matador about to misdirect a bull; instead he misdirected the audience.

Throwing the flag to one side, the blue-haired girl, now dressed in a black dinner suit, has replaced Luca on top of the sub trunk. She jumped off the trunk, speedily removed the padlocks and threw open the lid before untying the rope and revealing Luca who was wearing the blue mini skirt and cropped top. Sheepishly, he stepped out of the mailbag. Like me, the audience is blown away. It all happened so quickly. Little did I know what an integral part the girl with bright blue hair would play in my future life.

The Italian duo must have thought they had stolen the show, but they had not witnessed Snowflake in rehearsal, the final act on tonight's bill. Sarah completed her routine with great aplomb and the audience was clapping and cheering as one. The show was a resounding success. My predictive cards had delivered the correct outcome.

At the after-show party, I was about to approach John Todd, who was deep in conversation with Micky Marks and another man, but decided it was not the time to talk about my future. I searched the hotel and backstage for Penny but couldn't find her. In need of fresh air, I sat on the concrete steps at the front of the hotel and became lost in the sparkling lights at the end of the Palace Pier, shimmering on the ripples of the vast sea as it gently made its way to shore just 30 feet away. Suddenly, I sensed someone behind me.

'Why it's simply impassible, Alice said. Why, don't you mean impossible? Door: No, I do mean impassible,' Penny giggled before adding, 'Nothing's impossible!'

Immediately I jumped to my feet. 'How did you get here?'

'My mother brought me.'

'Sorry, what were you saying? What's impassable? I mean impossible?'

Penny smiled. 'Oh, it's a quote from *Alice in Wonderland*, haven't you read it?'

'No,' I declared, my cheeks turned as red as the taillights on the passing cars. I guided Penny to sit next to me, so close our knees were touching. Filled with fear, I fell silent in case I said something stupid like how beautiful the moon looks. Penny sensed my tension.

'How are you able to write and perform comedy when it's obvious your past is full of tragedy?'

'You think my past is full of tragedy?'

'Whenever I hear your voice, I hear sadness.'

I'm amazed Penny can work this out just from my voice. I want to put my arm around her but can't find the courage. 'I guess my sadness comes from having no parents.'

'You may not realise how lucky you are, Gee. Parents hold you prisoner until you find the courage to say, "I'm beyond your command". Gee, do you know my mother has never rented the room you were born in? Dad is always complaining it's stupid not to let it. So, once you reached 16, she thought it was time to have the room redecorated. Whilst clearing the room, my dad found the guest book of 1948 under the bed.'

Like a light bulb, I was illuminated inside by the mention of my parents. I looked at Penny. 'Does it contain my parents' names?'

'My mother has it with her. She plans to show it to you in the morning.' A momentary silence fell between us. As usual, I was lost in Penny's eyes. I was just about to lean across to kiss her when we were rudely interrupted by the same man I saw arguing with John Todd and Micky Marks earlier.

'Hey kids, where can a guy get a late-night drink in this godforsaken town?' he ask d, sounding like a cowboy in a Wild West movie.

'I don't know. I'm not a drinker,' I reply.

'Hey, aren't you that kid with the wacky imagination doing the slapstick thing?'

'Imagination is the only weapon in a war against reality,' stated Penny, courteously.

'What in hell's name is that supposed to mean?' remarked the yank.

'Oh, it's a quote from *Alice in Wonderland*,' added Penny.

'Whatever, kid. I need to find a drink.' With that he skipped down the steps and headed towards the Old Steine.

'I assume that was the so-called Great Zantini?'

'Yes,' confirmed Penny. 'I heard him arguing with John Todd, demanding to still be paid, plus all his expenses too.'

'Will Toddy pay him?' I asked.

'Not a chance, Toddy's ruthless when it comes to money.'

'Right, young lady, it's time for your bed.' I looked up to see Annie about to curtail our evening.

By the early hours of the following morning, and with my debut show still swirling around my head, I was wide awake – unsure if sleep had given up on me or vice versa. Recently I'd taken up a new pastime that helped pass the night - walking the hotel corridors. Zig-zagging along each one from the basement to the top floor and back again. Often I'd come across bizarre situations. Last week I passed a man locked outside his room wearing just his underpants.

I set about ascending the 447 stairs. The second floor was where all the plush suites were situated. Playfully I imagined my parents would have booked one for our summer holiday. Further along the floor, the sound of "You Really Got Me" by The Kinks was blaring out from Suite 63, enticing me to join a party. For a moment, I thought I could hear Lana singing along. I looked at my pocket watch. It was 2.25 am. Eventually, I reached the top floor, where I was treated to the 3 am chimes from my watch, along with the sound of a man snoring heavily in room 365. Finally feeling ready for sleep, I almost took the lift down but instead decided to walk. By the time I returned to the second floor, the hubbub from the party was no longer, and the door to Suite 63 was invitingly open. Looking at my watch it was now 3.28 am. I don't know what compelled me to slowly push open the door. Perhaps I thought Lana would still be inside. Maybe I was just too quizzical for my own good. Either way, I wished I'd taken the lift. The magician known as the Great Zantini was sat upright in his bed, still fully dressed, with two Scabbard swords protruding from his mouth. A mixture of vomit, blood and mucus dripped from his nostrils and mouth, splattering upon his white wing collar shirt. A half-empty bottle of vodka pointed up to the ceiling from the bedside table, and the ace of spades card was used as a drinks coaster. There was a strong smell of cigarette smoke but no sign that a party had taken place here just under an hour ago. Terrifyingly, the tap was running in the bathroom. Zantini's death stare alerted me I was not alone. Shivering uncontrollably, I had no wish to meet whoever was in the bathroom. Softly I backed out of the room, my eyes unwilling to leave the dead American's body until finally, I pulled the door to. Back in my room, I contemplated who may have been in the bathroom. I didn't know what to do. If I told the police I'd entered the room because I heard Lana's voice, that would place both of us at the scene. I decided to say nothing; though I had an idea what Lana would say about the Great Zantini.

'It's a good way for a bad magician to die.'

Early the following morning, and through the reception window, I saw Luca packing his stage props into the back of his van. Trying to shake off the horror of what I'd witnessed, I approached, asking the whereabouts of his blue-haired assistant.

'Oh, she went back to London after the show.'

'Surely you're not driving all the way back to Italy today?' I asked.

'Paris first. I'm appearing at The Moulin Rouge for the next three weeks, then home to Turin.' Luca took out a pen and scribbled down his address on a piece of paper before handing it to me. 'If you are ever in Turin you're welcome to come and stay at my apartment. With so many beautiful Italian girls, we'll find out if you're Italian or not!' he winked. '*In Bocca al lupo,*' he shouted out of the van window as he drove along Marine Parade. *I must find out what that means*, I thought, as I went in search of John Todd.

Entering the hotel lobby, Walter grabbed my arm and hurriedly led me to his office. Inside were two uniformed police officers. Instantly, I felt I was done for before my promising career had barely begun.

'This is Gee Valentine. He starred in last night's show,' remarked Walter. The taller of the two police officers was as thin as a seafront lamp post, and I craned my neck when he spoke.

'You were seen talking on the steps outside the hotel last night with the American guest, Zantini. What was said between you?' I am relieved he hadn't asked if I'd been in his room.

'He asked where he could get a late-night drink. Why what's happened?' The policeman ignored my question.

'Did he say anything else?'

'Not that I remember.'

'Did he speak to the blind girl you were with?' I threw the copper a disapproving glare, disliking the way he referred to Penny.

'Have you read *Alice in Wonderland* by Lewis Carroll?' I asked.

Both policemen looked at each other before answering, 'No.'

I smiled, adding, 'Then you won't understand a word she said.'

'Where were you between the hours of 2 and 6 this morning?' The second officer asked.

'In my bed.' I was too afraid and untrusting of the men in blue to tell them the truth.

The policemen left the office to look for John Todd as Walter mentioned he'd seen him and Zantini in an animated discussion the previous evening. Walter looked at me before blurting out,

'I told you this place was haunted. Zantini has been found dead in his bedroom.'

'Holy cow, how?' I responded as if unaware. Walter sat behind his desk and went into storytelling mode.

'Tom, Gordon and I were having a late-night drink in the sing-song bar when around 1.30 am in staggered the Great Zantini, drunk. He insisted on performing a few tricks, you know, showing off to the audience what they'd missed earlier. He did a few stock card tricks before performing the razor blades from mouth routine, which for a drunk he did very well, before finishing off by swallowing two swords at once, again pretty impressive.'

'Then what?'

'He picked up his props and wandered off to bed. The policeman thinks he continued rehearsing with his swords back in his room, where it appears he vomited and choked to death on the two swords.' Walter handed me a brown envelope.

'What's this? Am I fired?' I said jokingly.

'You made a big impression on John Todd last night.'

I removed the papers from the envelope and began to read.

John Todd Entertainments hereby agree to solely represent Gee Valentine, aka Radio Valentine from the date 31/10/1965. Performing a minimum of five shows a week. Salary of £832.00 per annum, paid weekly.
Automatic renewal date with a guaranteed wage increase, providing the act receives favourable reviews.

A small fortune. What I signed, however, was a contract without a release clause. Walter gave me one of his gurning smiles, which I'd have to put up with for a further three months. Leaving his office, I searched for Annie and the Capri guest book of 1948. I found her with Gordon, anxiously waiting for me in the hotel's busy coffee bar. At first, all the talk was about the mysterious death of the Great Zantini, then eventually, Annie handed me the guest book. As the book was almost 20 years old, I cleared the teacups from the table. I carefully turned the pages until I reached my birth date, 14th February 1948. There was just one entry, and it was not written in English. Gordon asked if I would like him to translate the words and I nodded, passing him the book.

We are sorry to leave the baby here. He was not due until March when we should have been back home. Babies not allowed in our workplace. We hope to one day return, please take care of baby. Sofia.

Gordon handed the book back to me. Softly, I traced my fingers across the words as though my mother and I were connected by blue biro. A passing tea trolley with a squeaky wheel broke the silence.

'So, my mother's name is Sofia!' At last I have a name. Annie pulled my hand into hers. Her smile dipped as she spoke.

'Like Penny, it appears you were also born prematurely.' She opened her purse, taking out a small silver charm in the shape of a heart with the initials SB engraved on one side.

'I found this on the carpet just after you were born, but thinking nothing of it at the time, I dropped it into my purse where it's been ever since. Now we know your mother's first name it ties in with the GB sewn into the towel.'

The café's overhead lights reflected in the charm Annie placed into my hand. I now had the second piece of my complicated jigsaw.

'Right Gee, once Penny, Lana and Tom return from their walk along the seafront, we'll be on our way home.'

Annie dropped off the room key to reception, leaving Penny and me alone.

'Where will you go when you leave here?' Penny asked.

Trying to be cool, I said, 'Maybe Blackpool at the end of October.' She shoved a pebble from the beach into my hand, and without looking, I moved my fingers across its smooth surface, realising it was shaped like a heart. Annie returned and took Penny's arm to leave. Turning her head, Penny called in my direction,

'If you don't know where you are going, any road can take you there.'

'*Alice in Wonderland* by any chance?' I called back. Penny smiled, a smile I would have to store in my memory until I returned to Blackpool.

Later, back in my room, I translated what Luca had called to me. *In bocca al lupo* meant into the wolf's mouth, similar to break a leg when wishing someone luck before a show. Italian custom stated if someone said *In bocca al lupo,* you're expected to reply with *Crepi il lupo,* meaning; *may the wolf die.* As I stretched out on my bed in search of sleep, I thought it odd that showbiz folk wished someone bad luck when in fact, they meant good luck.

The only luck Alex Lockhart, Vincent Leach, Tracey Mac and now the Great Zantini succumbed to was bad luck.

Chapter 9

Blackpool, 1966
Italian Embassy

Lana's freshly baked bread wafted up through the cracks of the wooden floorboards, gently waking me like an old friend. I made my way down from the mezzanine, greeted by Angel who screeched, 'Gee, Gee!' and excitedly flapped his wings.

'He's not missed me then?' I called to Gordon.

'Don't kid yourself. He says it every bloody day,' moaned my mentor whilst he sorted through the post. The Magic Attic had become my giant comfort blanket. I quickly fell back into my old routine, helping out in the shop and delivering magic tricks around town on the bike. After one such delivery I noticed how close I was to Palatine Road. Hoping Penny was home I took a detour, until I saw Tom's car outside and thought better of it.

I'd been summoned to John Todd's office to discuss the semantics of the contract I was about to sign. His office reflected a man at the very top of his game. There was no visible wallpaper in his office, instead it was plastered with billing photos - well over two hundred – of every type of act you could think of. Many of them famous, most of them just journeymen and women scratching a living at what they did and loved best. Though it soon became clear John Todd's pride and joy was not the successful entertainment agency he set up just after the Second World War, but his beautiful, talented daughter Sarah, aka Snowflake - a name her father conjured up when she was born during a heavy snowfall on

New Year's Eve 1939, the day his wife, also named Sarah, died delivering their newborn. There was nothing Toddy (as he was affectionately known by all) wouldn't do for Sarah - including providing her with a private education at the prestigious Roedean High School for Girls in Sussex. Come 1957, Toddy kept a promise to Sarah, enrolling her into The School of Performing Arts in New York for initially twelve months. It would be two years, however, before she returned home with a painful secret which she kept locked away for a further ten years.

'What's your ultimate ambition, young Gee?' he asked whilst typing numbers into a desk calculator, expecting me to have my life mapped out like his daughter's. In fairness, of all the questions he could have asked, this was one I had a stock answer for.

'To one day travel to Italy and locate my parents.'

Toddy's eyelids fell disappointingly. Pulling open the top drawer of his desk, he tossed me a glossy programme. 'This, young man, should be your ultimate ambition.' The programme heading read *The Royal Variety Performance*.

'Look at the names, Peter Sellers, Arthur Haynes, Hope & Keen, all funny men and legends of comedy. I could have Radio Valentine on the Royal Variety Performance before man takes his first steps on the moon.' Considering man had only recently taken his first stroll in space, I doubted it would be any time soon. Toddy encouraged me to work on extending my act to at least 30 minutes. I encouraged myself to buy a road map of Italy and keep searching for my parents.

Back at the Magic Attic, Gordon was in conversation with a hobbyist magician, they were skirting around the current state of magic and the ethics of magicians stealing ideas from one another. My ears locked into their conversation when the hobbyist revealed he worked for Blackpool welfare. The man was a doppelgänger for the comedian and all-round funny man, Eric Morecambe; I half expected him to lift his glasses at any moment and call for 'Little Ern'. Sadly he was lacking in humour. He bought a few magic tricks, the type used for children's parties. Gordon gave him a good discount, hoping to soften him up, knowing I was in need of obtaining my birth certificate. The following week he was back in the shop. I explained to him the story of how I was sent to Australia but jumped ship at the last moment. I then enquired how I would go about attaining my birth certificate.

'Not a problem,' he said. 'Leave it with me.'

Within a few days he returned again, this time with my birth certificate. In conversation, he also explained to me that earlier in the year a foreign-speaking lady came into the welfare offices and spoke to one of his colleagues. The foreign lady broke down in tears when she explained she'd left her baby in a hotel named Capri back in February 1948. I barely contained my excitement as he said her name was 'Sofia from Italy.' Instantly I was filled with excitement, encouraging my newfound friend to give me more information. Sadly, the next piece of information left me as deflated as a punctured tyre. He informed me the welfare official pulled out my records, informed the Italian lady I was sent to Perth, Australia in 1962 as part of an adoption project, and they had no further details of me on record. I asked if his colleague had any type of description of Sofia. As though in deep thought, he cocked his head and looked up at Angel.

'Yes, my colleague wouldn't stop going on about how the lady had the lower part of her right ear lobe missing, like her earring had been yanked out forcefully.' Automatically I lifted my right hand and touched my ear. He suggested I try getting in touch with Perth immigration, just in case the lady had sent them a letter. Though disappointed, for the first time in my life I felt unconditional love. My mother had travelled from Italy to Blackpool to try and find me. I felt it was only a matter of time before we would be together again. Encouraged, I decided to write a letter to the Italian Embassy in London in the hope of obtaining more information on my parents. On an A5 piece of paper, I laid out every bit of information I'd accumulated over the years, which sadly was not a lot. In fact, I spent more time trying to locate the address of the Italian Embassy than I did on the letter.

(*)

You always knew when the illusionist Danny Mac was in the vicinity. He was a constant whistler, and his favourite tune was Colonel Bogey. Gordon hated it, as it reminded him of the army. I loved it because Angel tried to imitate him. When we heard the tune echoing up the outdoor stairs, Gordon looked across the counter at me, his eyes closed, whilst he tied an imaginary rope around his neck, then held it above his head. Danny pushed open the door and strutted in like a gun slinger in a Wild West saloon bar. I half expected him to say 'Whiskey'. I wasn't far wrong.

At long last, he was about to order the Bullet Catch illusion. He'd also brought along his new stage assistant, Julie. She was similar in looks to Tracey. Same mousey brown shoulder-length hair, naive eyes, in her early 20s and she was the ideal size for an illusionist's assistant. I doubted she knew what she was getting herself into. Sarcastically I suggested Julie would be safer if Danny took up a knife-throwing act rather than the Bullet Catch. Gordon chortled at my teasing.

'That's not a bad idea, Gee.'

Julie, expressionless, folded her arms and glared in Danny's direction. Danny squinted through his beady eyes and shook his head.

'We'll stick with the Bullet Catch, and we'll present it differently to how it's been done before,' he bragged. Spinning a coin into the air, he caught it on the back of his hand. Danny tightened the elastic band around his ponytail and continued. 'At each performance, I will toss a coin to decide who fires the rifle or catches the bullet in their teeth.' Now it was Gordon's turn to shake his head.

'How will that improve the performance for the audience?'

'By creating a sense of danger,' was his quick reply. 'Neither of us will know who is going to be shot at.' Gordon shrugged his shoulders in disbelief. Julie, confused at Danny's tomfoolery, departed to pick up her new show costume. No sooner had she closed the door, the shenanigans continued. Danny tossed another coin into the air, but before he could catch it, Gordon beat him to it, slapping the coin down on the counter and declaring,

'There's enough danger in the Bullet Catch without complicating it with whose turn it is to fire the rifle.'

Danny placed two more one penny pieces from his pocket onto the counter near the glued down threepenny bit coin. Both Danny's coins were double-headed, one tails, the other heads. Danny told of his underhand tactics with a smirk. 'I decide who fires the rifle and who catches the bullet by using the double-headed coins.'

It got me thinking. Had he used the same scheme, ensuring Tracey ended up in the red sack complete with the venomous snake? Perhaps he also helped a drunken Alex Lockhart into the lions' cage? What of Vincent Leach? Had a sinister Danny Mac killed him too?

'Julie is my third assistant, you know,' Danny proclaimed as though girls were collectables.

'Eileen Collins was my first, a very talented multi-instrumentalist. Still to this day, she's one of life's great mysteries.'

'That's right, summer of 1955 if I remember correctly,' said Gordon.

'1956 actually,' Danny corrected menacingly.

'Ok, are either of you going to explain what you're on about?' I asked. Danny beat Gordon to it.

'Eileen and I were touring the theatres of the North East. We performed the Spirit Box Illusion made famous by the Davenport Brothers. Eileen was tied to a chair inside a box not much bigger than a police phone booth. The box also contained a collection of musical instruments, including a flute, violin, tambourine and trumpet. Once the door to the box was closed, the instruments started to play. Upon opening the box door, Eileen would still be tied to the chair in the same position. Those who witnessed the effect were made to believe supernatural forces were at play.'

I knew Danny was waiting for me to ask what went wrong, and though I didn't really care, it was the only way of getting him to leave the shop.

'So, go on, enlighten us to what happened next.'

'She vanished,' Danny stated.

With a look of cynicism, I said, 'After the show, you mean?'

Danny shook his head and ponytail.

'Danny, come on, it's an illusion. People don't just vanish.'

'Well Eileen Collins did. We were at the Empire Theatre, Sunderland. The audience were loving the show, so much so I had them call out which instrument they wanted the spirits to play next - violin, trumpet, flute. It was going really well until some cad shouted out 'piano'. The audience fell about laughing. I decided to end the routine early, so I opened the door to the box; Eileen had vanished.'

Gordon looked at me, his shoulders lifted, head tilted to one side as though confirming, before stating, 'It was headline news for weeks. She simply disappeared, no trap doors, no false compartments, she vanished.'

I looked at Danny. 'What did you do?' Danny gave the widest of smiles. 'I placed an ad in *Variety* for a new assistant.' He laughed so loudly that Angel flew to the far side of the shop. 'One thing I know for sure, Julie's definitely going to be my last assistant.' Danny, about to leave, moved his hand to pick up his two double-headed coins, along with the glued down threepenny bit.

'Stop thief, stop thief,' called Angel. Gordon and I wore twin smiles as wide as Angel's wingspan. Danny skulked out of the shop like an unwelcome bad smell with the threepenny bit still on the counter.

In his workshop, I spoke with Gordon in great depth about an idea I had to increase the length of my show. He took up his leaning position against a workbench, folded his arms and said,

'Tell me what ideas you have, and I will tell you if it can be built.'

'Well, it's complicated,' I said, raising my eyebrows. 'In my mind, I imagine a small cocktail bar. On top sits a radio along with a lifelike hamster. I enter the stage with my comedy walk whilst polishing a wine glass. I look surprised to find a hamster sitting on top of the cocktail bar. I place the wine glass on the bar and carefully pick up the hamster, placing it behind the bar. As I turn to my bistro table, the wine glass travels across the top of the bar on its own. The audience sees it, I don't. When I turn to look at the bar, I notice the glass has moved, and with a puzzled look, I return the glass to its original position. I ready myself to pull the tablecloth from the table without disturbing any of the crockery on top. Behind me, the glass again glides across the bar. The audience's laughter alerts me that something isn't right. I turn to see the glass has moved again. Finally, I pluck up enough courage and pull the tablecloth off the table; the crockery remains in position. The audience applauds my action until the table collapses, sending all the crockery crashing to the floor. The knock-on effect of vibration causes a flap to fall open on the front of the cocktail bar, revealing the hamster running around a hamster wheel travelling from one side of the bar to the other, simultaneously moving the wine glass.'

Gordon unfolded his arms and ran a finger where his eyebrows used to be before asking, 'Gee Valentine, what the hell goes through your mind?'

'You don't think it possible?' I asked in a disappointed voice.

'Leave it with me. I will give it some thought.' Which usually meant he would spend hour upon hour staring out of his window on the world until he came up with a solution.

Chapter 10

Blackpool, 1966
Cocktails for Two

John Todd worked tirelessly at placing my act into the right type of venue. Social clubs, holiday parks, hotels and, most pleasingly, the theatre at the end of the North Pier. Blackpool had two other piers, Central and South. The latter was also staging a summer show. Come the high season, both show promoters would be at war with each other. Come early March, Gordon had a surprise for me in his workshop.

'Gee, sorry it's taken me much longer than I thought to complete, but Tom Camberwell had to engineer most of the parts I needed.'

With a feeling of anticipation, I waited as Gordon removed a dusty old sheet to reveal my new stage cocktail bar. It was stunning, better than I imagined. Three feet high by four feet wide, *Radio Valentine* was written in chrome on the gloss, black frontage. Sitting proudly on top was a white Art Deco radio. I was really touched that this one-time stranger was doing so much for me. If the kindness Gordon showered on me was to keep alive his brother's memory, then I had to do his memory proud. He explained that the cocktail bar worked on the same principle as my pocket watch. Opening the top of the bar, I noticed the inside did in fact look like a giant pocket watch - coils, springs, wires, gears and pulleys all zigzagging across each other.

'It's all quite simple really, but never overwind it. Though it all looks harmless, I'm afraid it's quite the opposite. The wires are very tightly strung. For safety, best never leave the top open. If just one of the highly tightened wires comes away from its fixing, it will take off the tip of your nose.' Gordon went on to explain the most difficult learning curve I faced was not how to operate the cocktail bar but learning how to drive a car. His way of declaring he wouldn't be driving me to any more shows.

Layton Institute was your typical workingmen's club, renowned for its entertainment. Locals and holidaymakers lapped up the nightly shows from spring through to autumn. It was the first opportunity to try out my new stage set. On the bill were several acts, unfortunately, one being Sean Cameron, son of Billy, a notorious gangland boss whose activities included protection, extortion and prostitution. Sean had little talent, at best a compere. I once saw him perform as one of the clowns in the circus; he was more sinister-looking than funny. We'd performed on the same bill in a few social clubs, and each time he died on his arse. Up to now he'd come across as wanting to be my best friend, that is until after the show. I caught Sean snooping around my new cocktail bar. He was attempting to draw the inner workings in his notepad. Confronting him, he simply ignored me, as though he'd been given approval. His eyes focused on the workings of the bar without engaging mine. I moved between him and the bar, so close our noses were almost touching. The following words tumbled through stale breath.

'You need to share your ideas with your fellow performers, pal.' He spoke in a strong Glaswegian accent. I snatched the notepad from his hand.

'Understand this, I share nothing of my ideas with you or anyone else, and I am not your pal.'

Sean took one step backwards. Reflecting from the above lights, I caught sight of a knife by his side. I was slow to react as he lunged at me, slicing through my right ear. I felt shock before pain. Instinctively I lifted my hand to my ear. Looking at my hand, I saw it was awash with blood. Sean was ready for war, eyes bulging, mouth foaming with rage. The flyweight's left boot connected with my groin. I felt my heart in my throat as my legs gave way, and my knees collided with the floor. In a prayer-like position, I tried to regain my composure. Towering over me, Sean's chilling voice and action left me with no other option.

'Stay where you are and I won't cut you again.' Casually he picked up his biro and notepad and, like a college student, he continued to draw.

Fate was about to lend a hand. Sean's biro ran out of ink.

Meekly I declared, 'I have a pen.'

'Then let me have it.'

Slowly I placed my blood-stained left hand into my trouser pocket. With my other hand, I removed a penknife from my back pocket. His eyes fixed on my left hand as it opened. Besides the blood, it was empty. Climbing to my feet, I composed myself as I used to when playing Split the Kipper. I threw the penknife into his right foot. He did not scream but simply bent down and pulled the knife from his foot. Unflinching, he plunged his knife into the top of the bar, cutting through the wires, and the sound of swishing and pinging followed as wires flew through the air. Then I felt excruciating pain as one of the steel wires hit my left eye. In slow motion, I rocked back and forth like the laughing clown. My hands grabbed at fresh air to try and steady myself as I could no longer see. Sardonic laughter was coming from Sean's direction. Finally, a punch to the back of my neck removed the breath from within me, knocking me unconscious.

When I came to, it was dark, and instantly I knew the bed was unfamiliar, as was the room - I couldn't hear the creaking of the Magic Attic. My bedsheets were so tightly tucked in I could barely move my arms. Sensing a strong smell of antiseptic, I tried working out where I was but must have fallen back to sleep.

The next time I awoke, the sun was up, casting shadows across my bed. I could see, but only out of my right eye; a bandage was covering the left half of my face. I could hear Gordon and Lana talking softly. Turning my head left, then right, I saw them sitting on either side of my hospital bed. Gordon's face was filled with fear. He noticed I was awake and quickly stood, clasping his hands together prayer-like.

'I am so sorry. I should have explained more, should have fixed a safety top, should have…'

'Gordon, Gordon, stop, sit down please,' interrupted Lana before informing me I was in Blackpool Victoria Hospital. She asked how I was feeling.

'Angry and in pain.'

Gordon immediately apologised again.

'Gordon, it was not your fault,' I exclaimed.

Now Gordon looked confused.

Lana said calmly: 'Gee, in your own time, tell us what happened.'

'After the show, I caught Sean Cameron, one of the acts, trying to copy the workings of the bar. When I approached him he attacked me with a knife and sliced through my ear.' Instinctively I lifted my hand to my right ear, so heavily bandaged it felt like a pillow. I felt rage building inside as I explained what happened next. 'He plunged the knife into the top of the bar, cutting at the wires. I heard the wires snap and felt something hit me in the eye. It must have been one of wires, I don't know. Then I felt a punch to the back of my neck and I blacked out.' Lana's eyes became violent. Her lips remained sealed.

'Are you sure it was Sean? He said he phoned the ambulance, and he helped stop the bleeding from your ear.'

I smiled, knowing Cameron had lied. 'It was definitely him,' I confirmed.

'Then we must call the police immediately,' demanded Lana.

Gordon asked, 'Gee, are you sure it was Sean Cameron?'

I nodded my head. 'He and his family are real nasty pieces of work. Going to the police will make things worse for all of us.' Gordon's brow crunched into a mass of vertical lines. The arrival of Doctor Sarin, a close friend of John Todd's, helped ease the tension, but his diagnosis did nothing for my anxiety.

'You have a piece missing from the bottom corner of your right earlobe. It needs attention. As for your left eye - it's not good. It appears the point from one of the wires penetrated your cornea anterior chamber and iris; how deeply, at this point, we don't know. Behind the back of the eye are many bundles of nerves, only time will tell if there is long-lasting damage. For now, there is a high risk of infection, which could lead to permanent blindness. You will need to remain in hospital for at least another two or three weeks.'

Before leaving, Gordon placed a Bicycle deck of cards on my bedside table, tapping his index finger to his temple as a reminder to practice.

With Penny's home less than a mile away, I lay in hope she would visit, something not possible without help from her parents. Though I did get a visit from Toddy and Sarah. The former thought it would add extra comedy if I wore an eye patch for my show. I was grateful for him trying to lift my spirits and for arranging for Doctor Sarin to help in my rehabilitation. Sarah acted like my big sister, gently brushed my hair out of my eye, stating what she would do to Sean Cameron the next time she saw him. She also asked if Penny had visited.

With a deep sigh, I replied, 'No.' I spoke like a child whose parents had forgotten to collect him after school.

Sleep, as usual, was difficult. If I got a couple of hours a night I was lucky. During the day, I kept a towel over my eyes, drifting in and out of restless sleep. Occasional twitching dreams had me riding on the rear grill of a Blackpool tram. Bizarrely another placed my mother sitting next to my hospital bed. I couldn't make out her face but noticed the piece missing from her right ear. Usually, my dreams were broken by the sound of a passing tea trolley, but not today.

'The things some people will do to get attention.'

The warmth of Penny's voice engulfed me. I removed the towel from my eyes. Penny was holding onto her mother's arm, dressed in light blue dungarees. She looked beautiful. Her hand found the back of the chair before sitting.

'I'll be back in an hour. We'll catch up then,' said Annie. Penny gripped my hand, holding it between both of hers. We didn't speak for the first couple of minutes. I broke the silence, explaining the bandage would be removed from my eye later today.

'Are you scared?' Penny asked. I was not going to try and be brave.

'Yes.'

She squeezed my hand tighter. 'Accidents happen, my mother says you will be fine. Gee Valentine is destined for greater things.' Penny's eyes were full of tears. As they fell I let them softly soak into my hands whilst holding her face.

'Penny, I hope you don't mind me asking, but what, if anything, can you see through your eyes?'

She smiled. 'You don't see through your eyes; you see through your brain. Close your eyes, now tell me what you see?'

'Nothing,' I replied.

'It is the same for me, though I have a good idea how handsome you are!'

'How?' I asked, embarrassed.

'I once asked Sarah to describe you. She said you are a good two inches taller than me, your skin is olive in colour like the bark from an olive tree, and your pupils are like black marbles. Your nose is pointed and your cheekbones are high.'

I smiled at her description. 'But how do you understand colours?'

'My mother is an amazing woman. When I was a little girl she explained all the colours through touch, smells and sensory feeling.'

Penny sensed I was confused.

'Mother took me into the garden when the sun was at its hottest. She asked how it felt on my skin. "Heat", I replied. Well, heat can burn, so it's associated with the colour of red, as is embarrassment and even anger. She did this with every colour over time until I built up my own versions of colours. My rainbow, Gee, is very different to yours.'

Penny had let me into her world, a world I never wanted to leave, where time did not exist. Then Annie returned and sat down beside Penny, who instantly became quiet.

'Gee Valentine, why is your life full of trouble?' Annie said, smiling. 'I have just spoken with Doctor Sarin. He'll be along in a few moments to remove the bandages from your eye. It looks like you'll be discharged today. You're coming back to our house.' My spirits lifted instantly.

'I've cleared it with Gordon. He agrees it will be too difficult for you to climb up and down the ladder of the mezzanine at this stage.' I glanced at Penny who gave nothing away. Annie continued: 'Tom will pick you later. For now, I need to get Penny home, and don't worry, everything will turn out fine.'

Annie took Penny's arm to leave. It's said a person's walk reveals much about their mood. Penny's was sombre, similar to the doctor who now approached, flanked by two of his medical team. One of his team removed the last of the bandages from my eye before applying a patch over my good eye.

'Now open your damaged eye,' asked the doctor.

'My vision is a blur, a dark grainy blur with no focus,' I felt anger bubbling up inside.

'This is not unusual after a trauma of this kind. It may take many months to heal, if at all.'

'Will I be able to perform on stage again?' I asked nervously.

'Sorry, that's not a question I can answer.'

His answer left me feeling frustrated.

Gordon arrived with Tom to take me back to Palatine Road. I explained what the doctor had said. Gordon sensed my anger and in a calm voice, he said,

'Be patient, Gee. I promise you Sean Cameron will not get away with this. For now, you have to concentrate on recovering.'

Tom interrupted Gordon. 'Right, let's get him back to Palatine Road.'

We made the short drive from the hospital, past Stanley Park. Spending time with Penny was at the forefront of my mind. This was a chance for our relationship to grow. I hoped Annie and Tom would allow me to take Penny to the Italian Gardens. Perhaps we could take a picnic, even hire one of the rowing boats on the lake.

'Welcome home, Gee,' Annie threw her arms around me as I arrived. 'We've put you in Penny's room while she is away.' My heart plummeted as low as the plush pile beige carpet.

'While she's away? Where's she gone?'

Annie sensed the disappointment in my voice. 'Tom thinks it best that whilst you're here, Penny stays with our friends in the Lake District. Anyway, let's get you settled into your room.' Adding torment to my disappointment, I'd be sleeping in Penny's bed. I smelt her, touched the everyday items she touched, a virtual Penny without Penny. Downcast, I laid down on the top of the bed. Something bulky under the cover poked into my head. Pulling back the quilt, I discovered the Alice in Wonderland book. Inside was a typed note from Penny:

Dear Gee,

I am so sorry that I am not with you as you convalesce in my room. My mother and father know I have feelings for you and believe it will not be good for my future to become emotionally attached to you. I don't think it is you. No one is good enough for me, as far as my father is concerned. I hope you make a full recovery, don't give up your dream of performing again.

To help pass your time, I bought you the Alice in Wonderland book. Below is my favourite quote from the book.

"If I had a world of my own, everything would be nonsense. Nothing would be what it is because everything would be what it isn't. And contrary wise, what is, it wouldn't

be. And what it wouldn't be, it would. You see?"
My love always.
Penny. xx

Surrounded by everything Penny, I threw myself into reading my first ever novel, taking it with me everywhere I went, including my first two hospital check-ups that showed no improvement in my damaged eye. Doctor Sarin spoke about repairing my earlobe, which I declined, knowing my mother had a piece missing from her ear too, which gave us something in common. Three weeks after moving into Palatine Road, I informed Tom and Annie I was ready to move back to the Magic Attic. Before leaving, I finally plucked up enough courage to talk to Tom and Annie about my feelings for Penny. Sitting opposite them on facing sofas, they listened intently, both shifting awkwardly at times. They were not surprised when I said Penny felt the same way. Tom moved his bad leg to a more comfortable position before speaking.

'Look Gee, you have no understanding of what's required to look after someone who's blind.'

I nodded in an understanding way before I replied respectfully, 'I never will if you don't give me a chance.'

Annie looked at Tom and Tom looked directly at me.

'Chances are Gee, Penny will never leave here. Find a girl you have something in common with.'

I knew as soon as I said: 'Like someone who's got two good eyes,' I'd made a terrible mistake.

Tom exploded with rage and jumped up from the sofa – I saw a side of him I had not witnessed before. He called me a spoilt little bastard and I was no longer welcome if I continued to pursue Penny's affections. I tried to apologise, but he didn't give me the chance. I would not give up on my feelings for Penny, and Tom would never release his butterfly. Before I left Palatine Road, I placed a silver necklace on Penny's bedside table.

I hadn't been long back at the Magic Attic before I received a visit from John Todd, who delivered more bad news about my up and coming summer season on the North Pier.

'My concern, Gee, is not about your ability, it's more about what has happened. Sean Cameron has produced a summer show on the South Pier.'

Gordon had mentioned the many posters around Blackpool concerning the *"South Pier Spectacular"*. It was no surprise to see Danny Mac on the bill - there's only room for one illusionist in Toddy's North pier production and it would always be Snowflake. Though I was amazed to see Dravern Leach on the South Pier show as billed as *The Mind Reaper*, a hypnotist. I'd no doubt the whole show thing was no more than money being laundered through his father's illegal businesses.

'Gee, Gordon told me about the injuries Sean Cameron inflicted on you. His family are no better than gangsters. I can't afford to continue in a war with them. Last week one of Cameron's men placed padlocks on the main entrance to the North Pier Theatre, leaving the cast unable to get in to perform the first show. I ended up having to refund the audience. Two weeks before that *"Show cancelled"* banners were placed outside the theatre, Sean Cameron laid on buses to take our audience to his show at the South Pier.' I understood Toddy's fears and was grateful he was willing to pay me half my salary until I was able to return, hopefully in the autumn. Time enough for me to fathom out what to do with Sean Cameron.

Chapter 11

Blackpool, 1966
Eye for an Eye

Most of England was about to come to a standstill. The national football team had reached the World Cup final. Gordon, not surprisingly, decided to close the Magic Attic for the day, not that he wanted to watch the game, quite the contrary. He summed up his feelings when he told me,

'There's no point opening up the shop, all you bloody sachanacs will be crowded around your TV sets, and this Scotsman won't be watching.'

Although not surprised, I was almost bent double with laughter. I was surprised, though, at being invited by Penny's parents to a picnic in Stanley Park. After more than three years of keeping me away from Penny, suddenly and gratefully, I was Mr Popular. A few days back, Annie phoned the Magic Attic in a panic saying Penny was missing. An instant shot of adrenaline raced through my body. I grabbed the shop bike and hurried across town to Stanley Park. Annie and Penny often went there for an afternoon stroll, and it wouldn't have surprised me if Penny had mentally mapped out the route and taken herself off there. At least I hoped. Relentlessly I pedalled, turning the wheels as fast as I possibly could, cutting every corner, and taking every shortcut. By the time I cycled past the metal entrance gates into the park I was dripping in sweat but relieved. I could see Penny in her white summer dress, sitting alone on a park bench near the table tennis tables.

'Penny,' I shouted from a distance. 'Everyone is searching for you.'

Dismounting, I leant the bike against one of the tables.

'You win, Gee,' retorted Penny. She picked up her handbag from the bench, inviting me to sit down, to which I complied.

'I win what?' I asked, panting for breath, thinking we were heading for our first lovers' tiff.

'I placed a bet with myself that you would be the first person to find me.'

'Is this a game to you?' I ask as I wipe the sweat from my face on my t-shirt.

'No, but my parents treat me like a caged pet. I told them I would choose my friends, and they are no longer to put obstacles in the way of me being with you.' Without warning, Penny stood up and started to walk back along the drive I'd just cycled down.

'Come on, slow coach,' she pronounced. 'Get your bike.'

Slowly, and with aching legs, I pushed my bicycle as I walked Penny back home where she repeated to her parents about seeing more of me and should they continue to stop her she would not return so quickly next time. At least that's what Penny later told me, as I was too afraid to go into her house and face her parents.

(*)

Stanley Park and July go together like pork pie and pickle, as do the many various sounds of oars slapping onto the water, children's laughter, working bees and a cricket match taking place somewhere in the distance. The weather was far more suitable for a picnic than the last time I came here for my 14th birthday. Gone was the white blanket of snow, replaced by a multitude of colourful picnic blankets, dotted around the Italian Gardens. Beyond the flowing fountains, I saw the Camberwells setting up. Annie positioned the white crockery onto a bright red tablecloth. Penny was in white shorts and a red shirt, probably in support of the England football team playing later that day. She sat in a deckchair neatly folding white paper napkins. Meanwhile, Tom struggled to erect a sun umbrella above Penny's head. He noticed me arrive, though it went by without acknowledgement. I read Annie's lips as she smiled and informed Penny, 'Gee is here'. To which Penny smoothed out the creases in her shorts.

There was always a shyness about Penny when we first met up. Today she avoided eye contact with me, though she constantly twirled the silver necklace I'd left in her bedroom. It reflected the sunlight each time there was a break in the clouds. Annie had put together a feast of a picnic and we all tucked in, including the wasps and seagulls we continually had to fight off. Tom quietly took me to one side and laid down the rules about my courtship with Penny. I would be allowed to go walking with her in Stanley Park unaccompanied, but we could never be alone in the house. Nor would I be allowed to sleep over. I agreed and offered to shake Tom's hand. He declined, opting to help Annie pack away the picnic.

'Let's go for a walk,' called Penny, helping to ease the tension. She locked her arm into mine and we started our first official courtship stroll by the boating lake.

'Well, now that we have seen each other, said the unicorn, if you'll believe in me, I'll believe in you.'

Penny smiled at my remark. 'Well, well, so you have read the book.'

I gently squeezed her hand in response.

Unlinking her arm from mine, I locked my fingers into hers. Penny smiled, a smile I adored, forcing the sunshine from behind a cloud to join our walk.

'Do you not find it odd there are no olive trees in the Italian Gardens?' she said.

Now where had I heard that before, I thought? More importantly, I wondered how she would have known there weren't. Perhaps her mother or father mentioned it, or perhaps she could just sense there weren't. Either way, I promised myself to do something about it one day. As we turned and made our way back to her parents, a butterfly decided to break its journey, resting on Penny's shoulder and fluttering its wings. It was as comfortable in Penny's company as I was. When I mentioned it to Penny she asked,

'What are its colours?'

'Orange and brown, I think, but it won't keep still for me to be sure,' I replied.

'Then it is a Painted Lady, Vanessa Cardui, with four mottled brown large eyespots.' The once crawling caterpillar took flight, continuing its journey, and I was in awe at Penny's never-ending knowledge of all things.

I asked why her father called her his butterfly? Penny stopped walking, faced my direction, and placed her hands on her hips. Her head was skew whiff, as though dumbfounded at my question.

'Gee Valentine, have you never heard of a Camberwell Beauty?'

'No.' She'd caught me out again on my lack of knowledge about anything but magic.

'It is a butterfly that travels here from North America, and because it's rare and beautiful, and we share the name, my father decided to call me his butterfly.'

I took a step closer to Tom's butterfly and tilted my head. Our noses touched. Without seeking permission, I gently kissed her on the lips. A tingling sensation ran through my body. Penny locked her arms around my neck. Neither of us was sure who was supposed to pull away first. When our lips eventually parted, I muttered,

'Holy cow. I just kissed a butterfly whilst you kissed a moth.' I said, smiling like a Cheshire Cat.

Penny laughed. 'Don't worry, one day I'll turn you into a butterfly.'

Later in the afternoon, we all piled into Tom's bright red Austin Mini. He dropped Annie and Penny back home before continuing to the Magic Attic. Breaking the stony silence between us, Tom turned on the radio, just as England's fourth goal had been scored, securing victory over West Germany.

'Gordon will not be happy that England has won, Tom,' I commented, hoping to break the unease between us. Tom pulled the car into a parking bay, still about half a mile from the Pleasure Beach. He turned off the radio, fixed me his most intimidating stare and delivered the following threat.

'And I won't be happy if you get my daughter into trouble. In fact, it will be the end of you.' He leaned across me and opened the door. 'Get out of my car. You can walk the rest of the way.' As I stepped out, he sped away before I had the chance to close it.

At least I was guaranteed a warmer welcome from Gordon. As I made my way up the wooden staircase, I was surprised to hear him talking with a man, especially since the shop was supposed to be closed. Through the obscure glass door, I made out the familiar voice belonging to my knife attacker. *Why would Sean Cameron be here*, I wondered? More importantly, why would Gordon even speak with him? Deciding not to enter, I crouched down on one knee and manoeuvred into a position where I could spy on the proceedings through the keyhole. In the centre of the shop sat a large metal milk can, similar to the one used by Houdini in his great escapes. Gordon held the dull grey lid. Sean, peering inside the milk can, which was almost half his size, was doing most of the talking. His voice echoed inside the empty can.

'Is 20% discount the best you can do me, Gordon?'

'Shit,' I whispered angrily under my breath. Gordon was selling Sean the milk can trick, knowing the bastard tried to blind me, and he's giving him a discount.

'The extra discount is a thank you for helping Gee after his accident. Who knows what would have happened had you not been there.' It then dawned on me Gordon was convincing Sean he had no idea he was my attacker. I shifted position quietly as my knees were starting to ache. Squinting through the gap, I watched Gordon looking Sean up and down, like an undertaker sizing up a body to fit the correct coffin. Gordon knew I was there.

'First, you will need to strip down to your pants,' Gordon instructed. 'Have you brought the handcuffs?' Sean removed them from his back pocket and took off his shirt to reveal his scrawny protruding ribs. I almost laughed aloud, thinking I could play a xylophone tune on them.

'I can remove the handcuffs in under five seconds whilst lying in a bath of water,' bragged Sean. With my ear now pressed against the keyhole, I listened intently as Gordon told him what to expect.

'The difference comes when you're squeezed inside, and the lid is fastened on tight. It's dark, there's the pressure of your mind, the water and very little space to remove the handcuffs.'

'Aye, I'll be fine.' The more nervous he became, the stronger his Glaswegian accent became. I swapped my ear for my eye, taking pleasure as fear was now etched onto his face. Gordon secured the handcuffs onto Sean's wrist as he slithered down inside the can. We were both now in a similar crouched position.

'We will first try the escape without water inside the can. I don't want it soaking through to the bakery below.'

I chuckled at what Lana would say if it did.

Just before Gordon fixed the lid, he explained the presentation. 'You don't want to make it look easy, the lid is slightly dome-shaped, just enough room to tilt your head up out of the water to take a breath. Don't be too quick; the audience needs to think you're in danger. On the other hand, don't be too slow, or you'll drown,' he explained in a tone more in keeping with an executioner than a shopkeeper. Just as Gordon was about to screw the lid closed, Sean, in a frightened tone, grumbled,

'You won't let me die, will you? You know my father will never forgive you.' As the squeaking lid was secured, Angel started flapping his wings. Gordon removed his pocket watch and nonchalantly leaned back against the shop counter. Three minutes went by, again, I had to switch knees. Still no sign of Sean. He surely should be out by now. Slowly Gordon returned the pocket watch to his waistcoat. Methodically and slowly, he twisted the top off the milk can and, looking down, he called,

'You're dead, son.'

I should feel ashamed, as I'd done nothing to help. Unexpectedly, Sean appeared like the genie from a battered lamp, covered in so much sweat I thought the tank had been full of water. Panicking, panting, fighting for every breath, the handcuffs were still fixed around his wrist.

'I dropped the fucking key,' Sean blurted out, exasperated.

'There, there, son. Don't panic. You'll be fine,' patronised Gordon. 'You just need to practice more. Just think when you get this right, your peers will regard you as the Houdini of the north.'

I was sure Sean had no understanding of the word tapiaphobia and most likely never would until it was too late.

(*)

There was still no improvement in my damaged eye. I was coming to the conclusion it might always be like this. Trying to cheer me up, Gordon asked if I would like to go with him to judge a talent show on the South Pier. On arriving, I noticed the billboard above the entrance:

"Summer Comedy Spectacular", Illusionist Mac Attack. Hypnotist Dravern Leach. Including Comedy Magician & Producer Sean Cameron.

'Please don't tell me we are going to watch that,' I begged.

Gordon laughed, saying he wasn't that cruel. The talent show was taking place in one of the small bars halfway along the pier, and as one of the judges had failed to turn up, Gordon roped me in to help. I started to think I was part of a bigger picture.

'I'd better get some drinks in. It's going to be a long night,' Gordon postulated as he made his way to a busy bar. He returned after twenty minutes with several pints of beer delicately balanced on a tray. After judging eight of the sixteen acts on show, the interval was most welcome, probably due to the amount of beer I'd drunk. On my way to the toilet, I noticed streams of people making their way off the pier. *Odd*, I thought, *perhaps the "Comedy Magic Spectacular" is not that spectacular.* I saw Danny Mac twitching like a sparrow at the bar. As I approached, he appeared agitated, his hands were shaking, and his eyes were darting everywhere like a burglar expecting a policeman's hand any second.

'Hey Danny, you ok?' For a moment, he stared at me with his beady eyes, like he was about to divulge a secret he shouldn't.

'There's been a terrible accident at the theatre. They've told the audience to go home. The show's cancelled. That's right, the policeman said, "go home the show's been cancelled".' Taking hold of his arms, I tried to calm him.

'Danny, you're making no sense.'

'He got stuck, stuck inside,' he said, pushing my arms away.

'Who got stuck?' I asked. Danny gripped the handrail running along the bar to steady himself.

'We dragged him out, but he was out of time, then the stage curtains wouldn't close, people in the audience were confused.'

I interrupted. 'Danny, Danny, slow down, slow down.'

Ignoring me, he carried on at speed.

'We all told him he hadn't rehearsed enough, told him to wait. Now he's dead. He's fucking dead!'

'Who?' I demanded.

'Sean Cameron.' Danny let go of the rail as a glass was placed before him. Raising the tumbler to his mouth, he swallowed the drink in one. I asked the barman for a refill – a large one, this time.

Returning to my seat, Gordon looked beyond me towards the bar.

'Danny Mac looks like he's seen a ghost.'

'Yeah, you could say that, Mr Kingsley.'

I sat down beside Gordon and picked up my score sheet. Hopefully, the talent in the second half would be better than the first. Through the window, I noticed a seagull perched on top of a bench seat, part masking the sun setting over the Irish Sea. I closed my good eye, and the seagull, sun and sea became one big blur.

Rightly or wrongly, I couldn't help feeling it was a good way for a bad magician to die.

Chapter 12

Blackpool, 1967
Badger

Instead of sleeping that night, my mind tried to process what Gordon said about Sean Cameron's death. Not that I was struggling to come to terms with it; as far as I was concerned, as you sow, so you reap. No, it was more the lengths Gordon went to to try and prove he had nothing to do with Sean's death, and neither did Tom Camberwell. Was the picnic in the park just a ruse to get me out of the way so Sean could visit the Magic Attic? Gordon assured me it was not.

During breakfast with Gordon and Lana, I asked Gordon how come he'd sold Sean the milk can after what he'd done to me. As always, Gordon was careful with his choice of words.

'Sean came into the Magic Attic back in June, asking if I would supply the milk can trick, which I did. I even gave him a discount for helping you after your accident.' Lana glared at Gordon. 'I know he didn't help, Gee, but if he thought I knew what happened, then my idea was dead in the water if you'll excuse the pun.'

'But you said you had nothing to do with his death.' Gordon put down his toast, stood up from the table and folded his arms. I knew he was about to lean back on the shop counter, a trait of his I found endearing and one I'd seen so many times before.

'Sean Cameron drowned in his own inadequacy as a magician.'

'But you were gone for twenty minutes when you went to the bar.' I started thinking it was more than a coincidence that we were both on the

South Pier last night.

Gordon now fixed me with a stare, one I'd not seen up until now. 'Why, Inspector Brock, you are on the ball. I popped into the theatre to offer Sean a pair of easy opening handcuffs, where no key is required, which by the way, he declined.'

I realised Gordon had covered every angle. Even if he'd sabotaged the equipment, it would be impossible to prove.

'Gee, accidents happen. Back in the 1930s, American illusionist Robert James, known as the Wonder of Wizardry, was performing the Milk Can Escape. Unbeknown to him, the milk can had dropped and dented, so there was less space inside. Robert James couldn't remove the handcuffs, and he drowned. Now come and help me piece the guillotine back together.'

(*)

Manchester Eye Hospital was a tall, imposing building, built entirely of red brick. Once inside the labyrinth of confusing corridors, I was soon lost for the second day running. Toddy had paid for my visit to the eye specialist, and I was hoping yesterday's check-up brought news of my recovery. Having just turned 19, I'd recently contemplated that the sight in my left eye may never return. Eventually, I found my way back to the correct department after walking down another long narrow corridor where the walls were as white and bright as the doctor's coats. I sat on the chair outside the room. Waiting nervously, I looked up to see the name on the door - Dr Fortuna. Eye Ophthalmologist. *Now that*, I thought, *is a good sign* - hopefully, a sign of things to come. Still, it didn't stop me from touching my birthmark for luck.

A few days earlier, I'd received a letter from Australia regarding the search for my parents. With so many previous disappointments, I'd put off opening it, believing you couldn't receive two pieces of bad luck within a few minutes of each other.

Carefully, I broke the envelope seal and started reading.

Dear Mr Valentine,

Many thanks for your recent correspondence regarding the search for your parents.

Other than the letter received from you, we have had no other enquiries regarding a Gee Valentine.

The passenger list records the name Gee Valentine was aboard RMS Orion when it sailed from Tilbury dock England in 1962. When the ship docked in Perth he did not disembark. It was presumed he must have been lost at sea.

Yours sincerely,
Jacqueline Vincent
Perth Care Services

At least I had received a reply, unlike the Italian Embassy in London.

Hearing Dr Fortuna's creaking door open, I felt apprehensive. A chubby, middle-aged man with skin a similar tone to my own beckoned me into his examination room.

'Did you stop in Manchester last night or travel home to Blackpool?' the doctor enquired.

'I went home and got the early train back to Manchester this morning.' I was not good at small talk and the fact the doctor started this way made me anticipate bad news.

'You are a very lucky young man, Mr Valentine, not many patients get the use of radiography. Having had time to review your results, I am afraid there's not much more I can tell you that you don't already know. It's impossible to determine how deeply the wire penetrated your iris. Sometimes these tears heal given time. In your case, however, time has not helped.'

Standing to leave, I felt despondent. My plan that two pieces of bad news can't come at once appeared to have failed. 'Should I assume my vision will never return?' I grumbled.

Dr Fortuna shuffled my notes into a large brown envelope. As he returned them to the filing cabinet, he turned with a reassuring smile. 'I'm not saying you won't ever get back some kind of vision, but it is unlikely you will wake up one day and have the vision you once had. On the bright side, medical advances are made every day, and you are still a young man.'

It wasn't quite the answer I was hoping for, but I returned the smile. 'Will I be able to return to performing?' I asked, desperately hoping for some good news. The filing drawer closed with a thump as the doctor swung around.

'Of course, your brain will adapt, and you could become a leading light for blind and partially sighted people everywhere.' Penny would be proud of that. I shook hands with Dr Fortuna and wished him well. As I made my way out of his room, he called out,

'*In bocca al lupo.*'

I turned to say, '*Crepi il lupo,*' but the doctor interjected.

'Remember, the wolf's mouth is the safest place for its pup.'

'I know, this pup longs to be in the wolf's mouth,' I replied.

(*)

Trudging up the stairs to the Magic Attic, I heard the distinctive Mancunian accent of Jack Brock. Voices raised, I was unsure whether to enter. Then Gordon called,

'Come in, Gee.'

'Bloody mirrors,' I cursed. Opening the door, the service bell welcomed me, unlike Jack Brock, who glared in my direction, like a snake would its prey, ready to circle me at any moment.

'Gee, this is Detective Jack Brock of Blackpool—'

Brock interrupted Gordon. 'It's Detective Inspector now, no need for any introduction. Gee Valentine and I go back a long way, or is it Giovani Valentino?' His mouth moved in an exaggerated way as though speaking with an Italian dialect. I placed my Italian phrasebook on the shop counter, and turned my head to face him, so I could make eye contact.

'*Va' fan culo, ispettore.*'

I shook hands with Gordon over the counter, winking with my good eye.

'I take it that is some kind of Italian welcome,' remarked Brock, his collar turned up like an American special agent.

'How did it go at the eye hospital, Gee?' Gordon enquired.

Brock pounced on the remark immediately. 'Oh, that's right, wasn't Sean Cameron with you when you had your unfortunate eye accident? Draven Leach mentioned to me that Sean and you were the best of enemies.' He slowly opened his notebook. 'Let me read you a quote from Sean Cameron. "If I ever wanted to kill myself I would climb to the top of Gee Valentine's ego then throw myself off, landing at his IQ".' Brock closed his notepad like a traffic warden who'd just issued his first parking ticket.

'It sounds to me, Jack, from what you just read, you already know what happened to Sean Cameron. He committed suicide by jumping from a great height,' I uttered, with a smirk as wide as a policeman's pencil.

The DI rubbed his ear with his index finger, then scratched his top lip with his bottom teeth, appearing to buy himself some time before speaking. 'My official title is Detective Inspector Brock; you will do well to remember that, orphan boy. I will determine what happened to Sean Cameron, and suicide is not a consideration. Someone,' he said, looking directly at Gordon, 'damaged the outside of the milk can, limiting what space Cameron had inside, meaning he was unable to retrieve the handcuff keys found at the bottom of the can. Sean Cameron ran out of time, luck and breath.'

From behind the counter, Gordon casually lifted a large book off one of the many shelves. Blowing off the dust, he gave me a look of *I thought I'd asked you to clean these*. Business-like, he scanned through it until he reached the desired page. Gordon carefully placed the book on the counter in full view.

'As you can see, detective inspector, the diagram shows a man inside a milk can in the crouched position wearing handcuffs. The problem you're having is your lack of understanding of how the magician performs in a magical apparatus when under pressure.' Closing the book, he returned it to the shelf and Gordon advised the DI to seek the advice of a leading figure in the world of escapology.

'And where would you suggest I find such a person?' inquired DI Brock.

Gordon held out his right hand towards Brock. 'Gordon Kingsley MIMC at your service.' I covered my mouth so my giggle didn't burst out. The DI was losing his battle with Gordon. He fumbled for his notebook until he found the desired page.

'Tell me, Mr Kingsley, why were you backstage on the night of Sean Cameron's murder?'

'Murder?' Gordon and I blurted out.

The DI continued to read from his notebook. 'The hypnotist Dravern

Leach stated, "I noticed Gordon Kingsley snooping around backstage near the milk can. He was up to no good".' The detective closed the book adding, 'What do you think he meant by, "up to no good"?'

Gordon was about to deliver his straight flush. Slowly opening a drawer, he removed a pair of handcuffs, handing them to me.

'Gee, put them on, please.'

Without question, I followed his instruction.

'Now remove them.'

Again I did as requested. Gordon threw the handcuffs to the DI, which he just about caught.

'I went backstage and suggested that Sean wear these handcuffs as they did not require a key. Had he done so, he would still be alive, but he refused.' The DI looked surprised. Gordon continued, 'It was Dravern Leach who was snooping around the milk can. Let's not forget the previous criminal activities of the Leach brothers. Vincent was found dead trying to break in the bakery downstairs. Dravern was involved in the cash robbery at the Pleasure Beach.' Just as I thought Gordon had got the upper hand, DI Brock stood upright, straightened his red tie, and corrected Gordon.

'Dravern Leach was savagely attacked by someone,' his eyes locked onto mine, 'wearing a knuckle duster, and by the way, there was insufficient evidence to bring any charges against Mr Leach.' Brock was now in full attack mood. 'His brother was found with one of your magic linking rings around his neck and the ace of spades card stuffed into his throat. The same suit of playing card was found inside the mailbag, supplied by you, alongside a dead Tracey Mac. Now Sean Cameron is found drowned in one of your illusions, Mr Kingsley. Should Sean's father, Billy, think for one moment you were involved in his death, it would be the end of you.'

The room fell silent. Inside I prayed for Angel to say something as the DI had just delivered his royal flush. Confidently, he placed his hand inside his long overcoat, took out a white envelope and removed a playing card. Smiling like a Las Vegas croupier, he placed the playing card face down onto the shop counter. I was convinced I knew which card it was.

'Is it all just a coincidence, Mr Kingsley, or something far more sinister? This card was recovered from the bottom of the milk can. Turn it over.'

Gordon, showing no sign of tension, glided his hand over the card and flipped it over in the same motion to reveal the 7 of hearts - not what DI Brock expected to see. His face had the look of a child who'd just arrived at a birthday party that was about to end. He was convinced he'd placed the ace of spades on the counter. How could it possibly become the 7 of hearts?

'It's magic, it's magic,' Angel screeched. 100% correct. Gordon's lightning sleight of hand was far too quick for the slow eye of the detective inspector.

'There we are, detective inspector, even Angel agrees.' Gordon's smile had returned. 'We're going round in circles here. Sean Cameron drowned in his own inadequacy as a magician, and as you happily said when you found a dead Vincent Leach, it's one less common thief for you to deal with.'

'Stop thief, stop thief,' called Angel. Jack Brock removed his hand that hovered above the threepenny bit piece that was glued to the shop counter. Flustered, he made his way out of the Magic Attic. He'd never met a man like Gordon Kingsley before, and he would have to think of a different way to approach the wise old Scotsman again. And he would, for it was in his nature and his name: Brock, a badger whose nature was to be persistent.

Chapter 13

Blackpool, 1967
Opera House

Toddy arranged to meet me for lunch at his favourite diner, The Palm Court, inside the Imperial Hotel. He arrived dressed resplendently, as though attending the opera. The room was reminiscent of the Ocean Ballroom at the Carlton Hotel. The high ceilings were supported by palladium pillars, matching white tablecloths and more silver than a jewellery shop. We took our seats at a table overlooking the sea. Toddy was a well-known figure in these parts and renowned as a good tipper, hence why the head waiter visited our table before I'd picked up a menu, asking if Mr Todd would like his usual bottle of St-Emilion wine.

'Yes, and two plates of garlic snails to start.' Before I had time to protest to the waiter, he was on his way to fetch the wine and snails.

'I don't like snails, thank you.'

Without lifting his head from the menu, Toddy replied, 'They're not for you.' Embarrassed, I buried my head inside the menu. Eventually, I decided on potato and meat pie with chips and lashings of gravy. Toddy frowned at my choice and called over the waiter to add frogs legs in a garlic broth to his order - my turn to frown. He tied a table napkin round his neck, ready to tuck into his snails, bringing a whole new meaning to don't talk with your mouth full.

'Having spoken with Dr Fortuna, it appears fortune is on your side. He said there should be no reason why you cannot return to performing.' My face lit up like a pinball machine. 'Radio Valentine will be included in what will be the greatest show staged anywhere in the UK this summer,' proclaimed Toddy, wiping the garlic butter off his chin with my napkin.

I'd never even been inside Blackpool Opera house, but I knew the theatre contained just over 2,500 seats. The usual top acts were on the bill, such as Sarah aka Snowflake, the Brighton Belle Dancers; Tom and Gordon's band The Sandy Grains fronted by Penny, and from France *La Magie*, a brilliant card manipulator. Toddy being the wise businessman, also tied-in illusion act Danny and Julie Mac as *Mac Attack;* and unfortunately, Dravern Leach, ensuring neither act could stage their own summer spectacular.

'Staging a show of this magnitude requires a huge headline performer,' stated Toddy. 'A big name with a big reputation. My Sarah will, of course, be on the bill, but I've managed to negotiate a deal with Harry Larry.'

The name meant nothing to me. Why should it? Toddy waxed lyrical about Harry Larry, stating he'd just completed his third year as a headline performer at the Sands Hotel in Las Vegas.

'Harry performs magic, big box illusions, picks pockets, reads minds, he's funny, oh, and did I say he can sing too?'

Perplexed, I asked Toddy why he was swapping Las Vegas for Blackpool if he was that good? Toddy carefully returned a half-eaten frog's leg into the bowl.

'Well,' he started, lowering his voice and turning his head left and right to ensure no one was in earshot, 'regrettably, he picked the pocket of a guy who turned out to be well connected, you know, friends in high places.' I'd no idea what Toddy was on about but played along. 'Now he's had to get out of town for a while until things quieten down.'

'So, in a nutshell, Harry Larry will be knocking back pints of pale ale in the rain rather than Pina Coladas in the Nevada desert,' I chortled.

Toddy thought about my remark, pushed the bowl of devoured frogs legs to one side and started on a bowl of spaghetti bolognaise, ordered as an extra.

'The problem is, Gee, Harry not only comes with a big reputation but also a big price tag. He'll take a share of the profits each time the *House Full* sign is placed outside the Opera House. He's also insisted on having artistic direction, meaning nobody's act is safe.'

I bet that does not include Sarah, though, I thought.

'I'm having to insert a rider into everyone's contract stating so. Unfortunately, that includes you too, Gee. Though I've told Harry my daughter is untouchable.'

I thought so.

'Harry will obviously be top of the bill. The show will be run every Wednesday at 6.30 pm and 8.30 pm.'

'Wow, that's over 5,000 people!' I exclaimed. Too complicated to work out how much Toddy would make over the summer, I remarked, 'I take it lunch is on you, Mr Todd?'

He leaned back in his chair whilst removing his napkin, smeared with garlic butter, red wine and pasta sauce.

'Mr Valentine, just make sure you impress Harry Larry with your performance.'

(*)

The headline banner outside Blackpool Opera House read, *"Direct from Las Vegas, Harry Larry, Magic & Illusion…miss it if you dare!"*.

Arriving for rehearsals with 12 acts on the bill, I was full of excitement. Looking around, I could see there were quite a few egos needing to be massaged. I was sharing a dressing room with Dravern Leach and his awful BO, something I could well do without. On meeting up, he couldn't resist a sarcastic dig about my eyesight.

'I could smell you were behind me, Leach.'

It was the first time we'd been this close since I attacked him on the Pleasure Beach. He'd attempted to grow a beard, hoping to hide the scars around his face. I say attempted, the stitch line from nose to cheek and back across his mouth was still visible.

'You want to be careful, donkey. You'll get a punch in the back of your head, being cheeky to your elders.' I felt sure he still had no idea it was me who administered the punch and left him prostrate on the floor whilst listening to the laughing clown.

'You're no longer brave enough to punch me, or anyone else for that matter,' I said in a tone I reserved for lowlifes.

Dishevelled, scrawny, and unnourished, his clothes hung loosely from his frame, like a mannequin in the window of a second-hand shop. 'You look a mess, Leach; how can you go on stage looking like that?'

'It fits my stage persona, donkey.'

I kept my distance as spit shot through the gaps in his splintered teeth. 'Be careful. Remember how those teeth of yours got broken in the first place.' He gave me a stare like I'd just let him in on a much-guarded secret.

Toddy called all the cast together on the main stage for a group photo. It was also the first opportunity any of us would get to meet the much-esteemed Harry Larry. Despite his unfortunate name, Toddy said he was a top guy. I positioned myself next to Penny, placing my hand into hers, and she smiled. We waited in anticipation for the wise words our star attraction from America was about to deliver. When Harry made his entrance, Penny whispered in my ear to describe him.

'Well, he's making his entrance from the back of the theatre, straight down the main centre aisle. He's wearing a white, sleeveless t-shirt, denim flares, flapping with each long stride he takes, all topped off with a black Stetson. The only thing missing is spurs on his cowboy boots and the intro tune to *Bonanza*.' Penny laughed, asking what he really looked like. I squeezed her hand, saying, 'I was being serious.'

By the time he walked up the treads and reached centre stage, the entire cast had to tilt their heads upwards. He must have been 6 feet 6 inches tall. Before he even spoke, he oozed stage presence.

'Hi, y'all,' his southern drawl had the dancing girls in fits of giggles. Harry touched the brim of his hat and smiled at the girls. 'Happy to be here.'

They giggled even more.

'There are three types of people who go along to see a show containing magic and illusion. One, those who simply take the performance for what it is, entertainment. Two, those who are desperate to know how the magician did that thing. And three, those who don't want to be there, but their partner insisted they came along. 'The third one is the most important. When they leave this theatre, they have to believe this is the best show they have ever seen. If you're not up to what's required, I have a dozen acts in Vegas itching to fly over the pond and take your place. Now I have a hip restaurant booked for us all to have some fun and get to know each other. Let's go.'

We were three weeks into the run, and only four *House Full* signs had been put up outside the theatre. Whenever I saw Toddy talking with Harry, it was always animated with pointing fingers and in some dark corner. They tried everything possible to increase ticket sales, from the dancing girls dressed in skimpy costumes handing out leaflets throughout the town to full-page ads in the local press. Toddy warned me Harry was about to make changes to the cast.

I arrived early for the first show and was surprised to find Harry sitting on a stool in my dressing room.

'Why ain't you the early bird, Gee?'

'Props won't set themselves, Mr Larry,' I remarked, trying to make polite conversation.

'Have you ever watched Jerry Lewis?' he enquired.

'No, I can't say I have.' I continued to set up my props whilst Harry held court.

'Well, he's a friend of mine. He started out a bit like you, slapstick and clowning around, and now he's a big film star in the States.' Harry had a way of complimenting performers, but I was about to discover his other side.

'I'm about to make some changes, Gee. You don't need to worry, though.'

Good, I thought as I'd just removed all my props and set up, but the sting from his tail was about to follow.

'As for Dravern and your girlfriend, sadly one of 'em has to go. I'm bringing in a Tamla Motown girl group from the States.' If Harry had punched me in the face, it couldn't have hurt me any more.

'Should you decide on Penny, then you'd better buy an extra plane ticket for your friend Jerry Lewis, for if Penny goes, so does this clown.' Harry stared at me in surprise.

'Kid, come on, dig it. You're taking this far too personally, and it won't end well.'

I thought carefully about what I said next. 'No, it's you taking things too personally. This is Blackpool, not Vegas. You'll get full houses when peak season arrives. You can fly in Sinatra if you like, but you still won't sell 5,000 tickets on a wet Wednesday night in June.'

Harry rested his chin on both his fists before saying the oddest thing I'd ever heard. 'Kid, you got spunk. I like that.' With that he was gone.

Alone, I thought about what he'd said. There was no way I would allow Penny to become the sacrificial lamb.

Dravern Leach was a run of the mill act. He'd never be a bill topper. He switched acts between hypnotist and comedy magician, the latter being his act today, and he was the second act tonight. The highlight of his performance was the linking rings. I'd seen it performed in many formats. At best, the performer invited a young boy or girl onto the stage to assist, and the routine was then funny and endearing. At worst, the performer attempted to educate an adult audience into believing he could melt steel, which linked each of the steel rings together. As Dravern Leach never shared a stage with anyone, he chose the second option. The routine usually contained eight 10-inch steel rings, one ring was known as the "key", plus there were two individual rings, one double ring and three triple rings. Dravern was a lazy performer. He never checked his equipment before a performance. He would not realise until he was partway through his patter that there was no "key" ring in his case that proclaimed, "Master Magician". He was simply holding eight solid steel rings. When realising the dire situation he was in and with nothing to fall back on, he tried to dig his way out with a few stock gags that fell as flat as a dancing girl's belly. He lasted five minutes before someone in the audience shouted, 'get him off.' Harry hooked him and sent on the dance girls.

I took up my usual position in the wings to watch Penny close her set with "I Will Follow You". I felt the warmth from someone's breath behind me. It was a whispering Harry Larry.

'I just told Dravern he's out of the show. Your girl is safe. I trust you will honour your contract.'

'Of course, now Penny is safe.' I should feel guilty that I'd sabotaged Leach's props, but showbiz was ruthless, and there was nothing I wouldn't do to keep Penny in the same line-up as me.

Throughout peak season, the *House Full* sign remained outside on the pavement. Harry put it down to the change in cast. I put it down to the number of people now on holiday. Either way, both Toddy and Harry were happy with the extra profits they shared. So was the Opera House management who rebooked the show for the summer of 1968, including the charismatic Harry Larry who offered me the chance of a lifetime. He would pay for my travel to Las Vegas and arrange a residency in one of the top hotels. As tempting as the offer was, I still believed my parents would return again and try to find me. There was also Penny to think of. I'd have no idea how long I'd be away from her. I declined Harry's offer. As he shook his head in disappointment, he bent his knees so his eyes were level with mine, and in his best Texan voice, he said,

'Ok, kid, someday you're gonna live to regret this. You're going to be stuck in this one-horse town till ya die.'

Harry may have been correct. On the other hand, should I find my parents and marry Penny, then I'd be happy to see out my days on the Golden Mile. Harry also made the same offer to Sarah, who, before accepting, ran the idea by her father, who gave his blessing providing she took on a stage assistant as security. Toddy asked me what I thought of Francis P David or FPD as everyone called him. Would he be the right choice as Sarah's new stage assistant? We'd met a few times at the Tower Circus and the Pleasure Beach, where he was a ride operator. Toddy described him as not quite the full shilling. His lanky 6 feet 4 frame, long arms, and Mona Lisa smile brought a quirkiness to everything he did. He reminded me of Lurch from *The Addams Family*. Why he was always dressed in a camel overcoat, even in August, was a little strange. As for the small brown case he carried everywhere, well, let's just say it was bizarre. When anyone asked what was in the case, he always delivered the response: 'The future.'

It's fair to say I was not convinced about FPD. Toddy, on the other hand, believed adding FPD as a fetch and carry man to the act would bring the one thing missing from Sarah's show, comedy. In fairness, FPD did have a funny look about him. Eventually, Toddy decided to take him on.

(*)

Throughout the summer of '68, Snowflake's act included FPD. He did bring comedy to the act, though it was not always welcomed by Sarah. Unfortunately, he left the keys to one of the illusions in the dressing room. Sarah was not best pleased at being locked up in a cramped and painful position. It took almost five minutes of fumbling by FPD before he inserted the right key, releasing Sarah and sparking much laughter from the audience. When Sarah was finally released, her face looked like thunder, which sparked even more laughter from the audience.

As the season wore on, Sarah and I became like sister and brother. In fact, should I have a sister, and I may have, for all I know, I hoped she would be like Sarah. We shared the same dressing room throughout the summer, and we were always the first acts backstage to catch up on gossip as we readied our faces in the makeup mirrors. One evening she let slip that Micky had asked her to marry him, and she'd accepted.

'You mustn't tell anyone; I've not even told my father yet.' I promised her secret was safe with me. She asked if I would propose to Penny one day.

'Penny and I do talk about our future together, which is better than always searching my past,' I answered, adding a thick black pencil to darken my eyebrows even more.

'Did you ever hear back from the Italian Embassy in London about the letter you sent?'

'No, it's over two years now since I sent the letter. I doubt there's even an Italian Embassy in London.' Sarah twitched her nose while applying more slap before sighing.

'I guess we will both always be associated with the word abandoned.'

I felt disappointed at Sarah's comment. Her mother died whilst giving birth. My mother left me in a guesthouse. I tensed, noticing how my voice altered in my reply.

'I was abandoned, Sarah. Your mother died giving you life,' Sarah bit at her lip and put her hand over her mouth as if trying to stop anything else from tumbling out.

'If I tell you this, I need your strictest confidence, Gee. You must promise me you will never tell anyone, especially my father.'

I nodded, knowing whatever Sarah divulged would have to go to the grave with me.

'You know I attended The School of Performing Arts in New York in 1957?'

I nodded, trying to ensure my face didn't reveal my jealousy.

'Well, one evening, I stayed late rehearsing a new show production. When we finished around 9.30 pm and my dance teacher offered me a lift home. As I was only three blocks away, I declined and decided to walk.'

Sarah's shoulders dropped, her neck sank into the top of her chest, and she began to cry. I held her in my arms, watching through the mirror until her tears stopped falling and she regained control.

I pleaded with Sarah, 'Don't tell me any more if this is hurting you too much.' She positioned herself on a high bar stool, dabbed her eyes dry with a tissue and blew her nose.

'I need to tell someone, Gee, as I've never told anyone. Best I tell you.' I stood, holding both her hands as she continued.

'It was Halloween. They go for it in a big way over there, dressing up in weird and wacky costumes. I was just a block away from home. Lots of people were milling around. I didn't feel in any danger. Suddenly I was grabbed around the waist. At first I thought it was part of a trick or treat. Then I realised it was the complete opposite as I was bundled into the back of a van.' Anger filled Sarah's eyes, and the delicate hands I was holding became fists as her rage built.

'I was raped by two men, both taking turns while the other one drove.' I searched my mind to find the right words to console Sarah, but I can't find any.

'Fucking raped, Gee, on my way home, with families walking close by hand in hand with children, tricking and fucking treating.' No sobbing now, just pure anger that she'd waited to release for ten years.

'Did you go to the police?'

'No, I was too scared. I had to lie to my father – "hey Daddy, sorry I failed my exams. I need to stay another year" - all because those two lousy bastards made me pregnant.' Sarah was now engulfed in both anger and despair. Again, I held her close. She moved half a step backwards whilst holding onto my arms. Looking directly into my tearful eyes, she said:

'I abandoned her, Gee. I abandoned my baby like your mother abandoned you.' Her tears flowed uncontrollably. 'How could I come back to my father and say, "hey Dad, thanks for spending all that money on my education, oh and here's your bastard granddaughter"?'

'Sarah, you had no choice. There was nothing else you could do.'

'And do you not think that may have been the same for your mother?'

'What? Do you think she had been raped too?'

'No, Gee, but I think she may have been in an impossible situation. I do understand what your mother was feeling. She's tried to find you once;

she will try again.' Looking into the mirror, both our faces needed fresh makeup before we took to the stage in less than an hour.

'Have you tried to find your daughter?' I asked tentatively.

Sarah started redoing her makeup and gathering her thoughts.

'She will be ten years old next month. Regrettably, I will never be able to locate where she is. I gave her up for adoption without the legal right to ever find her. Though I do keep an image of her in my head.'

'Tell me what you think she looks like.'

Sarah's smile returned at last. Turning back to the mirror, through which our conversation continued, she said, 'She has long blonde hair, of course, she's tall for her age and very clever. She's not going to be in showbusiness, probably a doctor or a lawyer, oh and she definitely has my eyes.'

I'm amazed Sarah has such a beautiful description of a daughter she will sadly never meet.

'I've tried to imagine what my parents look like, but the faces are always blurred.'

Sarah put down her makeup brush, turned away from the mirror and looked directly at me. 'Then we'd better make a new start,' she said. Rummaging through her shoulder bag, Sarah removed a *Vogue* magazine.

'Let's flick through the pages until we find some famous couples. You get three choices to select which one you hope your parents look like.' Only showbiz folk can go from the depths of despair to choosing make-believe parents in the swish of a magician's cape. The first picture she stopped at made us both burst out laughing - Margot Fonteyn and Rudolf Nureyev.

'Hell no, they're no way hip enough.'

'So, you don't imagine your parents were ballet dancers?' I looked at Sarah as though I'd just been served blancmange at a care home. She continued flicking through the pages. Stopping, she gave me a look like she'd just discovered ice cream. 'Richard Burton and Elizabeth Taylor, they're so yummy.'

I looked over her shoulder.

'Have you missed the one blatantly obvious thing?'

Sarah tilted her head to the photo, then looked at me blankly.

'They're white, and my skin is olive.' I laughed loudly.

'Oops, sorry!' Sarah turned to the next page, and with a large grin she proclaimed, 'Found em.' 'Sophia Loren and Carlo Ponti.'

'Ok, they're not only hip but groovy too!' I said in a cool type of way.

I took the magazine from Sarah to get a closer look.

'Yes, she's how I imagine my mother looks and my father is probably bald by now. Do you have any scissors?'

'Why? You're not going to cut your hair, are you?' Sarah asked with a gasp.

'No, I'm going to cut out the photo and keep it in my stage set!'

Sarah said I was the oddest boy in the world. Our mood was much lighter now. It had to be. Overture and beginners were called over the intercom, and we both took up our usual positions on stage for the opening song, "All You Need is Love".

Chapter 14

I'd spent most of the afternoon staring through the dressing room window, killing time, and practising my faro shuffle whilst listening to the whimpering Irish Sea in the distance. The early evening sky revealed a faint outline of the moon, reminding me Apollo 11 and her crew were still up there. Peering upwards, I made out the man in the moon, but sadly not the men on the moon. Earlier today, I'd witnessed the impossible becoming possible through Gordon's window on the world. Now my thoughts turned to tonight's showcase.

Great magicians proclaimed to turn the impossible into possible. They thrived on creating a sense of danger, captivating their audiences with life-threatening illusions such as The Head-Chopping Guillotine, Sawing a Girl in Half, and The Bullet Catch to convince them the magician's or assistant's life was in great danger. In truth, the magician was in no more danger than those watching. Unless, of course, the performer became careless in failing to prepare.

Out of the corner of my eye, I noticed Gordon. Bag of chips in hand, he was strolling along towards the Marine Hall. Seagulls hovered just above his head in the hope he'd drop a chip or two. With one hand shading his eyes, he glanced upwards. Seeing me, he smiled and pointed to the banner above the entrance door: *John Todd Showcase: featuring Snowflake - the UK's Leading Female Illusionist.* Gordon was very proud of what his goddaughter had achieved, especially in a male-dominated world.

Arriving in the dressing room, he wore the oddest of smiles and was whistling a familiar tune. Under his arm was a rolled-up poster; he looked more like an explorer than a rifle marksman for tonight's showcase.

'Why have you got that expression on your face, like you've just discovered a treasure map?' I asked.

Gordon, complete with a silly grin, cleared a space on the dressing table and unravelled the poster. 'The Tower Circus decided to redecorate the performers' dressing rooms; most of the old posters that lined the corridor were so faded they decided to throw them away. Fortunately, Tom Camberwell thought otherwise and passed them onto me, thinking they may brighten up the Magic Attic.'

He secured the four corners of the poster to the wall and I recognised it immediately. *Rossini's Traveling Circus of 1948*. Gordon looked at me. His mouth dropped in mock surprise.

'I was about to throw this poster away, with it being so faded, but then I removed it from the frame.'

Taking a closer look, I noticed something I'd not seen previously. I could clearly read Italian Circus around the edge thanks to the frame. The artistes' names were as clear as the day the poster was printed. I wasn't as excited as Gordon until he pointed at the illustration of the bearded man throwing knives at the young girl. I'd thought the man was called *Otto Coltelli* – Italian for "eight knives". Gordon pointed to the name at the edge of the poster: *"Otto Coltelli: Gabino and Sofia Bellini"*. Just seeing it jolted me like the Wild Mouse car ride on the Pleasure Beach.

'Gabino Bellini? GB were the initials sewn into the blue towel I was found in as a baby,' I said.

Gordon pointed at the other name, Sofia Bellini.

'The silver heart found by Annie outside room 9 in the guesthouse was engraved with the initials SB, surely your mother's Sofia Bellini?' Gordon's words sent a shiver through me. My whole body twitched like someone had just walked over my grave. Had I at long last discovered the identity of my parents? Were they the knife-throwing act in *Rossini's Travelling Circus* based less than a mile from where I was born? Had my mother gone into labour confused and disoriented at what to do in a foreign country? Perhaps she was searching for a safe haven to have her baby and settled for Capri Guesthouse as it reminded her of home? Maybe the links were tenuous, but after all these years, I'd grab at anything. Gordon pointed to the bottom of the poster, where, printed in bright red ink it read: *Promoter: Daniel Doyle, Bethnal Green, London.* We looked at each other like we'd just discovered the entrance to Tutankhamen.

Gordon spoke first. 'If these are your parents, you were born into a showbusiness family after all!' The silly grin returned to his face, a smile that said, *I told you so.*

'Holy cow! Holy cow! Is that why I'm such a good knife thrower? Handed down by my father? Either way they'll have to stop. It's too dangerous.'

'I need to get in touch with this Doyle guy. He must have my parents' address. I'll also write to Luca Baldino; he may know of some knife throwers in Italy. Perhaps they all belong to a club or something?'

Gordon returned to whistling the tune from earlier.

'Don't whistle backstage. You know it's bad luck,' I said like I understood all the theatre superstitions. 'Why is that tune so familiar?' I asked.

'*Torna a Sorrento,*' replied Gordon. Somehow, and I don't know how, I had to put this to one side and concentrate on the evening ahead.

(*)

Showcases could be fractious affairs. Insecurity and rivalry between acts often bordered on hatred. Performers were in fear of being rejected by bookers and agents alike. So much depended on a good review in the *The Stage* newspaper from David Blottingdale, sarcastically referred to as "Blot-your-book-dale" by the acts - his pen was more potent than any magic wand. Then there was the waiting game; tech crews going through every performers' sound and light checks made the lead up a tedious affair. Added into the mix were acts who were bickering and complaining about either more time or better positioning on the running order, and there was tension you could almost taste. On the flip slide, there was also a chance to catch up with fellow performers you once shared a stage with, and of course, the opportunity to impress, leading to a summer season.

Tonight's event would be presided over by John Todd, giving Snowflake whatever time and position on the running order she wanted -

especially as tonight, she was performing her latest illusion, Discombobulation. As for the other nine acts on the bill, we would each be allowed a maximum of 10 minutes to impress the booking agents, hoteliers, theatre managers and impresarios travelling to Fleetwood from all parts of the British Isles. Dravern Leach would be given another chance to impress, but only for the smaller venues with a low budget. Surprisingly, he'd honed his craft as a hypnotist, though Penny thought his billing name of "The Mind Reaper" sent chills through most females. Danny Mac, who I helped earlier with the Bullet Catch, ensured it would be a busy night for Gordon, not only replacing Julie Mac as the rifleman but backing Penny with his band The Sandy Grains. Tonight would see me reunited with Walter, my old entertainments manager from the Carlton Hotel. I was out to make a big impression on him as he'd given me my first chance. Like Sarah, I'd also be introducing a new illusion made by Micky Marks. I'd make my entrance by climbing out of a radio no bigger than a two-foot square.

Tonight's venue, the Marine Ballroom, was once graced by the Beatles in 1962. The room's focal point was a stunning Art Deco glass dome in the centre of the ceiling, which I hoped would feature memorably for those in attendance who were now starting to arrive. For some, showcases were more often a catch up with old friends. Many spent their entire evening in the bar without seeing a single act. Unfortunately for Toddy, his annual event would be overshadowed by man's moonwalk. Being the great salesman he was, Toddy told anyone who'd listen that Snowflake's final illusion would be to lasso the moon and make it vanish before letting out one of his big hearty laughs. All in his vicinity joined in, except FPD. He was a little concerned about what would happen to Mr Armstrong and the other nice man who'd walked on the moon with him that day if Sarah made it vanish.

No sooner had the running order been attached to the notice board did the grumbling and discontent start. The first act up was Danny Mac.

'Why is your daughter topping the bill?' he demanded, sounding like Bill Sykes.

'Snowflake is the final act on the running order for two reasons,' Toddy answered, toning down his voice into a reassuring one.

'Discombobulation is the most exciting illusion ever to be built. Next year, if you present me with an illusion as unique, you can top the bill.' Danny, unsure he'd actually got the answer he wanted to hear, returned backstage, ponytail swinging from side to side. Dravern Leach was next up, trying to bend Toddy's ear for more time. Toddy was used to this. It's all part of showbusiness. He compared pacifying cabaret artistes to being in charge of a children's nursery. As a comedy speciality act, I didn't worry about what position I appeared in. My act doesn't clash with other performers, though Dravern Leach may disagree.

With curtain up only minutes away, the nerves and tension were starting to show, the atmosphere quickly turned sour. Sarah was running through her final paces with Discombobulation. It certainly looked more complex than anything I'd seen before. She found it tricky to fit her slender frame inside the star shape illusion. Danny Mac couldn't resist having a dig.

'She can't fit into the illusion cause she's got three arses,' to which Dravern and FPD burst out laughing.

Sarah overheard the comment and quickly fired back: 'Yes, I have got three arses - they're all watching me now, they're called Danny, Dravern and Francis,' to which the stage crew and myself fell about laughing, it certainly wiped the smiles off the three arses' faces.

Carrying out a final check of my own stage set, I noticed a shadowy outline moving away from the Discombobulation illusion. Surely it had to be FPD making one final check? The shadow passed stage right and I thought I caught the outline of a ponytail. Taking a closer look, Discombobulation had been moved a little closer to my own stage set. As I was on before Sarah, I edged her illusion back around two feet.

'Up to no good are we, donkey?' Immediately I knew Dravern Leach was close by. The putrid smell of his BO replaced the sweet smell of makeup and perfume. I turned to face him.

'I see your stage attire has not improved, Mr Leach.'

Dravern glared at me. 'What doesn't kill you, Valentine, disappoints me.' I guess the saying was true. There was no business like showbusiness.

The call went up for overtures and beginners. Dravern scurried away.

John Todd waited in the wings, ready to perform his duty as compere. Though he'd be the first to acknowledge he was no Bruce Forsyth, he certainly knew how to get his acts across to bookers. In fact, his booming voice guaranteed it. Feeling two hands wrap around his one, he instantly knew his little Snowflake was beside him.

'Break a leg, Daddy,' Sarah whispered. Toddy stooped down and she kissed his bald head.

The band struck up Toddy's intro music, "Money, That's What I Want" by the Beatles and the curtain was raised. By the time Toddy reached centre stage, the irony of the music had not been lost on an audience of almost 800. Applause and laughter broke out, letting Toddy know he was much loved and respected by his peers.

'After such a warm reception, I can hardly wait to hear myself speak,' he said, resulting in only polite laughter. That was the problem with showcases. Those who attended had seen and heard it all. The acts knew it would be a tough evening as most of the audience had not come for a good night out. They were there to work, to take notes on what was hot and what wasn't.

Toddy was banking on Danny Mac starting the show off in the right mood. Danny's own mood was becoming darker, unlike his brandy bottle, which was becoming increasingly lighter. I'd warned Gordon about the blood capsule gimmick Danny inflicted on me earlier. He'd shook his head disapprovingly. The Sandy Grains opened up the evening with a couple of instrumental tunes before Toddy introduced Danny Mac onto the stage. He opened up with a standard fire-eating routine, not the quick start Toddy was looking for. Taking hold of the microphone, Danny slowed the pace further by explaining the Bullet Catch routine. I noticed Walter looking at his watch and shaking his head disapprovingly. Danny finally got round to introducing Gordon Kingsley as his rifleman. Two stagehands positioned the glass screen the bullet was supposed to travel through. Gordon went through his paces of loading and unloading the bullet. Danny took up his position, exactly the way we'd rehearsed in the afternoon. As Gordon lifted the rifle, Danny held up his hand to signal stop.

'You will let my mother and father know if something goes horribly wrong, won't you?' Danny called out, to which he received a few titters from the audience.

Gordon steadied his aim. Bang! The glass shattered; Danny hit the floor. He lay motionless - 5, 10, then 15 seconds went by. Gordon stood soldier-like, rifle still raised, room silent. Eventually, Danny staggered to his feet, spitting the bullet from his mouth onto the metal plate. Applause rang out, but no blood seeped from his mouth this time. Later, he explained he'd forgotten to put the blood capsule in his pocket. I couldn't help but think if Danny lay off the booze, his routine would be so much snappier.

As the eighth act on the bill, I had plenty of time to kill. I sat behind the tabs waiting for Penny to complete her set. My thoughts should be on my act, but I was lost in Penny's beautiful voice. The photo of Sophia Loren and Carlo Ponti was fixed behind the bar of my stage set, silly really, but it helped keep my parents in mind. As the applause faded for Penny, I awaited Toddy's introduction. My act went by, as always, in a blur of fear, sweat and laughter, but not always in that order.

With just ten minutes left, I had to introduce Sarah; she thought it bad luck to be introduced by her father - all showbiz folk have their superstitions. Every measurement of Discombobulation was built exclusively for Sarah. At just under 5 feet tall, her diminutive frame needed to slither inside the box illusion. Her stage assistant, FPD, would display five 8-inch square steel blades. One by one, FPD would plunge each blade into a perfectly sized slot where Sarah's arms, legs and head joined her body. Each box section containing her limbs would then be pulled apart and placed around the stage, leaving just her torso. No screams, no blood, just rapturous applause was all Sarah expected. She'd be presenting Discombobulation in front of a live audience for the first time – if you can call agents and bookers a live audience, that is. Having built up a record collection of some 500 vinyls over the past few years, I was asked by Sarah to select her pre-show music and something for the illusion. I selected "Bits and Pieces" by the Dave Clarke Five. The drumming intro and words fit the routine perfectly. My only concern was whether FPD would be able to keep up with the timing of the song.

A nervous Toddy approached me. 'I trust the effects you've put in place will do justice to my Sarah? I want everyone talking about Snowflake for years to come, not some bloody Yankee's footprints on the moon.'

'Don't worry,' I replied.

On arrival earlier, I'd arranged for a large mirror ball to be erected underneath the glass-domed ceiling. Now with everyone in their seats, I gave the cue to the lighting operator to turn off all the lights. The darkness was met with sarcastic whoops and soft cheers from the audience. I gently lowered the stylus onto the vinyl. "Bad Moon Rising" crackled into play, and immediately, I got the effect I'd hoped for. The only light in the venue came from the moon, bursting through the multicoloured stained-glass dome, showering a kaleidoscope of coloured beams off the mirror ball, thrown like javelin poles around the room, searching for the wooden dance floor. The hairs on the back of my neck stood erect, as I hoped they did for most in attendance. It was the only time I'd ever witnessed a showcase audience stand, clap, and stamp their feet as one. I felt rather pleased with my work. Quickly I was brought back down to earth as Sarah approached me.

'I can't rely on that fool FPD. I've just caught him drinking brandy with Danny Mac in his dressing room. He's a liability, Gee. I've asked Micky to step in.'

'Are you sure?'

'Yes, I'm sure. FPD has locked himself in the dressing room. Can you help get him out?'

'Of course I will,' I replied as she climbed the ladder to reach her starting position above the stage. 'Sarah,' I called. She glanced down at me. *'In bocca al lupo.'*

With one hand, she blew me a kiss before continuing upwards. The music and light show came to an end, and I cleared my throat and moved to the microphone to make the introduction from backstage.

'Ladies and gentlemen, this evening's final performer is the UK's number one illusionist. A young lady who is about to take your breath away. Please welcome, Snowflake.'

Sarah, wearing a white catsuit, appeared from the fly tower above the stage, tumbling and twisting towards the floor. Gasps from the audience only ceased when Sarah suddenly stopped just three feet above the stage. Her left ankle was bound by a long, white piece of rope. Softly she swayed from side to side as thousands of tiny paper snowflakes fell from above. She quickly untied the ankle rope and somersaulted, landing in the splits position. Applause rang out from the audience. She cupped her hands together and scooped up handfuls of paper snowflakes, throwing them high above her head. As they fell, Sarah pirouetted, arms outstretched with two white doves fluttering in the palms of her hands. Carefully she placed both doves into a gilded birdcage. She clapped twice and the gilded cage vanished, bringing rapturous applause from the audience and those backstage. Sarah took hold of the microphone.

'Good evening and thank you for such a warm reception. Two years ago, illusion builder Micky Marks told me of a new and baffling illusion. He said it would be the most dangerous illusion he'd ever build, and he wanted me to present it. Thanks, Micky!' she said sarcastically, bringing much laughter, as most in attendance knew the couple were engaged to be married in the coming weeks.

'So, tonight, for the first time, we will present Discombobulation.' Sarah returned the microphone to its stand. "Bits and Pieces" was only 1 minute 57 seconds long - too short for the whole routine - so I'd suggested the only sound when Micky entered the stage should be a continuous heartbeat. The base beat was so strong the tables on the dance floor vibrated, causing the glasses to clink together and toast at the marvel they'd just witnessed.

Micky Marks appeared stage left carrying the blades. His stature, in both height and reputation, was considerable. Casually dressed in dark blue slacks and an open-neck white shirt, complete with his trademark orange spectacles, he looked more suited for a stroll in Stanley Park than Snowflake's stage assistant. He helped Sarah into the star-shaped illusion, leaving only her bare feet, hands and face visible. Sarah's face was protruding from a box section containing a small door that Micky was about to close. She cheekily puckered her bright red lips to be kissed. The audience urged Micky to comply, which he duly did. At the same time, I lowered the stylus onto the record, "Bits and Pieces" kicked in alongside the continuous heartbeat. Micky only had 117 seconds to insert all five blades, then dismantle the box sections supposedly containing her arms, legs and head. He showed no nerves. Why should he? He built the damn thing. Slicing through a raw carrot he demonstrated the sharpness of the blade. Confidently, he inserted the first blade into the slot where Sarah's left leg joined her body and repeated the process on the opposite leg.

Micky, with a blade in each hand, simultaneously plunged both blades into the shoulder slots, leaving only one blade left.

Looking at my pocket watch, I noticed time was running out. He needed to quicken his pace. Easily, he removed the section containing Sarah's left arm and then did the same with her right. Then each leg section, one leg placed up stage, one leg placed down stage. Legs and arms amputated. The only sections left were her body and head. I increased the volume of the heartbeat. Micky picked up the final blade and inserted it, only for it to appear jammed. *Good showmanship,* I thought. He removed the blade and tried again, this time with added force.

The noise that followed would torment Micky for the remainder of his days. Sarah let out a squeal, a cry, a gulp. The box moved violently, and then stillness. I noticed the blood pooling around Micky's feet, unlike everyone else in the venue. Micky knew he'd sliced through Sarah's throat. His white shirt was splattered with red. Toddy looked at me, hoping it was a secret part of the routine. Micky's begging eyes met mine, searching for a real magician to turn back time. Unsure what to do, he treaded circles of Sarah's blood around the illusion. I called the stage crew to close the safety curtain. Frantically, Micky started to pull the illusion apart; his screams echoed throughout the ballroom. A reappearing scream I'd hear for the remainder of my life each time I tried to sleep. Finally, the safety curtain was lowered. I raced onto the stage, quickly joined by Doctor Sarin, Toddy's guest. Micky continued pacing in circles. FPD finally appeared. He lifted Sarah's twisted body out of the illusion and laid her on the floor. Her white catsuit was drenched red; she'd bled to death.

It was definitely no way for a magician to die.

Turning away from the horror, I witnessed Dr Sarin performing CPR on John Todd, who was lying next to Sarah, having had a heart attack.

Five hours later, I lay shivering in the foetal position on the damp grass outside the Marine Hall. Alone with the horrors of what I'd witnessed, my eyes were too sore to close. I was afraid of what images I would see. Toddy's echoing, booming voice telling the world that his little Snowflake would lasso the moon and make it vanish kept repeating in my mind. The moon had taken up its usual position in a dark starless sky, shimmering off an Irish sea as empty as I was. I was unsure if Toddy was still alive. I deliberated about my choice of music, "Bad Moon Rising". My own guilt kicked in. Was it my fault? I'd moved Sarah's illusion - did I dislodge something? What of the shadowy person I saw backstage? Dravern Leach and FPD - had they tampered with the illusion? Why did Danny Mac leave so early? Micky Marks inserted the final blade - a suspect? Surely not. I saw and heard his pain.

The gentle sound of *"Torna a Sorrento"* chimed and I placed my hand in my pocket. It brushed against a playing card, the one from my pre-show ritual; the death card, ace of spades - a ritual I promised myself I'd never do again.

I thought about the words I'd chosen to introduce Sarah. 'This young lady is about to take your breath away.' It turned out to be the other way round. Someone had taken the breath away from Sarah Todd, Snowflake, the UK's number one illusionist...but who?

Chapter 15

Italy, July 1970
11 Months Later

When the Sanremo sign finally came into view, I patted the steering wheel of Alice like a proud dog owner pats a trusty hound for retrieving the ball. Having driven 2,200 kilometres from Blackpool via London, Paris, Lyon, Marseilles, and Nice, I was at last on Italian soil, well beach actually, ensuring Alice was out of reach of the incoming tide. In need of some sleep, here was as good a place as any. Though I'd only been in Italy for a matter of hours, I had a strange feeling of belonging. My journey so far had taken four months. Tomorrow after sunrise, I'd be meeting up with my old friend and fellow performer, Luca Baldino aka The World's Fastest Sub Trunk, who I performed with at the Carlton Hotel a few years back.

'If you're ever in Turin, Gee, drop in and say *Ciao*, then we will find out if you are Italian or not!' How on earth I'd find his address, I don't know; my sense of direction so far had been awful. After Lyon, I should have turned left for Turin, but I carried straight on, ending up in Marseilles. Not that I was in any kind of rush. Driving through Provence with its wonderful sights and smells was truly a fabulous experience. With the evening now drawing in, I made up my bed in the back of the van and hoped I'd enough battery left in my torch to read a little before attempting sleep. This was always the worst part of my day since that fateful night at Marine Hall, almost a year ago. The moment I shut my eyes, the horror of what took place switched on like a bad horror movie. Always the same.

First, I heard the scream from Micky, then his harrowing look into the wings, his eyes directly locked onto mine, begging for help as he walked Sarah's blood around the stage. Then I was awake with no chance of returning to sleep.

The only way of breaking my grief after Sarah's death was to get as far away as possible. Fortunately, Toddy survived, though his heart will always be broken. He remained in hospital for almost two months, too poorly to attend his daughter's funeral. I visited him almost every day, doing my best to lift his spirits, but it was an impossible task as he had lost his true reason for living. Though my nights were disturbing, my mornings were filled with bright optimism. With the camper's split-screen windows opened, it allowed the nightmares to escape whilst inviting in the freshness of a new day. Alice was a 1967, type 23, VW campervan. Her vibrant colours of orange and custard attracted as much attention as the scantily-clad girls already on the beach this morning. As well as a pop-up roof, convertible bed, two-ring gas stove and mini-fridge, Gordon engineered a shower attachment at the tailgate. My daily ritual started with firing up the gas stove, carefully balancing a tatty old coffee pot that I'd bought in Marseilles, then patiently waiting until the fresh coffee aroma kickstarted my senses. Every day started the same. Every day ended the same; the nightmares returned.

(*)

Blackpool 11 months earlier

Having never attended a funeral, I had no understanding of the traditions that took place. Toddy was still recovering in hospital after his heart attack. Dr Sarin had given strict instructions he was not to be involved in organising his daughter's funeral. The task was left to her godfather, Gordon. Toddy gave Gordon a list of must-dos. Burial only, the coffin and flowers must be all white. A photo of Sarah's mother was to be placed inside the coffin. Annie was to ask Penny if she would sing "Amazing Grace" at the service.

On a wet August morning, Gordon and I visited the funeral parlour to pay our final respects. The door to where Sarah lay was open. Entering the room of approximately 20-feet square, I felt an extreme cold. Sarah's white coffin was laid out on a table with two white trestle legs. There were no windows to interrupt the flow of white painted walls. The only light came from a dozen or so candles, thoughtfully placed around the coffin. Incense filled the air. Placed in one corner of the room was the coffin lid. Faintly I heard gentle piano music - from where I didn't know. Sarah's body was covered in a white silk shroud, finishing just below her ears and chin, I guessed, to ensure there were no visible scars. Two openings in the centre of the shroud showed her delicate hands, fingers interlocked. I was startled when I noticed the two copper one-penny pieces laid over each eye. I looked to Gordon for an answer.

'It's become a habit to put pennies on the eyes of the deceased to stop them springing open with muscular contraction – if it happened while someone was visiting it would be deeply disturbing.'

Trust Gordon, I thought, *he seemed to know everything.* I watched him carefully place the photo of Sarah's mother inside the coffin, along with one of her father. Gordon then produced two small pots, one from each blazer pocket. Again, he noticed the puzzlement on my face.

'Sarah was sand-grown, so I took a little from the South beach yesterday for her afterlife. The second pot contains salt. It is not uncommon to put salt in a coffin; Satan hates salt because it's the symbol of incorruption and immortality. Sarah has met the devil once, and once is enough.'

From the courtyard, we heard the horses pulling the hearse across the cobblestones. The funeral director informed us he would be closing the coffin in a couple of minutes. Gordon leaned in and kissed Sarah's forehead.

'Your daddy asked me to say goodbye, Snowflake.' For the one and only time in my life I saw tears fall from Gordon's eyes. 'Say your goodbye, Gee. I'll wait for you outside.' I paused for a moment before taking hold of Sarah's hands. I was surprised how cold they were, and desperately wanted to make them warm again. No magic could do that. I, too, couldn't stop my tears from falling, strangely thinking how laughter and tears are drawn from the same well. I kissed Sarah on her cheek and softly whispered,

'Rest in peace, little one. I promise I will find out who did this to you.' Removing the pocket watch Gordon and Lana gave me for Christmas, I placed it inside the coffin, feeling sure it would be safe with her. Time had little meaning to me anymore. As we were about to leave, I noticed Dravern Leach was part of the funeral team, moonlighting – a trade that fit him perfectly. Our eyes locked; his face was expressionless.

The funeral cortège drove along The Golden Mile. Undeterred by the heavy rain, thousands of mourners lined the route to pay their respects, including holidaymakers, locals and showbiz folk who had all heard of Sarah's tragic demise thanks to the media. Upon reaching St Anne's cemetery, our black limousine came to a halt. Gordon got out of the car and walked in front of the four white horses drawing the hearse. Through the window, I saw Micky Marks flanked on one side by a policeman, the other by DI Brock. Handcuffed to both, he was unable to lift his hand to wipe away the rain dripping from his nose. Mickey had a look of desperation, his eyes were empty. He looked as though all he wanted was to be reunited with the girl he'd planned to marry. DI Brock refused Micky's request to be a pallbearer, insisting it was too risky. Carrying the coffin would be down to Gordon, Tom, FPD and myself. We bent our knees ready to lift the coffin and made our slow procession into the church, greeted by the angelic voice of Penny singing "Amazing Grace". Sarah weighed probably no more than eight stone when she died. I carried her everywhere I went for the rest of my life.

(*)

Italy Turin, July 1970
11 months on

Driving through Turin was a terrifying experience, not helped by my awful map reading skills and Luca living on the opposite side of the city. Gordon told me driving in Italy was similar to driving dodgem cars on the Pleasure Beach; you'd bump into someone at some point.

'Use France as a driving exercise,' he said. 'It will help you get used to driving on the opposite side of the road before you reach Italy, where they drive on whatever side of the road they like!'

I'd sent Luca a letter from Blackpool informing him of Sarah's death and asking for his help to try and find my parents. I explained about the circus poster and asked if he could do some investigating about knife-throwing acts in Italy over the past 30 years. When I eventually found Lucas' apartment, he greeted me like a long-lost brother. Within no time, Luca took me on a tour of Turin and onto his favourite *Tavola Caldato*, which translates to "hot table". As we sat down to eat, Luca grabbed both my wrists.

'Firstly, Gee, before we talk about the search for your parents, I am so sad to hear of what happened to Sarah. She was a beautiful person; please tell me it was not Micky who did this?' I could see in Lucas' eyes he was truly upset about Sarah.

'No, I don't believe it was Micky. I had hoped it was just an accident, but according to Detective Inspector Brock it wasn't, and Micky was charged with her murder. At one point, even I was a suspect.'

Luca tried to lighten the mood. 'How is Lana?' Pouring us both a glass of red wine, his remark took me by surprise.

'She's fine. I didn't know you knew her?'

'*Sì*, yes, after Zantini had completed his mini-show in the late-night bar, Lana and myself went back to his room for a, how you say, nightcap, which turned into several nightcaps.'

'Was Lana still in the room when you left?' I asked, knowing I was also in the room around the same time.

'No, we left at the same time. The conversation was getting a little heated between Lana and Zantini about professional standards in magic. I was a little drunk, and with English not being my first language I was struggling to understand everything, so we left.'

I decided not to tell Luca the American was found dead the next morning. No point in distracting Luca from the task ahead, helping to search for my parents, which the conversation now turned to.

'There have been many Italian circuses throughout the years that have toured Europe including, Togni, Luca-Luca - no relation, though. Franconi and Rossini's all had knife-throwing acts that toured with them. Rossini's did tour Northern Europe in the late 1940s and again in 1965.'

The latter made perfect sense as my mother returned to Blackpool in

1965 and visited Blackpool welfare. I unravelled the faded poster. Luca studied it while I finished off my first-ever serving of *rigatoni pomodora* along with another glass of red wine. I swore I'd never eat pie, mash and gravy ever again. Luca rolled up the poster and returned it across the table with a look that said, *I wish I had more information for you.*

'Rossini's Circus was based in a town near Florence named Lastra a Signa. It's a small commune. I say *was* as Rossini's Circus no longer exists. I have a friend who lives nearby in Florence who's offering to help in your search. Zappa speaks better English than me. I have arranged for you to meet up in Florence next Tuesday at 16.34.'

That's rather a precise time, I thought.

'You will meet at the Il Porcellino, outside Mercato Nuovo.' As I wrote down the details, Luca explained that Il Porcellino means "the little pig". 'That's four days from now in case you have forgotten what day it is.'

He was right. Time had little meaning for me until September.

'I would have come with you, Gee, but in a few days I'm joining a cruise ship for six months as a resident magician.' Luca went on to ask me if I had thought of performing on the ships. 'It will be the future of entertainment one day,' he insisted.

That night I had the luxury of sleeping in a bed for the first time since leaving Blackpool in March. Not that much sleep was possible in Turin; the overbearing heat and constant traffic noise would wake the Devil himself. After much tossing and turning, I glanced at my watch, 3.40 am. As usual, I'd woken in a sweat, not just from the heat, but my reoccurring nightmare of Micky's scream. By 4.00 am, I was sitting in the apartment's courtyard, surrounded by olive trees in giant terracotta pots. Gazing across the red-tiled rooftops of Turin, this felt like a different world to the one I was used to in Blackpool. The smell from the fresh lavender pots reminded me of the last time I was with Penny in Stanley Park.

'Coffee?' I looked up to see Luca wiping sleep from his eyes, holding two cups of espresso. 'The singer girl, Penny, you in love with her?'

'Is it that obvious?' I asked.

'You should marry her; she's got the voice of an angel.' I smiled, trying to give nothing away.

'I could be the best man at your wedding.'

'You could pass me my coffee cup and stop talking,' I said jokingly as we both laughed too loudly for the time of day. Luca sat next to me. He put his hand on my shoulder and declared,

'You look, eat and drink like an Italian, but you will need to work on your walk.'

'That I can't change. My show depends on it.'

Luca stood from the chair, stretched out to fill his 6-feet frame and announced pronounced, 'Then you will never be able to marry an Italian girl.'

I, too, stood from my chair. With no difference in our heights, I embraced Luca like a brother and quietly uttered, 'Good, because I'm going to marry Penny, she doesn't care how I walk.'

Later that morning, we said our goodbyes. I thanked Luca for his help and he told me not to forget his wedding invite. I promised I wouldn't. Had I known when I embraced Luca it would be for the last time. I'd have held the embrace longer. Eight months later, while returning home from a gig he was killed in a head-on car crash.

It was no way for a magician to die.

I turned the ignition key to spark the engine, Alice awoke with a shudder, and we set off in search of my parents, Gabino and Sofia Bellini, a knife-throwing act, somewhere in Italy.

Chapter 16

Blackpool, Six Months Earlier

My journey to Italy came about thanks to Gordon's kindness. So grief-stricken was I after Sarah's death I couldn't even raise myself to perform again for three months, let alone contemplate the search for my parents. With my 21st birthday approaching, I knew Gordon was up to something to help lift my spirits. Lana had previously asked me if I wanted a party to celebrate my coming of age. Thanking her for the thought, I told her I had little to celebrate. The night before my birthday, Gordon called me down from the mezzanine to give me my birthday card.

'When you get up in the morning, open your birthday card and follow the instructions.' I could not help but smile at Gordon's actions. Everything he did was a stage production.

'Follow the instructions to what?' I asked.

'You'll have to wait until tomorrow,' he replied in a manner that reminded me of Sherlock Holmes.

The next morning, before I opened the card, my thoughts turned to my parents, in particular my mother. Somewhere in the world, she would be thinking of me today. I tried to imagine what she would have written. Before I became too depressed and ruined my day, I opened the card from Gordon; it read:

To Gee
Happy birthday.

Close the book and open your mind again.
Meet us in the Italian Gardens inside Stanley Park at 10 o'clock this morning.
All our love
Gordon and Lana.

I couldn't help but think it was another picnic in the snow. Though one thing was for sure, it was typical Gordon Kingsley, man of mystery.

Arriving in Stanley Park, I was grateful there was no snow, quite the opposite, in fact. It felt odd wearing sunglasses in February. Gordon's VW Beetle was nowhere to be seen. Thinking I had arrived before them, I strolled on past a maintenance man repainting the café's entrance doors green, then along by the boating lake and into the Italian Gardens. On arrival, I was greeted by a small, assembled choir of Gordon, Lana, Tom, Annie and Penny.

All in perfect key harmonising "happy birthday", my cheeks turned as red as Lana's hair. Tom and Annie handed me my birthday card, inside was a cheque. My eyes widened when I saw it was for £50, the most money I'd ever been given. Penny, too, gave me a card and present. Unwrapping it, I discovered a gold St Christopher pendant on a chain.

'This will keep you safe wherever you travel,' she said.

'Why, am I going somewhere?'

Penny turned her head towards Gordon. He was holding a blindfold.

'Oh, you've got to be kidding me?' I stated. Left with no choice but to put it on, Annie and Lana took hold of my arms as we commenced walking. The smell of paint lingered in the air, so I guessed I must have been back near the cafe. Underfoot gravel had me thinking we were in a car park. My ears tuned into the sound of a sail flapping nearby in the wind. Had Gordon bought me a boat for my birthday? Somehow Penny dealt with these conditions every day. Gordon finally removed the blindfold and, just as I predicted, we were standing in a car park. Unable to see Gordon's car, I asked where he'd parked it.

Without looking at me, he said, 'I didn't bring my car today.' Turning to face me, he smiled. 'We brought yours instead.'

I looked at Gordon, confused. The flapping sound was not a sail but a large blue bedsheet some 20 feet away. Slowly I was drawn towards what was beneath. It was definitely not hiding a boat or a car. The wind rushed by to take a peek, danced through the trees, and then ruffled my hair like a parent would.

'Every journey throughout life has a starting point, Gee.' Gordon took hold of one corner of the blue bedsheet. In one swoop, he yanked it off like a showman unveiling an illusion. My excitement turned to dizziness; it was love at first sight.

'Holy cow, how cow!' were the only words I could muster for the following five minutes. Half a dozen times I must have walked around the campervan before I realised the blatantly obvious and blurted out, 'The driver's steering wheel is on the wrong side.' My words were met with giggles and chortles that had me thinking I was the only one not in on the secret. I felt an arm around my shoulder. Turning my neck, I come face to face with Gordon. His forehead wrinkled as though trying to raise eyebrows he'd never had.

'That depends where you're going, young man.' He placed the van keys into my hand. Seconds later, I was sitting behind the steering wheel. Turning over the engine we were treated to a rumbling roar, resembling a group of percussionists warming up in the orchestra pit. Gordon inserted a tape cassette into the deck. The gritty voice of Rod Stewart singing "Dirty Old Town" was now in perfect harmony with the engine's percussionist, and I was in heaven. Gordon mentioned Lana contributed, too, ensuring his brother Gino was not forgotten. How could he be? Later, after finishing a few beers in Gordon's workshop, we looked out through his window on the world. The Pleasure Beach was closed, the evening was too cold even for the wildlife to show their faces.

'Gee, what are you going to do about finding your parents? You have their name and their profession.'

I had an idea where this conversation was going. 'Well, I can't just drive to Italy, asking passers-by if they know a knife-throwing act named Bellini, can I?'

Gordon tended to simplify moments like these. 'Why not?' His face muscles barely moved.

'Because it'd be like looking for a needle in a haystack, Mr Kingsley,' I replied, bringing a wry smile to his face.

'First, Mr Valentine, you have to find the haystack. Then you can look for the needle.'

I thought about what he said. 'So, you think I should drive to Italy in an attempt to find them?'

Without hesitation, he slapped his hand on the workbench and replied: 'Yes, don't you?'

My answer was also immediate.

'Yes, but what will I say to Penny? I'd be gone for months and what of the shows I've got booked in? Let alone how would I survive without money?' I exhausted every excuse possible.

Gordon, as always, reassured me. 'Firstly, it was Penny who suggested you should travel to Italy once I'd found the circus poster. She said you'll never settle until you find your parents.'

Sleep that night was almost impossible. Throughout the night, I planned my route and tried to work out how much money I'd need. Gordon had never taken any rent whilst I'd lived at the Magic Attic instead he'd encouraged me to open a savings account. If I was careful, I could probably survive a year away. One thing was for sure, I had no intention of being in Blackpool for the anniversary of Sarah's death. The magnitude of what happened to Sarah was so great, the eye specialist, Dr Fortuna, believed it may have led to the recovery of sight in my left eye. The next morning over breakfast I asked Gordon if he thought Tom would allow Penny to go with me. He lifted his head from his plate of scrambled egg and bacon, put his hand across his mouth as he swallowed, then warned,

'Don't poke the bear, Gee, don't even ask him.'

The next few weeks I diligently went about planning my expedition to Italy. As I would be away from Penny for six months, I delayed setting off until the 22nd of March, the day after Penny's 21st birthday. The next time we'd meet up would be on the Isle of Capri for her parents' 25th wedding anniversary in September. Saying goodbye was not going to be easy after we strolled through the Italian Gardens in Stanley Park.

Penny was wearing her blue dungarees. I loved her in that outfit, I loved her in any outfit really. The fact was, I think I loved her, but I was just not sure what love was. I once read the greatest love was supposed to be that of a parent. There's nothing a parent won't do for their child, and there's little a son or daughter could do wrong for a parent to disown their child. So, you see, that's why I didn't really know what love was.

Neither of us wanted to say goodbye, but after hours of walking, we finally returned to my VW camper.

'Don't you think the van should have a name?' I had a good idea where Penny was going with this. I leant my back against the side mirror as I tried to scratch an itch below my shoulder.

'Thumper?' I suggested in a very deep voice.

'Thumper, like the rabbit from Disney's Bambi?' I had no idea what Penny was on about.

'No, because the engine makes a kind of thumping noise!' With my itch now gone, I opened up the passenger door so Penny could sit inside. She ran her fingers slowly over the clock on the dashboard.

'I was thinking Alice,' smiled Penny, a smile I found hard to disagree with.

'I assume the reference is from *Alice in Wonderland?*' I asked as I took my seat behind the steering wheel.

'Yes of course,' Penny remarked in a matter-of-fact way while her fingers still played with the clock face.

'Then perhaps I should have written, *We're all mad here!* on the side too?'

Penny shook her head and chortled. 'No silly, just Alice will do.' Our hands locked together as one and we said the first of our many goodbyes that day.

'I know you will be safe,' she whispered into my ear. 'St Christopher will see to that.'

For Penny's 21st I gave her a silver charm bracelet containing a wishbone and the promise of more charms as I continued my journey through Europe. I looked at the dashboard clock wishing my time away until September.

I'd packed a map of Europe, my passport, teabags, sugar, soap, sticky plasters, a penknife, 12 new decks of Bicycle cards, a Rod Stewart cassette, a *Rossini's Travelling Circus* poster and, of course, my blue towel. It was my final morning in the Magic Attic before setting off in search of my parents. Lana and Gordon were already waiting for me as I made my way down the ladder from the mezzanine. Lana, through untrusting eyes I hadn't seen for a long time, told me not to trust anyone, that way I wouldn't be disappointed. Gordon pushed an envelope across the shop counter in my direction.

'Inside is an address in Sorrento where I convalesced just after the war. They're good people, and if you need help, contact them.'

As I turned to pick up my shoulder bag, the doorbell rang. Gordon's face came alive.

'Why Detective Inspector Brock, how nice to see you.' Noticing my shoulder bag, he was straight on me.

'Going somewhere, Mr Valentine?'

Jack Brock never seemed to age. He looked no different from the first run-in I had with him when I was only eight years old. Same old loose-fitting red tie, jet black, wavy hair, dark brown eyes. I doubt he was a pound overweight.

'I'm going in search of a needle, Jack. Can you help?' I said, knowing nothing riles the DI more than addressing him by his first name. He removed a brown envelope from inside his jacket, and for the first time since we'd met, I actually think he had half a smile on his face.

'I'm personally serving you this summons, Mr Valentine. You must appear in person this October as a witness at the trial of Micky Marks - who, as you well know, has been charged with the murder of Sarah Todd.'

Without opening it, I placed it into my bag before delivering my reply. 'Of course. By the way, you're completely wrong. Micky Marks did not murder Sarah.'

Brock ignored my protest. 'Administrators at the station would normally just pop this kind of letter in the post, but Mr Kingsley may have magically changed the summons into a toilet roll.' A reference no doubt to when Gordon switched the ace of spades card to the 7 of hearts. Gordon burst out laughing, putting his arm around the DI and patting him on the back.

'You're a funny man, detective. I'll ensure that Gee is back by October.'

Brock manoeuvred Gordon's arm. 'Make sure you do or he'll be in contempt of court and arrested.'

The DI, for once, closed the door behind him. I felt relieved I wouldn't be seeing him for at least seven months. When I looked over to Gordon, he was dangling Jack Brock's red tie from his index finger. I hadn't even noticed him removing it.

'When do you think he'll notice it's gone?' I laughed.

'Probably when one of his team at the station asks where his red tie is?'

Moments later, I followed through the same door. Angel called, 'Ta, ta,' as I closed it behind me. Excitement filled me with what lay ahead. Alice roared into life. Rod Stewart was my only companion. Sunglasses on, I turned down the visor, Gordon had left a handwritten note.

In Bocca al lupo.

Into the wolf's mouth, indeed.

Blackpool to London was the first of many journeys that lay ahead. Danny Doyle was the promoter of Rossini's Travelling Circus. I found his address near the back of *The Stage* newspaper under the heading "Promoter of Fine Entertainment". His address was listed as 22b Brick Lane, Bethnal Green. I was lucky and managed to find a parking space directly outside number 22, a material shop owned by a lady in her mid-50s who, on entering her shop, informed me 22b did not exist.

'It's just a PO box. You know, a redirecting address for some dodgy business without premises.'

I almost wanted to ask if she was related to Danny Mac. They sounded so much alike.

Not quite the start I was hoping for. I wrote a short letter to Mr Doyle requesting help in my search for my parents, then posted the envelope into the red post box, ironically outside number 22 Brick Lane.

Chapter 17

Italy, Five Months Later
Zappa Russo

With music blaring out of the radio, and wind gushing in through the open windows of Alice, I continued my journey towards Florence. It suddenly occurred to me I'd forgotten to ask Luca what Zappa looked like. I didn't know if he was tall or small, young or old. My only hope was Luca had given Zappa a good description of me.

Ten kilometres from Florence, I noticed a road sign for *Lastra a Signa*. That was where Luca had said Rossini's Circus was based. My spirits lifted. For all I knew, I could be driving near to where my parents lived. Arriving in Florence, the heat was intense. I parked Alice on a busy side street next to the River Arno, knowing when I returned the inside would be as hot as a pizza oven. My map stated I was now in the historic centre; in fairness, everything around here looked pretty much historic. To my left was a bridge named *Ponte Vecchio*. Lined with old wooden, ramshackle jewellery shops, I felt I'd been transported back to medieval times. I was a little early for my meet up with Zappa, two hours, in fact. Temptation was everywhere, mainly in the shape of ice cream. Using my phrasebook, I decided to treat myself to one from a cart positioned on the corner of the bridge. I also sought advice from the vendor on how to find *Il Porcellino* (little pig).

He looked at me with a puzzled expression, answering at such speed I caught very little of what he said. It's one thing trying to speak a foreign language from a phrasebook, quite another trying to translate what's said in return. Fortunately, he did what most Italians tended to do when they spoke, he used his arms and hands. Eventually, I came across a large group of 50 to 60 tourists taking photos of what I assumed was another statue. Fighting my way to the front for a better view, I came face to face with the brass pig. How I'd find Zappa amongst this lot, I didn't know. I attempted to read a plaque placed nearby. It stated the Boar was placed here in 1634. Oh no! Had I misunderstood Luca when he said meet Zappa at the brass pig at 16.34? Had he just meant the pig was placed here in 1634? I'd probably got the time completely wrong. The plaque also stated you should rub the nose of the boar with one hand and hold a coin in the animal's open mouth, letting it drop. If the coin fell through the mouth's grating, good luck was guaranteed. If not, you should try again. I did not have spare money to throw away, so I decided to sit, soak up the sun and people watch. Locals and tourists alike came and went throughout the afternoon. Garlic occasionally wafted by as the *trattorias* readied themselves for the evening's trade. A single strike from the church bell tower reminded me it was 16.30. Most of the crowds had now dispersed.

'You could be Luca's brother.' A voice spoke from directly above where I was sitting.

Shading my eyes, I looked up and quickly had to avert them as I was looking directly up a young lady's shorts.

'I'm Zappa,' she said in an American accent. Luca hadn't mentioned Zappa was a girl, a woman, in fact.

Jumping to my feet, I blurted out, 'I was expecting a man.'

'Sorry to disappoint you.'

Quickly addressing my stupid remark, I complemented Zappa on her English.

'Your Italian is awful,' she said disapprovingly.

'How do you know?' I replied defensively.

'I was standing behind you when you ordered your ice cream.'

'Why didn't you say hello to me?'

'Like you, I'm a people watcher too,' she replied, which brought a smile to my face. I held out my hand in that English kind of way and introduced myself.

'Gee Valentine, very pleased to meet you.' She burst out laughing at my Englishness.

'Zappa Russo, my friends call me Zap.' She did a mock curtsey, adding, '*Vieni*, come, let's get a drink.'

Within two minutes, we both had a bottle of beer in our hands as Zap held court. She was loud, funny, and very forward. There was a quirky, prettiness about her. Short jet-black hair - like a public schoolboy's - a pointy nose, and pupils as dark as my own. She was similar in height to Penny, but whereas Penny's body line was shapely, Zap was the complete opposite. In her mid-twenties, she told me she was educated in America and studied as a sculpture artist at St Mark's School of Art in London. Within an hour, I felt like I knew everything about her life. Her parents owned a vineyard near Greve in Chianti as well as a holiday home close to the centre of Florence. More bottles of beer were consumed.

'Did you meet Luca because you like magic?' I asked.

'Hell no, I met Luca because I like sex.' She knew how to shock people. 'Though it was kind of magical, he had good hands, if you know what I mean, probably all that dexterity you get from constantly playing with cards.' Like the afternoon sun covering the bar terrace, I felt myself glow a bright shade of red. Zap expertly rolled a couple of cigarettes and placed them between her thin lips before lighting. Presuming I smoked, she offered one to me, which I declined.

'You don't smoke?'

'No,' I said adamantly, shaking my head.

'What about drugs?'

Again I was shocked that she'd even asked me. Aghast, I said, 'God no!'

Zap laughed out aloud. 'It's not just help with finding your parents. You need help in finding out about life. Show me your hands.'

My embarrassment grew by the second. She examined them like a Romany gypsy.

'I thought you said you were a magician. These are not magician's fingers.'

How she came to that conclusion by just looking at my hands, I didn't know. To cover my embarrassment, I proclaimed, 'I'm more a comedian than a magician.'

'Well, with your walk and the piece missing from your ear, you look funny!'

Zap was unlike any girl I had ever met before.

'Can we just stop?' I pleaded. 'It feels like I am in a game of tennis with you, and you're winning every rally! I just need help finding my parents.'

It was Zap's turn to feel embarrassed, and I felt awful for throwing water onto her teasing. We both fell quiet as she rolled and lit another cigarette.

'You must be fit to perform the acrobatics in your show. It's also very funny too. There you are, a compliment for you from Zappa Russo!'

'You've seen my act?' Zap's eyes widened as she nodded.

'When, where?' A wide smile appeared across her face knowing she held a secret. She walked over to the jukebox, dropped a coin in and selected a track. Hearing the stylus connect with the vinyl, I instantly recognised "The Twist" by Chubby Checker. Zap turned, swaying her slender hips from side to side, hands swinging in opposite directions. She danced her way back over to me. I was flabbergasted.

'Holy cow! You're Lucas' assistant with the bright blue hair at the Carlton Hotel in Brighton.'

The grin on Zap's face confirmed it.

'Where has the long blue hair gone?'

'It's a long and sad story for another day.' Zap ordered a plate of bruschetta, and I filled her in on the search for my parents. I hadn't noticed night creeping in, but it was getting late.

'Let's meet up in the morning by the brass boar at 11 o'clock. We'll get breakfast, then start your Italian education and how to go about finding your parents. Do you have somewhere to stay this evening?'

'Yes, Alice is just around the corner by the river.'

Zap's eyes almost popped out of their sockets. 'You have left your girlfriend waiting around the corner all this time?'

'No, Alice is my VW campervan!' I stated proudly. 'Would you like to meet her?'

Zap's face lit up brighter than the end of her cigarette. '*Vieni!* Let's go,' she said, grabbing my hand as I tried to finish the last drop of beer. From a distance we saw a group of teenage boys looking through the side windows of Alice.

'*Scappa scappa,*' Zappa called to the boys, chasing them away as we approached. '*Magnifica, sono innamorato, sono innamorato.*' Zap spread her arms along the split windscreen.

'I'm in love with her too,' I proclaimed like a jealous boyfriend.

'You can't leave her here; the police will tow you away in the night. You can park in our courtyard.'

I looked at Zap in a quizzical manner.

'Oh, don't worry, I'll not sneak into your bed and seduce you in the night,' she said before giggling at her own outrageous remark.

'Do you live nearby?' I enquired shyly, trying to distract my embarrassment.

'*Piazzale Michelangelo,*' she pointed at the hill rising up above Florence. I saw a collection of lights that must be from people's homes dotted about the hillside. Without asking, she opened the passenger door and jumped in.

'*Pronto,* let's go, let's go.' Alice gave a roar of approval and we crossed over the River Arno bridge just behind where I'd parked. Within minutes we were halfway up the *Piazzale Michelangelo.* Pointing out the entrance to her villa and without warning, Zap opened the door and jumped out to open the large courtyard gates. The courtyard was in total darkness; the only light came from Alice's headlights. Passing through the black wrought iron gates I felt I'd driven into an outdoor museum. There were sculptures, statues and monuments everywhere. Slowly Alice passed over a driveway of small white pebbles. It sounded like popcorn popping inside a glass case. Ahead of me, I saw Zap reach for a switch, and suddenly the outdoor lights illuminated the courtyard like a football stadium. In the centre was a circular fountain containing two marble statues. Both males, both naked, arms stretched over each other's shoulders forming a bridge, their heads leant in a passionate kiss. Zappa turned on the fountain, and water now flowed out of both penises creating the weirdest water fountain I'd ever seen. Now I was the one laughing.

'I take it you made it?' I inquired.

'No, my work is more about objects than people, far more interesting, though the men are cute, ain't they?' I declined to answer. The panoramic view from the villa's position on *Piazzale Michelangelo* was stunning. I saw right across the city of Florence below.

'At night, the historic buildings are ghostlike, the creaking sound their conversation, the flickering lights their eyes.' Zap now stood next to me. 'The dome shape is the Duomo, the bridge is *Ponte Vecchio* where you bought your ice cream.' She also pointed out Santa Croce and Fort Belvedere. Blackpool felt a million miles away. Somewhere in the night, I heard exotic music, unlike any music I'd heard before. It was both beautiful and enchanting. Closing my eyes, I allowed the song to cradle me as if in my mother's arms.

'Wow, am I in heaven? I've never heard music like this before.'

Zap smiled, ready to proudly educate me. 'It is opera, the song is *O mio babbino caro*, (Oh my dear papa). It is a soprano aria from the opera Gianni Schicchi and is sung by Lauretta. The story is of tension between the girl's father Schicchi and the family of Rinuccio, the boy she loves. They have reached a breaking point that threatens to separate her from Rinuccio. The song provides an interlude expressing simplicity and love in contrast with the hypocrisy, jealousy, double-dealing and feuding in medieval Florence.' The story reminded me of the tension between Penny's father and myself.

'The name Alice is the name for your van, yes?'

I nodded, still lost within the song and taking in the view.

'It is taken from Alice in Wonderland, yes?' The painting of Alice on the tailgate gave it away. Again, I nodded, confirming she was right.

'Then from now on, I shall call you Dodo.' Surprised, I twisted my mouth in Zap's direction.

'Why?' I asked, confused.

'Because you walk in a funny kind of way, like a dodo.' Zap laughed at her own statement, 'Do you like red wine?'

'Yes, wine is becoming my new version of Dandelion and Burdock.' Zap ignored my remark and went into the house. I sat by the fountain, trying not to think where the water was pouring from. Zap returned with two bottles of Chianti and two glasses; *it's going to be a long night,* I thought.

'Are these bottles from your vineyard?'

'Yes, of course. Tell me, Dodo, why do you have a photo of Sophia Loren and Carlo Ponti in your camper?' Zappa Russo missed nothing.

'A friend, Sarah, said I should imagine a famous couple who I'd like my parents to look like. In a game of chance, it turned out to be Sophia and Carlo.' I smiled at just the mention of Sarah's name. Zap raised her glass to mine, and as the two glasses kissed, Zap kicked off her shoes, putting her feet into the fountain.

'Ok, we have all night. I want to know everything about you, *il ragazzo smarrito che cerca i suoi genitori,*' she said. This is what I had become over the years, the boy in search of his parents.

Chapter 18

Italy, 1970
The Bullet Catch

Barking dogs, somewhere in the distance, jerked me awake. It was 3.40 am. The task of emptying both Chianti bottles was now complete. Zap, like most of Florence, was sleeping. I carefully lifted her from the chair by the fountain and carried her into the house. Not knowing which bedroom was hers, I laid her on the chaise longue in the library and returned to Alice. With very little breeze, even the shooting stars were on a go slow. I laid back on my mattress, returning to sleep too tricky a task. My mind wandered ahead to Capri and being with Penny again, and even further ahead. How, after such a short time in the land of my parents, would I ever be able to resettle in Blackpool? One thing was for sure, I had to return by the end of October when Micky Marks' trial got underway.

I still found it incomprehensible that Micky would have murdered Sarah. What could he possibly gain - money? But maybe Sarah's death was not about money? What if Micky was just one of those weird guys who got their kicks from murder? After all, he'd not only made the illusion but the five retractable blades too; the final blade which cut Sarah's throat and failed to retract due to the ace of spades being jammed inside the handle. That was enough evidence for DI Brock to charge Micky with Sarah's murder. Like Gordon, Micky had been in and around each of the mysterious deaths - including Alex Lockhart's, Micky had been working at the Tower Circus. Vincent Leach owed money to Micky for an illusion

he'd made and never paid for. Then there was The Great Zantini. I saw
Micky in an animated discussion with him after the show at the Carlton
Hotel. Micky also built the Milk Can Illusion for Gordon, who sold it
on to Sean Cameron.

Micky was a constant part of my nightmares. Perhaps his scream of
pain, which I thought was out of heartbreak, was actually out of rage? A
tortured soul that belonged to the Devil. At some point, I must have
dozed off, for the next thing I heard was Zap calling.

'Hey Dodo, come and get some breakfast.' Zap, cigarette hanging from
her mouth, was by the fountain. She wore her usual denim shorts and
bikini top. Thankfully the fountain was now switched off. Zap had
prepared some fresh coffee along with a plate of cold meats.

'So I now know everything about you, Gee Valentine, or is it Giovanni
Valentino? Oh dear, I'm starting to regret I opened the second bottle of
Chianti. The birthmark on your shoulder is shaped like the map of Italy.'

I interrupted, 'I showed you?'

Zap smiled.

'Yes, but you refused to take off your shirt.'

I laughed at my shyness. I had no idea why Zap repeated everything I
said from the previous evening, so eventually, I interrupted her.

'And your point is?'

'My point, Dodo, is that we don't have much to go on in a country of
53 million people.' Her eyes widened, directing her thin eyebrows in an
upward motion, an expression that stated we had little or no chance. It
felt as though my search was a hopeless cause. Why was I here? Why was
I always searching? Maybe I was more sand-grown than I realised, and I
would never belong to the *Bel Paese,* this beautiful country. Zappa tried to
remain upbeat.

'Today I want to show you Firenze, first, David - a masterpiece of
Renaissance sculpture, by Italian artist Michelangelo. Then the Uffizi
Gallery, onto Il Duomo then lunch at the Trattoria Sostanza.'

I held up my hand like a schoolboy. 'Hey, what about the search for
my parents?'

'*Domani,* tomorrow, we go to Lastra a Signa, and when we go, you stay
by my Vespa. The locals don't trust strangers who come asking questions.
They still remember the Nazis.' Zap's hands flapped around as she

knocked away the early morning flies. 'I have a friend who lives there, a retired opera singer who's lived in the town all her life. She will know where the Rossini Circus was once based.' Zap instructed me to open the gates while she fetched her Vespa, an Italian name meaning "wasp". Within a minute, Zap roared into view on her bright red, buzzing "wasp", kicking up gravel stones as she skidded alongside me.

'Get on, Dodo, and put your arms around my waist.' I gripped my hands onto the underside of my seat. Zap drove the Vespa fast and furious, like an angry wasp, and anyone who got in her way received a mouthful of Italian abuse. By the time we reached the centre of Florence, I was grateful to get off with my limbs still intact, though my legs wobbled like a newborn baby. Making our way towards David's statue, Zap suddenly stopped by a wooden newspaper stand, picked up a newspaper, and looked at the headline, then at me. From the look of shock on Zap's face, something in the headline bothered her.

'Mago inglese ucciso a colpi d'arma da fuoco.'

'What?' I asked.

Zap stared at me again before exclaiming, 'An English magician has been shot dead in Blackpool.' I swear my blood stopped flowing for a moment.

'Who? Who was it?' Zap paid for the newspaper. We sat side by side on the museum's steps while she translated what had taken place.

'It happened at the Tower Circus in Blackpool yesterday. The actors were performing a routine called The Bullet Catch. You know of this?'

Quickly, I nodded so as not to delay the story. 'The performers were known as Mac Attack. Am I saying this right?'

'Yes, yes,' I replied hastily. 'Does it say which of the Macs was killed?'

Zap continued reading and skipping parts to try and find a name. 'Danny Mac.'

I froze with shock.

'Danny Mac? Holy cow, I need to find a phone.' Moments later, we were back on the wasp and roaring back up the hill to the villa. Zappa took me to the library and handed me a black and gold telephone that was more reminiscent of a miniature statue. I quickly dialled the number. It only rang once before Gordon picked up. It was the first time I'd heard his voice since Paris, three months ago.

'Is it true?' I asked in a panic.

'Gee, how are you? Is everything ok?'

'Yes, I'm fine, but is it true? Was Danny Mac killed performing The Bullet Catch?' There was a pause before Gordon toned down his excitement at hearing my voice.

'Yes, it's true, at yesterday's matinee performance.' *Oh my God*, I thought, *in front of children*.

'How did it happen?'

There was a pause on the line before Gordon continued. 'Danny requested a member of the audience to select and sign the bullet, like always. Julie went through her usual preparation of loading and unloading the signed bullet. Danny explained to the audience the dangers of the trick, even quoting Chung Ling Soo's death of 1918. Danny informed the audience he would toss a coin to decide who fired the rifle. Julie won as usual. Danny took up his position holding the plate. Julie lifted the rifle into the firing position. In that melodramatic way he always does, Danny lifted his left arm calling out stop! to Julie. Saying he was sorry for not washing the dishes before they left home, 'I'll do them when we return home," to which the audience laughed. Julie stood upright gently rocking from one foot to the other foot until she was steady. Then she squeezed the trigger and bang! The glass screen shattered, and Danny was knocked off his feet. When his body hit the floor it was spread in an unnatural way. Blood poured from a wound in his head. Parents covered the eyes of their screaming children.'

I interrupted the line. 'So it was an accident?'

For a moment, Gordon's voice was lost. The phone was crackling like a typewriter with a bad stammer. 'No, Julie placed the rifle onto the floor and calmly walked over to the vanishing girl illusion. She opened and then closed the door behind her. Stagehands rushed onto the performing area. An announcement was made to clear the venue, and by the time I got into the middle of the arena…'

Again I interrupted. 'You were there?'

There was a pause on the line before Gordon confirmed, 'Yes, yes, I was there with Lana. By the time I got to Danny, FPD was covering him with a blanket.' Another surprise. FPD had said at Sarah's funeral he was done with showbusiness.

'What's happened to Julie? What did she say?'

Gordon's answer was a puzzle in itself. 'I rushed across to the vanishing box illusion, opened the door to the box, and the only item inside was a dagger stabbed through the ace of spades on the rear of the door. No Julie.'

I thought for a moment before asking the next question, knowing how stupid it would sound. 'Are you really saying Julie just vanished?'

Gordon did not answer my question but stated, 'By the time the ambulance arrived, Danny was dead. He had been shot right through his left eye.'

Standing alongside, Zap listened, looking as bewildered as I was. Gordon's voice was fading due to the poor connection.

'Gee, Danny had been knocking Julie about for a long time. Do you remember the night you and I stepped in to help Danny Mac at John Todd's showcase, the night of Sarah's death?'

'Of course I do. Danny said Julie was unwell,' I replied.

'She was unwell because Danny had broken her nose in one of his drunken rages.'

As I tried to process the information, Gordon sounded like he was describing an accident; it obviously was not.

'I bet DI Jack Brock is all over it?'

'He's just left the shop. I gave him your regards, saying you were in Italy, so he won't suspect you were involved.'

For the first time, I felt anger at Gordon. 'Why the hell would the DI Brock suspect me?' I demanded in a high pitched voice.

Gordon sensed my anger. 'Stay calm, Gee. When the coroner arrived, Dravern Leach was part of the team. He babbled to DI Brock that Gee Valentine probably arranged Danny Mac's murder with the help of Julie because you both believed Danny Mac had murdered Sarah.'

'Bastard, Dravern Leach,' I said angrily down the phone.

I tried to calm myself down by asking about Penny, knowing the Camberwells were about to set off for Capri.

'Penny is fine. She is very excited about being reunited with you. She's missed you very much.' I sensed Zap heard what Gordon said, and then the line dropped out. I replaced the statue-like phone on the table. Zap was no longer in the room.

I told myself I did not believe that Danny Mac was involved with Sarah's death. He was a bully and to my surprise a wife-beater, but surely not a murderer? I felt annoyed that I'd agreed to help him at Toddy's showcase. I also thought back to the double-headed coin Danny used. Did Julie work out his cheating system of who fired the rifle and who caught the bullet? Perhaps Julie evened up the score for Danny's previous stage assistants - Tracey was bitten by a venomous snake whilst performing Metamorphosis; Eileen, who, like Julie, simply vanished into thin air. Either way, being shot between the eyes in front of a matinee audience is no way for a magician to die.

'Who's Penny?' Zap asked, now back in the room.

'She's my girlfriend.'

'You never mentioned you had one.'

'You never asked,' I replied, not allowing our eyes to meet.

'Is she the girl with the angelic voice I heard at the Carlton Hotel show?'

'Yes she is,' I said with pride. I spent the next hour telling Zap all about Penny. How she was blind, and we were born in the same house, just a few weeks apart, both premature babies.

'In a few weeks, we will meet up for the first time in six months on the Isle of Capri, where I will ask her to be my wife.' I lifted my hands to show her my fingers were crossed for luck.

'How romantic. You were born to be together.' Zap's disappointment was obvious from the tone of her voice.

Lastra a Signa was a town of around 20,000 people, made up of small industrial units, individual shops and many beautiful villas topped with traditional red tiles. So different to the dull grey slates that covered the terraced houses of Blackpool. We arrived at the apartment where Zap's opera friend lived. I did as Zap instructed and waited by the Vespa under an old olive tree, avoiding the midday sun. It was two hours before Zap returned.

'Well, what did you find out?' I asked impatiently.

'She's fine, though her knees ache as the apartment has no lift.'

I was not sure if Zap was teasing me or if she'd forgotten why we were there. 'Rossini's Circus?' I reminded her in an animated way.

'Oh, yes, the circus,' she said, smiling out of one corner of her mouth. 'The Rossini family did once live here, but after a failed tour of Europe in 1965, the circus was disbanded. Ticket sales were so bad in England. The performing artists had to pay for their own travel back to Italy.' She changed the subject and rather randomly said, 'Let's go and buy some fresh bread from Alfredo's,' and then gave a look of *'I know something you don't know.'* As we walked on, Zap teased me with a little more information.

'Alfredo owns the bakery shop; he was one of the trapeze artistes in Rossini's Travelling Circus.' I felt my heart skip a beat at the thought of meeting someone who actually knew my parents.

'Let me do the talking,' were Zap's final instruction as we approached a row of shops.

The shop door triggered the tinkling service bell, instantly reminding me of the Magic Attic. The smell of fresh bread was like a virtual hug from Lana. Everything in the room was white except for the glass counter displaying a multitude of coloured pastries. *La vita è un circo* was painted in large red and green letters on one wall. Even with my basic Italian, *Life's a circus* was easy to translate.

Alfredo was a powerfully built man in his mid-thirties, jet-black hair, and a broad shoulder span which indicated you needed great strength to be a trapeze artiste. How he kept in physical shape with so much temptation at his fingertips was a mystery. Zap and Alfredo talked at such speed it was only possible for me to catch the odd word like my name, earlobe, and circus, until finally, Alfredo's lips went into slow motion. His face lit up as he said my mother's name, Sofia. Looking directly at me, he lifted his hand, touching the lower part of his ear and smiled. Zap turned in my direction.

'He says you have your mother's ears.' We all burst out laughing.

Zap continued. 'Alfredo was not on the European tour in 1948, but he did know babies under five were not allowed in a travelling circus. If you broke the rule you would be immediately dismissed without pay.' Was this why my mother had to leave me in the Capri Guesthouse? Knowing that if Signor Rossini discovered she had a baby, my mother and father would be abandoned as well as me? Alfredo motioned for us to go through to the back of the bakery. On the wall were several circus posters, *Rossini's Traveling Circus of 1948* was up there. Was this third time lucky? Alfredo exchanged words with Zap.

'Alfredo says you are Sofia's son. He can see so much of her in you. He also says your father was not the best of knife throwers. With your mother's wrists and ankles fixed to a wooden board, your father would spin the board; your mother hated this. Once in rehearsal, your father missed with one of the knives and cut the right ear lobe of your mother.' Zap doubled up with laughter.

'Why do you find that funny?' I snapped. Zap looked away in embarrassment. *What kind of a man is my father,* I thought, *throwing knives at my mother, who was carrying an unborn baby?* I looked again at the poster. It was in pristine condition.

'Please ask Alfredo if he knows where my parents are now.'

Zap and Alfredo talked for the next five or six minutes and partway through their conversation something Alfredo said took Zap by surprise. Her eyes jumped to me, then back to Alfredo. She exhaled and then took in a long breath to compose herself.

'On the 1965 tour of Europe, your mother told Alfredo she had left your brother back home in Italy with her parents.'

Turning to Alfredo, I croaked, 'I have a brother?' Do you know his name? Or how old he is?'

'Slowly, slowly,' Zap pleaded.

Now I felt an even deeper pain. My parents had rid themselves of me but kept my brother. Alfredo told Zap the 1965 tour was a disaster. Ticket sales in England were very bad.

'After the show in Manchester, Signor Rossini called us all together saying there was not enough money to pay any wages and we would all have to make our way back to Italy.' Alfredo travelled back with the rest of the trapeze artistes; they offered my parents space in their truck, but Sofia had refused, insisting they go somewhere else first. That somewhere, I presumed, was Blackpool. In that moment I believed the Bellinis were definitely my parents.

'Ask if he knows how my parents returned to Italy without money?' Zap asked Alfredo; he simply shook his head.

I paused, trying to take it all in. 'Does Alfredo have any idea where they came from originally?' Alfredo must have understood my question as he answered,

'Napoli.'

'Signor Rossini?' I asked. 'What happened to him?'

Alfredo dropped his head forwards and mumbled a few words to Zap, who copied Alfredo's stance before stating,

'Sadly, Signor Rossini never made it back to Italy from Manchester.'

Alfredo placed two fresh cakes into a box, giving them to Zap. He removed the poster from the wall, rolled it up, and handed it to me before saying, '*In Bocca il lupo.*'

I smiled at his warmth. I now had a different understanding to its meaning, the safest place for a wolf pup is to be in the mouth of the wolf. *Crepi il lupo* (death to the wolf) no longer sounded suitable.

We made our way along the small parade of shops. Zappa popped into a bar, returning with a newspaper under her arm and two fresh coffees to go with our cakes. Sitting under the olive tree, we enjoyed our cakes and coffee. Zap opened the newspaper. Her face changed as she read the headline.

'*l'assistente magico svanisce nel nulla.*'

Zap repeated in English, 'Magician's assistant vanishes into thin air.'

I almost spilt my coffee over my shorts. I couldn't believe Blackpool was world news. Though in fairness, it was a great story.

Zap continued to read aloud. 'Detective Inspector Brock of the local police said, it appears after Julie Mac murdered her husband Danny Mac, she simply vanished into thin air, her whereabouts unknown. Detective Inspector Brock also stated they had little to go on, and commented he'd sought advice from Magician and Historian, Gordon Kingsley MIMC, who confirmed in the right circumstances it was possible for someone as knowledgeable as Julie Mac to simply disappear.'

I couldn't help but smile, knowing that Gordon had got one over DI Jack Brock again.

Zap gave me a baffled look before enquiring, 'How did she vanish? How did she do it?' I smiled, giving the stock answer all magicians give when a layperson asks a conjurer to divulge the secret of a magic trick.

'Very well,' I declared. 'Very well indeed.' In truth, I hadn't got a clue.

Chapter 19

Italy, August 1970
13 Ways to Kill a Magician

Zap offered me a proper bed in the house rather than being cramped up in the van. Due to my odd sleeping pattern, I declined. Come 1 o'clock in the morning. However, I was regretting the decision - air conditioning would have been most welcome. The night was as still as a Florentine statue. Opening the camper windows was not an option as it would only fill my nostrils with the stench from the city sewers. In a few days, I would reach Naples, the door to the Mediterranean Sea. Should the search for my parents in the Neapolitan area result in failure, I'd have no alternative but to return home after my holiday in Capri. I was trying to remain positive, though, having now met someone who actually knew my parents. The thought of having a brother and not knowing where he lived was tormenting me, as was finding continuous sleep.

Come 5.35 am, I was disturbed by the sound of a hammer and chisel on stone. It was the first time in months I hadn't woken without my reoccurring nightmare. I climbed out of the camper feeling like I'd stepped out of a hot shower. The volume from the hammering and chiselling increased. Wearing just my night shorts, I looked out across Florence, the view as wide as it was high, the rising sun in all its glory. There wasn't a cloud in the sky to hide her blushes. It was another hot Tuscan day. I followed the working sound, now just chisel on stone coming from Zap's workshop. Due to the heat, both of the large sliding doors were open. Zap was standing in front of a large slab of marble with her back to me, holding a chisel and hammer in one hand and small watering can in the other. Besides the protective eye goggles, she was completely naked. My eyes fixed to her form, I forced myself to look away, then walked away quietly - not quietly enough though.

'What's wrong, Dodo? You never seen a naked girl at work before?' I didn't respond nor look back. Quickly, I made my way back to Alice. A few minutes later, Zap appeared in shorts and a bikini top. 'It's hot and I'm not used to having visitors while I work.'

My guilt was obvious by the colour of my face.

'I'm sorry, I followed the sound of the hammer and chisel. I didn't know you worked without clothes. Does it not hurt when the marble chips off and hits you?' Avoiding the word naked, I tried to move the conversation onto her work.

'I'm used to it. Firenze girls are tough. Working at this time, there's less heat, even though it's still hot. By 10.30 this morning, my workshop will be like a baker's oven.'

Zap went to make fresh coffee as I tried to cool down my embarrassment. She returned not just with coffee but also a plate of sliced tomato and mozzarella. I was still unable to meet her eyes.

'You've been a great help, Zap, but tomorrow I think it's time I move on down to Naples.'

Zap quickly turned her head towards me. Her disappointment was clear.

'Why? Because you saw me naked?'

The word naked brought a glow back into my cheeks. 'Please don't go now, it's my birthday this weekend and my parents have invited you to their home at Greve. It's on the way to Naples anyway. You can continue your journey from there.'

How could I say no? Zap had got me closer to finding my parents than anyone. The least I could do was spend a few extra days.

'Ok, It will be good to celebrate your birthday and meet your parents, just don't expect a present. And there's one condition.'

Zap, with a smile now back on her face, spoke first. 'If the condition is I have to keep my clothes on when working, then the answer is no, I can't work in this heat fully dressed.'

I laughed. 'I understand. Perhaps you can whistle while you work so I know you're in there.'

'Is that your condition?' Zap asked.

'No, will you help me choose an engagement ring for Penny before I leave?' Zap looked at me across her cup as she swallowed her last mouthful of coffee, pausing long before she answered.

'Are you ready for marriage, Gee? It took you quite a while to avert your eyes from my nakedness earlier.' She must have felt me watching her.

'Zap, you are very beautiful, but my heart belongs to Penny. So will you please help me buy the engagement ring?'

She lit a cigarette. 'I'll shower first, then when the shops open I will take you to a friend who makes jewellery.'

Nino's jewellery shop was on the Ponte Vecchio bridge, next door to the ice cream cart where I'd bought an ice cream cone on my first day in Florence. Zap breezed into Nino's shop like the main attraction arriving for a film premier.

'Nino, do you remember showing me the silver dodos you made the other day? And I said hey, look at the boy passing the window he walks like a dodo?' Nino looked at me and they both laughed. So that's how Zap came up with the name Dodo? I knew my walk was a little odd, but I couldn't change it. Nino offered to make an engagement ring for Penny. I told him Penny wouldn't want anything too fancy or overstated, just a thin gold band with a single diamond.

'What size is Penny's finger?' Nino enquired.

'I don't know,' I said, embarrassed again.

'Well, is she big like me, or slim like Zappa?' Nino must have been at least 16 stone. Zap was probably nine stone and Penny slightly heavier.

'She is more Zap than you, Nino.'

Nino looked at Zap chortling, 'So, he doesn't like big girls then?' To which they again both laughed. Nino asked me to take hold of Zap's hand.

'Now, does that feel like Penny's hand size?' As I held Zap's hand, I felt guilty, almost like I was cheating on Penny.

'They're similar.' Nino produced a selection of brass rings for sizing. 'Try this one first.'

'It's too big,' I declared.

'Ok, now try this one.'

Zap shook her head.

Nino muttered, '*Terza volta fortunato*.'

Zap, thinking I did not understand repeated, 'Third time lucky.' Then she smiled as I placed the ring on her finger; it fitted really well.

'*Perfecto*, now ask her to marry you,' announced Nino. I was still holding Zap's hand and she jokingly fluttered her eyelashes and stared directly at me. The room fell quiet. Without averting her eyes from mine, Zap cut through the silence.

'Dodo is already spoken for.'

I let go of her hand.

Nino shook his head, muttering, '*Pazzo*, you make a lovely couple.' As we were about to leave, Zap called to Nino,

'Be quick please. We leave for Greve in a couple of days.'

Having missed out on lunch a few days ago at the Trattoria Sostanza when we discovered the newspaper headline about Danny Mac, Zap arranged to take me there. As we made our way through the busy streets, she announced:

'Lunch is my treat today, Dodo, to celebrate you buying your first engagement ring.' I was grateful, as I was starting to run out of money, especially after buying Penny's ring. Then realising what she said, I stopped.

'Eh, what do you mean by me buying my first engagement ring?' Zap winked at me.

'Well, you men give out a ring, then you think the girl is yours to lock away forever.' Zap's smiling face turned to sadness. 'Nothing lasts forever, Gee.' I hoped Zap wasn't referring to Penny and me.

We ordered lunch. 'Any news on the vanishing girl?' Zap enquired.

'No, to be honest, the detective in charge is not very bright. Seven magicians have mysteriously died or been murdered, depending on your viewpoint, yet only one person has been arrested, and that was for just one of the murders.' Zap was fascinated, asking me to tell her the circumstances of each murder. It took so long that Zap had to put the main course on hold with the kitchen.

'Wow, the way you've described Blackpool to me sounds like nothing ever happens.'

Lunch finally arrived and I was about to tuck into a dish of lasagna.

Zap asked the significance of the dagger plunged through the ace of spades card inside the vanishing cabinet.

'All those who have died had the ace of spades placed on their body or attached to their equipment,' I said, spoken like I was DI Brock's assistant.

'What about the guy eaten by the lion? You never mentioned if the ace of spades was found on him.'

'Alex Lockhart had the ace card tattooed on his neck. The pathologist report on Vincent Leach stated the ace of spades card found in his throat did not, in fact, kill him. He was electrocuted.'

Zap interrupted: 'You mentioned the ace cards were also found inside the mailbag containing Tracey's body and in the milk can Sean Cameron drowned in.'

'Yes, and as for The Great Zantini, found with two swords protruding from his mouth, Brighton police concluded he'd accidentally killed himself whilst rehearsing. Perhaps if Brighton police had mentioned to their Blackpool counterparts about the ace card under the bottle of spirits, then they would now be searching for a serial killer. The ace of spades card was jammed inside the handle that led to Sarah's death. According to DI Brock, it had to have been placed there by Micky Marks. DI Brock also stated in the newspaper that Micky was locked up in a police cell at the time Julie Mac shot her husband Danny, therefore dismissing any link with the ace of spades theory.' I realised I'd done that much talking I'd barely touched my lasagna. Zap jumped in to talk as I dived into my food.

'So, who do you think could be the murderer?' Realising my mouth full was of pasta, she chortled, 'So this is how to keep you quiet!'

Until my plate was empty, I didn't say another word. I just took the odd gulp of red wine. Then I was ready to go again.

'I believe whoever murdered Sarah also murdered the other five magicians and at some point wants to be found.'

'Why do you say that?' Zap enquired.

'Why else do you leave your calling card?'

Zap edged forward in her seat. 'Who do you think could be the murderer?'

In full flow, I reeled off all the suspects.

'Well, Micky Marks is an obvious one, but I don't believe it was Micky.'

Zap tilted her head thoughtfully. 'Is he the guy with the orange spectacles?'

I nodded.

'Who is the one with no eyebrows again?'

'That's Gordon, but it can't be him.'

Zap again looked quizzically, trying to chew on an octopus leg partly sticking out of her mouth.

I started to mutter to myself. 'I don't think it could be Dravern Leach either. He didn't have the guile to carry out a murder.'

'You don't think it's Gordon, Micky, or Dravern, so who do you think it could be?'

'Zap, that's a question that's been racing through my head from Blackpool to Florence. The only other person present at each murder and disappearance was FPD, though he had the perfect alibi being locked inside his own dressing room at the time of Sarah's murder.'

'That's the boy in the brown overcoat who always carries a case? I remember him from the Carlton Hotel. I thought he was a psycho.' We both fell silent. Zap had just lifted her wine glass to her lips when suddenly she spat the contents all over me.

'Wait!' she yelled. Everyone in the restaurant turned and looked our way.

'There is one other person you haven't mentioned.' I tried to think who she was referring to.

'Who?' I enquired.

'You!' I nearly choked on my ice cream.

'Me?' Zap transformed into DI Brock, pointing her dessert spoon in my direction.

'You were present at each murder. Perhaps you locked Alex Lockhart in the lions' den. You've already confessed you didn't like the Leach brothers. Admit it; you knocked Vincent down the stairs. And you certainly had a motive to kill Sean Cameron after he almost blinded you.'

She'd worked me up into a cold sweat.

'Maybe you didn't like the way The Great Zantini spoke to Penny, so you shoved the two swords down his throat? Come on, Valentine, own up!' At that moment, Zap stood up in the middle of the restaurant and shouted: 'Oh my God, I'm harbouring a murderer!' She laughed loudly before slumping back into her chair. I wiped the sweat from my brow on a napkin, thinking Zappa Russo was, without doubt, the craziest person I'd ever met and thankful she did not work for Blackpool police. When the restaurant returned to normal after Zap's outburst, we ordered coffee and I changed the subject, asking Zap what she was currently creating in her workshop.

'Oh, just a simple headstone. It's been commissioned for the Day of the Dead Festival this November; I'll show you before you leave.'

During my last few days in Florence, Zap continued her work on the headstone. I kept away from her workshop to save any further embarrassment and spent my time cleaning Alice, practicing my faro card shuffle and visiting art galleries. On my final morning in Florence, it felt different. There was at last a breeze in the air and gone was the sound of hammer and chisel on stone. I smiled, knowing it was my fourth consecutive night without nightmares. I felt sadness at the thought of leaving a city where I wish I'd found my parents. Zap was sitting by the fountain; the marble statues recycling water now looked a dirty brown.

'The day starts better with Lavazza,' called Zap, referring to the fresh coffee she'd just made. She also gave me a small box.

'It's not a present, just something I think you will find useful when you get back to England.' I opened the box to find an Italian coffee pot. 'The one you have is imitation. This one's the real deal. It's Italian.'

Fresh coffee, something else I'd become accustomed to, along with lasagna, Chianti and sunshine. I thanked Zap for the gift, saying it would get much use in the coming years. As we prepared to leave the villa I took one last look over Florence from the courtyard. Although I had yet to find my parents or brother, I'd found peace within myself for the first time in my life.

The sound of running water in the fountain suddenly stopped. I turned to see Zap standing next to the camper, watching me take in the view.

'*Vieni,* I want to show you this before we leave.'

I nervously followed Zap into her workshop.

'Now I want to thank you for giving me the idea for the Day of the Dead headstone.'

Had I? I was intrigued by what it could be. Zap removed a sheet revealing a gravestone. A chill shot up my spine. On the stone, Zap had chiselled the ace of spades card. Underneath, she had also chiselled an inscription.

Tredici modi per uccidere un mago which translated as "13 ways to kill a magician".

I ran my fingers across the letters of the cool, marble stone before enquiring, 'Why 13?'

Zap shook her head, unwilling to speak. She turned and made her way out to the courtyard. I called again,

'Why 13, Zap?'

With eyes full of tears she answered, 'I feel bad luck is coming your way, Gee.'

We made our way to Nino's to pick up Penny's engagement ring. It was magnificent. I swear Nino had set a larger diamond in place than the one I'd paid for. I bought Zap an ice cream from the cart vendor next door, and we ambled our way through the streets until I noticed we were by the brass boar where we first met. As usual there were many tourists. Animated, Zap moved towards the boar as if clearing a space for the arrival of some VIP.

At the top of her voice she announced to the throngs of people in English, 'It is said if you rub the boar's nose it will bring you luck and one day you will return to Firenze. Dodo step forward please.'

Totally embarrassed, I focused on my feet, pretending I was not Dodo.

'Come on, come on, Dodo.' Zap was in full flow like a market seller about to sell their prize bull. I shyly walked forward and rubbed its nose, trying not to make eye contact with anyone. I made a wish that one day I would return with Penny. Zap immediately started a round of applause and the tourists joined in. Reverting to type, I took a bow before quickly making my exit.

Alice trudged over the River Arno and out of Florence like she was leaving a party far too early. Zap kicked off her flip flops and put her feet up on the dashboard. She pulled her hat, which looked like a terracotta plant pot, over her eyes and said,

'Remember what I say, when you see nothing but cypress trees either side of the road wake me.'

'Don't rely on me to navigate. We'll end up in Rome!'

A wide smile broke out on her face. 'That would be nice.'

Within seconds she was asleep. Boy, I wished I could sleep like that.

Within the hour, I was driving past the tall, never-ending skinny trees that Zap had referred to. I turned on the radio, hoping it would wake sleeping beauty. Matt Monro's "On Days Like These" did the trick. Zap awoke singing along in Italian - a memory I'd always carry with me.

'*Casa mia, casa mia!*' Zap called excitedly.

'Which is your home?' I asked jokingly. There was only one house – or should I say mansion? - and it could be seen from miles away. It was surrounded by vines running mile upon mile. *Russo Vigneti est 1776* stated the large wooden sign. *Almost 200 years a vineyard, that's a whole lot of wine*, I thought. Alice made her entrance up a driveway that was as long as Blackpool's North Pier. Zap's parents were waiting for us at the front of the house. Zap, as exuberant as always, jumped out of Alice before I'd even applied the handbrake. She ran across the gravelled entrance throwing her arms around her father and embracing her mother. Life was just one big stage to Zap. Onstage, I too was as exuberant as Zap and offstage, I was as shy as a lamb. Quietly, I made my way over to join the three of them.

Zap's parents were both welcoming and friendly. Her father, Roberto, was a powerfully-built man, similar in looks and build to Toddy. Her mother's name was Zona. She was a carbon copy of Zap. I was amazed at how well her parents spoke English. Zap later informed me it was because of dealing with distributors who placed their wines in the UK.

'So, he does walk like a dodo,' Zona remarked. Both daughter and mother laughed whilst I turned my usual colour of red. Zap took me on a tour of the nine-bedroom house, and her mother insisted I sleep in a proper bed for the next two nights. Zappa was about to become my tour guide.

'We will swim later, but first, let me show you around the vineyard.'

'You have your own swimming pool?' I enquired.

'Of course, don't you?'

'Sort of, it's called the Irish Sea.' I laughed at my own joke.

Zap enthusiastically marched ahead.

'*Vieni* no time to dodo walk, the vineyard measures 17.8 hectares.'

This meant very little to me. 'Tell me something I understand, like how many bottles of Chianti do you produce a year?'

Still marching, Zap replied, "Around 100,000."

I stopped in my tracks. 'What? Are you serious?'

'Plus we make and export olive oil to America.' We walked amongst the narrow vine lanes; the grapes were still weeks from reaching ripeness.

'Six weeks from now, the pickers will arrive to harvest. It's all hands on deck. Even I have to help. Perhaps you could lend a hand on your return home?' As tempting as the offer was, I explained I had a prior court appointment back in England.

'How come you're not involved full-time here instead of playing with marble?'

'I'm too independent, too headstrong for my father, too much like my mother. Why he married her, I don't know, and why she said yes is even more baffling.' We walked for what seemed like miles until we could no longer see the house. Zap mentioned she was the only child left, and one day, all of this would be her responsibility.

'I'm trying to enjoy my wild side because one day, when my parents pass, the fun will end. I will have to become the man who takes over Russo vineyard.' It was the first time I had seen real seriousness in Zap's eyes, the girl who never really wanted to grow up.

'I want an invite to your wedding, Gee Valentine,' she said matter-of-factly as she rolled and lit a cigarette.

'You would travel to Blackpool for my wedding?'

'Of course, what is it that the priest says?'

I interrupted: 'We call him a vicar; we're not catholic.'

'Ok, but the moment he asks, is there anybody here who has an objection to this wedding? I will jump up from my seat and shout, "yes, I do".' We both laughed loudly, and it echoed all around the vineyard.

'Why?' I asked.

Zap's head turned away, and I saw the tears return, rolling down her cheeks. I took a deep breath, trying to keep myself composed.

'Zap, there is someone out there for you, but it is not me.'

As soon as I said those words, I remembered they were the same words said to me by Annie regarding Penny. I knew exactly how Zap was feeling. I held her in my arms while she sobbed. 'Love is cruel,' I whispered as I dried her tears with my fingers like a brother would hold his sister after her heart had been broken.

When we returned to the house, I asked Zap if it was ok to telephone Gordon so I could find out where and when I was meeting the Camberwells in Capri.

'Of course. Let me check with Mother which phone to use.'

Zap went in her search of her mother whilst I sat looking at the various photos of Zap's abstract sculptures lining the hallway. The white walls and high ceiling reminded me of Manchester Eye Hospital. Zona appeared and led me into the library. She kindly dialled the number, then passed me the receiver and left the room. It was early evening, so I knew the Magic Attic would be closed. I let it ring five or six times and was just about to replace the receiver when Gordon answered.

'Hello?'

There was a delay before I could speak. 'Hi Gordon, it's Gee.'

'Hey, Gee. Great to hear from you again, you ok?'

'Yes, tomorrow I'm making my way to Naples. Are Penny and her parents in Capri yet?'

The line was not good. Gordon's voice was coming and going. I could just make out him telling me we were no longer meeting in Capri as no cars were allowed on the island.

'Meeting in Sorrento this Friday. You're booked into the Syrene Hotel.' The line dropped again and there was silence for a moment before Gordon's voice reappeared.

'He is dead. Sadly, it appears he's taken his own life.' With that, the phone line went completely. I tried to redial but couldn't get another connection. I told Zap what bits I'd heard and what Gordon had said.

'Who's dead?' Zap asked.

'I don't know. I can't think of anyone I know who'd take their own life.'

Chapter 20

Italy, 1970
See Naples and Die

Throughout the night, my mind played its own guessing game. Who could have taken their own life back in Blackpool? I knew it wasn't any of the Camberwells, who were now en route to Sorrento. I prayed it wasn't Lana and hoped it wasn't Walter. I didn't really care if it was DI Jack Brock, Dravern Leach or FPD.

The early morning brought laughter and the sound of splashing from the swimming pool down below. I opened wide the heavy wooden shutters in my room. I was treated to the warmest of good mornings by a Tuscan sun, half peering across thousands of swaying sunflowers in the adjacent field. It had me thinking - what was birthright? To taste your mother's milk, or perhaps one day inherit all this? Laughter was rising from the pool area. Zap and her parents were having fun. Remembering it was Zap's birthday, I leaned out of the window, and in my best operatic voice, I sang Happy Birthday like the stage player I was. The sound of hands slapping on the water acted as my round of applause.

'*Vieni,* join us,' Zona called. I duly did. After breakfast, Roberto showed me around the huge wine barrels and the family's private collection of wine, some bottles as old as the estate itself.

'Zap tells me you are in Italy trying to locate your parents?' Roberto's voice was soft and calculating; whenever he said something, you tended to listen. 'Am I correct? You think they may have lived in Naples?'

I nodded.

'I have many associates in that area. Would you like me to make some enquiries?'

I was grateful for any help and thanked Roberto in advance.

Zap continued with my tour of the estate. This time we found ourselves amongst the olive groves. Hidden amongst the trees, we came across a marble globe on a plinth. Sadly, algae and fungi had been allowed to grow wild on this once beautiful carving. Zap wrapped her arms around it, her fingertips just about touching to complete the circle. She instructed me to do the same. I did and was left with a green stain on my white t-shirt.

'You're giving the world a big hug,' Zap said in a sad voice. I wiped some of the algae away. I could see it was a sculptured map of the world, but the countries were not in their finalised locations. Zap remarked that I was not the first person confused by it.

'The world according to Zappa Russo.' She explained she based her sculpture on how she thought the world should look.

'Why is it hidden away out here? It should be cleaned up and on view near your house,' I said as though I understood art.

'You asked when we first met what happened to my blue hair? Back in 1967, my younger brother was killed in an anti-war demonstration whilst at university in America. He was on a peaceful march in Washington. The students were protesting at what was taking place in Vietnam. The police attacked the protesters with batons, and he was trampled to death in a stampede to get away. He was just 19 years of age.'

For a moment, Zap's face was empty, like a garden without flowers. Looking at the map, I noticed all the countries were in different positions. Vietnam was where the USA would normally be, the USA situated next to China. Africa replaced England's position as they needed more rain. England was next to Italy, so it would be easier for Zap to visit London. Germany had swapped places with Australia just in case the Nazis reformed one day. I realised Zappa Russo was more complex than I first thought.

'I'm sorry for the loss of your brother. What was his name?' From the look on Zap's face, she still found it painfully hard to say.

'Giovanni,' she whispered. Perhaps that's why she came up with the name Dodo for me? My name was too reminiscent of her brother.

'Why is the globe hidden away here?'

'It's too painful for my parents to see it each day.' It had been too painful until now for Zap to open such a recent wound on a day which should hold only joy. Attempting to lighten the mood, I gave her a small parcel wrapped in sunflower birthday paper I'd bought in Florence. Zap excitedly ripped at the paper, stopping when she saw it was a box.

'How did you buy this without me knowing?'

I didn't answer. Taking the necklace from her hand, I fastened it around her slender neck. Zap, for once, became shy. Her fingers played with the silver dodo pendant.

'*Lo terrò per sempre.*' I knew she meant it too; she would keep it forever.

We drove around the region of Chianti, ending up in the beautiful town of Greve for lunch. Neither of us wanted the day to end.

'When we get back, you must phone Gordon.' Zap was still as intrigued by events in Blackpool as I was. On our return, we made our way back to the ornate library; it contained more books than the Magic Attic I was about to telephone. Gordon answered immediately, asking if I'd heard all the conversation yesterday.

'No,' I replied.

'Micky Marks has taken his own life in prison.'

'Holy cow, but how?' More than anything, I was disappointed he did not stick around to prove his innocence.

'Deadly nightshade, last Thursday.'

'What the hell is deadly nightshade?' Gordon, as always, was happy to educate.

'Also known as Belladonna, it's a native plant to parts of Asia, so toxic that even a small quantity of its leaves or berries can be fatal to humans.'

'But you said Micky was in a remand centre. How could he possibly have got hold of it?' As usual, the telephone line started fading in and out. Within a few seconds, the line dropped out. As I opened the door to leave the library, I saw Roberto waiting for me in the hallway. He spoke in a tone even softer than I'd previously heard, as though he was about to let me in on a secret.

'South East of Naples, on the road to Pompeii, there's a town called Torre Annunziata. About a year ago, a commune of circus acts arrived. They erected a large circus tent and put on a show. They have yet to leave.

I suggest you move quickly before they get moved on.'

I was grateful to Roberto and thanked him for his kindness. Just as I reached the end of the hallway, Roberto called out my name. I turned. Roberto was beckoning me to return to him.

'Can I ask a favour of you?'

Without thinking, immediately I said: 'Yes, of course.'

Roberto placed his arm around my shoulder as we walked. 'I have a client, though more of a friend, he owns a restaurant in the centre of Naples. It would do me a great favour if you delivered six cases of wine to him. It's on your way to Sorrento.' I tried to answer, but he stopped me. 'My client will feed you well and make sure you have a safe passage through Naples, which can be very dangerous, especially in a vehicle like yours.'

What could I say? After all, he had welcomed me into his home and tried to help locate my parents. 'Yes, of course.'

Roberto's hand gently squeezed my shoulder. 'No need to mention this to my daughter. She may think I'm taking advantage of you. I'll get one of my staff to put the boxes into the back of your camper before you leave. I will also call Antonio, who owns the restaurant, let him know to expect you, and serve you his finest pizza.'

That evening, the family served a birthday dinner fit for their princess. Out of Zap's earshot, Roberto advised me to keep the van doors and windows closed whilst driving through Naples, no matter how hot it may be.

'My wine is not only very expensive, but it's, shall I say, sought after.' I noticed Zap giving her father a stare of disapproval. Zap's mother smiled at me, then insisted I return one day.

'Next time you stay longer. In 1976, the vineyard will be 200 years old. Perhaps you will come and entertain us?' I promised I would, and for free. Zap's parents both said their goodbyes at that point as they would be at work when I left the next morning.

By mid-morning the next day, and after another excursion around the vineyard with Zap, I was ready to continue my onward journey. Zap placed my backpack onto the front seat of Alice and noticed the boxes of wine.

'Did my father ask you to take these?'

'It's not a problem. I'm told Antonio will feed me well.' I could see Zap was not pleased her father had roped me in to deliver his wine.

Shading my eyes, I looked up. 'Have you noticed the Tuscan sun is starting to brown the top of the cypress trees?' I was desperately searching for small talk as I knew saying goodbye was painful for both of us. Sweet, crazy Zappa Russo had got to me. I needed, more than wanted, to move on. We stared at each other for what seemed an age, no words spoken. It wasn't that I couldn't find the right words, I just couldn't find any words at all. Continuous tears streamed down Zap's face, each one tracing the path of the previous. I was too afraid to hold her, not sure I would ever let go. I moved first, opening the driver's door. Through the passenger door window, Zap, statue-like, was fixed to the spot, her fingers fumbling with the dodo necklace, shoulders gently shaking as she sobbed. We were no more than three feet away from each other, I dared not get out of the camper, in case I never got back in.

'*In Bocca al luppo*' she uttered, wiping at her tears.

I choked on my reply.

Turning the ignition key, Alice was reluctant to leave too, failing to fire the engine on the first turn of the key. Motoring down the long gravelled driveway, my eyes were fixed to the rear view mirror. Zap faded into the distance but never faded from my memory.

Greve to Naples took me a few days, I contemplated visiting Rome, but with six cases of wine on view I thought better of it. In two days I would be in Sorrento. Remembering Roberto's instruction that it was too dangerous to park overnight in the centre of Naples, I searched for a quiet woodland area. The village was Russo and about 20 kilometres north of Naples. I smiled at the thought that Zap's family may own this place too! I found a spot under the pine trees and parked up Alice for the night. Having filled my new coffee pot I fired up the gas stove and waited. My mind drifted back to saying goodbye to Zap and how difficult it proved. Strangely, I felt we would meet again.

I was now alone for the first time in weeks. The evenings were at last cooler, and sleep was easier to find but not to keep. The nightmare of Micky Marks returned but was now different. As I stood in the wings I watched him frantically trying to free Sarah. He turned his head, looked directly at me and winked. Did I now see Micky as guilty because he took his own life? Perhaps he took his own life because he felt life was no longer worth living without Sarah? I truly hoped it was the latter. Alongside illusion work, he also had great hands and performed a wonderful version of a routine called Multiplying Billiard Balls. His dexterity was superb. Each ball moved effortlessly between his fingers, and each one vanished at will. I was convinced Micky would not have murdered Sarah. One thing was for sure, taking one's own life is no way for a magician to die.

The sunrise came into view beyond the pine trees surrounding Alice. My thoughts were still with Zap. Trying to lift my own spirits, the way I always do, through music, I slid Rod Stewart's new album, Gasoline Alley, into the cassette deck. "Cut Across Shorty" kicked in. Now I was up for anything, or so I thought until I started driving through the busy streets of Naples. Entering the city I noticed a police car in my rear view mirror. I was paranoid they were following me, my eyes constantly darted from the police car behind to the road in front. A police car behind - bang! A Vespa hit the side of Alice; I'd knocked a girl off her bike. I was travelling down a one-way street, so was the girl, only she was travelling in the wrong direction. Though she still thought it my fault. I caught a little of the foul words she shouted at me from the floor. To add to my problems, the same police car pulled up alongside me. One of the officers approached. He ignored the fouled mouth girl lying on the floor. I was about to get out of the camper to help her and assess the damage.

'*Non*,' said the police officer. '*Vieni*'. Pointing at his car he motioned me to follow him. I did exactly as instructed. I was sure my next stop would be the police station. Was I about to be charged with careless driving? What of the girl travelling the wrong way? Why wasn't she taken in? Within a few minutes, we approached the police station, and to my surprise, the police car drove straight past. Where were they taking me? I thought of turning off at the next junction and trying to outrun them, but I had no idea where I was. Eventually, the police car turned down a side street and pulled into a small car park. Painted black graffiti adorned the whitewashed wall.

'*Vedi napoli e muori.*' Translated into English, it read, 'See Naples and die.' *Holy cow*, I thought, *I was only delivering a few boxes of wine*. My heart thumped in my chest as though trying to escape. Sweat slowly dripped down my back. I was terrified at what happened next. Averting my eyes from the police car, I noticed *Antonio's Pizzeria* written above a door leading from a metal fire escape. The door sprung open, and a short, stout man in a white t-shirt and apron came bouncing down the stairs. He made his way to the police car and shook hands with one of the policemen. I swore he placed something in the officer's hand!

'*Ciao,* Gee,' the man shouted before beckoning me out of Alice.

'I am Antonio, friend of Roberto, Vieni Pizza.' I felt relieved, if not completely safe.

He took the van keys off me and threw them to another man who'd appeared, also dressed in white overalls.

'*Vai a prendere le scatole.*' Antonio told the man to fetch the boxes. We made our way up the fire escape and into the restaurant where I was greeted by a waitress who instantly placed a bottle of beer in my hand and led me to a table. It wasn't only the beer I drank in, but the music and smell of fresh oregano; at last I felt safe - thanks to Zap's father who must have arranged for a police escort to keep Alice and me safe, or more likely his wine. Either way, I was grateful. I hadn't ordered the pizza the waitress brought over to my table, but I was thankful for it. The aroma alone made me think this was one of life's great inventions. I devoured it.

I waited for what felt like an age for Antonio to return with my van keys. Eventually, I finished my beer and went in search of the restaurant owner. Through a half-open door in the kitchen, I noticed the man in white overalls from the car park. It wasn't the bottles of wine he removed from the cases I'd brought, but small packages, each one the size of a house brick, wrapped in a grey tape. I knew very little about drugs other than they're illegal, but I suspected that was what they were. It now appeared Roberto had used me as a drug mule. I decided to make a quick exit, hoping the keys were inside the camper. They were, along with a box of wine left on the back seat. On top was an address in Sorrento. I picked up the box and went back into the restaurant, searching for Antonio. He was sitting at the table where I'd eaten the pizza.

'*Ciao* Gee, you enjoyed your pizza?' I placed the box of wine on the table.

'The pizza was great, thank you, but you left this box behind.' Antonio stood up, placed his hands on the table and, looked at the address on top, then glared at me. The scar that zig-zagged from one eye to the other widened in anger.

'You going to Sorrento, no?' I knew he was playing a game with me, a game I could not win.

'Tell me what is inside the box?' He gestured for the waitress to come over, the one who served me earlier.

'*Tradurre,*' he said to her. I understood he asked her to translate, which the waitress did, word for word. Antonio sat back down.

'My business arrangement with Roberto Russo goes back a long time. He said to me, Gee Valentine is a good kid. He will deliver the box for you, Antonio. He owes me a favour.' I took it the "favour" I owed Roberto was his help to locate my parents.

'You've still not told me what's inside the box?' Antonio leant back in his chair and stared at the table. Shaking his head, he spoke softly without looking at me. Again the waitress translated,

'The girl you knocked off the Vespa earlier sadly died from her injuries. You are too young to spend the next 15 years in Naples prison, though pretty enough for the many beasts inside to play with. It takes one call to my friend at the police headquarters.'

Antonio dismissed the waitress and left me in no doubt that if I did not carry out his instructions, these were my last moments of freedom. I picked up the box and left the restaurant. Being in and driving through Naples proved a harrowing experience. This part of Italy was far different to anything I'd experienced. I was desperate to find my way out of a city with such a dangerous edge. Lost, I followed the sign *Porta.* Knowing once I reached the port with the sea on my right, I would be on the road to Pompeii where, according to Roberto, I would eventually find the Vasserlino Circus. Just before dark, I approached the small fishing port of Torre Annunziata. In the distance, through the sea mist, I could just about make out the big red top of the circus tent. Sailing boats peacefully bobbed along on the tide.

I parked up as close to the circus tent as possible. Paint had been scratched off the near side of Alice by the Vespa's handlebars. Alice was no longer looking pristine. I also knew the girl on the Vespa wasn't killed.

Rather, Antonio was showing me how powerful he was. I made my way towards the circus tents, hoping to find someone I could talk with who could shed some light on my parents. The main entrance door was hanging off its hinges. I squeezed through and into a corridor that led into the big top. If darkness was a welcoming spirit, its mysteriousness invited me into the open space. Deserted and dilapidated, carefully I walked to the centre of the ring and was startled by a bat that flew low over my head. I shuffled my feet, turning full circle. There was nothing more dramatic than an empty theatre, waiting in anticipation for the show to commence. I imagined myself as the ringmaster, dressed in a red tailcoat, tipping the brim of my top hat. I introduced the clowns and was surrounded by elephants, lions, and zebras. Above my head, the daring trapeze artistes flew without fear. I commanded a drum roll from the orchestra as I announced the world's greatest knife-throwing act, The Fabulous Bellini's. In reality, the only performance was the sound of the wind that whistled under the empty benches. This circus had not seen entertainment for a long time. Retracing my steps back out of the circus tent, I felt the search for my parents was at an end. It was ironic that the closest I'd got to them was being in a circus tent where they once performed.

Back in the campervan, I looked at the address on the wine box:

Otto Coltelli Forno
Via Correalee
Sorrento

The *forno* indicated my delivery address was a bakery. I continued my journey to rid myself of the clutches of Roberto and Antonio. By the time I reached the outskirts of Sorrento it was still dark. I remembered Lana never opened the bakery before 5.30 am. I presumed Otto Coltelli Forno to be no different. I parked up and waited. Though apprehensive at getting rid of the box, I was also very excited that in just a few hours I would be reunited with Penny. Remembering Gordon had given me an envelope, I decided now was a good time to open it. Inside, I found an address and a postal order in my name for £250. There was also a short note from Gordon, it read:

Hi Gee,

I trust you are having a great time and are now in Sorrento. The money order is just in case you've got no money left. You can repay me when you start back performing. The address below belongs to the people who helped me at the end of the Second World War. Please try to go along and say hello to them.

Always
Gordon

Giovanni and Anna Agosto
Lemon House. Via Casarlano. Sorrento

Chapter 21

Sorrento, 1970

U nlike me, Sorrento slept. It was not the ongoing nightmare of Micky Marks that kept me awake, more my questioning conscience and the guilt associated with the box of "wine" I was about to drop off. I felt trapped in one of those awful late-night B movies where the cops suddenly appeared just as the illegal switch took place. By 6.45 am I was running out of patience. There was still no sign of life inside the bakery. Anxious and in desperate need to rid myself of this burden, I decided to leave the box inside the bakery doorway.

As I returned to Alice across the deserted road, it suddenly occurred to me that perhaps the bakery opened later on a Sunday? About to turn around and retrieve the case, I stopped, again telling myself it wasn't my problem if they didn't open till later; my part was done. I'd delivered the case. Sitting behind the steering wheel, I put the key into the ignition. Then I questioned myself again. What if the case was stolen? Antonio would no doubt send someone after me. Just as I was about to get back out of the camper, I noticed a car approaching in the distance. By the time I realised it was a police car it was too late to retrieve the case. Quickly, I slid down in my seat, pretending to be asleep. My hands were clasped together and I prayed they didn't spot the case outside the bakery. I tried to squint from the corner of one eye. The policeman picked up the case and was heading my way. Shit! I was done for. The thought of spending the next few years in a Naples prison as some beast's toy filled me with dread. He banged hard on the windscreen.

'*Ragazzo, ragazzo, svegliati.*' Boy wake up, he shouted, unconcerned the rest of Sorrento was sleeping. Slowly I opened the door as if unaware of what he was holding.

'*Fai il tuo lavoro stupido ragazzo e consegna.*' He told me to deliver the box, angrily shoving it onto my chest. I was shaking with fear at the Neapolitan version of pass the parcel as he returned to his police car. To calm myself I put a coffee on the gas stove. Nearby, a squeaking shop sign added to my nervousness, gently swaying in the early morning breeze. Then I realised there was no early morning breeze. It was coming from a bicycle ridden by a young boy. He dismounted outside the bakery, and whilst he picked up a set of keys from the bike's basket, he noticed Alice. Like a magnet, she pulled him across the road to take a closer look. As I opened the side door, the boy startled, and jumped back, shouting,

'Madonna, Madonna.'

'Sorry, I didn't mean to make you jump,' I said as I picked up his worn deck of playing cards that had fallen from his pocket.

'Madonna,' he said again. 'I have to stop saying.' His English was better than my Italian. I asked if the cards were for performing magic.

'*Sì*, yes I am learning.' I asked him to show me his dealing position. He smiled and held the deck in his left hand. I could tell he was more than a novice. From his neatly fanned deck, he asked me to take a card, to which I obliged. My chosen card was the 5 of hearts, which I slid back into his deck. His eyes fixed on me throughout, he could tell I practised. Competently, he completed a Hindu shuffle that even I was jealous of. Turning over the top card, he revealed the 6 of clubs, oh dear.

'Shame,' I observed. 'You were doing really well until then.' I turned to pass him the box of wine; my chosen card, the 5 of hearts, was placed on top of the wine box. By the time I looked back to congratulate him, he'd already crossed the road to open up the shop. I followed him and entered with the case in my arms.

'You were expecting me, weren't you?' He flashed a half-smile, then confided in me.

'Yes I'm expecting an English guy to deliver the case, but this is not something I like to do. It is something I'm forced to do.' From the sad expression on his face I believed him. 'This is my father's shop. He's too lazy to open up. He'd rather put me at risk.' I felt really sorry for someone so young to be mixed up in smuggling drugs, then I remembered, I was only 21.

'Your magic is very good, but your cards are very old.' I threw him a new Bicycle deck.

'You are a magician too?'

I nodded with a kind of glass-half-empty expression.

'When I complete school I will leave here and become a full-time magician, maybe Las Vegas.' His reference put a smile on my face. He was no more than 14, but he'd already mapped out his life.

'You will need many more years of practice before you can call yourself a magician,' I said.

He opened the new deck of cards ready to show me another trick. 'Your name is Gee, right?'

Again I nodded.

'My name is Danny.'

I distanced myself as far away from the case as possible. I was in no mood to start another magic trick. '*Ciao* Danny,' I said, closing the door behind me. I crossed the road and climbed back into the camper. Sorrento was starting to awake. At that moment, I promised myself I would never deliver anything for anyone ever again, against my will.

'Now Alice,' I called out. 'Let's go and find Penny!'

Majestically placed overlooking the Bay of Naples, the Hotel Syrene sat proudly in her own grounds, looking every bit of her five stars. It was probably no more than a five-minute stroll from the centre of town. The hotel driveway was gravel, so I turned off the engine to let Alice roll the final 30 yards in an attempt to leave the guests sleeping. The noise from the gravel reminded me of the night I drove into Zap's courtyard in Florence - a name I would do well to avoid whilst around Penny. I quietly closed my driver's door and made my way past the ornate ponds, hoping reception was open.

'You're right. You should have called her Thumper.'

Hearing Penny's voice for the first time in over five months was music to my eyes. She was sitting elegantly on a deck chair outside her garden room, wearing a white dressing gown with a matching headscarf to protect her from the early morning chill. Even at this early hour, she looked like a film star waiting to go on set. I rushed over, sunk to my knees, and wrapped her in my arms. Of all the things Penny could have remarked on she said,

'You need a haircut.'

'I've missed you too,' I said jokingly. 'How long have you been sitting here?'

Penny gave me one of those expressions I'd so desperately missed.

'Well, I know you can't sleep properly, so I thought I'd better be up early for when you arrived.'

'Penny, I have a brother,' I announced.

'So you have found your parents?'

'Not exactly. I met a man who performed with them.'

'How old is your brother?'

'I don't know.'

'Do you know his name or where he lives?'

'No.' I started to realise how vague this all sounded. Penny sensed from the disappointment in my voice I still had no idea where my family were.

I guided Penny to where I'd parked Alice. Taking hold of her hand, I ran her fingers gently over the brail sign I had made in Marseilles.

'Alice,' observed Penny with a smile as bright as the rising sun.

'How was the journey from England?' I asked.

'Very, very boring, how was yours?'

'Wonderful! Incredible sights, the people are so friendly, well mainly.' I stopped, feeling stupid at my phrasing, almost forgetting the woman I was about to ask to marry me was blind.

'Meet any nice girls?' she remarked. I felt my cheeks start to burn.

'Penny! What are you doing out here at this time? Come inside. You'll catch your death of cold!'

Annie, fortunately, saved my blushes.

'Gee Valentine, you and that bloody noisy thing have woken up the whole hotel, except Tom, of course, who can sleep through anything!' Annie gave me a big hug. It was another hour before Tom appeared. He was less frosty than the last time we met.

'I have cleared it with the hotel for you to leave the campervan in the car park, but they won't allow you to sleep in it overnight. Annie and I have paid for you to stay in the hotel.'

By the look of this place it must have cost a small fortune, I thought.

Tom handed me an envelope. 'Looks like you won't have any trouble paying us back.'

Inside was a letter from Toddy explaining since Sarah's death, he'd decided to venture into a new emerging market - cruise ship entertainment. I remembered Luca telling me cruise ship entertainment was the future. I took a peek inside the envelope – there was a new contract for me to sign. I'd be performing on various cruise ships throughout the world. The money was more than ten times what I was previously paid. Tom must have peeked too, as he threw me a knowing grin.

'Not bad, eh?' Tom remarked. 'Toddy's also asked Gordon and I to remake the cocktail bar so it's easier to transport.' He seemed rather pleased with himself. I couldn't help thinking his pleasure came from keeping Penny and me apart. 'I've organised a holiday itinerary, planning different excursions each day. Starting with Pompeii tomorrow, then Positano the day after, followed by Mount Vesuvius, an Amalfi coast tour and Naples. That'll take up the first week.' Their 25th wedding anniversary fell in the second week when we would be spending a couple of days on the Isle of Capri where Tom had convalesced at the end of the war.

Being back with Penny reminded me it was her more than anyone else I needed. Tom and Annie ensured we were never left alone, other than a short stroll each morning. When the day arrived for us all to visit Naples, I came up with an excuse not to go. Visiting Naples once in a lifetime would suffice. Knowing my luck, we'd end up in Antonio's pizzeria for lunch. I asked Tom if I could take Penny with me to visit the house where Gordon had convalesced after the war. Tom refused; no surprise there. The Camberwells set off to Naples and I went in search of The House of Lemon.

Casa sull'albero di limone, was surrounded by high, whitewashed walls bathed in mid-morning sunshine. With Alice parked on the main road, I made my way through the driveway gates. Immediately I was taken aback by the hundreds of lemon trees surrounding the house, along with the powerful smell of the fresh lemons. Across the courtyard, I could see an elderly couple sitting at a table having breakfast. They were yet to notice me.

'*Ciao, sono un' amico di Gordon Kingsley.*'

They both stared at me before transferring their stare to each other. I tried again, but this time in English.

'Hello, I'm a friend of Gordon Kingsley, do you remember him? Do you speak English?' They just stared at me, taking hold of each other's hands. I was starting to think I'd got the wrong house.

'*Piccola, sì, a little,*' the old man replied, 'are you his son?' The old man was now standing.

'Yes,' I called. It was too complicated trying to explain anything else. Slowly I explained I was on holiday with my girlfriend's family at the Hotel Syrene. I thought they didn't understand English very well. The old man moved from the table and went inside the house. His wife motioned for me to sit at the table with her. She continued looking at me, probably thinking I looked nothing like Gordon, then she smiled and said: ·

'Anna,' pointing a finger at herself, then pointing towards the house, she said, 'Giovanni'. I was sure she'd referred to her husband and not the house.

'My name is Giovanni, too,' I said, thinking it may give a little more credibility as to who I was. Her smile widened. The old man, slow on his feet, returned holding a book, which he opened and removed a photograph. Anna spoke to her husband in Italian, which I partly understood.

'He says his name is Giovanni.' The old man looked at me and then the photo, then at me, then back to the photo. He handed it to me. It was very old and faded, though I could still make out Gordon sitting at this very table along with Giovanni and Anna. There was a date written in the top left corner, 12/6/1947.

'How did Gordon end up here?' They looked at each other quizzically.

'Please, I will be back in a moment,' I said and dashed off to Alice to get my phrasebook. When I returned, Anna was crushing lemons into a press. Giovanni was still looking through the book he'd brought out with the photo. I repeated the question, but this time in Italian. Giovanni smiled and broke into good English.

'Good, I needed to see if you could make an effort to speak Italian, even if only a little. I taught Gordon Italian. He helped me with my English. I was the better student. His Italian was awful!'

I laughed, saying: 'It's better than mine!'

Anna returned to the table with a jug of cloudy water and three glasses, pouring a glass for each of us.

'Limonata,' she stated. Above, an old bed sheet shaded us from the sun. The lemonade was most welcome, and unlike any lemonade I'd tasted before. I felt relaxed in their company like I had known them longer than the 40 minutes I had been there.

'I take it you know the story of your Uncle Gino and what happened to him in Bari?'

I nodded.

Giovanni continued. 'Gordon was based in Naples; he was sent to this very house to defuse an unexploded bomb, dropped, may I say, by the allies.' He pointed to under our feet where we were seated. 'He arrived with two other soldiers, and we were moved out to stay with friends. We were not allowed back for a week until the bomb was made safe. When we received the all-clear to return to our home, we found Gordon living in the shed at the bottom of our garden. He was in a bad way. I think he'd had a breakdown. He told us the bomb was safe, it was still under where we sat.'

I moved uncomfortably in my seat and looked down as if expecting to see something. Giovanni told me Gordon was not ready to go back to Britain. 'We were grateful he'd saved the house, as well as all our lemon trees, so we said he could stay. He refused to live in the house as our teenage daughter was still at home. He insisted on living in the shed. Each day he helped with the land, and we fed him in return,' Giovanni stood from the table.

'*Vieni,* come follow,' he said.

We ducked our heads as we made our way past row after row of lemon trees until we reached an area overgrown with old olive trees almost ready to harvest. Giovanni brushed past the branches until we made our way into a clearing. There stood an old, dilapidated shed. I helped Giovanni and pushed open the shed door. I didn't think it had been opened in years. The room filled with light as sun rays cut through the floating dust particles.

No bigger than 14-feet square, it contained a single camp bed and a small table with discarded playing cards scattered on top. The ace of hearts was so faded it was barely visible. It was hard to believe that any man could live like this for almost two years, but Gordon Kingsley was not just any man. I noticed Giovanni staring at me.

'What happened to your ear?' he enquired. Automatically I lifted my hand as if I didn't know I had a piece missing.

'I was involved in a fight.'

Shaking his head he muttered: '*Pazzo!*' He turned to walk back through the lemon groves.

'Why did you not keep in touch?' I got no reply.

Anna had set the table for lunch. Throughout the afternoon, Giovanni told me all about how he helped his grandfather in the lemon groves when he was a little boy. I couldn't help feeling more than a tad jealous, as, like Gordon, he could trace his family back generations. Giovanni's mood became sombre as he explained how he and Gordon would go fishing early each morning to avoid Gordon being seen. Again, he picked up the old photo.

'The morning after Anna's 40th birthday party, I waited for Gordon to go fishing, but he did not show. I went in search of him at the hut, but it was empty. Gordon had gone. On the bedside table, he left this book.'

With that, he passed me the book he'd brought out with the photo earlier. The book was A4; the kind used to sketch in. I turned the page to see a message written by Gordon in pencil.

Dear Giovanni and Anna,

I cannot thank you enough for your kindness these past two years. As you know, I have found life very difficult since the loss of my brother. But I have to face up to my responsibilities and help those I have let down. I hope one day we can meet again.

If I am lucky to have a son, I will name him Giovanni and hope he grows to be a man like you.

Yours sincerely
Gordon Kingsley

I continued turning the pages that contained Gordon's many sketchings, each page something new. I'd no idea he had such a talent. From detailed lemon and olives trees pre- and post-harvest, and early morning fishing trips to the dreaded ace of spades card, plus at least a further 20 pages explaining various card sleight of hand techniques. The final page in the book had been torn out. Lifting my head, I looked to Anna and asked:

'Do you know why this page has been torn out?'

Anna looked to Giovanni, neither replied.

I had a feeling they were harbouring a secret, one they would not divulge with a stranger. As the day wore on, I didn't want to outstay my welcome, so I explained my girlfriend would soon return from her day trip to Naples.

'Please say hello to Gordon. It would be good to hear from him again, and you must come back with your girlfriend before you leave.'

'I will try my best,' I answered, knowing Tom would never allow it.

Anna walked to one of the many wooden sheds. When she returned, she gave me a bottle of her homemade Limoncello then kissed me on both cheeks before whispering in my ear,

'*Torna a sorrento.*' (Return to Sorrento.)

'I will come back, I promise.' That's why Italians were so endearing. You only needed to spend a little time with them to feel you were part of their family like you had known them all your life.

The night before we set off to Capri to celebrate Tom and Annie's 25th wedding anniversary, I finally plucked up enough courage to ask Tom if I could marry Penny. Like a good performer, I'd rehearsed what I needed to say - starting with Penny and I were both mature for our age. With my new cruise ship contract I'd save enough money to put down a deposit on a house within a year. Then we would get married. Throughout dinner, Tom was in a jovial mood. A violinist strolled by playing *Torna a Sorrento* - now a firm favourite of mine. Perhaps Penny and I would have it played at our wedding. We could even come back here for our honeymoon. Annie and Penny left the table in search of the ladies' room. I felt a window of opportunity to ask Tom for Penny's hand, but he spoke first.

'Gee, over these past few months, both Annie and I have been pleased to see Penny return to her normal self. She's starting to understand a normal life for her will be without a husband and children.'

I couldn't let his remark go unchallenged.

'Why not? Penny deserves more than just a normal life; she deserves an extraordinary life.'

'And there lies the problem, Gee, you filled her head with stupid talk of love. Penny will never lead a normal life.' With that, Tom pushed back his chair and walked away to the bar. He'd not only knocked the chair over but kicked the wind from within me, leaving me deflated.

The next morning I waited in reception with my overnight bag, as today we were all sailing off to the Isle of Capri. Tom and Annie arrived, but no Penny. Annie took me to one side.

'Penny is not feeling well. She says she has an upset stomach and there is no way she could travel on a boat. Tom is furious. It's cost him a small fortune.' I looked across at Tom and he looked livid.

Annie continued. 'I have asked the lady behind reception to keep an eye on her at lunchtime and dinner. If they think she is no better, they will call the hotel where we're staying. Will you please keep your eye on her too? If she feels better later in the day, you could both catch the last ferry.'

I promised Annie I would take care of her. Tom refused to make eye contact with me. Annie took Tom's arm, and they left the hotel. I watched from the hotel gardens as the ferry boat sailed out of the harbour below, then walked around to Penny's room expecting the curtains to be closed. Penny was sitting outside on a deck chair looking as bright as the day. She was wearing just a bikini whilst soaking up the sun.

'You took your time getting here,' she said without her usual smile. I was always amazed she could tell I was nearby.

'So, are you not poorly?'

Penny threw me a smile. 'I can do misdirection too, you know. Now come and put some sun lotion on my back.' With the help of her cane, she made her way back into her room, like an obedient pet, I followed.

'Close the door,' she said - more an instruction than a request. Her room was in semi-darkness. Floor to ceiling lace curtains gently swayed in the breeze. The Tyrrhenian Sea framed Penny's beauty as she removed her bikini top, breasts so perky they barely moved. Holy cow! I was gobsmacked. Penny was standing half-naked in front of me.

'If I wait for you to make a move, I'll be an old spinster.' For once I was not embarrassed. My eyes explored her form, my hands explored her body, our tongues discovered each other. I knew we were both virgins, no protection, reckless in our desire to lock our lives together forever. Creating a bond so strong her father would never be able to break. I removed her bikini bottoms, and we made love, laying in each other's arms, legs interlocked, no thought of time. I told her of the lemon tree farm, and she told me of her fear whilst in Naples. We made love again. There was a knock at the door, I immediately felt panic, had Tom tricked us? No, it was one of the receptionists checking on Penny.

'I am fine, thank you,' Penny called from the bed before giggling into my arms.

The afternoon turned to evening. Penny decided she would not travel on the last ferry to Capri.

'I am almost 22, and it is time my parents stopped treating me like a child.'

'Would you like me to sort some food?'

Penny rested her chin on her knees and giggled. 'Yes, pizza.'

Returning from the pizzeria, I stopped by Alice and grabbed the bottle of limoncello Anna Gusto had given me. With the sun setting, we sat on Penny's balcony overlooking the bay of Naples. Pizza and limoncello proved to be a great mix. From the cocktail bar, we could hear a piano. The occasion and setting were about as perfect as they would ever be. Tom Camberwell no longer had a speaking part in what I was about to ask. I tried to do the gentlemanly thing and get down on one knee. Due to the small size of the balcony, what should have been the most romantic of moments, became a comedy farce as I almost knocked Penny off her chair.

'Gee, what the hell are you trying to do?'

I snorted at my own stupidity.

'Why are you laughing so much?' Penny asked, joining in the laughter. I'd found myself in the kneeling position.

'Because I am trying to ask you to marry me.'

Silence fell between us. I placed the ring into her hands and watched as her fingers traversed slowly across the gold band, then delicately over the diamond. I looked into Penny's eyes, the ones that captured me when I was just 14. Her misty outer grey rim, thin, delicate black circle, bold planet-like pupils were as spellbinding now as the first time I saw them. Only now they were full of tears, not like the tears of anguish when she sat next to my hospital bed after Sean Cameron's attack. These were tears of happiness. She placed the ring over her finger. I was about to say, 'marry me', but she placed her index finger to my lips and said 'yes'. I lifted Penny from the chair and carried her back to the bed, where we made love one more time. Penny and I agreed it was best I slept in the camper that night, in case her parents returned early from Capri. As I was about to leave her room, Penny called,

'Do you mind if we don't tell my parents until we're back in England? I just don't want to spoil the last couple of days in Sorrento in case my father gets angry.'

I totally understood though I knew her father never would. Locking butterflies away should be made illegal.

Chapter 22

Italy, 1970
Retorna da me

High above Marina Piccola harbour, the early morning sun was in dazzling form, reflecting off the water as the fishermen brought home their daily catch. I had a gut feeling Tom and Annie would be on the first ferry out of Capri, as over the horizon it loomed into view. Shortly after mooring, and even from a distance, I could make out Tom's limp as he made his way down the gangway ahead of Annie. I thought it best to keep out of the way on their final day. I ambled into the town of Sorrento in search of a gift to take home for Lana. Weirdly, I found myself outside *Otto Coltelli Pane* where I'd delivered the case of wine a couple of weeks ago. Through the window, I watched the young boy, Danny, stack bread onto the shelves. Presumably, his lazy father was still in bed. To my shock I noticed Antonio was also in the bakery. Worse still, I swear he saw me. I moved backwards and made a swift getaway.

The Camberwells were leaving for home first thing in the morning. I will follow on later. That evening, as Penny missed her parents' 25th wedding anniversary celebration, we were all going out to dinner at the nearby Grand Europa Hotel. I felt like the luckiest guy in the world as I escorted Penny into the Al fresco dining area. Penny's white and silver dress attracted the eyes of all in attendance and the twinkling lights which looked like stars in the ceiling above. The tables were dressed with fine white cloths adorned with premium white porcelain. Each table's centrepiece was graced with an 18-piece candelabra. The candle flames danced to the sound of a trio playing in the corner. Tom was back to his usual frosty self, hardly speaking throughout dinner. The ladies excused themselves and arranged to meet us at the poolside bar.

I asked Tom if he enjoyed being back on Capri and he gave me the briefest of answers.

'Too many bloody tourists.' Tom Camberwell does not like change. Soon he would have to accept it. Though I knew the answer to the question I was about to ask, I still had to ask it.

'Tom, I would like Penny to travel home with me in the camper.' His cheeks reddened. Like the mouth of Mount Vesuvius pointing out of the water across the bay, he was ready to explode.

'Are you bloody stupid? Where would she go to the toilet, for starters? Definitely not.'

I also knew what I was about to say would not change his mind, but Tom Camberwell had said his final no to me regarding Penny.

'Do you think it fair to keep Penny locked away like a prized butterfly?' The volcano that was Tom Camberwell spewed its lava. His eyes dilated as his mind searched for the most hurtful words he could serve up.

'Do you know why you were abandoned as a baby, Valentine?'

I remained silent.

'Because your parents knew you would turn out to be nothing. You ponce about the stage thinking you have talent, which by the way, you have very little of. You have no prospects for my daughter, and I thank God I never tried to adopt you as a child.'

I don't know why I smiled, but I did. He wasn't finished with me yet.

'Should I ever find out you slept with my daughter while we were in Capri, I will do everything in my power to keep you away from her. Everything.' His last words were as venomous as the Saw-Scaled viper that killed Tracey Mac. I'd known for a long time Tom that didn't like me. I'd tried very hard to keep on his good side, but if just being around upset him, then tough, I was going to be around for a long time. As I stood up to leave the table, I looked directly at Tom and let him know.

'You don't have to like me. You just have to get used to me being around more,' I said as I walked away. My own red mist had started to descend. I retraced my steps back to the table where Tom was still sitting.

I placed the palms of my hands onto the table, our faces were no more than six inches apart, and I reposted my own revengeful bile.

'As for sleeping with your daughter, there was no sleeping involved.'

Before he could reply, I'd turned on my heels and didn't look back. Penny and Annie were already at the bar. It wasn't long before Annie reminded me they were leaving early in the morning, so it was best to say our goodbyes. Penny and I strolled back to the hotel. As we passed a row of olive trees, to break the silence, I jokingly said:

'Did you know there are no olive trees in the Italian Gardens in Stanley Park?'

Penny squeezed my biceps and said: 'When you get home, you'd better do something about it.'

On a more serious note, I explained her father and I had just exchanged the most hurtful of words. Penny again squeezed my arm, ready to proclaim where her future lay.

'Don't worry, so did I this afternoon. When we get home, things will settle. If not, we will find a place of our own.' I took off my St Christopher necklace and attempted to fasten it around Penny's neck.

'I want to make sure you get home safely.'

Penny pushed it back into my hand. 'No way, it's kept you safe this far.' We kissed passionately, neither wanting to let go. Ahead, I saw Annie was waiting. We both continually kept saying 'I love you' before I finally uttered,

'You'd better go,' as her mother approached.

Walking away Penny called, 'Gee, remember if you don't know where you are going, any road can take you there.'

'I know where I'm going and I'll see you there. *In bocca al lupo,* Penny Camberwell.'

'What does that mean?' she called.

'I'll tell you in when I get back to Blackpool,' I shouted through the night air.

Later that evening as I lay in the camper I regretted what I'd said to Tom. I'd apologise to him at my first opportunity once I got home. I drifted in and out of sleep. At one point, I swore I could hear Penny singing "I Will Follow You" in the late-night bar. Partway through the night, I definitely heard people talking near my campervan. At first, I thought they were just passers-by. But then someone tried the driver's door and then the passenger door. I picked up a monkey wrench, trying to make as much noise as possible and then threw open the side door.

'Madonna, Madonna,' shrieked a startled Danny, accidentally knocking Antonio to the floor.

'Danny!' I exclaimed. 'What the fuck are you doing here?' Fear raced through my body. Danny helped Antonio to his feet.

'*Scusa, scusa,* sorry Gee.' Unlike Antonio, I saw fear in Danny's eyes.

'It's 3 o'clock in the morning?'

Danny's eyes were unwilling to meet mine. Internally, my heart beat loudly. Externally, the noise came from the waves crashing against the rocks below. Danny looked like he'd rather be anywhere than here. He shuffled his feet, and nervously blew on his hands, pretending to keep warm.

'You leave in the morning, no?' stuttered Danny.

'Yes, I'm on my way back to England.'

'Would you do Antonio a favour? He'll make it worth your while.' Poor Danny, roped in by Antonio to translate.

'Let me guess. You'd like me to deliver a few small boxes for you?'

Danny's face lit up at how easy it was to convince me. '*Sì,* yes, it's on your way, a place called Livorno, do you know it?'

'Yes, but no.'

Danny looked at me, confused.

'Look, so far, Italian favours tend to mean something illegal, something Roberto and Antonio are unwilling to chance in case they get caught. Yet they're happy for me to take that chance because if I get caught it will not matter. So yes, I know where Livorno is, but no, I will not deliver the boxes for Antonio.'

Danny looked from me to Antonio and back to me with fear in his eyes. His face began to twitch. Turning back to the restaurant owner, Danny translated what I'd said. Antonio suddenly became animated, arms and hands gesturing like a British bobby in Piccadilly Circus. His speech was so quick I caught little of what was said, though I was sure I caught the word 'girlfriend'. Antonio tried to pass me a roll of banknotes secured with elastic bands. His English had suddenly improved.

'Gee, it's simple, just a few boxes you drop off in Livorno. I'm happy,

Mr Russo too, and you make £100.' I couldn't believe Zap's father was involved in this. I wondered if Zap knew too. I attempted to hand the money back to Antonio, but he refused, holding up his hands like someone who'd just stuck a gun in his back. He told Danny to go to the car and fetch something. What? I didn't know as his dialect was too strong. I was no longer scared, as I was the one holding a monkey wrench. Danny returned with half a dozen pizza boxes. Trying comedy as my last line of defence before violence, I said thanks, but I'd already eaten.

Antonio jabbered away; Danny listened intently. I looked at Danny and wondered how a boy so young ended up in this kind of mess. Antonio eventually ran out of words. Danny was about to speak. I put my index finger to my lips in a shush-like motion.

'Save your breath, Danny. I don't want to hear what he says. Tell him if he leaves now and takes the boxes with him, I won't crack open his skull with the wrench.' Danny twitched his head like a bird in a tree, wary of the neighbourhood cat.

'Gee, they will kill you, do you not understand? Antonio knows you have a girlfriend in the hotel. They will kill her too. Please just take the boxes.' Danny placed the pizza boxes on the front seat of Alice. I wanted to smash the life out of Antonio. Penny's safety was everything to me. I looked to Antonio and nodded slowly. The smirk on his face said he knew all along I would.

'*Lo tengo per le palle,*' declared Antonio. He was right. He had me by the balls, for now. As Danny walked past me to leave, without him realising, I placed the £100 notes into his trouser pocket, hoping it would help him flee his situation.

I'd barely slept as the sun came into view. I still pondered what to do with the pizza boxes on the front seat. I fired up the gas stove and got a fresh coffee on the go. I opened the side door and on the grass sat a small olive tree in a terracotta pot, with a card attached that read:

For our Italian Gardens. Drive carefully. Love Penny xx.

I looked for Tom's car but it had already gone. Their journey plan included stopping near Pisa tonight, onto Lyon the next day, then Calais, and home in four or five days tops. With my gig not for another five weeks, I had no need to rush back. In fact, it was probably better for me to be in another country when Penny told her father we'd got engaged. I secured the olive tree in the back of my campervan before closing the door. I took one final look over the Bay of Naples. My search was over. I was disappointed not to find my parents and frustrated knowing I had a brother somewhere who I couldn't reach. I knew for sure I would return here one day. For now, I turned the ignition, and Rod Stewart's gritty voice lifted my mood. *Take me back, carry me back, to the gasoline alley where I belong.* Alice pulled out of the hotel car park, and I glanced into the rear-view mirror as the neatly stacked boxes of pizzas faded into the distance. Antonio no longer had me by the balls.

(*)

Sorrento was now three days behind me. After stopping the night on the outskirts of Lyon, I readied myself for the final push to Calais and the ferry back to England. Whilst washing out the coffee pot, I noticed I was standing in a pool of oily water; it turned out to be petrol. I looked at the underside of the vehicle and saw petrol dripping from the tank. There was no way I could continue driving Alice in this condition. Three weeks later and with a £300 bill (ouch!) I had just enough money left to get home.

My journey had taken me past many monuments, the Eiffel Tower, the Tower of Pisa, David's statue in Florence. Yet oddly, Blackpool Tower had a hold on me like none of the others. I drove along the seafront with the window open, my arm resting in the cool breeze. I saw and heard the sound of day-trippers having fun on the Pleasure Beach. Gordon's VW was parked in its usual place. I parked Alice alongside and made my way to the Magic Attic. I was taken by surprise to see there was no queue of customers outside Lana's bakery. As I approached, I noticed a sign on the window.

Closed until further notice.

Odd, I thought. Walking up the stairs to the Magic Attic, I half expected to hear Gordon playing his saxophone. I was greeted by the same sign that was on Lana's window. I turned the handle. The door was locked. I banged on the door. No reply. I banged again, harder this time with my fist.

Gordon shouted, 'Can't you read? We're closed!' His tone was unfamiliar.

'Gordon, it's Gee,' I called.

For a moment, there was silence, followed by whispering, then the rustling of keys. I felt tense, unsure of what I was about to discover. Slowly the key turned in the lock and the door opened. The only welcome came from the service bell above my head. I hardly recognised Gordon. He was dishevelled, unshaven, and he looked like he'd slept in the same clothes for days.

'I tried calling you from Calais, then Dover. Did you get my letter about the van breaking down?'

Gordon didn't answer. Slowly, he shuffled his feet back towards the counter.

'Hello, Gee.' I turned to see Lana was also in the room. Like Gordon, she looked as though she hadn't slept in days. Her eyes were as red as a Tuscan sky that predicted tomorrow would be another beautiful day. I was about to discover that beautiful days were a thing of the past. Lana began to cry.

'What's wrong? What's happened?' I pleaded. Gordon brought a chair from behind the counter.

'I need you to sit down, Gee.'

'I don't want to sit down, just tell me what's wrong?'

Gordon paced the floor. His eyes reminded me of Micky Marks', searching for the hands of time. After what seemed an age, he eventually spoke.

'I haven't been answering the phone. I needed to tell you face to face.'

I was losing patience. I shouted, 'For God's sake, tell me what?'

Gordon struggled to find the right words. Of course, there were no right words for what I was about to hear - the three most devastating words of my life.

'Penny is dead.'

My heart, lungs and reason to live all collapsed at that moment. I needed to sit down before I fell down as my body craved for air.

'How? When?' I yelled as I gasped for air. Gripped in both Gordon's and Lana's arms, as though protecting me from the Devil waiting to take me on a road of self-destruction, I clutched for a memory of Penny in the Sorrento sunshine. My world had just imploded. Sunshine would never feel the same again.

Chapter 23

Blackpool, 1970
Abyss

When you have nothing to search for, it's much easier to find. My existence passed without meaning. Preston, Bury, Rochdale, Salford, Southport were just a few of the places I roamed around aimlessly, never knowing how I'd arrived or moved on. It's not that I was trying to run away from Blackpool, the Magic Attic or my show. I was simply trying to get away from myself. As Penny often quoted, 'If you don't know where you are going, any road will take you there.'

If there was a town called Farouche or Vagabond, that's where I was. I'd barely caught Gordon's last words to me that Tom also died in the car crash and both funerals had already taken place. Lana and Gordon tried to restrain me, but my inner rage demanded I smash the magic display cabinets before I stormed out and ran away.

Most of my nights were spent in doorways, doss houses, or refuse bins; the latter at least brought some kind of warmth. I was unrecognisable from the young man I used to be; unwashed, unshaven, and undernourished. Thankfully, I was now used to my own BO, though people avoided me like a bagful of rotten onions. I never begged on the streets. I just took unashamedly, obtaining my daily needs from shoplifting, picking pockets, and even breaking into shops late at night. My only companion was guilt. It followed me everywhere, as did the Devil dressed as alcohol, reminding me daily of my crime, causing Penny's death. I needed to be held to account. My punishment came in many forms, silence being one of them. I'd not spoken a word to anyone in three months and hoped I'd no longer remember how to. A more severe form of punishment came at closing time when the pubs emptied and the drunks poured onto the streets. I'd pick a fight with one or two staggering their way home. Every punch, kick and stamp I received was payback for what happened to Penny. I'd wake up in some cobbled entry as my tongue searched for new gaps where my teeth used to be. Sarah's nightmare was now replaced by Penny's haunting voice singing, *Hello darkness my old friend,* constantly echoing in my mind, like a stuck record. Once, though, I couldn't recollect where or when I thought I saw FPD. He looked so warm in his long brown overcoat, carrying his little brown case. I thought of mugging him and taking both his coat and case. I might have done. I didn't remember. Often, I gravitated back to the Italian Gardens in Stanley Park, in particular, the park bench where Penny and I used to sit. Forcibly removing anyone sitting on it, my actions usually guaranteed a warm cell at the police station for a few hours. I was once held in a cell for two days as the local authorities tried to decide what to do with me for my most recent misdemeanour, throwing bricks through the windows of a certain Fleetwood care home. I even received a visit from Detective Inspector Jack Brock, who cryptically lectured me on my behaviour.

'There's no need to invite death. It will visit when it's ready.'

'Well, tell it to fucking hurry up then,' I replied humourlessly.

His remarks did nothing to jolt me out of my misery. Once out on the street, I simply reverted to my tramping ways. My memory no longer allowed me to wander back further than the day I returned from France. Dismissed were the happier times of my journey through Italy or the time spent with Penny in Sorrento.

Sometime around December, I found myself back in Blackpool on a deserted North Pier. I was coming out of another drunken slumber in the middle of a raging storm. It appeared dark, though I had no idea of time. Huge waves crashed against the pier, creating a volcano-like eruption of sea spray shooting through the gaps in the boardwalk. I'd lost my shoes but couldn't remember where. Defeated, soaked to the skin, I remembered shivering. The constant nagging guilt was exhausting. I needed to find Penny and say I was sorry. At last, I'd found the courage to end my life. My final punishment was about to be administered. I walked to the pier edge, stepped up on top of a bench, and told myself Penny was only a moment away. I wondered if this was how it was for Micky Marks, so desperate to be with Sarah. In the wind, I heard Penny's voice calling to me.

'Come across. I'm waiting for you.'

I convinced myself that's what I heard as the wind pushed then pulled me back. *Go on, it's easy,* I told myself, *one more step and the guilt will vanish forever. Go on. Penny's waiting.* Grabbed by the wind or a wave, I knew not which, it lifted me off my feet. I wasn't sure if I'd been thrown forward into the Irish Sea or pushed back onto the pier deck. My mouth, eyes and nostrils were full of salt water, and I struggled to breathe. With that, I stopped fighting, allowed my arms and legs to float, and I waited, desperately I waited for the moment that DI Brock had promised. Death would visit me when it was ready.

Disappointedly, death wasn't ready for me. I awoke to another miserable grey dawn, dismayed the waves had pushed me backwards. Dejected at my failure to take my own life, I sobbed at the thought of another punishing day for what had happened to Penny. My hand was wet with blood, probably from my head; too sore to touch. My tongue searched for more lost teeth; my ribs ached as I tried to take each breath. Drifting in and out of consciousness, the next time I awoke, the smell of TCP had replaced the smell of seaweed. I was in a hospital bed, Gordon and Lana sat on either side. I knew of the expression déjà vu but had never experienced it until now. Had time stood still? Was I in hospital because of the attack by Sean Cameron? Had Penny's death been a nightmare? Dear God, please say yes. Lana noticed my eyes were open.

'Gordon, he's awake.'

Gordon must have been dozing because he jumped out of his seat and rushed away, calling for a nurse. I mumbled something, but I don't know what.

'You've been in a coma for almost two weeks. Do you remember what happened?' Lana asked. I tried to shake my head, but it hurt too much. Gordon returned with a nurse. I mumbled again.

'Is it 1966?' Gordon's turn to shake his head.

'I was on the North Pier.' The nurse placed her hand on my forehead and told me not to talk. She shone a torch into my eyes, which had me thinking I'd partly lost my sight again. The nurse instructed Lana and Gordon not to let me talk too much. Lana smiled politely to the nurse, ignoring her as she walked away.

'You were found in a bad way, Gee, near a pub in Old Turnpike Street in Fleetwood.'

'Ah, polite drunk,' I said, remembering the anagram game I played as a child. Lana looked at Gordon like I had something wrong with my memory too.

'You had been attacked and badly beaten by some drunks outside a pub,' Gordon interrupted. 'You're not in a good way, Gee. You have a concussion and four fractured ribs. There is a gash in your head that required 18 stitches. Your left arm is broken, and you have lost a lot of teeth.'

'And Penny, is it true what you told me?'

Lana took hold of my hand, and my tears started to fall, knowing what Lana was about to say.

'Yes, Gee, sadly it is. Penny would hate to think you are throwing away your life like this.' Gordon's concern increased.

'Where have you been? We searched every day for you. Jack Brock phoned me weeks ago saying you were at the police station, but by the time we got there, you were gone.'

'I'm sorry I've caused you so much worry; it's not your fault. But it's my fault what happened to Penny.' Gordon shook his head.

'Gee, listen to me, it was not your fault what happened to Penny. You didn't give me time to explain what happened when the Camberwells travelled home from Italy.' I looked at Gordon, unable to move. I had no choice but to listen now. As always with Gordon when delivering important information, he stood.

'What I'm about to tell you is upsetting, but you need to know the truth. What happened to Penny is not your fault. On the journey home, she told Tom and Annie that you had proposed to her whilst they were in Capri, and she'd accepted. Annie was pleased, but Tom was furious. They were near Birmingham on the M6. Penny said when she returned to

Blackpool, you and her would get your own place. That is all Annie remembers before the crash.'

I was stunned and immediately retreated into myself again, searching for the abyss. Then an inner voice called to me, 'Hey, Annie is alive, you selfish bastard!' In my own self-pity, I had not thought of the woman who saved my life at birth. I asked Lana if she would ask Annie to come and visit me, but sadly Annie's injuries were so severe she wasn't up to it just yet. Gordon explained the local authorities were looking at having me committed to a secure mental home for treatment if I tried to go back on the streets.

'This is the crossroads of your life, Gee. You either come back with us and live at the Magic Attic or be committed. Within a few months, you won't even know your own name.'

Had I been offered that option when I'd first received the news Penny had died, I would have gladly accepted. I knew I owed it to Penny to get my life somehow back on track. However, there was a puzzling question to which I couldn't find the answer. If I was found in Old Turnpike Street in Fleetwood, then what took place on the North Pier? Was it simply a dream? Or was it what I've heard described as being stuck between life and death? Perhaps God did not need a comedy slapstick artiste that night.

Chapter 24

Blackpool, 1972
Palm Court

It was a further two weeks before I was allowed to leave the hospital. I looked out through the window from my bed. The morning was as dull as the slate topped roofs; winter grey. Not that I expected a Tuscan sun glowing over red roof tiles. After all, Blackpool was not Florence. It just put into perspective - many challenges and demons lay ahead. The first of those was returning to the Magic Attic. I watched and listened to the rain play an unrecognisable tune against the glass. When I noticed Alice in the car park, a smile started to grow, like the first shoots of spring. I would not be allowed to drive, that would be down to Gordon. It would be a while before my ribs completely healed, though the doctors felt I was well enough to be discharged, providing I remained in the care of Gordon and Lana Kingsley. Climbing the wooden stairs leading to the half-glazed door left me breathless. Along with the shop bell, Lana also greeted me. Everything looked as it did the first day I entered. The glass cabinets I'd smashed were now repaired.

'Hello Gee, hello Gee!' called Angel. Gordon stood behind the counter, serving another wannabe magician, trying to convince them the change bag would become a mainstay in their act. A polished wooden staircase had replaced the makeshift ladder to the mezzanine. My room looked the same as when I left for Italy. The olive tree Penny had bought in Sorrento sat on my bedside table. My psychiatrist had warned me there would be testing moments like these. Should I process them negatively, I would probably end up back on the streets. Next to the olive tree sat a small box. Knowing Penny's engagement ring was inside, I struggled to bring myself to open it. Also inside were the charms for her bracelet I had bought around Europe. I couldn't allow moments like these to send me spiralling back down into the depths of depression. Sitting next to the box was my St Christopher. God, how I wished I'd insisted on Penny wearing it. On the bed, neatly folded, lay my blue towel, and the silver heart inscribed with my mother's initials was placed on top. I threaded Penny's engagement ring, the St Christopher and the silver heart onto a silver chain before fixing it around my neck.

Waking up the next morning to the smell of Lana's fresh bread gave me a sense of belonging again. I found Gordon in his workshop, tea in hand. He looked out of his window on the world. We talked at length about my journey through France and Italy, visiting his friends Giovanni and Anna Gusto at Lemon Tree Farm. I apologised for the damage caused when smashing up the glass cases when he told me Penny had died. He winked, saying he would deduct the repair cost from my wages. Whilst in an apologetic mood, I had to broach something else.

'I'm so sorry, Gordon. You lost your best friend, Tom. I know your friendship was a long one.' I wanted to raise the subject of his brother Gino but felt now was not the right time, asking instead when I was stronger would he take me to visit Penny's grave. Gordon's face turned a shade whiter. He stared at his work benches, hoping he could fix the answer right for me.

'Penny was not buried, Gee. Tom had left strict instructions should anything ever happen to any of them they were to be cremated.' No grave for me to visit to lay flowers, Tom Camberwell had delivered the final word on my relationship with Penny.

(*)

Meeting with Toddy for the first time in almost a year brought a feeling my life was returning to normality. To help cheer me up, Toddy had booked us a table at the Palm Court, his favourite restaurant inside the impressive Imperial Hotel. Knowing we both now shared terrible grief had brought us closer together. The question of why was I here hung in the air like an inflated balloon waiting to be popped. Toddy, dressed immaculately as always, surprised me with his food selection. Gone were the snails, frogs legs and spaghetti bolognaise. They were replaced by poached salmon and a salad on the side.

'It's good to see you're taking care of yourself,' I observed with a wry smile.

'I plan to live long enough to discover who murdered my Sarah. Like you, I don't believe it was Micky Marks either.' Toddy pointed at my plate of lasagna and smirked.

'Too much of that young man, and you'll not fit in your radio illusion.' He placed *The Stage* newspaper on the table. I felt the balloon was about to be burst.

'When do you think you'll be ready to return to performing, Gee?' Quickly I shoved my mouth full of pasta, buying time to answer. Toddy smiled; he knew my game.

'I'm not sure I have enough fun left inside me; how can I make others laugh when I rarely smile?'

'Gee, the world is full of sadness. You have a gift, a gift that adds smiles to other people's faces. At 22, your best days are still ahead of you.'

I looked at my fingers, bitten beyond the quick, exposing painful whitlows. The tips had all split from the extreme cold due to living on the streets. 'At this moment, it doesn't feel that way,' I confessed. The waiter delivered another bottle of wine to our table, asking Toddy if he'd like to taste it.

'Yes, by the glassful, please,' he replied, letting out one of his big hearty laughs. He may have got his food consumption under control, but the same couldn't be said of his alcohol intake. Picking up the newspaper, he rifled through the pages until he found the classified section. Handing me the paper, he pointed to one of the ads, circled with a red marker. *Shaman… the truth awaits from beyond the grave.*

My eyes lifted above the newspaper.

'Toddy, I don't go in for all that crap.' Folding the newspaper, I returned it across the table. Toddy refilled his glass and savoured the smell before tasting. He looked over both my shoulders to ensure no one was listening; he was ready to open up about his newfound world.

'Last August, late in the evening, someone rang my doorbell. It was after 11 o'clock, so I ignored it. But they were persistent and climbed over my garden wall and banged on the lounge window. They almost gave me another heart attack. I edged back the curtain, but it was pouring down and difficult to see who was there. I thought I could make out two women.'

'Lucky you,' I remarked. Toddy frowned at me as though to say, *you don't have a speaking part in my story.*

'I switched on the garden lights to get a better view. They couldn't have been any wetter if they had climbed straight out of my swimming pool. One of the girls was familiar, so I invited them in out of the rain. To my astonishment, Gee, and this has to remain a secret.'

I nodded, intrigued to know who the girls were.

'In the light of my kitchen, I clearly recognised one of the women. It was none other than Julie Mac.'

'What the hell?!' I exclaimed. 'As in Julie Mac, who shot her dead husband at the circus and then vanished?'

'Keep your voice down, Gee, it's a bloody secret!' Toddy's head bobbed like a chicken, ensuring no one was earwigging. 'Did you ever hear the story of Danny's first assistant Eileen Collins?'

'Yes, Danny boasted about her in the Magic Attic – she'd also vanished from inside the spirit cabinet at the Sunderland Empire if I remember correctly.'

'Well, Eileen Collins was the other woman with Julie Mac.'

'Holy cow! This is mad.' I pushed my shoulders back into my chair, tilted my head and asked. 'Is this some kind of gag to shake me out of my slumber?'

Toddy fell quiet whilst the waiter placed two bowls of apple crumble and custard on the table. Toddy pushed both bowls in my direction, then continued.

'I've never been more serious, Gee. I sat the girls by the fire and made some tea. It was only a few weeks after Julie had shot and killed Danny. I asked Julie why she'd killed him. Eileen, taking the lead, took hold of Julie's hand and explained that Danny had violently abused both of them over the years. She explained how she'd escaped from his clutches 15 years ago. Unbeknown to Danny, Eileen had a new identical spirit cabinet made, except this one had a secret compartment he knew nothing about. When he opened the door to the cabinet he was too stupid to realise she was still inside; he simply fell for his own trick. Several hours after the show at the Sunderland Empire, Eileen simply let herself out of the secret compartment, then headed to Portsmouth where she started a new life as a spiritualist.'

'Wow, that's mad, man. But how did she come to meet up with Julie?'

'Gee, close your mouth whilst you are eating, please.' Toddy waved *The Stage* in my direction.

'Eileen advertised in the *The Stage* for an assistant, one with performing experience. Julie was amongst the many selected for an interview. At the interview, Julie told Eileen she performed with an illusionist, who she needed to escape from, as he was knocking her about. When Eileen learnt his name, she offered Julie the job and they immediately bonded. Eileen explained she'd secretly opened a seance parlour in Fleetwood where they hoped to run the business together. The girls knew there was no way Danny would allow Julie to leave.'

I interrupted. 'I know what Danny did was wrong, but did Julie need to kill him, and in front of a live matinee audience? And how on earth did Julie vanish in front of a live audience at the Tower Circus?'

Toddy took another sniff of his wine and swilled it around his mouth before swallowing. 'Firstly, Eileen said death by bullet was the only way to completely rid themselves of Danny forever. By the way, when she says forever, she means from beyond the grave. Eileen believes the spirits and mediums won't mix with those who died by a bullet. As for how Julie vanished, it was exactly the same way Eileen did all those years before - in the very same secret compartment of the spirit cabinet.'

I shook my head at how stupid Danny Mac really was.

'So, had they come to your house to clear their conscience?'

'No, Eileen told me she was living in Portsmouth the night Sarah was killed. I asked how she knew Sarah? She said they'd never met in person.'

'What is that supposed to mean?' I grumbled whilst eating a second portion of crumble.

'Eileen is a proper medium, Gee, not a phoney. She's fine-tuned her extrasensory perception and can talk to the spirit world.'

My eyes lifted with an expression of *yea sure man,* which Toddy ignored.

'Within days of Sarah dying, she contacted Eileen for help.'

I couldn't believe what I was hearing from Toddy. Had he had too much to drink? Was he still grieving from Sarah's death? Either way, if it helped him cope, I played along and listened.

'Sarah contacted Eileen through the spirits and told her she'd been murdered, but not by her fiancé as people thought. She needed Eileen to contact me as she had something to tell me, something she could not have told me whilst she was alive.' Toddy then fell quiet, and I couldn't help but think Eileen could have read about Sarah's death in the newspapers. Inside, my stomach was doing somersaults. Sarah did have something to tell her father, something she'd made me swear I would never repeat to her father.

'What is it Sarah couldn't tell you?' I asked.

'Eileen said she had not heard from Sarah for the past two months, but there was a way of getting back in touch with her.' Toddy dug deep into his trouser pocket and pulled out a piece of paper. He unfolded it like a sweet wrapper, then started to read.

'If you gather together six people who have lost a loved one or a relative for a seance, then the spirits will encourage Sarah to attend. Oh, and they must have been an entertainer of some kind when they were alive.'

I'd heard enough. Throwing my hands in the air, I protested, 'Oh come on, can't you see it's just her way of drumming up business?'

'No, Gee. I manage the two girls. They're going to perform this seance for free.'

'Toddy, I'm educated enough to know flickering candles, knocking on the underside of tables, and floating balloons with faces painted on is all fake.'

'Don't you want to know what really happened to Penny?' he asked.

Aghast, I said: 'You want me to attend?' I sat on my hands to keep my fingers out of my mouth.

'What have you got to lose?'

'How about my dignity?' I lamented.

'You'll be doing me a huge favour. After all, you once said there was nothing you wouldn't do to help me after Sarah's death.' It's true I did say that, and though I was a non-believer, I didn't have much dignity after sleeping rough for the past three months anyway.

'Are you paying for lunch?' I said with a rueful smile.

'Don't I always?' he replied as he beckoned the waiter. 'Cointreau coffee, please, and for you, Gee?'

Grinning at the waiter, I asked, 'Do you have any Dandelion and burdock?'

Chapter 25

Seance

In Gordon's workshop the next day, I told him Toddy had roped me into attending a seance. He bent over double with laughter, slapping his workbench with his hand at my misfortune. Without mentioning his brother, I asked him if he had a spirit he'd like to be in touch with.

'Aye, I do, about eight o'clock this evening, I'll be in touch with my favourite spirit, going by the name of Johnnie Walker!' he said, laughing at his own joke.

I'd also asked Lana to see if Annie would attend the seance, but she said Annie wasn't up to it just yet. Lana was, though, as she hoped to have contact with her late husband. I'd also been roped in as the taxi driver. Along with driving Lana, Toddy asked me to collect him from his home in St Annes. As he settled his large frame into the front seat alongside me, he stretched his hand towards the cassette deck and turned down the volume:

'I can't bloody stand Rod Stewart. Now young Gee, along the way, I'll need you to stop in Cleveleys and pick up Maggie Marks.'

'As in Micky Marks' mum?' I asked, surprised.

'The very one. Remember, her son was an entertainer too. His mother has every right to be at the seance.' Just the mention of the word seance made me feel like a non-believer.

My left hand found the volume button, and Rod Stewart belted out "Street Fighting Man". Toddy's eyes fell disapprovingly. The drive ahead took us along the Golden Mile, another test of my rehabilitation, as I would be evoking many past memories. First up was the Stargate tram, travelling in the opposite direction. I shook my head as I remembered how I used to ride on the front grill as a nine-year-old. The tip of the Tower was engulfed by fog and out of sight. How different life could have been had I not jumped ship. Looming on my left was the red brick hotel of Butlin's, where I first heard Penny sing. I smiled inside at the memory.

Arriving in Fleetwood, I dodged Old Turnpike and the care home where I grew up but could not avoid the Esplanade. Neither Toddy nor myself could bring ourselves to look to the left as we passed the Marine Hall, where Sarah so tragically died. The town itself had barely changed in my 22 years of existence. Continuous rows of terraced, back to back houses, all with the same sad black and white expressions. Kemp Street contained many of them, along with our destination, Fleetwood Workingmen's Club. I'd sort of performed here about three years ago. I say sort of, as a brawl broke out in the bar area partway through my act, suffice to say I didn't complete the show. The car park entrance was at the back of the club, where a few young boys were using it as their football pitch. Locking the doors to Alice, one of the boys called,

'Do you want me to look after your car, mister?'

I knew from experience it was better to negotiate with the ten-year-old than return to scratch marks all down one side of Alice. Handing the boy a new 10 pence coin, I promised another if he was still there when I came out. I held onto Lana's arm as we made our way down a few icy steps. Toddy did the same with Mrs Marks. I looked above the shoddily painted entrance door, a handwritten sign read, *Return to me....Shaman.* It was the first time I'd noticed the cold all evening. Toddy tried to open the door, but it was locked. Before he could lift his hand to knock, the door slowly opened. I was about to see the first of many surprises. FPD stood in the doorway, complete with a long camel coat and small brown case, and he beckoned us in. I couldn't resist the opportunity to ask, even though I knew the answer.

'What's in the case, Francis?'

'The future, Mr Valentine,' he replied in his West Country drawl. I politely smiled as we entered the cellar of the building.

It was the complete opposite of what I'd expected. "Get it On" by

T.Rex boomed out from two floor-standing speakers, positioned on either side of a raised platform. Placed in the centre of the platform was a red and gold high back chair, the type used to crown a beauty queen. The room was bright, and hanging from the ceiling, six individual bare lightbulbs formed a large circle. The ceiling was so low I traced my fingers around the shapes of a beautifully painted mural, a blue sky dotted with fluffy white clouds, where cherubs sat talking to angels. The walls were completely the opposite, adorned with a dozen or so framed paintings of sinister-looking gargoyles. Eerily their pupils had been replaced with miniature light bulbs. One picture contained three Devil-like gargoyles; each was sitting on their hands with *See evil, Hear evil, Speak evil* written underneath. The smell of incense was overbearing, and there was a coldness to my feet that kept me on the move until Julie Mac approached, carrying a tray of small sherry glasses. She almost tripped over the threadbare carpet, and I reached out to help steady her.

'Hello, Gee, long time no see.' Considering we had only met once, it was kind of her to remember me.

'Nice, cosy place you have here,' I remarked. 'Though you could do with a new carpet!' She smiled, then winked at me.

'It's all part of Eileen's setting.' I couldn't help but think she wasn't entirely happy in her role. I hoped she hadn't brought the rifle she shot her husband with.

'Sherry?' She pushed the tray towards my chest. 'It helps the spirits enter knowing you're relaxed.'

'No thanks. If I drink one of those, I become the Devil himself.' Julie asked which spirit I wanted to hear from.

As a non-believer, I chanced my arm. 'I'm trying to locate my parents and brother; they were entertainers,' I confirmed.

Julie looked at me enquiringly before asking, 'Have they passed on?'

'I hope not, I've not even met them yet, but I do think they live somewhere in Italy.'

Her eyes avoided mine as she spaced out the sherry glasses on the tray. 'We're not private investigators,' she said before moving on to Maggie Marks, hoping she wasn't looking for a lost cat. I was surprised to see Lana and FPD deep in animated conversation. I couldn't possibly imagine what they had in common.

I scanned the room for the seance table, but there wasn't one. After Julie had finished her rounds, she emerged carrying two wooden chairs, a task she repeated three times. Each chair was carefully placed below a bare lightbulb and spaced 12 inches apart to form a circle. Toddy appeared to be getting on very well with Maggie. Lana looked happy with a glass of sherry, and I was starting to think we were a couple of people short of the six mourners required. FPD helped Julie roll up the carpet to reveal a large wooden circular board on the floor. Around the edge of the board were the letters of the alphabet. My eyes followed Julie as she placed the carpet across the high back chair. As stage settings went, I was really impressed. Without warning, the needle was snatched from the T.Rex record.

'Ladies and gentlemen, when I call your name, please follow me to your seat.' I looked up to see Julie had gone from being dressed in jeans and a t-shirt into a long, white, ethereal-like gown. No wonder she didn't look happy; she appeared to be doing most of the work.

'Lana Kingsley,' called Julie.

A rather tipsy Lana replied, 'Oops! That's me.' Julie led her to the chair positioned at ten past the hour. John Todd was called next, and he whispered something into Maggie's ear before taking the chair set at twenty past the hour. Next up was Maggie Marks. Wearing a wide smile, she sat next to Toddy at half past the hour.

'Francis P David.' Now I didn't see that coming. *Which deceased entertainer was he related to,* I thought? His seat was positioned at twenty to the hour. With two empty chairs left and just Julie and myself to fill them, there was a loud knock at the door. Perhaps it was Eileen's way of making an entrance. Julie went to open the door, and in walked the giant, intimidating frame of Sean Cameron's father, Billy.

'Holy shit!' I mumbled. My left eye went into a twitching frenzy.

Billy removed his overcoat, leaving a pool of water where he stood. 'Sorry I'm late,' he declared in his broad Glaswegian accent. 'I had to get some change from the shop for the bairns to mind my car.' *You should have just told them who you are,* I thought. *They'd have washed and waxed it for you.*

'Gee Valentine.'

I looked at Julie as she pointed to my seat. 'Next to Francis,' she said in a fed-up kind of way. My chair was positioned at ten to the hour.

'Billy Cameron,' bellowed Julie.

'Please don't sit next to me, please don't sit next to me,' I kept mumbling to myself. Billy Cameron sat at the top of the circle, on the hour, 12 inches from my chair. His head almost touched the light bulb. Julie, white gown flowing behind her, momentarily walked behind the high back chair, only to re-emerge a couple of seconds later, wearing a black jumpsuit. *Impressive,* I thought. Though, besides Toddy, I didn't think the others had noticed. Julie handed each of us a slate the size of an A4 clipboard. Attached to the slate was a blank sheet of paper and a black marker pen.

'Please write the name of the spirit you want to contact, and also the question you want the spirit to answer. Then fold the paper. Don't let anybody see what you've written.'

Billy Cameron threw his slate to the floor: 'I can tell you why I'm here, my son Sean drowned in a fuckin milk can and if I find…'

Julie bluntly interrupted Billy: 'If you don't write down your message on the slate, then you will have to leave.' Billy glared at Julie, picked up the slate and reluctantly started to write. Julie pulled up the dust-laden carpet. With one swoop across the chair, she produced Eileen, sitting regally and dressed in a white gown. Julie had vanished. How could I have missed it was a Dekolta Chair?! The move was so slick I wanted to applaud. This time, everyone noticed. The room suddenly became colder. Eileen appeared to glide rather than walk as she made her way around the circle. With papers folded and put away, the room was plunged into semi-darkness. The only light in the room came from the gargoyles' eyes, just enough to make out each other's facial expressions. Eileen returned to the platform and began moving her hands upward as though encouraging a magic flower to grow.

'Spirit table, join us, please.' The wooden alphabet disc on the floor slowly raised up, stopping with a shudder as it reached table height. Holy cow! Again I'd missed Eileen's quick-change costume. She was now wearing a turquoise gown.

'Did each of you bring something that once belonged to your loved one? If so, place it on the table next to the letter it symbolises, starting with Lana.' Lana removed an envelope from her purse and placed it on the table next to the letter E. She was followed by Toddy, who, surprisingly, produced one of Sarah's live doves. I had no idea he could perform sleight of hand. Still fluttering, he placed the dove onto the letter D. Maggie placed Micky's orange spectacles on the letter M - technically, she should have placed them on the letter S for spectacles. FPD bizarrely placed an urn on the letter U. I still didn't know which spirit he wanted to engage with and wondered if it was the person whose ashes were inside. I placed Penny's engagement ring on the letter R. Billy Cameron sent me into a flat spin as he removed Sean's flick knife – the one that had once been rammed in my ear. His eyes were burning into the side of my head as he placed the flick knife tormentingly on the letter R. With a puzzled look, Julie asked Billy why he'd placed the knife on the letter R and not K. Billy stared at me and pronounced,

'Revenge.'

From the platform, Eileen held her arms aloft. She started to sway her hips in a sidewards motion. Smoke appeared through the floorboards and covered her ankles. It had to be dry ice.

'Spirits, your loved ones have connected with you. They have spelt out the password "EDMURR" for you to enter.'

Was I the only one who realised the anagram of EDMURR was MURDER? The room became even colder.

Eileen continued. 'Francis, place your case on the table, please.' FPD diligently lifted his small case onto the table. 'Inside Francis's case are six envelopes, numbered one to six. Starting with Lana and continuing clockwise, please call out a number. Francis will then hand you the chosen envelope. Do not open it until asked to do so at the end of the session.'

FPD looked at Eileen, waiting for her next instruction. Lana, obviously feeling the cold, asked for a blanket, but Eileen simply threw her a look of disapproval. FPD removed a piece of string about six inches long from his top pocket and, gripping it between his thumb and index finger, he held it above a lit candle. A bright flash of light brought a temporary blindness to my eyes. Now dangling from FPD's finger was a six-inch silver chain with a key attached. It was a smooth production, though out of place for a seance. FPD inserted the key into his case. So, at last, here comes the future. I smirked as he fumbled with the catches. I was half expecting a flying bat to swoop out, or giant spider legs to slowly appear. But there were neither, just the six white envelopes as promised. Lana called out number three. Toddy number one. Maggie number five.

FPD, confused, looked at Eileen.

'Yes, you too, Frances.'

He called out number five.

Eileen gave him a look that asked why Julie had invited you. 'Try again, Francis. Five has already been called.'

'Number four,' he said.

I chose number two, leaving number six for Billy.

By the time I looked back to the platform, Eileen was sitting in the red and gold chair. She'd changed her clothes again and was now wearing the same black jumpsuit as Julie, who stood behind the chair. Both girls, despite the age difference, looked almost identical. Black hair tied up in a bun, dancing girl height and shape, and sinister black make-up around the eyes. It was Julie's turn to speak.

'Each of you wrote down the name of a spirit you wish to make contact with, along with a question you would like to ask. It is only you who can summon the spirits to this room with your love, your energy, and your thoughts.'

'Will they need the password again?' asked FPD innocently. Eileen looked to Julie, who made her way over to him and whispered something into his ear. She then stood behind FPD and continued.

'Should the spirits visit, Eileen is the medium the spirits will talk through. Do not attempt to talk to the spirit. If you do, they will leave immediately and never return.' So convincing were the girls I was starting to believe they could actually summon the spirits. Julie gently rang a small, brass service bell before speaking.

'Each time you hear the bell, it indicates we are ready to invite the spirits into the shaman's cellar. Now take hold of the person's hand to your left.'

Oh, you've got to be kidding me. I glowered at Toddy for persuading me to attend. With Billy to my left, I glanced at my hand, unsure I'd get it back. Slowly I placed my hand into his. It felt clammy. He closed his hand around mine, swallowing it whole like a whale swallowing a school of mackerel; only my wrist was visible. Billy then squeezed hard to let me know he was in control. Eileen looked like she was searching for the cracks in the ceiling; her head twisted and shook from side to side, then she started calling out names.

'Gino Kingsley, Sarah Todd, Micky Marks, Vincent Leach.' Instantly I looked across at FPD, now knowing whose ashes were in the urn. 'Penny Camberwell, Sean Cameron, are any of the spirits in Shaman's cellar tonight?' Julie observed Billy and me were no longer holding hands. She called out,

'You must all hold hands for the spirits to visit.' Billy looked at me, his eyes barely visible due to the size of his beard. Again Eileen started to shake; her pupils moved in opposite directions, impressive! The voice coming from Eileen's mouth was that of a much younger woman. On hearing it, the dove wildly fluttered its wings.

'Daddy, Daddy,' instantly I recognised it as Sarah. 'Gee has the secret. Tell him I said he's got to reveal it to you!' Toddy's eyes flashed across at me. Every hair on my body stood to attention. I couldn't look at Toddy. Holy cow, how could Eileen possibly know what I knew? Eileen's voice transformed into a much deeper one. Her eyes were begging, reminding me of Micky, whose voice we now heard.

'You know I didn't do it, Sarah. I could never have hurt you.'

Incredibly Eileen instantly metamorphosed back into Sarah.

'Of course, I know it was not you, but why did you take your own life?'

'I didn't,' called Micky.

Maggie jumped up, shouting, 'What happened, Micky?' Julie instructed Maggie to sit back down as she was chasing the spirits from the cellar. Maggie sat down and began sobbing in her chair. Toddy's eyes were still locked onto me. Julie reminded us to remain silent. I was now a believer, so close to finding out who killed Sarah and Micky. Suddenly Eileen stood up and spoke in a gravelly voice that immediately reminded me of Vincent Leach.

'I won't enter while that murdering bitch is in the room, and that's final.' With that, Eileen slumped back into her chair. Who was Vincent referring to? Julie, Maggie, Lana, Eileen?

Julie passed a glass of something to Eileen. Whatever was in it did the trick because pretty quickly, Eileen looked refreshed and ready to go again, or so I thought until she cupped her head into her hands and started crying uncontrollably. Lana removed a tissue from her handbag, but Julie gave Lana a warning look to stay in her seat. Eileen started to shout. It appeared she was quarrelling with herself.

'Stop arguing, both of you and reduce your speed. Do you hear me, Tom? Tom, look at the road, Tom, look at the road!' Eileen then let out a piercing, violent scream and fell from the chair onto the floor. Julie helped Eileen back into the chair. Her voice now made a noise like she was drowning, gasping for air, her arms pushed upwards. Billy Cameron jumped to his feet and exploded with rage.

'Is this some kind of sick joke, you fucking freaks?' Julie quickly moved behind Eileen's chair.

Eileen's voice became boy-like and gargled when she said, 'You're done for Kingsley when my dad finds out it was you!' I kicked over my chair as I stood, hoping to chase Sean's spirit out of the cellar. Billy grabbed me by the throat. We were eyeball to eyeball. His stale breath was obvious to all when he said:

'Tell him he's a fucking dead man waiting.' I knew he was referring to Gordon. His eyes suddenly widened, frog-like, as though they were about pop out of their sockets.

'Let go, Cameron, otherwise your crown jewels will be out of use til Hogmanay.' Lana had forced herself between the giant Scot and me. Her hand was gripping Cameron by the balls. Instantly he let go of my throat, and slowly she let go of his balls. Gradually, Billy's eyes returned to their sockets. Lana's eye's informed Billy Cameron it was time to leave. He picked up his overcoat and left the room like a hurricane, searching for the next town, destruction behind and ahead of him. The room fell into a period of silence. Eventually, Julie broke the silence asking if the evening was proving helpful.

'What about my husband Gino?' asked Lana. Julie explained they couldn't continue as all the spirits flew out of the door when Billy left. Lana's face was full of disappointment. Toddy's eyes were still on me. Eileen sat down on the chair vacated by Billy. Her voice brought a calmness to the proceedings.

'Earlier this evening, you were given an envelope. Each one contained a playing card that predicted your future. Remember, you could have chosen any number.'

FPD piped up. 'Not any number Eileen, I asked for number five, and you refused.' Eileen gave FPD the same look as earlier.

'Number five had already been taken, Francis. Gee, starting with you, remove your chosen card.' Tearing open the envelope, I removed the 5 of spades. Eileen asked me to read what was written on the reverse. I cleared my throat.

'You will soon be moving on, leaving behind what you currently know. A new job and new location await.' I slipped the card back into the envelope and hoped the prediction was right.

'Francis, you're next,' informed Eileen. FPD had already removed the 9 of spades. He read the reverse triumphantly.

'A sign that soon you will no longer be held to ransom, though it could result in the death of someone close to you.' FPD's face remained expressionless. He placed the card into his brown case, closed the lid, then let out a huge sigh.

Toddy looked at Eileen before declaring.

'This better be good, or I'll leave you standing in the rain next time.' He pulled out the king of diamonds. 'A powerful and successful businessman about to travel,' he declared, reading from the card. 'I'm happy with that.' He turned to Maggie and said, 'Come on, let's see what you've got.'

'Ace of hearts,' proclaimed Maggie, flipping the card she reads. 'A new beginning, such as a relationship or marriage.' Toddy and Maggie looked at each other. I hoped they were both about to discover happiness again.

Eileen sat next to Lana and announced, 'And finally, the lovely Lana.'

Lana slowly peeled the seal off the envelope and peered inside. 'The queen of spades,' she said, then read the reverse before placing it back in the envelope.

Toddy asked. 'Well, what did it say?'

'Oops, sorry,' said Lana before she removed the card and read aloud: 'Stability will soon return to your workplace; your troubling times are almost at an end.' She placed the card back onto the table. I knew she was not telling the truth. What she just read was the reverse of the 4 of spades, not the queen.

'What troubling times?' FPD asked Lana. She fixed him that stare that always had me worried.

I diverted attention by asking Eileen what card was inside Billy's envelope that he'd left on the table. Eileen grabbed the envelope and handed it to Julie. Without hesitation, she ripped it open, producing a smile that lit up the room. With two crossed fingers, she held aloft the ace of spades, the death card. There was no need for Julie to read the reverse. As we collected our items from the table, I observed Lana had picked up Sean's flick knife. Unexpectedly, she handed it to FPD, and without acknowledgement, he placed it in his overcoat pocket. She left the playing card face down on the table. I palmed it for the one I had.

The return journey home was a silent one. Outside Toddy's house, he asked if I was going in to reveal Sarah's secret.

'Maybe in the morning. Too much has taken place this evening for me to fully explain.'

Toddy nodded. 'Tomorrow then, back here at 10 o'clock. I'll have the kettle on.'

'It will suit you,' I said, trying to lighten the mood after such a traumatic evening, an evening that still had one more surprise for me.

Back at the Pleasure Beach, I made sure Lana was home safely before I returned to the Magic Attic. Lying on my bed, I tried to take in the enormity of what I had just witnessed. Did I truly believe what my eyes had seen and what my ears had heard? I remembered I had Lana's card, so I shoved my hand deep into my pocket and retrieved it. Turning over the card, I read the reverse.

A cruel woman who is extremely manipulative, malicious and dangerous.

Chapter 26

Blackpool, 1972
Window on the World

L ast night's seance was at the forefront of my mind. So much of what had taken place kept me awake, churning over in my mind. At one point, I swore I heard the shop doorbell, and I shot up in bed thinking it was Billy Cameron coming for Gordon. It wasn't. It was just the Magic Attic stretching and contracting as it did through the night.

The next morning I made my way downstairs and into the workshop. Gordon, mug of tea in hand, was looking out through his window on the world. There were so many things I wanted to discuss with him about what had taken place, like Julie and Eileen resurfacing and organising the seance. Did he know FPD and the Leach brothers were related? Or that Sarah and Micky Marks spoke to each other through Eileen? And Billy Cameron's threat to murder him? Had I told him, he would have taken me straight back to the psychiatrist! Anyway, Toddy had sworn me to secrecy until I had told him Sarah's secret.

As I drove along Toddy's driveway, the popping and crunching under Alice's tyres brought back memories of Zap's villa in Florence. I parked outside the double garage then paused to gather my thoughts, knowing I was about to break a promise to Sarah. Elvis Presley singing "I Just Can't Stop Believing" enticed me into the garden through an open gate. I was welcomed by splashing water, and then I noticed Toddy's bald head bobbing up and down in the pool like an inflatable beach ball.

'Have you brought your swimming things?' he called.

'You never told me to,' I shouted back, looking up at the March sky and thinking the weather was kinder than usual for this time of year.

'I didn't know it would be this warm,' he said, then climbed out of his pool and secured his dressing gown as we made our way into his kitchen.

'Oh, I do like a room you can land a helicopter in!' I remarked sarcastically.

'You see, Gee. That's why you need to get back on stage. You're able to pluck out funny lines from nowhere.' It was so long since Toddy had last seen me perform he'd forgotten I didn't even speak on stage. I noticed an Italian coffee pot on the side, and Zappa Russo came to mind for the second time that morning.

'Any chance of a fresh coffee?'

Toddy rummaged through the kitchen cupboards before declaring he was out of coffee. I settled for tea. If the kitchen was the size of a helipad, then the lounge was the size of a nightclub. The dining room table could sit more friends than I had made in 22 years. Above the ornate fireplace hung a photo of Sarah, dressed in her white catsuit. The picture had caught her by surprise. Her mouth was slightly open, forming one of her beautiful smiles. I made my way to the sofa, and her eyes followed me, eyes that said, *be gentle with what you are about to tell my father.*

Again I tried to compose myself. I didn't know where to start.

Thankfully, Toddy took control. 'So, after last night, are you still a non-believer in the spirits?' he asked as he tapped his teaspoon three times on the china cup before resting it on the saucer.

'As you once said to me, John Todd does not book bum acts. The girls are a quick change act in their own right.' I didn't want to tell Toddy the reason for the low ceiling and light bulb was so Eileen could spy from above, reading the names and questions we wrote down. Though I had no idea how they arranged the items we placed on the alphabet table to spell out murder.

'Firstly, Mr Todd, don't shoot the messenger. What I'm about to say is not about whether I do or don't believe. It's more about me telling you something you have a right to know. Something, if Sarah was still here, she would surely have told you herself one day.'

Toddy fidgeted uncomfortably in his big leather armchair. I'd thought long and hard at how to soften what had happened to Sarah, but I had to be truthful. I looked up at her photo again.

'The reason Sarah had to extend her stay in New York wasn't because she failed her exams. Late one evening, after rehearsals, she was attacked by two men who abducted and raped her.' Toddy's eyes instantly widened as large as Billy Cameron's had the previous night. His hand wiped across his face. I hoped it would change his expression.

'Did she go to the police?'

'She was too scared she'd be deported.' I paused, knowing what I was about to say would greatly affect Toddy for the rest of his life. 'By Christmas, Sarah discovered she was pregnant.' This time his face twisted with anguish. He clenched his fist and punched the sofa. Then he stood up, then sat down, before standing again and pacing up and down like a wild wolf ready to kill.

'How long have you known this?' he demanded.

Remaining seated, I gave a soft reply. 'She told me at the end of the summer season in 1968.'

'And you've waited until we attend a bloody seance to tell me?' His anger escalated and his face changed shape again, like a man possessed by the Devil.

'Sarah swore me to secrecy. I'm not telling you now because the spirits said I should. I'm telling you because you need to know.' My voice now drowned out Elvis, still playing on the gramophone in the kitchen.

'Damn right, I need to know!' He left the room. I looked at my fingernails and desperately tried not to bite them. Toddy returned, clutching a bottle of Cointreau and a wine glass.

'Is that wise?' I asked. He ignored me as he half-filled the glass then emptied it into his mouth as though it were prescribed medicine. It certainly calmed him.

'What happened to the baby?'

I threw Toddy a smile. He'd already suffered too much torment for one lifetime.

'She delivered a baby girl in a New York hospital. Sarah put her up for adoption and was told by the authorities that she had to give up any right of ever seeing the child again.'

'But that can't be right? You're telling me I have a granddaughter somewhere in America who I'm never going to see?' I looked up at Sarah's photo and hoped for a sign that I'd done the right thing. It was now time for me to put a smile back on Toddy's face.

'When I was discharged from hospital, I needed to focus my mind on something good.'

'You think this is something good?' Toddy barked, then swallowed another half glass of Cointreau.

'Obviously not but hear me out. I did some digging to see if maybe the law had changed on finding adopted children in America. I came across a company named Amara. Between 1950 and 1959, Amara placed around 800 children into various homes. They were adopted in a time of secrecy, with the understanding that the parental records would remain sealed. I decided to write to child welfare in New York explaining what took place in 1957 and how Sarah Todd had been a shining light for women in the world of magic and illusion. I included paper clippings of her work and how she had tragically died. Also, I explained there was a grieving grandfather who would never see his granddaughter unless someone with a heart and conscience in the New York office did something about it.'

Toddy's face softened. He placed his empty glass on the grand piano as I removed a letter from my Harrington jacket.

'Unlike the Italian Embassy I wrote to years ago, I received an immediate response from New York.' I took the letter from the official envelope, and Toddy sat next to me on the sofa. He read it aloud.

'Dear Mr Valentine,

'I am in receipt of your letter and newspaper clippings regarding Sarah Todd. As a former revue dancer (now retired!) I completely empathise with Sarah Todd's tragic and inspiring story. Searching through the hospital records of 1958, I came across Sarah's file. She was admitted to Lower Eastside hospital and delivered a baby girl on 31ˢᵗ July 1958. The girl was adopted by American citizens, John and Mary Johnson.'

Toddy dropped the letter to the floor and burst into tears. His arms hung heavily from his shoulders, unable to carry on reading. I asked if he wanted another Cointreau, he shook his head. I picked up the letter and continued to read.

'As the Johnsons still lived in Manhattan, I decided to visit them and explain the delicate situation. I took along your newspaper clippings. John and Mary were also touched by Sarah's story. They are open to Sandy meeting her biological grandfather.'

Toddy gripped my arm. 'Her name is Sandy!' He had the widest grin I'd ever seen.

'Shall I continue, Mr Toddy?' He shook his head.

'Sandy is now 14. I passed on her grandfather's address, which you included in your letter, the Johnsons have promised to write within the week.
Yours sincerely.
Janet Kowalski.'

For a brief moment, there was silence. I swear Sarah's eyes smiled directly at me when I looked up at her photo for approval. Toddy jumped up, ready for action, a spring in his step I'd not seen for a long time.

'I've got to get to New York! I'll book us tickets on the QE2, no wait, that's too slow!' I tried to interrupt, but he talked over me.

'We'll fly, yes, that's much quicker. We can even meet up with Harry Larry. Did I tell you he's appearing in a show at the Radio City Music Hall?'

'Toddy, stop! This is your journey now, not mine. I need to get back to performing. Is the offer still on the table for me to perform on the cruise ships?'

'Is it still open? You bet your bottom dollar it is!' He sounded like a New Yorker already.

'As soon as I've booked my flights to the Big Apple, I'll be in contact with my man at Royal Caribbean.'

'Then I'd better get back to rehearsals,' I said as I stood ready to leave.

Outside his garage, he grabbed my arm. 'Gee, I'll never be able to thank you enough for what you have done in helping to find my granddaughter.'

I was just about to open the door to Alice, I decided to chance my arm.

'Does that mean lunch is on you next time at the Palm Court?' I smiled. Toddy threw his arms around me. 'Free lunches for life, my friend!'

'Let go!' I protested. 'What will the neighbours think?!'

Alice thundered into life, moving slowly along his gravelled driveway.

Toddy's voice bellowed: 'How about *Radio Valentine* appearing in the Radio City Music Hall's Christmas Spectacular?'

'Penny would be proud of that,' I smiled.

On the way home, I thought about becoming a private investigator, reuniting lost families throughout the world. Then I remembered I couldn't even find my own parents.

Within a couple of days, and out of the blue, Annie contacted Lana asking if I would like to visit her at Capri Guesthouse. As much as I wanted to meet up with Annie, revisiting Palatine Road at this stage of my recovery, I felt, would set me back. We arranged to meet in the Italian Gardens in Stanley Park for what would have been Penny's 22nd birthday. I parked Alice in almost the same spot where Gordon had handed me the keys just over a year ago. I must have looked like the onsite gardener, carrying an olive tree under one arm, flowers under the other and a small shovel. With no graveside to visit, I decided the Italian Gardens was as good a place as any to plant the olive tree given to me by Penny.

Ahead, I saw Annie already sitting on a park bench. Unlike the blue skies of a few days back, today was overcast. No songbirds or children to help lighten the mood. I'd no idea what to say to Annie. Did she feel the same as Tom had? Did she too wish I'd been abandoned next door or on some other road in Blackpool? However she reacted, I would pay her the respects she fully deserved.

'Hello Annie,' my voice shook on the last part of her name. Looking up at me, her face was expressionless. She straightened out her long dark skirt as she stood up, the way Penny always did.

'Hello, Gee.'

I passed Annie the small bunch of daffodils. Without looking at them, she placed them on the bench between us as we sat back down. For two people with so much to say, we remained silent. Nearby a magpie searched for food; we both knew the significance of a lone magpie. Annie looked at the olive tree I'd placed on my lap, and I broke the silence.

'I've always thought it strange there are no olive trees in the Italian Gardens.'

'Is that the one Penny bought you in Sorrento?' Annie's voice was softer than I remembered. 'I've ordered two rose bushes to be planted at the Blackpool Crematorium. One for Penny, the other for Tom, when spring finally arrives, that is.' By the look on Annie's face, I could tell she wanted a gravestone to visit too. I took hold of her hand.

'I'm going to plant the olive tree here; would you like to help?'

'Are you allowed to?'

'Probably not.'

We found a place behind a low bush and dug a hole just large enough to fit the plant. Annie appeared with a cup of water from the fountain and poured it around the base of the tree. We were joined by the magpie looking for worms in the disturbed soil.

'Tom had left strict instructions. In the event of any of our deaths, we would not be buried but cremated. I should have ignored his stupid bloody instructions.' Tears were silently falling down Annie's face. I put my arms around her and held her tight, wanting her to know she still had me for what it was worth. I felt Annie's arms around me, and gently she began to sob.

'I thought I had no tears left. This is the first time I've cried since Valentine's Day.' As we returned to the bench, I noticed Annie was limping. She took my hands in both of hers.

'I wanted to visit you when you were in hospital, Gee, but I couldn't walk at the time. I'm not angry with you. I'm so grateful to you for making Penny happy. You treated her like the normal girl she was. You made her feel special. She told me when you were both together, she could see everything clearly. At breakfast on the final morning in Sorrento, Penny showed me the engagement ring. I was so excited for you both, though I said it was best not to tell her father until we were back home. Penny told me everything, Gee, including that you made love whilst Tom and I were in Capri.'

I felt my cheeks burn. 'I loved her, Annie. I truly loved her.'

She squeezed my hand then started to tell me about their journey home.

'Tom was frosty with Penny from the moment we left the hotel in Sorrento. It all came to a head when we got back into the country. We were driving up the M6, only a couple of hours from home. Tom had barely spoken for hours when he blurted out that you were no longer welcome at our house, and Penny was not allowed to see you again. I told Tom that if Gee was not welcome, then neither was he. Penny was sitting in the middle of the back seat. She simply leant forward, stretched out her left hand in between Tom and me, and showed off her engagement ring, calmly announcing you would be married at the earliest opportunity, and with any luck, she was already with child. Tom's hands tightened around the steering wheel, his face a raging red. The overhead bridges passed by much faster than necessary. I told Tom to slow down. He turned his head to face Penny, and it was like he'd forgotten he was in a car. I screamed at him to turn around, but his eyes remained fixed on Penny.' Annie's hands tightened around mine as she relived the moment. 'I pleaded again with Tom to look at the road. There was a piercing scream. I think it was mine. Waking up in a Birmingham hospital is the next thing I remember.' There were no tears from Annie now; she just stared into the distance.

'Tom was jealous of you from the day you were left abandoned in our house. He blamed my early labour on your arrival. I wanted to keep you, Tom didn't. When you turned up at our house at the age of 14, Tom realised the connection immediately and tried everything to keep you away, whilst I did the opposite.' We sat in silence again for a while.

I asked, 'Will you open Capri Guesthouse for the summer season?'

Annie opened her handbag and took out the details of a property and handed them to me.

'No, I've decided to sell up and buy this bungalow in Cleveleys, where there will always be a room for you.' Now I squeezed her hand. 'What are you going to do with your life, Gee? You know Penny would be disappointed should you not use your talent.'

'Toddy has arranged for me to join my first cruise ship, mainly performing around the Mediterranean to start with.'

'You've done well for a little boy once lost. Will you continue to search for your parents?'

'I think my searching days are over, for now, I'll let fate take a hand. Anyway, you've been as kind as any mother could have been. When I return from sea, I'll come home to you if that's ok?' Annie rubbed my cold hands, like a mother would her child. I saw the shape of a smile on her face, probably the first in months.

'Thank you for planting the olive tree. You've given me a place to visit and talk with Penny.'

'I have the campervan with me. Would you like a lift home?'

Annie let go of my hand and stood. 'Thank you, but no, I've got to get used to this damn plastic leg.'

We hugged like mother and son. A contrasting sun broke through the clouds. Annie pointed at the olive tree, noticing there were now two magpies and again we both knew the meaning. I watched her limp out of the Italian Gardens. Annie Camberwell was a proud lady making her way to an empty house. A house that should have welcomed her grandchildren. Her life was, at this time, without reason. As for Tom Camberwell, no doubt he was stoking the fires of hell, awaiting my arrival.

I sat back down on the bench and reflected on what Zappa Russo had said to me on our last morning in Florence: 'I feel bad luck is coming your way, Gee.'

What could she have possibly known? Nothing, of course. Having now gone through my own period of discombobulation, I owed it to Penny to pull my life together. Walking away from the Italian Gardens that morning, I felt the sunshine on my face. Penny's smile beamed down on me. From now on, it would always be this way.

Before leaving hospital, the doctor told me I would probably be alcohol dependent for the rest of my life. However, it had been almost three months since I'd last had a drink, and up to now, I'd not wavered. Strangely, I felt I needed to test myself. On my way home, I decided to call into a pub and buy a Coca-Cola. The Sun Inn was a traditional South Shore alehouse, one street back from the seafront. With the lunchtime session about to close, I parked up nearby. The alehouse had two rooms: the saloon where the men tended to drink and the snug for couples. I chose the latter due to the thick fog of smoke in the saloon. Opening the snug door, the smell of hops, malt and spirits engulfed me like the scent of a woman. I knew immediately this was a stupid idea. I was ashamed of my weakness. Even the jukebox thought it a bad idea as 'We Gotta Get Out of This Place" by The Animals blared out in the empty room.

I made my way across the sticky carpet to the bar and ordered a pint of beer. Eagerly I watched as the barmaid slowly pulled the pump arm until the white head topped off the pint glass, like surf settled on the beach. I could taste it before it even touched my lips. The room quietened as the tonearm lifted the stylus off the vinyl and back into its resting position. I stared at the pint sitting on the bar, hoping another song with another cryptic message would play.

Unexpectedly my ears pricked up at the sound of "Return to Sorrento". It could only have come from my pocket watch, the one I'd placed in Sarah's coffin. I looked across into the saloon bar, my *bête noire*, Dravern Leach, was in deep conversation with the gangster Billy Cameron, cigarettes hanging from their mouths. They were haggling a price for the stolen jewellery spread across the bar, which reflected in two half-empty pint glasses. Dravern Leach downed the remainder of his drink. As he did so, his eyes caught mine through the bottom of his glass. I tried to hold his gaze, but the barmaid interrupted as she placed my change on the counter. By the time I looked up again, they were both gone. Leach must have stolen the pocket watch out of Sarah's coffin after Gordon, and I left the funeral parlour. Anger stoked my fire. I left the untouched beer and hurriedly followed them out into the street. Dravern was scurrying along the road like the rat he was. Billy was nowhere to be seen. Trying my best to keep out of sight, I watched Dravern turn down one of the back alleyways. By the time I arrived, he was swaying from side to side whilst flooding the cobblestones with his urine. Walking up behind him, I rabbit punched him in the back of the neck. He collapsed to the floor and lay in his own piss, which flowed like a mini river between the cobblestone cracks. I waited until he staggered to his feet. The pocket watch struck the quarter-hour chime.

'You bastard,' I said. 'You took that out of Sarah's coffin.' Leach tried to catch his breath, then coughed and spluttered.

'She'd no use for it where she was going, donkey.'

I fixed my feet to the floor and delivered a punch to his stomach. He collapsed to his knees, gasped for breath and vomited over his trousers, then tumbled the remainder of the way to the floor. Stood over him, I looked into his sunken eyes. I tasted his fear on my tongue. Bending my knees, I reclaimed my pocket watch from his coat. Time was now back in my hands again. As I looked up, I caught the back of Billy Cameron at the end of the alleyway; he must have witnessed my assault.

As I made my exit, I turned to take one last look at Dravern. Billy Cameron, like the giant vulture he was, rifled through Dravern's pockets as he lay prostrate on the floor. He removed the jewellery they had just haggled over, then placed his foot on Leach's throat and pressed down hard until his meaningless life ended.

I returned to Alice and the safety of the Magic Attic. I found Gordon in his workshop with his feet up on a stool, reading his favourite magic magazine, *Abra*. On seeing me, he placed the magazine on the workbench.

'Well, are you going to tell me what took place at the seance?' Now I'd told Toddy about what happened to Sarah. I could tell Gordon everything, including the return of Julie Mac and Eileen Collins. I also passed on Billy Cameron's message, *tell him he's a fucking dead man waiting.*

Gordon simply shrugged his shoulders.

'Are you not worried?' I asked.

Gordon smiled. 'He'll make the same mistake others have made.'

'What's that?' Gordon simply shook his head.

My pocket watch struck 3 o'clock.

'I've not heard that in a long time,' he remarked. I gave him a reassuring smile that he would hear a lot more of it in the future. Gordon rifled around in one of his workbench drawers.

'I have something for you. Now, which drawer did I put it in? It came in the post a couple of weeks after you set off for Italy, and with everything that has taken place I forgot to pass it onto you. Ah, here it is.' Gordon handed me an envelope post-marked London.

'Ah, it must be a reply at last from the Italian Embassy,' I presumed as I waved it in triumph. I opened it to find I'd presumed wrong. I sat on the window ledge and read the letter out loud.

Dear Gee,

Sorry I did not get to meet you when you came to visit me at Brick Lane. I wish I had known you were coming. We keep our address a secret as Signor Rossini and I live together as a couple in London. We were very fond of your mother, Sofia. Below is her address in Sorrento. Next time you come to London, drop me a line and we will show you the sights. Do pass on our best regards to your mother and father.

Yours sincerely

Daniel Doyle

Her address in Italy.
Sofia Bellini (nee, Agosto)
The Lemon Tree House
Via Casarlano
Sorrento
Italy

Also in the envelope was a black and white photo of my parents performing on the 1965 tour of England. I handed it to Gordon, his face immediately transformed into a younger man, his eyes scrutinised the photograph. It appeared to transport him back to a time he'd previously refused to visit. I must have called his name two or three times before he finally dragged his eyes away from the photo. We now stared at each other, both of us trying to take in the enormity of the connection. Lips so dry my tongue had to prise them open to speak.

'If the lady in the photo is my mother, then Giovanni and Anna Agosto, who took care of you in Sorrento, are probably my grandparents?'

I took the photo from Gordon to look again at my mother and father. Gordon remained silent. His eyes avoided mine as he stared out at his window on the world.

Chapter 27

Blackpool, 1971
Lies

The incessant hammering on the shop's front door invaded our quiet contemplation.

I tore my eyes away from my parents' photo. Gordon forced his stare from the window.

'Who the hell could that be? It's nearly midnight?' I asked.

Gordon removed a framed painting of Houdini from the wall and revealed a hole the size of a box of matches. Tilting his head to one side, he peered through the cavity. I could only think it must contain another tunnel of mirrors that led to the shop door. Returning Houdini to his original position, Gordon rubbed at his hairless eyebrows as though to make his brain work quicker. Frustrated, he complained,

'It's DI Brock with two uniformed police officers.'

Immediately I felt Billy Cameron must have watched my attack on Dravern Leach. I explained to Gordon what had taken place earlier. Gordon gave a startled look of, haven't we been in this situation before? The knocking continued. Someone called through the letterbox and demanded we open the door, now! Gordon ushered me to the fire escape door leading down into the Pleasure Beach.

'Make your way to Brighton. I'll contact Walter and explain.'

As we pushed open the fire escape door, two more uniformed officers were waiting at the bottom. DI Brock had covered every angle. Pulling the door closed, Gordon gave me an unconvincing smile.

'I'll sort this; admit to nothing. When he asks where you've been, tell him you spent the day here with me.'

Gordon made his way through the shop and unlocked the front door. DI Brock and two officers entered, three sets of eyes fixed on me. The DI was the first to speak.

'Gee Valentine, I am arresting you on suspicion of murdering Dravern Leach. You do not have to say anything...'

'What the hell?' I interrupted.

Gordon squeezed the top of my arm. 'Gee, say nothing.'

The detective continued. 'But it may harm your defence if you do not mention when questioned something which you later rely on in court. Anything you do say may be given in evidence.'

My whole being froze. One of the officers removed a set of handcuffs from his waist belt. Without question, I simply outstretched my arms in front of me, just like I'd seen in late-night movies.

'Where will you take him? asked Gordon calmly, as though I was about to be taken for a short walk around the block.

'Why?' remarked the inspector. 'Are you thinking of springing him out with one of your magic tricks?' All three officers laughed. The two in uniform took hold of my arms and led me down the wooden staircase.

Angel called after them from his perch. 'Stop thief, stop thief!' bringing more laughter from the lawmen.

My cell at the police station felt familiar. It was probably one of the many I'd stayed in during my abyss. The next morning, a bang on my cell door was accompanied by an unconvincing breakfast of stringy bacon, crusted fried egg and baked beans. Like revenge, it was served cold. Within the next couple of weeks, I should have been setting off on my first cruise ship adventure. My only destination now looked like prison. By the time I was led to the interview room, it was mid-afternoon. Besides a wooden table and three chairs, the room was as bare as a house on moving day. DI Brock, complete with his trademark red tie and open-neck shirt, had brought along a pretty WPC, dressed in her traditional blue uniform. She wasn't much older than me, though she looked far more relaxed.

'I always thought we would end up in this room. Me sitting on the right side of the law, you sitting on the wrong side of the table.'

I knew Gordon had given me instructions to keep my mouth shut, but

I just couldn't follow them.

'Where were you between the hours of 1.00 pm and 6.00 pm yesterday?' I was sure Billy would have told the DI he'd seen me in The Sun Inn, and no doubt the barmaid would back up his story. So I delivered my version.

'I'd been to Stanley Park to plant an olive tree for my deceased fiancée. On the way back to the Magic Attic, I decided to call at The Sun Inn. As you know, I've had problems with alcohol recently. Whilst waiting for the barmaid to pour me a pint, I heard the distinctive sound of my pocket watch. I instantly knew it was the same one I'd placed in Sarah Todd's coffin eighteen months ago. I looked across the bar and noticed Dravern Leach holding it. He must have stolen it from the coffin after I'd left.'

'Is that why you killed him?' DI Brock enquired.

'I didn't kill him.'

Jack Brock gave a sinister smile and sat upright in his chair. He had the arrogance of a man who believed he was superior to everyone. 'Do you know how I can tell when someone is lying, Valentine?' Uninterested, I simply shrugged my shoulders. 'Their lips move.' The WPC lifted her hand and covered her mouth as she tried to hide the wide smile that Jack Brock had just placed on her face.

'Do you know, Jack, you're only 44 minutes away from being a comedy act.' It was my turn to smile. I knew how much he hated me using his first name.

'And you are about the same time away from being charged with murder. So be very careful with your answers. You followed Mr Leach out of the pub. What happened next?'

'He made his way down a back alleyway, and by the time I arrived, he was pissing into someone's back gate.' I looked across at the WPC and apologised for my language. In return, I received a curt smile.

'I walked up behind him and punched him in the back of his neck. He fell to his knees and started to be sick.'

The DI blurted out, 'Then you placed your foot on his throat, pushed down as hard as you could and murdered him.' The M-word alone terrified me. I sat with my elbows on the table as my hands cradled my face. I knew my only way out of this was to tell the truth.

'No, I simply bent down and retrieved my pocket watch, which was rightfully mine.'

'What time did you arrive back at the Magic Attic?' he demanded. I paused, wondering if he'd already interviewed Gordon this morning, asking the very same question. Impatiently the DI raised his voice. 'Well, come on, what time did you arrive back?'

'Three o'clock,' I replied instantly, hoping Gordon remembered my pocket watch striking three as I entered his workshop.

Disappointment crept across Jack Brock's face confirming Gordon must have stated the same time. Removing his notepad from his top pocket, Brock flipped over a few pages in that policeman kind of way when they're about to postulate.

'I watched Gee Valentine as he followed Dravern Leach along Bond Street. Dravern turned into one of the back alleyways, and Valentine was just a few yards behind. By the time I got there, I could see Valentine pressing his foot on Dravern's neck. When he removed his foot, Dravern was no longer moving. Valentine bent down and stole Dravern's pocket watch and some other jewellery before making his way back towards The Sun Inn to finish his pint.'

DI Brock closed his notepad and placed it on the table. Billy Cameron, as I thought, had seen me retrieve my watch, though he'd lied about me stealing the other jewellery and returning to The Sun Inn. I had to somehow get control of my nerves. My request for a glass of water was ignored. My voice cracked as I tried to reply.

'Billy Cameron wanted revenge for his son's death.' I felt tears spill out of my eyes. The DI turned his head towards the WPC and gave her a wink from his charmless eyes, demonstrating his power over me.

'Where is the watch you stole from your murder victim? Be careful with your answer, Mr Valentine. My officers are searching the Magic Attic as we speak.'

The thought of policemen searching through Gordon's magic collection brought me the first bit of respite since my arrest. *Gordon's misdirection will have them all over the place,* I thought.

Without warning, the interview room door sprung open. A portly man in his mid-fifties entered, slamming the door behind him.

'My name is Charles Smite. I've been appointed by John Todd to act as the legal representative for Mr Gee Valentine. I am requesting full disclosure before another question is asked of my client.'

'I know who you are and what you do. You're wasting your time; we have a witness who placed Mr Valentine at the scene of the murder.' Smite, wearing a suit he may well have slept in several times, delivered a one-word answer.

'Had.'

DI Jack Brock had become used to Smite's cryptic remarks over the years. He leant back in his chair before throwing his pen onto the table. Looking up in my legal's direction, Brock called,

'What do you mean, had?'

'At approximately 12.55pm, Billy Cameron was found dead in his car, opposite the South Pier.'

Knocking over his chair, the detective quickly stood up from the table and instructed the WPC to find out the details. Charles Smite triumphantly brought the DI up to speed. The solicitor removed my pocket watch from his overcoat. He delivered the time in the same tone as the telephone's talking clock.

'It's now 4.25 pm precisely. I don't see any further reason to hold my client.' Charles Smite stretched out his arm, returned my watch to me with a winning smile, and proclaimed,

'In law, I believe this belongs to you.'

The WPC re-entered the room, confirming that Billy Cameron had been pronounced dead. A suicide note was found close by. Brock was left open-mouthed, and I was left relieved. I spoke at my first opportunity.

'Am I free to go?'

The DI stared at the empty chairs, and without eye contact, he grumbled, 'For now, but don't leave the country.'

Back at the Magic Attic, I helped Gordon return the discarded magic props left scattered across the floor by the police after their heavy-handed search.

'Half a dozen bobbies turned the place upside down. No wonder they can't catch any criminals. They're all too bloody stupid. I told them, do not pick up any of the magic apparatus, they're dangerous. One of the daft buggers opened a spring-loaded appearing cane and almost took out his eye. Another almost lost his head in the guillotine. I tried to convince the female police officer that the mousetrap she was holding did not contain a secret compartment. Only when the metal bar snapped on her fingers did she believe me. Anyway, she'll be taken good care of at A&E.'

The last 24 hours had left many unanswered questions. It was time I started asking some.

'Did you arrange for Charles Smite to represent me?'

Gordon raised his index finger and pointed at the telephone and confirmed, 'Kind of. I spoke with Toddy. He did the rest.'

'Did you arrange the death of Billy Cameron to look like suicide?'

Gordon fixed me a disapproving glare like a father would a child who'd pushed his luck too far. My next question had been queuing in my mind since I was a child, waiting to be asked of someone, that someone I never thought would be Gordon Kingsley.

'If the lady in the photo is my mother, are you my father?'

His glare transformed into a considered look, his head tilted to one side, as both corners of his mouth formed a caring smile. Angel paced back and forth on his perch, wanting to say something, but thought better of it. Gordon picked up the last of the discarded pieces of magic and made his way behind the counter. Removing a dust-covered book from a shelf, he knew exactly where to find the piece of paper. He carefully unfolded it, then placed it sketch side up on the counter like it was the final piece of a jigsaw he was about to give voice to.

'It was June 1947, Giovanni Agosto laid on a big party for his wife's 40th birthday in the garden of the House of Lemons. It was a day full of Sorrento sunshine, mixed with dancing, wine and limoncello, the former of which I drank far too much. I retired to my cabin, what time it was I couldn't remember, but it was late. When I awoke the next morning, Sofia was lying in my arms.'

'Did you?' I asked awkwardly.

'I honestly don't know. What I do know is that I had a thumping hangover and a terrible feeling of guilt. I was 35, Sofia just 17. She had a boyfriend at the time, so why was she here with me? I had breached her parents' trust. How could I ever face them again? In a panic, I told Sofia to go back to her room. I dressed, grabbed my belongings and left.'

An awkward silence fell between us. Thankfully, Angel began flapping his wings noisily.

I looked down at the pencil sketch on the counter, and instantly I connected it as the last page torn from the drawing book at the House of Lemons. The girl in the drawing was clearly my mother, Sofia. She was sitting at the table where I'd sipped lemonade the year before. Her hair was tied in a ponytail, the high cheekbones, and her smile was so shy I felt she was trying to edge off the paper.

'In answer to your question, Gee, I honestly don't know if I'm your father. As I mentioned, your mother had a boyfriend at the time.' I tried to digest everything he'd just said. Shuffling my feet, I stared into one of the many crystal balls on display in a glass cabinet. I hoped it contained answers to my many questions, one in particular forced its way to the front of the queue.

'Why did you never ask about Sofia when I returned from Italy?'

'How could I when Penny had just died?'

'Of course, I'm sorry,' I said. We fell back into silence, both now staring into the crystal ball. It was midnight, and my pocket watch played the full cycle of "*Ritorna a Sorrento*". Gordon's face glowed in the globe as it played, and I knew exactly what he was thinking.

Chapter 28

Into the Wolf's Mouth

I laid awake most of the night, listening to the March winds as they whistled under doorways and throughout the secret tunnels that made up the Magic Attic. I wished I could just get up in the morning and drive to Sorrento, but I had so much rehearsing to do over the next couple of weeks before joining my first cruise ship. Sleep must have crept in somehow, as I was startled awake by Angel furiously flapping his wings. I questioned whether I'd covered the cage with his blanket. It soon became obvious there was no way I could return to sleep until I'd checked. I made my way downstairs. The cage was covered by the blanket. About to return to bed, I was spooked by the sound of a doorbell behind me. In fight or flight mode, I spun on my bare feet to see Gordon standing in the doorway. Relieved, I asked,

'Are you home late or up early?'

Gordon marched straight past me, leant over the counter and grabbed a bottle of whiskey from one of the display cabinets, taking a large swig.

'I thought that was a magic prop,' I chortled.

He disregarded my comment.

'I'm amazed you slept through the bloody racket that took place. Didn't you hear the police sirens?'

'No, I was woken by Angel. That's why I'm downstairs.' Gordon looked agitated.

'Just after 1.00 am, Lana telephoned, claiming the police were trying to get inside the bakery. By the time I got downstairs, a police officer had put her in handcuffs, whilst another was reading her her rights. The only information the officer divulged was she was helping them with their enquiries. With that, they drove off, sirens blaring.' Gordon took another swig from the bottle, now gripped in his hand.

'What could they possibly want with Lana?' I gasped. Again, he ignored my comment.

'I immediately telephoned Charles Smite, informing him of what had just taken place. By the time I arrived at the police station, Charles was already there. He'd managed to ascertain that FPD had also been arrested yesterday in connection with the suicide of Billy Cameron.'

'But how does Cameron's suicide link to Lana?' I asked.

'At the moment, I don't know. I left Smite at the station and made my way straight back here.' Gordon looked at his watch. 'It's almost 4.00 am. You'd better get some sleep.'

'What about you?' I asked. He looked into the whiskey bottle as though it contained the answer to my question.

I flitted in and out of sleep, unsure if there would ever be another virtual hug from Lana's fresh bread.

I spent the next few days rehearsing in the cellar of Lana's bakery. Above my head, I could hear the constant coming and going of police officers, searching the bakery for what or who I had no idea. Deep into my third day of rehearsing, I was suddenly disturbed as a panel in the wall was kicked through. When the dust settled, two policemen were standing where a wall used to be. Behind them, the stairs led back up to the bakery above. I was told to pack up and leave, as this area was now part of a murder investigation. Sullenly, I made my way back to the Magic Attic. On entering, I recognised the voice of Jack Brock coming from inside. For once, I was pleased to hear his Mancunian accent, hoping he had good news of Lana.

'Why, Mr Valentine, perfect timing. Mr Kingsley's kindly offered to help us with our enquiries. Perhaps you can help too?'

Also with the DI was the WPC from my interview a few days ago. Her index finger was picking at the threepenny bit on the shop counter. The look on Gordon's face advised her to stop. Gordon then turned his attention to the detective.

'Understand me, inspector, until you tell me why you are holding my sister-in-law in police custody, I wouldn't help you cross the road.' DI Brock's face remained passive.

'The only information I'm willing to disclose at this stage is as follows. Francis P David was arrested after his brown case was discovered in Billy Cameron's car. Inside the case, we found a pen and paper identical to that used, in what we now believe was a forged suicide note, made to look like it was written by Mr Cameron. In my first interview with Francis P David, he broke down and confessed to being an accomplice in the murder of Billy Cameron. He stated he'd been coerced into the action by Lana Kingsley, who had been blackmailing him for several years.'

'Wait!' I called angrily. 'FPD is a fruit cake. Everybody knows that.'

Gordon told me to be quiet and asked the DI to continue.

'I started to think exactly the same, but on further inspection of Mr Cameron's car, we discovered a footprint that contained flour, the type used in bread-making. We believed that footprint belonged to Lana Kingsley. At this stage, that's all I am willing to reveal.'

I enquired how Billy Cameron took his own life. The detective held both his arms out straight. Palms up, he closed both fists tight, his veins and arteries in his wrists now prominent.

'At first, it was believed he'd used his son's silver flick knife to slice through his own wrist. We now know it was Francis P David and Lana Kingsley who carried out the crime.' In a casual manner, the DI locked his eyes onto mine: and asked, 'That enough information for you?'

My head was spinning. I remembered I'd watched Lana pick up Sean's knife at the seance and pass it to FPD. 'Are you sure it was Sean's knife?' I asked. The detective placed his hand into a brown holdall he'd placed on the counter, and he removed a see-through plastic bag. Inside was a knife. It was definitely Sean's. I struggled to take in the enormity of it all; how and why had Lana become embroiled in this?

The DI moved into overdrive. 'Now I have a few questions I trust you will both answer. Officer O'Reilly, the boxes, please.'

WPC O'Reilly inserted her hand into a black leather glove. Slowly she unzipped a pocket inside the holdall and methodically removed 13 packs of Bicycle playing cards, neatly stacking them on the counter, like a window dresser trying to impress passers-by. Jack Brock gave her a look of disdain before continuing.

'These packs of cards were found hidden in the bakery cellar below. Did you supply Lana Kingsley with these items?'

Gordon, without touching any of the packs, leant forward like an antique dealer ready to give his opinion on their authenticity.

'Well, they don't appear to have my fingerprints on them,' uttered Gordon.

Officer O'Reilly jumped in. 'You can't always see fingerprints with the naked eye.'

DI Brock turned his head to give O'Reilly another disapproving look.

Gordon got the reaction he wanted. He was enjoying the cat and mouse game between the officers. He observed, 'Yes, you are exactly right, miss. But had they contained my fingerprints, I'd have been arrested by now. Anyway, these types of cards are readily available from at least half a dozen magic shops in the Blackpool area.' Jack Brock knew Gordon was playing a game of misdirection.

'Of the thirteen packs on view, Mr Kingsley, seven of them have the ace of spades missing. Vincent Leach, Tracey Mac, Zantini, Sean Cameron, Sarah Todd, Danny Mac and Micky Marks had placed on or about them an ace of spades card. Now, I'm really not that interested in where Mrs Kingsley bought them from. The only part that really bothers me is why would Mrs Kingsley be involved in the murder of seven magicians?'

I looked to Gordon. His face revealed nothing, unlike mine, as I caught my reflection in a glass cabinet. Gordon was about to dispel the ace of spades theory:

'Inspector, you have no idea how often the ace of spades appears when a magician performs a trick. It's probably the most used of all cards, and it's used in at least two dozen table games. I sell beer mats, mugs, jewellery, t-shirts, t-towels and even ladies' underwear with the black ace card printed on. So, the fact that the ace of spades was found in a mailbag or the bottom of a milk can is purely coincidental. As for my sister-in-law's involvement with the said seven murders, you will find she's got a watertight alibi to every one.'

Without a word, Jack Brock nudged Officer O'Reilly to return the card boxes into the holdall. The pair was about to leave the Magic Attic without the cards being stacked in his favour.

Stony-faced, he delivered a final instruction. 'I want you both to think long and hard about where you were when each murder took place. Should I be able to place either of you at any of the murder scenes, then like Mrs Kingsley, you will spend a long time behind bars.' The inspector was just about to close the door behind him when Gordon called out,

'Officer O'Reilly, you've forgotten your glove.' The WPC, with eyes full of wonder, looked at her naked hand like a little girl who'd just seen her first magic trick. Just like when Gordon had removed Jack Brock's red tie, I had no idea how or when Gordon removed O'Reilly's glove. DI Brock knew exactly what Gordon Kingsley was up to. Did she or did she not have the glove on when she returned the card boxes back into the holdall? If not, then her fingerprints, like anyone else's, were all over them, contaminating the evidence. Smiling, she made her way back to the counter to retrieve the glove as Angel joined in the banter.

'It's magic, it's magic.'

Over the following couple of days, Blackpool was awash with rumours and gossip regarding the multiple murders. The *Evening Gazette* churned out nightly headline banners: *"The Ace of Death"; "Baker's dozen, foiled"; "The death of magic"*.

Julie Mac was arrested and charged as an accomplice to murdering her husband. Again the *Evening Gazette* was ready with a snappy headline, *"Vanishing assistant found at last… in Fleetwood"*.

As I would soon be leaving to join my first cruise ship, I asked Charles Smite if he would allow me to accompany him on a visit to see Lana. She was being held at Risley Remand Centre. The prison was famously known as "Grisly Risley" throughout the area. As we waited for Lana to be brought to the interview room, Charles agreed to leave us alone for a few minutes to talk privately.

The room's unpainted concrete walls belonged to another era. Above our heads, the fluorescent light tube buzzed as though a bluebottle was trapped inside. A small, partitioned booth was divided down the centre by a wire-mesh glass to separate visitor and prisoner. Two small wooden stools ensured neither of us would sit comfortably. Lana shuffled into the room, led by a female officer. Her wild red hair was now cropped into a basin-like shape, and her prison uniform of paper-thin, light blue denim hung loosely from her frame, giving the impression she had lost all reason for living. My stool scraped on the concrete floor as I sat down, echoing loudly like the door that closed behind Smite and the prison warden. Dominating the room was our silence. I glanced at my fingernails, which were, at last, starting to repair. Lana stared at me through the glass screen, which was misting over from our breath. Her eyes were no longer violent.

'The older you became, Gee, the more you looked like your Uncle Gino,' she said through her soft Scottish accent. I shouldn't have been shocked that she was convinced I was Gordon's son. Lana always had a different way of looking at life. I smiled.

'Hello Lana, are you ok?'

She tilted her head with what I thought was a smile, then lifted her hand to her left ear.

'The first day you arrived, I watched as you sat at the bottom of the stairs, shoving cakes and bread into your mouth like they were the last bits of food on earth.' The memory brought a smile to my face.

'What you don't know is I'd telephoned Gordon and told him to look at the boy sitting on the stairs. When he looked, he said he thought he was staring at a younger version of his brother. The next thing I heard was the saxophone playing, and you were enticed up the stairs. I phoned Gordon and said, "I don't care how you do it, but don't let the boy leave".'

And I'd thought it was all a coincidence. It turned out to be a cleverly worked entrapment.

'It was you who had been sent from God to make up for me losing my husband. You were the son Gino, and I should have had, and I was going to do everything to protect you.' She began to smile. I listened intently, searching for a reason as to why she would commit murder.

Eventually, I asked: 'Is this all true, Lana. Did you kill Billy Cameron?' Her smile became a grimace before her lips straightened. She wiped away the mist that had fogged on the glass between us.

'I did what any mother would do when their child is in danger.'

Wow, I thought, *she actually saw me as her son*. I gasped.

'Did that have to include murder?'

Lana tried to move her stool closer into the booth. 'Billy Cameron came to the bread shop a few days after the seance looking for you. He said you would never see your 23rd birthday.'

'Why did you not go to the police?'

Lana smiled at my naivety. 'DI Jack Brock was on Billy Cameron's payroll. He's fitting me up with all these so-called murders because he's just lost part of his income.'

'So you had no part in any of the deaths?'

Lana looked away as she bit at her thumb.

I sat tightly on my hands.

Ready to continue, she edged closer to the glass partition. 'I found Vincent Leach slumped outside my shop door. He was already dead. I hated bad magicians. Gino used to say every time a bad magician died, they should be buried along with the death card, the ace of spades. I had several of Gino's packs of cards gathering dust, so I removed the ace of spades from one and shoved it inside Vincent's mouth. I played no part in any other death.'

'What about Sarah Todd?'

'Absolutely not!' she exclaimed. I looked down at my fingers, now bleeding from pulling at the skin around the nails.

'Did you blackmail FPD?' I asked.

'He was a thief, and I was fed up with him stealing from my shop. Knowing he was terrified of his father, I used it to my advantage. The only time I roped him in to help was with Billy Cameron, and that was because I couldn't manage on my own.' I asked her to think back to the Alice in Wonderland party in Brighton.

'I passed Zantini's room in the early hours and a party was in full swing. I swear I heard you singing.'

Lana shimmied her shoulders and puckered her lips. 'He was a great kisser, but I played no part in his death, nor did I play any part in Micky Marks' suicide. As for Sean Cameron, though I wanted to be involved in his death, the closest I came was dropping the ace of spades into the milk can. Gordon was right; Sean drowned in his own inadequacy.' The room fell into silence.

I knew what Lana had done was wrong, but she was greatly affected by her husband's death. Having no body to bury had affected her state of mind. I was just about to ask Lana what she thought would happen to her when the door opened, and Charles Smite walked back in. Our time was up. We were both in tears as we hugged and said goodbye, not knowing if it would be for the last time. On the journey back to Blackpool, Charles Smite broke the news that in the last hour, FPD had confessed to the accidental murder of Sarah Todd.

'How the fuck is slicing through someone's neck an accident?' I blurted out angrily.

Smite said I should calm myself or I'd be an old man before my time. He went on to explain.

'FPD claimed he placed the playing card inside the handle, knowing Micky would get into difficulty and not be able to complete the illusion. He also said the choice of card was purely coincidental.'

I couldn't help thinking this new information would bring more heartache to Toddy, knowing he had suggested FPD to Sarah in the first place. Smite told me FPD had denied being involved in the murder of The Great Zantini but confessed to sending Micky Marks the Belladonna poison in prison with instructions on how to kill himself. He also accepted the charge of assisting Tracey Mac to kill her husband. In all, Francis P David was charged as an accomplice to the murder of four people.

(*)

The night before I was due to board my first cruise ship, I went in search of Gordon. He was repairing the damaged walls in Lana's bakery where the police search teams had smashed their way into the cellar. Gordon had been very low for a few weeks, and I was giving serious as to whether to leave him. Yesterday he'd told me he blamed himself for the mess Lana now found herself in.

'Would you like me to put off the cruise until this all blows over?' I asked.

Gordon sat upright, with a grimace on his face. 'Hell no, I insist you join the ship. I want to know what the Europeans make of your comedy waiter routine.' We both smiled at the thought, as laughing was off the menu for a while to come. Gordon asked which ports the cruise ship would stop at.

'Ah, that reminds me, I've yet to open the letter that came this morning containing the ship's itinerary,' I replied.

Gordon shook his head with a smile that turned into a grumbled voice.

'Open it up and make me jealous, why don't you?' Using my penknife, I carefully cut the envelope's seal and removed a crisp, white piece of paper. I ran my fingers across the embossed logo that read *Royal Caribbean Ships*. Penny came into my thoughts, as she always did when I felt any kind of achievement. Gordon folded his arms and leant back on his workbench.

Like a ceremonial toastmaster, I cleared my throat:

'*SS Capri* sets sail from Southampton the day after tomorrow. First stop is Bilbao.' I lifted my head and looked over the paper at Gordon. 'Where's that?'

'Spain,' he replied, raising his eyes.

'Next is Lisbon?' I said quizzically.

Shaking his head at my poor geography, Gordon bemoaned, 'Portugal!'

'Next up Tangiers, and before you say anything, I know it's in Africa.' There were three further ports the ship would dock at, but my eye was drawn to the final destination. I dismissed the paper to one side and peered across to Gordon.

'Naples. Naples will be the last port of call.' I looked out through the window on the world, knowing Sorrento would be only sixty minutes down the road. Sixty minutes away from asking my mother the most important question of her life … is Gordon Kingsley my father?

When I looked back at the man in question, his arms were still folded. The widest of smiles beamed from his face as he stared serenely out of the window, knowing my impending journey would end in Sorrento. His lips slowly parted.

'*In bocca al lupo,* Gee Valentine.' Into the wolf's mouth, it certainly was.

Epilogue

Blackpool, 31st December 1999

The Italian Gardens inside Stanley Park had always been my go-to place, where time paused, and nothing seemed to matter. Think I'll sit a while and see what nothing brings. My eyes focused on the olive tree I'd illegally planted almost 30 years ago, as it swayed in the easterly wind. A new millennium was hours away, but I felt reluctant to let the old one go. Although my past was complicated, I would turn back the hands of time in a heartbeat if given the opportunity. I'd even deny myself life if it meant a different outcome for my first true love. Sadly, neither time travel nor spell-casting magic wands had been invented yet, so my life journey could not be altered.

I'd returned to Blackpool for the first time in 15 years. Managing Russo Vineyard and the House of Lemons in Sorrento meant almost every hour of each working day was accounted for. Having not had a holiday in over 10 years, Zap, my wife, insisted I took time out to collect my 87-year-old father, who, after many years of persuasion, had finally agreed to live with us in Sorrento - a home we also shared with my mother, Sofia.

On the 25th of May 1971, under a sweltering Sorrento sun, I walked into the garden at the House of Lemons. Unbeknown to me, it was my grandfather Giovanni's 64th birthday. Instantly I recognised my mother, sitting at the garden table with my grandparents. All three looked across at the stranger in their presence. No words were spoken as I walked across to them and placed the blue towel I was wrapped in as a baby onto the table. Quizzically, my mother lifted her head towards me. Her fingers stroked the GB monogram, and her eyes floated in a river of tears. I placed the silver charm engraved with SB carefully into her olive tanned hands. In my mind, I'd rehearsed the moment a thousand times. I would say, 'Hi, Mam. You left this behind.' But at that moment, the words escaped me. My mother gripped the edge of the table to help her stand. I held her in my arms and cried out, 'Mama.' Her hand pushed aside the top of my vest to reveal the birthmark on my shoulder shaped like a boot. She cried, '*Valentino, perdonami, perdonami,* forgive me, forgive me.' It turned out Valentino was the name she had always referred to me as. But Valentino Valentine would never have worked!

Sofia Agosto never slept with Gabino Bellini until they were married in the autumn of 1948, which confirmed that Gordon Kingsley was, in fact, my father. My mother had sought refuge in the Capri Guesthouse to have her baby, and she confirmed Rossini Circus did not allow performers with children under five years old. It was Gabino who insisted that my mother left me behind. When in Italy the previous year, unbeknown to me, I'd met my stepbrother Danny in the bakery of Otto Coltelli pane, which my mother and stepfather owned. They'd named the bakery after their knife-throwing act, "Eight Knives". I would never get the opportunity to meet my stepfather Gabino; he died in a hail of bullets, along with Antonio, who owned the pizzeria in Naples, a drug switch that went badly wrong.

In the cold of New Year's Eve, I was brought back into the present as my pocket watch struck 11.00 am. On my lap sat an urn containing Annie's ashes. She died 18 months ago on what would have been Penny's 50th birthday. I didn't keep my promise of returning home to Cleveleys – I had not been the son I'd pledged to be. She had left me the bungalow in her will, which I sold and donated the proceeds to the Royal National Institute of Blind People.

The reoccurring nightmare of Sarah's death at the Marine Hall in 1969 still haunted me, just not as often. As for Toddy, we were still in touch. By 1975, he had sold John Todd Entertainments and moved to New York near his granddaughter. That same year, Lana took her own life whilst in prison. My father was devastated. FPD was committed to a mental institution somewhere in Cornwall. I had no idea if he was still alive. My father, whom I still referred to as Gordon, sold all his old magic props, except the large guillotine that had been in our family for over 100 years. It would take up residence in the dining room of the House of Lemons, along with my old stage props, which I hadn't touched in 15 years.

Before leaving the Italian Gardens for the last time, I scattered Annie's ashes around the base of the olive tree. Gently taking hold of one of its branches, I imagined I was holding Penny's hand - I didn't want to let go and never will. I searched my mind to remember her voice singing, "I Will Follow You", but it was no longer there.

Back at the Magic Attic, I placed Angel and his cage onto the back seat of Alice then climbed back up the stairs to the now-empty Magic Attic. Gone were the glass cabinets that once held such wonders, where Gordon mesmerised children and adults alike. My nose twitched, searching for one final smell of Lana's fresh bread. Gordon was calling me from his workshop. With his back to me, and for one last time, he looked out of his window on the world. He handed me an old dusty envelope, once white, now a shade of brown and covered with broken cobwebs.

'This is an old one,' I said. 'Did you forget to post it?'

'No, but it looks like you did. I found it this morning when the clearance men took away your old bed.' On the envelope was written...*The Italian Embassy. London.*

'Holy cow. I thought I'd sent this back in 1966. No wonder I never received a reply.'

We looked at each other and laughed. As we made our way out through the Magic Attic, I noticed the threepenny bit still glued to the counter, and I couldn't help but smile at what the new owner would think when they discovered the secret mirrored tunnels. As Gordon closed the shop door behind us, the doorbell rang goodbye. I traced my fingers across the obscure glass where *Kingsley's Magic Attic* was still written in gold leaf. Taking hold of Gordon's arm, I guided him down the stairs, like my life depended on it, just as I did some 35 years ago with Penny. Reaching the bottom run, I leant in towards my father.

'Shush, can you hear that?' I asked. Gordon tilted his head to one side as if pushing his ears back up the stairs.

I whispered to him. 'It's "*Ritorna a Sorrento*".'

Gordon smiled at the memory. As we passed the gumball machine, I reminded him today was his 87th birthday. Placing my hand in my pocket,

I removed the very same threepence he'd placed inside the Christmas pudding back in 1963.

'Do you want to try your luck?' I asked.

'Life, Gee, is full of opportune moments, some we take, like the shilling you took from Lana's counter, some we leave, like the ship that sailed to Australia, and some we keep forever.' Gordon took the threepence from my hand and placed it safely in his pocket.

I removed the warm scarf from my neck and placed it around my father, tucking it into his overcoat. He linked his arm through mine as we made our way to Alice - and the long journey back home to Sorrento.

Acknowledgements

My childhood day trips to Blackpool, and the endless hours spent on the Pleasure Beach, certainly helped to fuel my imagination. It was without doubt the best educational experience this young boy could have wished for. The surest thing I knew whilst growing up, was my mother dearly loved me. I drew on her love to help me complete this book.

I believe in luck and fate. It led me to the fabulous Michelle Emerson who has not only edited this book, but from the outset she gave me the confidence to carry on and tell my story. As an analogy 'If the book is a curry, I came up with the recipe, added the ingredients, then watched it simmer. Michelle added spices I didn't even know existed'. I implore anyone writing a book to get in touch with Michelle.

Thank you James Howells of Howells Magic, somehow you transformed my awful drawings into a book cover I'm so proud of. Craig Freer for equally doing the same with my website.

Throughout the book I make reference to many beautiful areas in Italy. I have travelled extensively throughout the country with my wife Kate and visited the splendid hotels Bellevue Syrene and Grand Europa in Sorrento.

Music played such a large part in my own comedy speciality act. If it were not for my fourth heart attack in 2020, I would be still treading the boards, and this book would never have been written. That's why I've drawn on so many great songs, I hope it helped to set the scene. I make no apology for my constant reference to my favourite singer Rod Stewart, his music has been a constant in my own life.

Luck also led me to the Butlins Ocean Hotel in Saltdean, Brighton where I met my closest friends. We sadly lost Jim Waldock to cancer in April 2022, R.I.P my friend. His wife, Sue, worked tirelessly with me on my non-fiction book, *The Art of Stage Craft*, which I'm truly grateful for. Everybody has a best friend, mine is Mike Sayer, another constant in my life. He helped get my first show, *El Loco*, off the ground. He was also the first person to read a draft of this book, encouraging me to get it published. His friendship has been unwavering.

My two sons Charlie and George, make their father so proud with their achievements. Your constant love lifted me to write every day.

My wife Kate has painstakingly had to correct every page of this book, many times over, because of my awful dyslexia. She is the most beautiful, caring person I have ever known. Kate and I met at the Ocean Hotel in 1984. She has supported me in everything I have done, was with me at my first stage performance, and when I almost lost my life just before a show on a cruise ship off Dubai.

Finally you, for parting with your hard-earned money to read my story. I truly hope you enjoyed Gee Valentine's journey through life, reminding us all -

"The greatest thing you'll learn is just to love and be loved in return."

Wayne Slater
www.wayneslater.com
28/4/2022

Your honest opinion of this novel is most welcome.

Printed in Poland
by Amazon Fulfillment
Poland Sp. z o.o., Wrocław
25 May 2022

0a514704-8c2d-45bd-a776-1309ecbc24cfR01